★

"What have you got there, big boy? A nice juicy bone?"

She risked a hand, but the dog retreated. She peered into the hole. For a moment, she thought she was seeing double. The bones were connected—and covered with dirt and shreds of discolored clothing. And something like a pointed rock stuck through a filthy shirt! She put a hand to her nose, though there was only the thick smell of earth. A gust of wind blew a pile of dead leaves in her face, and the bones seemed to move. She shivered. And then she screamed.

★

"...combines a finely wrought mystery with some superb local color.... Wright melds setting and character with the skill of Stephen Dobyns in his Saratoga mysteries."

—*Booklist*

Previously published Worldwide Mystery title by
NANCY MEANS WRIGHT

MAD SEASON

HARVEST
OF BONES

NANCY MEANS WRIGHT

W🌐RLDWIDE.

TORONTO • NEW YORK • LONDON
AMSTERDAM • PARIS • SYDNEY • HAMBURG
STOCKHOLM • ATHENS • TOKYO • MILAN
MADRID • WARSAW • BUDAPEST • AUCKLAND

In memory of Evelyn Wright McGregor
of Weybridge, Vermont,
model for the Glenna Flint of this novel.

HARVEST OF BONES

A Worldwide Mystery/October 1999

First published by St. Martin's Press, Incorporated.

ISBN 0-373-26325-2

Visit us at www.worldwidemystery.com

Printed in U.S.A.

Acknowledgments

I want to thank a number of generous persons who helped me develop an accurate ambiance for this novel. My appreciation goes to Harold Giard of Blue Slate Farm, Bridport, Vermont; to Ward B. Stone, wildlife pathologist for the State of New York; to Dr. Paul Morrow, state medical examiner, Vermont; to Scotti Devens of SAVE THE GREYHOUND DOGS—Vermont; to Irene Poole, massage therapist, who, in her "chair-on-wheels," gave me a massage and proved that "nothing is impossible"; to the Buttolph farm family of Shoreham, Vermont, for inspiring both books in this series; to Don Batchelder, whose bicycle and signs I borrowed; to Ed Barna for his expertise on catamounts in Vermont; to Joanie Cohen, postmistress of Hughsonville, N.Y., who kissed this manuscript for luck and sped it on its way; to my copy editor, Carol Edwards, who labored through the manuscript and kept me at task; and especially to my legendary editor, Ruth Cavin, who caught up the book in flight and compassionately edited it and gave me courage at a low point in the final stages. Finally, my love and thanks to my wonderful extended family, Vermonters all; and especially to my daughters Lesley and Catharine, and my husband, Dennie Hannan, who read the novel in early drafts.

Certain books were also helpful in providing atmosphere for the novel: *Hawk Hill* by Suzie Gilbert; *Cutting Hill* by Alan Pistorius; and from the Vermont Folklife Center: *Families on the Land*, edited by Gregory Sharrow and Meg Ostrum, and *Visit'n: Conversations with Vermonters*.

Keeping time,
Keeping the rhythm in their dancing
As in their living in the living seasons
The time of the seasons and the constellations
The time of milking and the time of harvest
The time of the coupling of man and woman
And that of beasts. Feet rising and falling.
Eating and drinking. Dung and death.

—T. S. Eliot, from
Four Quartets. East Coker

No Rack can torture me—
My Soul—at Liberty—
Behind this mortal Bone
There knits a bolder One—

You cannot prick with saw—
Nor pierce with Scimitar—
Two Bodies—therefore be—
Mind One—The other fly—

The Eagle of his Nest
No easier divest—
And gain the Sky
Than mayest Thou—

Except Thyself may be
Thine Enemy—
Captivity is Consciousness—
So's Liberty.

—Emily Dickinson, from
No. 384

ONE

ZELDA LEAPT AT the gate and the old wood split in two, making a path through to the outer pasture. The bawling in the early-morning field she'd just left quieted. The other cows were lined up along the fence to watch—unwilling, it seemed, to venture far from the barn. Already they smelled winter. Zelda, though, wanted out. It wasn't that she was hungry. She was off her feed; for a time, she'd eaten everything: hay, ground corn, prickly ash, and nettles. But now these foods didn't tempt her. She needed solitude, a quiet spot to drop the load inside her. She charged ahead on the hard October dirt, where a thin, cold rain was starting to fall. She shuffled about, peered back at her flanks as though she'd swat a fly—then rammed a second fence.

But this fence gave a jolt. Something sharp zinged through her, penetrated the bones. She wouldn't give up. She rammed again, and again, until the pole was knocked sideways, then, when a sharp pain scissored through her insides, gave up. She turned sideways into a declivity of dried underbrush, near a cold stream, into a hole partly dug; she smelled dog, but only on the bone that was half-unearthed there. She trampled it back in, almost; with her back feet shoved in damp red leaves, the wind did the rest. She beat her head against the fence, mewling. Somewhere a crow called, a cricket spoke. A soft grayish pink crowned the mountains to the east.

She thumped down on the frosty grass, cramped into a swollen sigh; the birth sack heaved with each bellow. Her noise was echoed by the wind, and by the other cows, watching at a distance, like women at a home birth. Her insides screamed; her breath squealed as she pulled in, pushed out, bellowed again. And then an ivory hoof kicked out, a black head, followed by white shoulders, and ribs like furrows of hard earth. Finally, it lay there on the ground, a bloody steaming package of spindly limbs. Zelda licked the soaked calf dry, then lifted her head and trumpeted her prize.

Back in the inner pasture, she heard answering cries.

Ruth Willmarth arrived on the scene a half hour later with Joey, the hired man's foster boy,—a bit backward but a sweet lad and useful for all that. He'd burst in that morning before she could even grind her morning coffee beans. The calf was already up on its stick legs and sucking. Zelda had tried to hide it, of course, but a bit of rummaging located the calf behind a pile of brush, by the stream that meandered over from the Flint farm to the south. There was no use scolding Zelda for breaking out. It was her first calf; she'd been ornery from the start, a dominant cow, though not always a leader. They'd gotten her to replace poor Charlotte, burned to death in last spring's barn fire.

And here the miserable heifer had broken through a gate—more work for them all when there was still late corn and alfalfa to be gotten in. It was already mid-October and the beast had practically battered down the pasture fence in its birth agony.

"Ow," said Joey, his bony fingers leaping back from the hot wires. Ruth clucked in sympathy and pulled him away.

Her husband, Pete, had electrified those wires. She'd been meaning to switch them off, actually. Pete was in New York. "We'll get Tim to fix the fence; you can help," she told Joey. "But we have to get this calf back in the barn. Now Zelda's had it, she won't want to feed it any longer—what do you bet? Not much of a mother, I'm afraid."

It was true. Already, Zelda was rolling away from the calf, her white switch whirling like a helicopter as she moved off through the open gate, toward the other cows. They parted to let her through, then followed her lead, over to the pond that already had a rim of ice on it. The calf just stood there on unsteady legs and gazed at Ruth with plaintive brown eyes, wanting to suck.

"I haven't got anything for you," Ruth said. "My milking days are over. But Jane Eyre does. She's a good mom. She'll share." Ruth had named her cows after favorite characters from books, like Jane or Esmeralda, and from movies, like Dolly Parton. Zelda, for example, had been named for the wife of a novelist, who'd claimed his wife had stolen all his subject matter. Of course, Ruth's husband thought her crazy; to him, cows were merely objects that gave milk. But Pete had taken off with that actress woman—though things weren't going so well with her at the moment, according to Ruth's daughter Emily, who spoke on the phone each weekend with her father. It gave Ruth a certain satisfaction to hear that.

She put an arm around the calf's neck, propelled it gently toward the barn. Already, the red and gold leaves were crackling down off the trees, the tourists heading home. In Vermont, winter came early. A hard winter—she could feel it in her bones. An aching in her joints.

Behind her, Joey yelled, "Hey, Ruth, Ruth, look what I got. Ruth—hey, look!"

She turned, and the calf sank down on its black knees, stumbled into a hole. She hardly saw what Joey held out; she was trying to tug the calf upright again. She needed the animal; the herd was down to twenty-nine, an all-time low. She couldn't afford to buy a grown cow, since times were bad: Everything was going up—farm machinery, chemicals, fertilizer—and her buying power was dropping. Some weekends, when Pete called, she wanted to give in, say, All right, all right, I'll sell; we can liquidate. You can have your half in cash, if that's what you want. And of course that was what he wanted....

"I thought, jussa bone," Joey said. "But look, look, Ruth, it's got a ring. A bone with a ring." His hair was almost white with frost, and his mouth, with its two missing front teeth, was set in a grin. His words came out with a slight whistle. "Ruth! You gotta come see."

She smiled. When Joey got an idea in his head, he wouldn't let go. She let the calf loose and it staggered on ahead, toward the barn, as if it knew already where the feed was. Sighing, she looked at the bone Joey held out, and was surprised to see it was a finger, a long brownish finger—not a hoof, not a skeletal paw, but a human finger. A finger with a narrow gold ring above the bony hump of knuckle joint. A ring with an etching—moss-filled. But on closer observation, it looked like an arrow crossed with a bone.

"You wanna ring? Pretty ring," sang Joey. "Pretty, pretty, pretty. What finger you want on?"

"No, leave it as you found it," she shouted, the shock of the calf and then the finger running through her like an electric pulse. "Give it here, Joey. We should keep it intact."

"Who's it?" he said, dancing around, excited by the calf, the ring, the rain that was turning to sleet. He thrust the finger at her, then stood on his gloved hands in the frosty grass, wiggled his skinny legs.

"Oh, probably came from that cemetery over there." She pointed at the Larocque farm to the north. There was a small cemetery on it, dating from Revolutionary times. Belle Larocque, for one, was buried there, killed by an assailant. Her septuagenarian husband, Lucien, still worked the farm, alone now. Lucien had once unearthed an Indian there, sitting up the way the Abenaki buried them. Though an ancient Indian wouldn't be wearing an etched gold ring, would he? She? And the stream it was found near flowed from the Flint farm, not Larocque's. She made a mental note to call her friend Colm Hanna, let him look into it. Colm was a Realtor, familiar with the town properties; he worked on the side for the town police.

Oh well. She had other things on her mind. Like barn work. Milking time already, and she hadn't even had her coffee yet. She couldn't function without her coffee! She dropped the finger into a pocket, then raced after the calf—a priority now—and steered it toward the barn, where two pregnant heifers and three calves were still inside. Birthing was year-round for her; she needed the cash flow. And with milk prices higher in the fall, it made sense to inseminate in late winter. Though it was getting more and more costly to buy the right semen. And then, just when she'd invested in Select Sires to get a better set to the leg, more curve, greater milk flow, a bull had broken out from a nearby farm and impregnated two of her cows.

That farm had been sold after a series of fires and had been bought by a couple from down country who thought anyone could farm—they didn't know about keeping up fences. As if farming were a hobby, not a hard, tough, backbreaking business! Well, they'd given up already, planned to develop the place. And now Ruth had heard, a woman named Fay was renting the Flint farm next door, meaning to open a bed-and-breakfast. The neighborhood was going commercial. It made her sick to think of it.

The calf took to Jane Eyre at once. Jane had plenty of milk; she was a good gentle girl, always baby-sitting for the other calves. Her three-day-old didn't particularly want to share, though; it kicked at the newborn with a hard muscled leg. Ruth shoved the newborn at the teat. It was a female calf; she was thankful for that. Annie, she named it; it was already an orphan apparently, its mother a renegade. The others kowtowed to Zelda; she was spoiled rotten.

Kowtow—funny how that sounded, she thought. In this case, "cowtow," female to female. Interesting to contemplate. Would there have been a pecking order among the Amazons?

Something jabbed her side as she moved about, hoeing out the manure to make space for two calves—something in her right pocket. It was the finger: She took it out, laid it on the edge of the stanchion, and bent to examine it. But she looked up when someone behind her squealed: Emily, coming up to say good-bye before school.

"Mo-ther. What's that? Oh, dis-gus-ting."

Ruth laughed. She was already quite fond of it, that finger, that ring. She was making up a story around it. It had belonged to some nineteenth-century female, young, wearing her lover's ring; took her life out of unrequited love.... "A soldier's wife," she told Emily, smiling. "Her husband dead in a war, and she died from heartbreak and was buried with his ring."

"Mom, you're going soft in the head. But how old do you really think it is?" Emily's interest was piqued now—she'd been assigned a school project on local history. She picked up the finger, examined it in the blur of light from a plastic-lined window. "I've seen rings like this. Some guy in town makes them—not exactly like this, but with arrows, moons, stars, things like that. 'Hex rings,' he calls them."

"An arrow's a pretty universal symbol—for good or bad."

"I suppose." The girl glanced at her watch, put the finger back on the wheelbarrow. "Bus is coming in a couple minutes. Got to get my stuff together. Wilder and I are having a showdown before school starts. I'm really pissed the way he's been acting lately— that Joanie Hayden. She's been after him, you know."

"She can't compete with you." Ruth stood up; together, mother and daughter watched the calves suckle on a placid Jane Eyre. It was always a thrill to see how a newborn took to the teat, even standing, and only two or three hours old. Jane was practically purring with motherhood.

"She'd never be able to clean out a feeding trough, that Joanie

TWO

FAY HUBBARD peered out the cracked window of the nineteenth-century farmhouse. She was expecting the new sign for the Flint's Farmhouse Bed-and-Breakfast she was opening up. She'd registered already with the local chamber of commerce, but not a single client yet. Though who would be attracted to a run-down place like this? House, barn, and silo all in disrepair, one leaning into the next like they were trying to prop one another up. And a hired man's shack that looked like it had been through a war. Even a coat of paint wouldn't do much for house or barn, but she'd try. Nine months ago, she'd walked out of a marriage with only a battered suitcase, a pile of wool she intended to hook into rugs, a knot of guilt heightened by the thirty-one-year-old daughter and the grandchild she'd left behind, and twelve thousand dollars in a money market that was already on a downward spin. And rent due Monday to Homer Flint down in Poughkeepsie, New York.

Homer Flint was a second cousin three or four times removed. She'd never met him, but he drove a hard bargain; he wasn't giving anything away, not to an obscure relative. Imagine, $250 a month for a run-down farm without even a cow. She'd had to rent one for the atmosphere. Fay was a flatlander, she had to admit. Though she'd lived thirty-two years in Vermont with a seventh-generation Vermonter, maverick as the old cow out in the falling-down barn. That cow kicked every time Fay tried to get near. But she had been born in New York State, the daughter of an Italian father who seldom practiced his Catholicism, and a mother who traced her ancestry straight to the *Mayflower*—all that Puritan guilt. Fay couldn't escape that past. Though she was trying. Trying to become a Vermonter, trying to make a new life in Branbury, Vermont, where at least there was a small college: concerts, lectures, a chance to meet people. Though she hadn't met a conversational soul yet, except the hardware store clerk, who frowned at her out-of-town checks.

She went over to the General Electric range to boil some water. It must have been bought in the thirties. When she had customers— no, "guests," they called them in the B and Bs—she'd have to get a decent stove. Another five hundred bucks. Yipes! Well, maybe a secondhand one. The water boiled slowly, and finally she filled a cracked cup with hot water and two Lipton tea bags. She needed the caffeine.

She didn't belong anywhere, that was the trouble. After leaving Dan, she'd gone back to the city: six months down in Philadelphia with an ancient college friend she'd had a crush on once. He was sweet, but it was obvious that he missed his first wife. He had ten grandchildren, who kept eating up the larder and pulling threads out of her hooking. Every night before bed, he removed his prosthetic leg, but he complained about pains down there. And then was impotent in the bargain—saltpeter or something he took for his angina. Even so, he wanted to marry her. That was the worst of it. They all wanted a live-in to do the dishes, vacuum up the dirt, be an ornament on the holiday tree.

Now Fay was a pariah. She had no future. At fifty-six, how was she going to make herself a future? A few more years and she'd be a senior citizen. Or was it even less now? They kept lowering the ante; youth ended at twenty-nine these days. But was she going to sag around and let old age happen? Was she going to sit in a rocking chair all day and hook rugs? She pulled her achy bones upright. No ma'am. She was damned if she would.

Whoa! She knew it. Just sat down with her tea and someone was at the door. The liquid trembled in the cup; her spine tingled. Well, she had the room ready. She'd spent a small fortune in the local Ben Franklin buying pale blue polka-dot sheets and curtains for the grimy windows and a rag rug (she'd charge Flint for repairs; that was part of the bargain—he had a cushy job in the city). She took a deep breath, peered out the window. Saw it was no guest, but her sign. It was just that she hadn't expected it to arrive in a gray cart dragged behind a rusted green bicycle.

"Come in—it's not locked," she hollered, and heard the man put a shoulder behind the door and bang it open.

"Hi," he said, practically falling into the room, along with a sweep of orange leaves, then catching his weight on the door. "Willard Boomer here. I brought your new sign." He jerked his head in the direction of the outdoors, then stood there, apologetically, as if he'd intruded on a tea party, hands clasped at the crotch of his paint-spattered jeans, an ingratiating smile on his lips. Nice face, though, rather sweet—hardly wrinkled, though he had white hair. She liked him. By phone, she'd ordered the old farm sign replaced, and he'd sent a sketch.

"Well, let's take a look," she said.

He squinted at the teacup still in her hand. "Gosh, I've come at a bad time. I should've phoned. Mother tells me that I'm impulsive. But I thought you'd of wanted it."

"Yes. Of course! I really didn't even feel like tea; I just poured it because...well, I was alone, I guess." She put the cup down with finality, grabbed a purple wool sweater from a hook on the door, and strode out. "Ooh," she said. And when he made a gasping sound behind her, she said, "Not the sign. The wind! I've been away six months. Forgot how cold and windy it gets up here—so quick. It's blowing all the pretty leaves off. And only half through October."

"I'm sorry," he said with an apologetic laugh, as if it were his fault, the wind, the chill.

She spread her hands, then went over to the cart to look at the sign. She grinned back at him, made a sign of approval. FLINT'S FARMHOUSE B & B, it read. Neatly painted in green and white, with the head of a black-and-white cow on the bottom.

"I've only the one," she said, waving her arm at the scrawny Holstein out in the pasture. "Cost me forty dollars a month to rent, and I had to pay for six months. But I can pass for a farm, can't I?" Seeing him look about, confused, she said, "The one cow. It won't let me near it, but it looks pretty out there in the field, doesn't it? Dandelion's her name. The woman who lived here had one, but it died. She's my cousin something removed—Glenna Flint. This is really her place. She lives now with her nephew, Homer, and his second wife. Married, but kept her maiden name. Know her?"

"Oh, yes, surely," he said, bowing west as though Glenna, whom Fay had never met, was there in the field, as well. "Nice lady. This was her home all right. I can't imagine she wanted to leave."

"C'mon in and I'll give you a check," Fay said. "Cup of tea?

I have some Lipton's, actually. Or would you like a glass of wine? There's some homemade in the pantry.''

"Oh, no, I don't—actually, I have to go. Got another sign to do. For a new lawyer in town. They expect it yesterday.'' He laughed, groped in his jeans pockets, then an inside pocket of his dungaree jacket. Then he laughed again. "I must have left the bill at home. But there's no hurry, no hurry.''

"Just tell me how much. You can mail the receipt.''

"No, no. I wouldn't presume. What we agreed on—sixty, I think? If that isn't too much? I mean—''

"That's fair enough. But if you want to mail the bill, mail it.'' Fay was pleased in fact; it would give more time to recoup. She was planning to sell a fur coat the Philadelphia widower had given her—it had belonged to his wife. He was pretty upset when she left, tears running down his face, but he insisted she take the coat. They mustn't lose touch, he'd said; she'd see how hard it was for a woman alone. The coat was his lifeline to Fay.

Well, one of them would soon be sinking.

"I'll be going, then," said Willard Boomer, "I'll send you— when I find it." He checked his pockets again, shrugged. "You're sure sixty isn't too much? I don't want to—''

"It's a sharp-looking sign," she said, holding up her right palm. "It should do the trick.''

"Well, then," he said, pleased, "I'll drop off the bill. Maybe... maybe take you up on that tea?''

"I'd love it. Do you know how to milk a cow?''

He looked worried. "Well, I...I've seen it done. I suppose I...well, yes, I could give it a try. Wait—wait, though. Yes, there's another farm next door. Nice man—Willmarth. No, no, he's gone. Wife running it now—Ruth's her name. She'll give you instructions. She'll know how.''

"But she probably has a milking parlor and all that, right? Does it by machine?''

Willard laughed. "Oh my, yes. Machine, yes. They don't do it by hand anymore. But I'm sure, if she had to—''

"*I* have to, beginning today. I got Dandelion only yesterday, and she's supposed to be milked twice a day. Twice a day! They didn't tell me that till they brought her here. By truck. She's a big girl. Skinny but big. Huge.''

"Oh my, yes, I see that," he said, squinting at the overgrown pasture, getting on his green bike.

"You're taking the sign back?"

He laughed graciously. "No, no, I'll just hang it out there on the post. You want that old one down? About corn and maple syrup? I don't think there's been any syrup sold here in...well, twenty-five years. Since the husband, um, left, you know. It was my first sign," he added. "I was just starting up the business. Not as, well, skilled, you might say, in those days."

"Down with the old. Up with the new!" she declared, remembering something out of a community play she'd played a part in. He looked startled; his eyes popped, and then he giggled. "And thanks, Mr. Boomer. I'm very pleased with it."

"Willard," he said, and the back of his neck turned red. He half-turned and waved; the bicycle wobbled up the leafy drive, almost tipped, then righted itself. He started out into the main road, then, remembering the sign, wheeled about and waved again. He got off the bike, removed the old sign, and hung the new one, his white thatch tangling in the October wind.

She wondered how old he was. Milk white hair but smooth pink cheeks, a nice lean shape—all that biking, she supposed. She wondered if he owned a car. For all her bad experience with men— well, Fay liked men. She did, she had to admit it.

But she wasn't getting involved. No way. Thirty-odd years of living someone else's life—now she'd live her own. She pulled her long cotton underwear firmly down over her white cotton socks. She'd make do. Her husband had called her a cockroach once when they'd had a fight. Because she was tough, she was sneaky, he'd said. She was a survivor, wasn't she? She had to be.

"Come on, folks," she shouted into the wind. "Flint's Farmhouse B and B! Smelly cheese and sticky syrup." She'd have to buy those, she realized. "And fresh milk from a horny old cow. Hurrah!"

THREE DAYS, the sign flapping in a north wind and no "guests" for Flint's B and B. The leaf-viewing season was over. Who'd want to be in Vermont, Fay asked herself, when your boots sink two inches into mud and dead leaves every step you take? Already, Fay had gone through three cans of beans left in Glenna's pantry (tops slightly rusted, so she was alert for botulism), two jars of applesauce, and a box of stale oatmeal cookies. Desperate for income, she'd gone first to the local craft center, where she was told, "We already have a hooked-rug artist but we'll keep you on file." Then she'd gone up to Burlington to audition for an advertising firm—they were looking for a woman to sell freezers. And she'd dressed her frozen best in a red wool pantsuit and fleecy boots. But they chose a young female in a low-necked pink silk blouse. So if nothing else turned up, she'd have to clean houses. Not that she minded that really; it just wasn't on the top of her agenda. She didn't always see the dirt, that was the trouble. It was hard enough to keep things neat, but now she had to be prepared for a guest.

When someone knocked on the door, she jumped. It was either a guest or a greyhound—she'd ordered one from a newspaper ad— a woman alone needed a dog. "Young greyhounds are being shot, clubbed, starved, hanged, electrocuted, and worse," the ad read; "forced to race rather than enjoy a run. The greyhound is meant to live in a home like other dogs, not at a racetrack."

Fay identified with that ad. To take in a greyhound, she felt, was like taking in a victim, a clone of herself. How could she not respond? A woman alone, she'd feel safer with a dog. She'd heard about that business with the French-Canadian farmer, knocked on the head one muddy spring night. But it was neither greyhound nor guest at the door; it was the woman farmer down the road. She announced herself at once in a husky, sensible voice: "Ruth Willmarth." Good-looking woman, Fay thought, in her forties somewhere. "I'm here to help with your cow," Ruth Willmarth said, holding her ground on the threshold of Fay's kitchen. When Fay invited her in, she refused, politely taking a step backward in her sturdy brown boots.

"I can't stay. Can we take a look at her now?"

"If we can catch her," said Fay, shoving an arm into her heavy purple sweater. "She skitters away when I come near, even with hay. I have to leave it in the stall. Reminds me of Cousin Glenna— what I hear about her, anyway." When Ruth raised an eyebrow,

Fay said, "Oh, we're related. Very distant, something-something-something removed. You knew her?"

"Oh, yes." Ruth looked interested. "She's coming back? They came up and hauled her off. I understood she was reluctant to leave."

"Not coming back, oh no. She's going into a nursing home down there. Losing her, um, faculties, according to her nephew."

"Really? I never noticed it. Too bad. I suppose Homer will want to sell, then. Is Glenna agreeable with all this?"

Fay shrugged. At the moment she had other things on her mind. Like learning to milk a cow. The farmer she'd rented it from had pinch-hit for a few days. Now it was her turn. "Do I need anything? Pail?"

"That might help."

They moved out toward the barn in silence. She saw Ruth looking at the leaning silo. Any minute, it could topple over on them. And the foundation was slipping away beneath the barn and adjacent trailer—into the stream, it seemed, that ran close by. But that wasn't her responsibility, was it? The Willmarth woman was a Vermonter all right: robust, pleasant enough, but one-track. So was the cow, Dandelion. For a ten-year-old, though, the cow was quite agile. Fay rather admired the way she skipped away from Ruth, her white switch whipping about her skinny ribs, her brown eyes snapping.

"Could be my Zelda's sister." Ruth slapped the cow's rump—quite familiarly, Fay thought. She laughed when Ruth told the story of the newborn, how Zelda had just taken off and dropped her calf in the bushes. "Sounds like a good old girl," Fay said, and Ruth nodded. Dandelion kicked up manure and they both jumped back.

Ruth cornered the creature with a headlock, pulled her into the barn, and pushed her into the only stanchion that wasn't broken down. "You'd think she'd want to be milked. They usually do, get cramped carrying it around inside. Now stand there and I'll show you. Haven't done this in awhile myself, you know. We have a milking machine. But I guess it'll come back to me." She grabbed a three-legged stool and plumped down on it.

"Looks like years since they ran this as a farm," Fay said, wanting now to slow the lesson. Anyhow, she was suddenly curious about the place. Her guests would want to know its history.

"Last time was when Glenna came up with her husband. A city fellow. He stayed maybe six or seven years. And then——" Ruth flung up her hands.

"Dead?" In the tiny spare room that was hardly more than a closet, Fay had found a man's black overcoat, quite fancy-looking, with a white silk scarf in the pocket, faded to yellow——a B. Altman label. The husband's?

"Died in some rooming house in New York City was the word. Left her, people say. Others say Glenna did him in, buried him here. You know, small-town rumors." Ruth looked amused. "I liked her, though. She was her own person. Eccentric but tough. Okay," she said, getting down to business, "you take the teat between your thumb and forefinger, like this." She gripped the long pinkish teat. "Relax the grip, and push up, see? Then start pulling down as you squeeze"——the milk squirted into the pail——"with the first finger, then the next, then the last two. You'll force it from the teat through the streak canal."

"Streak canal," Fay repeated. She watched the milk squirt into the pail, then squealed when a stream hit her foot.

"Sorry. It's been awhile." A tiger cat appeared out of nowhere, and Ruth took one of the teats and squirted it into the cat's mouth.

"I never knew that cat was here. Where'd it come from?"

"Barn cat. Must be several around." Ruth whistled, and, sure enough, two more came running up, clones of the first.

"I have to feed them, too?"

Ruth laughed. "They eat mice. Except that one." She pointed at a dead mouse, lying in rigor mortis, its short legs upright like a turned-over chair. "Could have poison in him or something. Cats know." She patted the cat. "Now you do it."

Fay sat down gingerly on the stool. The pink teats looked like stalactites on a cave she'd seen once, only warmer-looking. She'd nursed her own child, but briefly. At the time, she hadn't fancied having long pink teats hanging down to her waist. Now the daughter, Patsy, who was divorced, with a ten-year-old boy, accused Fay of ignoring her, of never being around when she'd needed a parent. Was it true? Fay wondered. But who had changed her diapers, she wanted to know, read to her, cared for the child when she was sick? And where was Dan those times?

"Don't be bashful," said Ruth, sounding impatient.

Fay frowned at the cow. When she'd rented it, she hadn't thought of having to milk it. She just wanted it as a kind of ornament for the B and B guests. Dandelion twisted her head, peered back suspiciously. She smelled warm, like sweaty flesh. Fay gingerly took a teat in her hand. Nothing came out. She was reminded of those newfangled faucets that never worked right in the ex-lover's house.

"You have to squeeze. Like this." Ruth grabbed a teat in each hand and pulled, hard, close.

Fay squeezed, and got a drop out. The cow sensed her frustration and urinated. Ruth snatched away the bucket just in time.

"Jesus." Fay felt weak in the knees. "I'll just have to practice. Twice a day, you say?"

"Yes, ma'am." The farmer woman was glancing at the barn door. "Look, I'd like to stay, but I can't. I have my own cows. Maybe my daughter Emily can come over and help when school's out. I'll give you a call. The older one, Sharon, she's pregnant— due next month. In the awkward stage now."

Fay remembered how happy she'd been when Patsy got pregnant. The thrill of the birth! The boy growing up, and then Fay went and left. How could she have done that?

Fay followed Ruth out, carrying the pail. It was half-full, although Ruth told her a cow had to be milked "clean—shouldn't leave a drop in the udder." And then what? She'd have to pasturize it or something? She didn't want to think about it. She found Glenna Flint a more interesting subject, actually. After all, the woman was her relative. "Glenna never said anything—about what happened to the husband?"

"No, she was always closemouthed, Glenna. Even more so after Mac disappeared—like she'd been violated somehow. Psychologically, I mean. Well, it could even have been suicide. Vermont has a high suicide rate in winter, you know."

"Oh," said Fay, contemplating a winter without guests. And her daughter, Patsy, calling up every other night to tell her mother to come home, that little Ethan needed a grandmother. Each call, she felt the stabbing wounds.

"My theory, though"—Ruth smiled at Fay—"is he went back to the city and died there. Of old age."

She started to leave, then swiveled to look at Fay—suspiciously, Fay thought. "You from the city yourself?"

"Oh, no," Fay said. "I mean, once, yes, but not for a long time. I lived in the Northeast Kingdom, near Cabot. My ex-husband has an egg farm there. I came down here—alone."

Ruth looked more sympathetic now. Fay had heard she was a single parent; obviously, she'd struck a note. "My son keeps chickens. Vic would like a whole barnful. We need to diversify, you see. We grow Christmas trees; I rent a pasture out for a friend's sheep. These are hard times for farmers. Well, look, Fay, I'll send Emily over; you needn't call."

Ruth started out through the stubbly field, stepped across the narrow stream that snaked between the barn and the hired man's trailer. She pointed, turned. "He lived there, they say, the husband. Rumor has it she wouldn't allow him in the house." She laughed aloud. It was a nice laugh, generous, deeply amused. She disappeared back across the rocky pasture, where scarlet sumac, Queen Anne's lace, and goldenrod still held on. Beyond, the mountains rose up, deep lavender and then the color of blood where the sun was trying to push out of the darkish clouds.

Fay peered into the trailer but could see nothing, because the windows were boarded up. The whole place seemed to slant to the rear—like if you sat on a chair on the front porch, it would soon slide down and out the back door. What was she doing here, anyway? What had she been thinking of, renting this derelict ghost of a place where a man had disappeared?

THREE

TIM, THE HIRED MAN, was taking down the diseased elm Ruth had marked. She hated to see it go; it had been there for the twenty years she'd lived on this farm, probably more than a hundred years before that. But they needed the wood for winter—used as many as eight cords for the old farmhouse with its poor insulation, which Pete had never gotten around to replacing. Tim had the Bush Hog splitter hitched up to the secondhand Harvester he'd persuaded her to buy, though it had put her in debt, and she hadn't paid off the last loan. The Bush Hog maneuvered nicely in the woods, Tim argued, had an efficient hydraulic system to power the splitter. He was struggling with the limb logs: They were dry, gray, and split off like popcorn. But full of bark-beetle tunnels—beetles partly responsible for killing the tree.

Beetles, she mused, were like people: big, bumbling, tunneling into the heart of things and festering there. Like her God-fearing sister-in-law, Bertha, who a year and a half ago had stirred up a brew of mischief in the name of God. But that was done with. They'd gone through more than a year without mishap. And her second grandchild due in a month's time. She'd feel better when Sharon delivered safely; Ruth wasn't sure about Sharon's determination to have a midwife, a home birth in Ruth's own bed, because the town apartment had thin walls. When Branbury had a perfectly good hospital. She'd had three safe deliveries there. Though she'd hated those stirrups they'd imprisoned her legs in. They reminded her of the eighteenth-century stocks. And just as much a punishment!

"You think this will do it for the season?" she called out. "We probably have another six cords stacked up already."

"Got my eye on another tree up in the woods, an elm. *Farmer's Almanac* predicting a tough winter. Pays to be safe."

"You're the boss," she said, and Tim smiled, put two fingers in salute to the brim of the cowboy hat he wore as an act of independence—most hired men wore the traditional feed cap. He was a fiftyish ex-hippie, had been through the sixties rebellion, dropped out of the establishment, "found himself." Pete had hired him in the late seventies, and he'd stayed on when Pete left. He seemed happy enough now as a hired hand, helping foster kids like Joey. She couldn't do without him. Nor could Vic, her eleven-year-old. Tim was something of a father figure to him now that Pete was gone. Though she knew the boy missed his own father.

"Think the kid could run the Deere, pull the manure spreader out to the woods, pick up a load for me? He knows how; I showed him."

"No way. Too young. I'll do it."

"Oh, come on. He's grown a foot since spring."

"You sound like Pete. The answer is no. A boy older than Vic lost an arm falling off a tractor down in Shoreham. Like I said, I'll do it. When? Today? Tomorrow?"

"Morning. After milking." Tim swung his sledgehammer against a log end, struggling to drive the log free of the wedge. They didn't really split, these logs, she observed, just wrenched apart, shrieking, like a bulldozed building. Like a mismatched husband and wife, she thought.

An ancient blue Horizon was sitting in the driveway. She recognized it when she got to the house. "Why didn't you just walk in?" she shouted at Colm Hanna. He was getting to be a familiar figure around the farm now—maybe too familiar. She wasn't a free woman; she had to remember that. Pete wanted more than a sold farm. He wanted a divorce, and for some reason, she was having a hard time giving in. Not for herself—it was over with Pete, wasn't it? Though after two years, she was still hurting, didn't want to give him the satisfaction.... And there were the children, Vic and Emily—especially Emily, who blamed her in some way, she felt, for Pete's leaving. She knew Emily still told her school friends that Pete would be back. The older one, Sharon, of course, even in her ninth month of pregnancy, could fend for herself; Sharon was a stubborn one, full of New Age ideas. If Ruth heard one more word about eating tofu... Though it was true, she couldn't eat beef anymore, not when she was thinking it might have been one of her own bull calves.

Here was Colm, his gray-black hair rumpled from the wind, grinning at her, waving a bone. "I checked Larocque's after you called. Nothing dug up there. I'll try Flint's, but there's no cemetery on that place."

She'd forgotten about the finger, too many other things on her mind: getting in the wood, cutting the last corn, mending tools and machines bought back in the seventies because she couldn't afford new ones. Work never done, and late fall was supposed to be the more lax time in a farmer's year. "How old you think that bone is?" she asked as she ran into the house ahead of him, and swept a pile of crumbs off the table. Emily's house job was the kitchen, but lately she'd been wrapped up in her quarrel about this city girlfriend of Wilder's.

"You should see my place." Colm settled into a high-backed kitchen chair and examined the bone, glasses down on his nose. It looked like any minute they'd slide into his lap. "Dad thinks it's been in the ground for a while—twenty, thirty years. But we'd have to get an expert. You know any guys got bumped off back then?"

"People are always dying. You should know that. You and your dad." She'd never related to the idea of Colm being a part-time mortician—or assistant to one—though what could he do when it was his dad's business? She set a cup of coffee in front of him, sank into a chair with hers, and then leapt up to throw a log into the woodstove. Tonight, she'd have a talk with Emily about keeping up with chores. "What makes you think it's male?"

"The size, I guess. Could be wrong. Dad thinks so, though."

"A man with a delicate ring like that?"

"Ring?"

"Oh, sorry." She'd forgotten to mention the ring. She rummaged in a drawer. Where had she put it? But the drawer held only napkin rings that she never used, and in the back a paper cigar ring left over from Pete. She crumpled it, tossed it in the trash can.

"Emily must have it. We pulled it off the finger—the knuckle-bone looked frail. It has some bone-and-arrow symbol on it, like a hex sign, she says. Didn't people use those a lot in the old days?"

"On doors maybe, yes—but on fingers? But hey, where did I see an arrow recently?" He shoved the glasses back up on his nose. They magnified his intense blue eyes. "Yeah, I know—that meditation group up the mountain, in East Branbury. I was up there yesterday, showing land.''

''What group is that?'' College kids, she supposed, or graduates returning to the area, starting up communes of sorts—usually didn't do much harm, though there could be drugs involved. Something to kick off the retreat into the inner psyche. Emily had told her the actress woman had Pete meditating. Imagine, pragmatic Pete! One would do anything for sex, she guessed.

''You're not listening again,'' Colm accused, his eyes probing hers. He looked thinner than ever, cadaverous. Those hunger lines around his mouth! Real estate, like farming, was depressed in these parts. ''Why don't you join up with them?'' he teased. ''Might do you good. This is an older group, seems like. Some of them look forty years old, maybe fifty.''

And when she gave him her ''How do you know?'' look, he said, ''They called me, wanting to buy up a couple extra acres of land. I tried, but no way old conservative Bagshaw next door was selling. I mean, he wanted an acre of *their* land. 'I ain't selling to no cult members,' he said. He remembers that Northeast Kingdom group, supposed to have been abusing their kids.''

''And the state took away the children. I thought it abominable. They had no proof of abuse.''

''Well, they thought they did. Anyway, I didn't see a single kid at the Healing House. That's what they call the place,'' he explained, and this time she had to laugh. He was wolfing down her doughnuts. His chin was a furry mask.

''Pig,'' she said. And suddenly she remembered what he'd said. ''What were you saying about the arrow?''

''On the sign. A bone crossed with an arrow—about to penetrate a moon, or what looks like a moon.''

''But that's it!'' she cried. ''That's the ring. I mean, almost, except that this one didn't have a moon.'' And she smiled, noticing a moon of sugar around Colm's lips. He caught her glance, and smiling himself, he licked it off with a pink tongue.

''I need a shave,'' he muttered. ''I thought I'd wait till after I saw you, though. You don't mind?''

''Should I?''

But he just looked at her, hard, then licked his lips again.

FAY WAS COMING BACK from the barn with a half pail of milk, painstakingly drawn, when a white car squealed its brakes in front of the house. Then Fay caught a glimpse of a girl, a decade younger maybe than her Patsy, dragging a paper bag from the car. Guests! And no one had called ahead. She hadn't been gone that long. But she mustn't prejudge, or assume they were staying. In her excitement, she stepped into the rivulet; it filled her socks. Oh well. The car had a New York license. There was a dent in front, but it was in better shape than her own ancient Dodge. They'd told her at the auto-parts place that her engine was in good shape but that the body wouldn't go through another winter; the bottom might drop out. A metaphor for me, she thought. But she'd worry when winter came. Who knew? By then, she might have found her future.

She stopped to button her jacket properly, ran milky hands through her hair; it needed cutting. No, she thought. I'll grow it into a long braid—yes, something different. Dan had always wanted her to grow her hair long—that's why she'd kept it short. "Perverse," he'd said, and she guessed she was. She'd had to be, or he'd have cooked her into an omelette.

Entering, she heard footsteps upstairs. Now that was a bit of an imposition. They might at least have waited in the kitchen. "Hullo up there," she called. There was no banister on the stairs; that could be a liability. She'd had to get a license, had barely met the fire laws. "Hullo—proprietor here," she said.

"Who?" a woman's voice called. "I'm the proprietor here."

And then a younger, sweeter voice said, "Aunty, please, Dad rented the place out; you're not the proprietor now. Hi, down there," and a girl came flying down the steps, her chestnut-colored hair a raggedy mop behind her. "Sorry, we just kind of took possession. We really hadn't planned to come; it just—happened. We got in the car, and next I knew, I was kidnapping my aunt! I mean, we're just here till my parents get back from some convention. They've got Aunty signed up for a nursing home. She sprained her arm, you see, chasing the cat." She grinned, stuck out a hand. She was a pretty girl, on the plump side, eyes the color of grass. "We brought some stuff for supper." She waved at a paper bag on the kitchen table.

"Wait a minute here," said Fay. "It's just breakfast you get, and

I provide it. You go out for dinner. I've got a list of nice places. You want fish? Try Elmo's. Steak?''

"I'm a vegetarian," the girl said. "So's Aunty—more or less. I brought pizzas."

A screech filled the upstairs. The girl dashed up, three steps at a time. "Aunty, you all right?"

"No, I'm not all right. They took everything out of my closet. You didn't think to pack a damn thing to wear."

"Aunty, I didn't know. I didn't know we were coming here."

"And I can't find my red sweater. It's my favorite. It cheers me up in the snow. Your mother never packed it when she rushed me out of here. It should be in the bottom drawer, and it's not."

Fay climbed the stairs slowly, afraid of what she was hearing. She remembered that sweater; it was full of holes. She'd packed it away in a box somewhere. Oh dear. At the landing she stiffened her shoulders, jerked her jeans around so the zipper was properly in the middle, and took a stand in the doorway of the guest room.

"Who are you?" said the old lady. She resembled some variety of hybrid shaggy dog. Under the unbrushed hair, the face was fierce. She looked like an Amazon, ready for battle, a sling on her arm. For arrows? Fay wondered. She was almost beautiful, in a feral way, like a wild hawk. Fay had to admire her. As she stared, the woman yanked off the sling and tossed it at the girl. "I don't need this thing anymore. It puts me off balance."

"I'm Fay Hubbard. I mean, that's my married name. My great-grandmother was a Flint. I rent the place out for a B and B. So who are you?" As if she didn't know. She took a deep breath, held on to the edge of the doorway. The old lady just sat back down on the bed, looking put-out, as if Fay had stolen her surname.

"I'm Hartley Flint," said the girl sweetly, "from Poughkeepsie, New York, and this is my great-aunt, Glenna Flint. This is her place. She owns it."

"You bet I do. Six generations on this rocky soil. And I'm not paying to stay in my own house." The old lady flopped back on the bed, throwing her feet up on the quilt Fay had just had dry-cleaned.

"Jesus," said Fay, and held on to the doorknob.

"I'll pay," said the girl. "I've got a credit card. I'm not supposed to use it except for food. My parents are in Florida. I mean, I told Aunty she should stay at the inn. She's so...perverse," she whispered in Fay's ear, and Fay's eyes widened. "But she insisted. They want to put her in Lands' End, you see, and she doesn't want to go."

"Lands' End's a catalog," said Fay.

"Same thing," said Glenna. "Freeze you in print, those places. Shut you up between covers. I won't have it."

Hartley sucked in her lower lip, looked contrite. "Just for a couple nights. Till my parents come back from Miami."

"I'm not leaving. Never again," said Aunty, spacing her words, her eyes narrowed. "I'll get a court order."

"Somebody has to take care of you," said Hartley, sounding prim. "You can't live alone. Who'll see that you eat right and don't fall down the stairs?"

"That one will," said Glenna, pointing a finger at Fay.

Feeling panic in her chest—any minute she'd have a heart attack, and the women in her family had all had them early on—Fay backed out of the room and ran for an Ecotrin.

EMILY WILLMARTH was cooling it altogether with Wilder Unsworth. It was just too much, this city girl Joanie Hayden, with her diamond nose stud. He claimed there was nothing to it, but Emily could hear the tremor in his voice when he denied any interest; she could see that flush of red across the cheekbones when she mentioned Joanie's name. So Emily was going underground.

Anyway, she had an assignment for her history project. She had to read a moldy book about the Branbury area in the local library and then interview a couple of equally ancient residents. Mr. Morinelli had assigned her one, an old fellow named Alwyn Bagshaw, who lived in East Branbury and whose family hadn't moved off the original pitch since they'd floated up the Otter Creek from Connecticut in 1769. But she had to find one other interviewee on her own.

"Try next door," her mother said, pointing to the south. They were in the barn, cleaning up after evening milking, scraping out the calf pens. Emily disliked the job, and she was wearing a scarf up over her nose. Another cow, Esmeralda, had freshened, but at least she was nursing her young, unlike that miserable Zelda. Emily didn't know why her mother kept that cow. Now Zelda's calf had the scours: loose bowels that stained its tail yellow. Her mother was pushing a huge pink pill down its gullet, while the calf laid its ears back in panic. Her hand was practically swallowed up inside the purply throat.

But her mother was still talking. "Glenna Flint just came home to roost."

"Oh?" Emily knew their old neighbor Glenna Flint. She had a voice like a crow. Emily laughed at her mother's choice of words. "Home to roost," she repeated.

"Or visit. I don't think she has much power anymore over the nephew and his wife. She's a little eccentric maybe, but she can probably tell you her life story." Her mother laughed. She looked years younger when she laughed, Emily thought. But she hadn't laughed much since Dad had left. But she wasn't doing anything to get him back, either. That annoyed Emily.

"What's so funny?" she said.

"Oh, I don't know. The whole situation. There's quite a crew of Flints over there now. That Fay Hubbard called again, in a panic herself. Wants to know if it's okay to drink unpasturized milk. I told her that her ancestors drank it and lived. Anyway, they're all ages over there—one of them just a little older than you. Fay hasn't had a single guest yet, I understand, though of course it's off-season. She rented a cow. Can you imagine? Renting a cow?" Her mother broke off into a paroxysm of giggles, and Emily laughed, too.

"You don't need me here anymore, right, Mom? You can finish up in a jiff? Well, maybe I'll call Flint's and set up a time to talk with old Glenna. Vic's tape recorder's in his room, you think?"

"Better not borrow it without asking. And for heaven's sake, don't touch his telescope. He saved for a year to buy a real one— I mean, other than the homemade. Your friend Wilder's family destroyed that one."

"Not *my* friend Wilder anymore, Mom. We broke up." Emily swept out one more stall under her mother's watchful frown. She was thinking about that girl at the Flint's. Maybe they could be friends. She could use a friend—she'd dropped other girls while she was so thick with Wilder. And where did it get her?

Okay, she'd interview old Glenna, type it up on the Selectric—when would her mother break down and get a computer?—and then go see that Bagshaw. She didn't know much about him. She'd just heard he was crotchety. That's what her conservative teacher said: "crotchety." And he lived next to that new meditation center, or whatever it was. "Stay away from that place," Mr. Morinelli had warned, like it was dangerous to sit and think.

Maybe she would and maybe she wouldn't. Her sister, Sharon, said there was a midwife who lived there; Sharon's midwife had used her once as an assistant. Well, Emily was ready for new experiences at this point in her life. Honestly, she was getting sick of cows. Sick of this whole family situation.

She ran to the door, leaping the cow patties, then turned and looked hard at her mother. "When are you going to call Dad?" she accused. "He's always calling here first, and you never give him the time of day. Don't you think he might come back if you'd give him an opening?"

But her mother just went on doctoring the calf, her head in its Select Sires feed cap like an extension of the animal's belly.

YOUNG VIC WILLMARTH watched his sister leave the house before he took the hawk into the house. It was a red-tailed hawk; he knew the broad blond wings and rounded reddish tail from his Scout work. He'd found the bird out in the east pasture. It had glared and hissed at him, but it couldn't fly; it was down. Beside it, its mate had lain motionless. The wings, during the bird's death throes, had left a feathery, four-foot-wide leaf angel on the field. The male—or was it female?—had flapped its wings furiously as Vic wrapped it in his coat.

"I'm sorry," Vic said, "I really am. But your mate's gone and you're still alive. And I'm gonna try and get you better."

But the hawk seemed to fall in a dead faint when he got it up into his room; it lay there with one unblinking eye fixed on him, accusingly. When his mother came in, before she could open her mouth to object to a nearly dead hawk on his clean quilt, or remind him he had chores in the barn, he said, "I know, Mom, I know. But I want it to live. Can you drive me to the vet's, Mom, please?"

The hawk made a noise then, a small pleading sound, and Vic

told about its mate. "They mate for life, Mom; I read that somewhere. It's sad. Can't we help it?"

She stood there a moment, looking down at the hawk, looking
like her eyes might explode in her face, and then she said, "Okay.
Get in the pickup. But we'll have to leave it there, because I have
work to do and I have to get right back." Vic smiled, wrapped the
hawk back in his jacket, and followed her out. His mother was a
pushover when it came to animals—birds *or* cows. It was just with
people she was tough. Too tough, he thought, thinking of his father.
He had his own theories about why his dad had left.

The vet, a woman, examined the hawk critically. It was a female,
she said, explaining that the female hawk was actually larger than
the male, its tail feathers redder. They'd have to do tests. "But my
assumption is that it's been poisoned. The way the eyes look, you
know. It's a healthy bird—good flesh—I can see that. It must've
gotten into something bad." She peered over her glasses at Vic's
mother, as if she was responsible, but Vic spoke up. "Mom doesn't
use pesticides. Not anymore. Dad did, but when he left...well, Mom
doesn't now."

He was proud of that.

The vet just shrugged. She knew farmers, the shrug said: how
they got around the law, tried poisons for this and that—lice, horn
flies on their cows.... "We'll try atropine," she told his mother.
"It's an antidote for organophosphate poisoning. That is, if my assumption's correct. We'll try," she repeated, her expression softening when she looked at Vic's face, though he tried to hold it
expressionless, immobile. "And I'll call you, Vic. I can't guarantee
anything, but I'll try."

He let his mother lead him back through the maze of rooms to
the outer door. A dog whined in a crate; a cat hissed on its owner's
lap. "If somebody's using poison," his mother said, "I don't like
it at all. Not with my animals out there in the field."

Vic nodded. He thought he might like to be a vet someday. A
small-animal vet, not a big-animal vet. Not cows.

FOUR

THE GREYHOUND Fay had ordered arrived at six in the morning. "Come in," yelled Fay, and stumbled into the kitchen, a blanket pulled around her—Fay slept in the nude—just as the old white cat Glenna Flint had brought with her was digging its claws into the greyhound's rear end. The dog had come from New Hampshire, where they still allowed greyhound racing—a disgrace, Fay felt, agreeing with the woman from Greyhound Rescue.

"Call off your cat," the woman said. "This animal tolerates cats. Some don't, you know. They train these dogs with mechanical lures—mice, rabbits, cats. But this poor fellow, we got him away, young. But look at the ears, all bitten away. The scars. Three toes where there should be four. They chopped it off at the track. Abuse!"

Fay looked doubtfully at the tall sleek animal. It was panting, and she could see its yellow teeth—would she have to brush them?

"What does it eat?" she asked, running her tongue over her upper lip.

"I feed mine Eagle Premium Select," the woman said. "Maybe a little boiled chicken or hamburg mixed in. They have tender stomachs, these dogs—all that crap food they got fed at the tracks. Look," she said, baring the animal's teeth. Fay stepped back. The white cat hissed and lurched menacingly toward the dog. It cowered.

"The cat isn't mine," Fay assured her. "It belongs to a guest."

"Who's a guest?" growled Glenna, bumping her way down the stairs in a pink flannel nightgown and huge fuzzy pink slippers. "Get that beast out of here. He'll kill my Puffy! Puffy," she cried, snatching up the bristly white cat while the greyhound stood warily by the door.

"In Spain," the woman said, "they hang these dogs when they're through racing. Hang them! You're saving a soul."

"That has a soul?" said Glenna, pointing at the cowering dog, but Fay saw the half smile. Glenna, she suspected, was more bark than bite.

Fay leaned down to pat the dog. It gazed up at her gratefully, its eyes a rich liquidy brown. It was all curves and angles, sleek gray fur. Already, Fay loved it. Already, too, her heart was racing—the presence of the old lady and her great-niece was causing tension. Her mother had keeled over at sixty-nine, and age was creeping up on Fay. Turning her into Old Mother Hubbard. Fay just wanted to live in peace with a dog. She thanked the woman and ushered her out the door. Two more greyhounds were gazing sadly out the window of a black van. LIVE FREE OR DIE the license plate read. "Enjoy," the woman called back, as if she'd just served up a meal.

"Oh, adorable," said Hartley Flint, running downstairs in jeans and an orange sweatshirt. She threw her arms around the dog's neck. "What does he eat?" She stuck her head in the old General Electric, hauled out orange juice, Phony Boloney, I Can't Believe It's Not Butter!.

"I'm supposed to make the breakfast," Fay said. "I forgot to ask you what time."

"I'm always up by six," said Hartley.

"Well, I'm not," said Glenna, and, grabbing up her cat, she stomped back upstairs to dress. She turned at the top and yelled down, "You'll have to keep that animal outdoors, then. I won't have my cat eaten alive."

Upstairs, there was a crash. "It's Aunty," Hartley said. "You need new springs on that bed." She crushed two pieces of whole-wheat bread into the dented toaster. "You can use a new toaster, too. This thing squeals when you push it down."

Fay sighed. "This place needs a new everything." She'd have to go out and get some kind of job. She accepted the glass of orange juice Hartley gave her. The greyhound was panting in its corner. "It wants water," Hartley said, and poured some in a cracked saucer. The dog lapped it up in a gulp and stuck out its tongue for more. "Got any hamburger?"

"Not yet," said Fay, sighing.

"Speaking of Aunty," said Hartley, "I can't sleep in the same room with her. She has these nightmares. I didn't sleep one single minute last night. Though I couldn't make out a word she said. What about that other room upstairs?"

"It's not ready. I've ordered the paint, but I still have to buy curtains—I haven't had the money."

"Oh, Daddy will buy them." Hartley waved her credit card. "Just put it on this. It's his house, really. I mean, he has power of attorney. He makes out all Aunty's checks since she hurt her arm."

"Oh?" Maybe the aunt's arrival wasn't such a bad idea after all. Fay had been too modest in her requests, afraid to ask for much. Now she had a buffer. "You can sleep in the room anyway," she told the girl. "There's a bed. The window's broken, but spring is coming."

"Yeah," said Hartley, looking out at the light snowflakes. They were flying this way and that, as if they couldn't decide which direction to snow in. Fay was identifying with everything these days. She squatted down beside the dog to give it a welcoming hug. "I think I'll sleep in that trailer out there," Hartley said. "It's kind of cute. I could fix it up."

"No, you won't." A voice boomed down the pipes. "Nobody uses that trailer. Nobody sleeps there."

"Why not?" the girl yelled up. "You got your old man buried there or something?"

The pipes were silent, except for the rattling of the gas furnace down in the basement. The furnace was a backup for the woodstove, which was always going out. Fay hadn't counted on having to cut wood, either. She'd done enough of that in her old life. Her ex-husband, Dan, was in love with his woodstove.

"There are rats, that's why," Aunty hollered down. "Your step-mother would wet her pants if she knew her little girl was sleeping with rats."

"You got to get a new toaster," Hartley complained, ignoring the comment about the rats. She slapped a dollop of butter on her burned toast.

"We'll go in this afternoon, with your credit card," said Fay. "How long you say your parents are gone for?"

"Six days. Well, they left yesterday. Five days still. Then I'll have to go back. You have a telephone here? Matilda—she's my stepmother—will want to know what's going on. I can call back from here. She won't trace the call, will she?''

"I don't know your stepmother.''

"She would if she was suspicious. We'll have to make sure she's not, right?''

"I rather think so.'' Fay watched the girl lather on the butter. *Her* butter. At this rate, she'd have to shop every day. The dog was sitting up now, staring at the water dish. It wasn't water he wanted—that was obvious. She wondered if they could put dog food on the credit card.

In the pantry now, Hartley gave a cry of triumph, came out with a can of ham spread, and dumped it in the dish. In one lick, it was gone. Fay watched in shock. She dropped the dirty plates and cups in hot water. Of course there was no dishwasher. She'd have to wash the eggy plates by hand. What had made her think she wanted to run a B and B? If anybody came today for a room, where would she put them? In the bathtub?

"I'll take doggy here out for a run," Hartley said. "That okay with you? Can I name him?'' Without waiting for a reply, she said, "How about Gandalf? That's a guy out of *The Hobbit*—Tolkien. Have you read it? I've practically memorized it. Now I'm starting on *The Lord of the Rings*.''

"No,'' said Fay, then added, "Whatever.'' She was thinking now she might send the dog back with Hartley and Glenna when they went. She might not be able to afford to feed it.

"I'll have to go back,'' said Hartley, turning at the door, as if she'd read Fay's mind. "Though Aunty here thinks she's staying for good.''

"I don't think so,'' said Fay. She had to take a stand against intruders.

"We'll see,'' said the girl, and whistled for the dog. It sprang up, knocking over a chair, and dashed out after her. The pair disappeared into the drive and down the dirt road.

Fay had just settled back for a quiet cup of coffee when the phone rang. A cheerful voice from the Branbury Chamber of Commerce informed her that a man wanted a room for that night. "He has business in the area. He might stay awhile. Isn't that good luck? He especially asked for a B and B in your area, seemed happy that it was your farm. Shall I say yes?''

"Tonight," Fay repeated, feeling her fingers jump on the receiver. "What time?''

The person on the other end of the line repeated Fay's question to another party, then replied, "After dinner, eightish.... Ma'am, are you there?''

"I think so," said Fay, and hung up.

"Jesus," she said aloud to the sink. She left the dishes soaking and went to throw on some clothes.

Once she was dressed, she went back to the kitchen and pulled a gallon of white paint out of a bag. She'd have to get painting right off. Then she remembered she hadn't milked the cow yet, and Dandelion would be ramming her head against the barn wall. She pulled on her boots, picked up her heavy purple sweater, and ran out.

Fay got waylayed up by the hired man's trailer. Hartley was yanking on the doorknob. "I'll sleep here. I want to," she hollered.

The door came open and the girl nearly fell inside. "It's cute in here! I don't see a single rat.''

As she spoke, a mouse raced out the door and around the side of the barn; it disappeared underneath. The dog raced after it, then began digging. "Quit that," Fay ordered, but the dog went on digging for the mouse. Fay gave up and followed Hartley inside the trailer.

It was trailer size, though not exactly a trailer: A tiny room had been built on—actually, two rooms cut out of one, and a Lilliputian bath. One could take a shower and pee all at the same time. The living room was painted canary yellow over old striped wallpaper that glared through where the paint was thinnest. There was a couch with the bottom fallen out and a plush velvet overstuffed chair that the mice had obviously chosen as home. When Hartley stood in the bedroom doorway, a bed fell out of the wall. "Neat," the girl said, and dropped onto it.

"If not rats, mice," said Fay, looking at the droppings. "But okay, if you want to sleep here, fine, but you can't clean it up today. I've a guest coming at eight tonight and a room to paint and curtains to buy, so I'll need you and your credit card. Oh, and how'd you like to milk a cow?''

"I'd rather paint.''

"Then get to it. Paint's in the kitchen. I'll bring up a second brush when I'm done with Dandelion.''

Outside, Fay yanked the dog away from his digging and clipped on his leash. It was a warmish day; a few red leaves still clung to the trees. But the place could fall in any minute; there could be a sinkhole, she thought. Out in California, she'd read, a whole house fell in while the family looked on in shock. A small girl watched her bed and teddy bear sink slowly into the muck. That image had stuck in Fay's head. It made her think of her sweet young grandson....

Well, I have to quit this guilt trip, Fay told herself. "C'mon, Gandalf, I'll give you a squirt of milk.'' And she headed into the barn, the greyhound panting behind.

JEEZUM. Vic Willmarth had found another downed bird—this time, a crow. It was in the pasture his mother rented out for sheep. Vic had a schoolmate whose mother owned the sheep, and when he saw them out in the field, he'd gone over to ask about the homework assignment—he had been in the bathroom when the teacher gave it out. Garth was in a bad mood because his mother had put him to work. "I hate sheep, I hate sheep,'' the boy chanted while his mother shushed him from the far end of the field, and told him to "Go wait in the car, Garth.''

But Garth Unsworth didn't. He wanted to see what Vic had found. "Ooh, re-vol-ting,'' he said, reaching out a finger to touch the purply black feathers. The crow gave a violent twitch, and then its head flopped over. The filmy eyes stared.

"Leave it,'' Garth said. "No loss. They're filthy birds. They eat dead things. Caw-caw,'' he cried, flapping imaginary wings and pretending to peck at Vic's ear.

Vic explained how crows were actually useful; his dad had taught him that. "They're part of a chain,'' he told Garth. "They clean things up. So only the bones are left. They pick the lice off our cows—you watch sometime—you watch. The cows like it; they lift their tails so the crows can perch.''

"Re-vol-ting," said Garth, who had been brought up in a city. He kicked the dead bird and raced, cawing, back to his mother's car. Vic watched him go, then wrapped the dead crow carefully in his jacket and carried it back to his house. They were intelligent birds, they were! His dad had said so. His dad had had a pet crow when he was a little boy. It kept saying *cu-koo*, as if it wanted to talk to his father. He'd remember to tell his dad about this when he called on Saturday. Sometimes he was mad at his dad for leaving, didn't feel like talking. But this time he would.

It could be that poison again. The stuff that had poisoned the red-tailed hawk. Though the hawk was still alive—it had to be! The vet had said she'd keep in touch. Yes, she should probably know about the crow. He'd call her when he got home. Maybe she'd let him come visit.

Poison, he thought. Jeezum. Who would do that to birds?

BY FIVE O'CLOCK, the room was ready, though smelling of fresh paint. Fay made a sign—DO NOT LEAN ON WALLS OR WINDOW!—and then propped it up on the guest's pillow. If he'd wanted this place, he'd have to take what it offered: cluster flies (Hartley had painted over several right on the wall) and primitive sleeping arrangements. The new ruffled curtains and rose-flowered quilt looked out of place, like thin paint over ugly wallpaper. There were fresh blue-striped sheets on the bed, though, and a pine rack at the foot for a suitcase. She wondered if the chamber of commerce had told the man that this wasn't a working farm, but then she swallowed the worry. He could take it or lump it. *Lump it* is right, she thought, looking at the mattress. Well, she was the only B and B in this part of town. That, at least, was an advantage.

"Mother would throw up if she saw those ruffles," Glenna said, squinting into the room, her mouth in an upside-down U. "This was her room." Glenna followed Fay down the creaky stairs. She shuffled in her huge pink slippers over to the pantry and banged around among the few cans and bottles there. "I know I had scotch," she said. "*She* won't allow it down in New York; it's got to be here somewhere. You been sipping?" she accused, squinting out the pantry door.

"I don't drink scotch," said Fay. "But have some wine, if you want. It's homemade. By my ex."

"I never had an ex," Glenna said thoughtfully. "Never needed one."

Hartley came flinging in with the greyhound on her heels, and Puffy leapt up on the kitchen table, fur rising like quills. The wine bottle clunked over on its side.

"They're going to have to learn to be friends." Hartley picked up the furious cat and brought it close to the dog. Gandalf quivered while the cat hissed and jabbed its claws at him. Glenna laughed. "That dog knows who's boss around here."

"Yes, he does," said Fay bravely, "and the boss has a guest arriving any minute. And she'd be very grateful if you would go sit in the living room. No one treads on anyone else's toes around here. Remember that."

"We'll see about that," said Glenna, and shuffled with dignity into the front room.

Outside, a taxi was already pulling up. A tall, lanky man in a dark brown suit got out, hauling a suitcase that could hold a month's clothing. He stared dubiously at a dog mess, stepped carefully around it and up onto the shaky porch, looked a moment at the disappearing taxi as though he might want to drive back to town, and then, with a quick intake of breath, knocked.

Fay met him in the doorway, her most ingratiating self. "We do have two other guests," she said with a casual laugh, "but they'll be leaving shortly, and we'll move you into another room. I mean, I have a room for you now, of course." And laughing again (it came out like a step creaking), she took his suitcase.

"Come on," he said, hefting it, and shook her hand with his free one. He appeared to be in his early sixties and was intimidatingly good-looking: thinning dark hair, gray around the temples; eyebrows still thick and dark; a straight Grecian nose. Nice and lean. And hungry? Fay hoped not.

"Kevin Crowningshield," he said, catching up her hand. For a moment, she thought he might kiss it and her heart quickened. "Any room's fine. I'm just in town for a bit of business; I won't be in the room much."

She couldn't think what business would bring him to this rural town, but she wasn't going to pry. She just wanted to keep him here while he did it.

When they got inside, the kitchen was empty, the table cleaned up except for a bottle of homemade wine. She saw him look wistfully at it. Was wine a part of the B and B deal? But already he'd dropped the suitcase, was sinking into a chair. "Tell me about this place," he said, "this farm. I like to know about where I'm staying. I like farms. The fresh air..." He stopped, coughed, smiled. He was quite charming. Yes, Fay liked men; She just didn't always want to live with them.

She told him what she knew, which wasn't much. "The farm has been around a long time. The owner is on the premises—briefly, that is." When she poured him a glass of wine, he took it and, with a subdued little laugh, thanked her. She saw how white his hands were, though there was the palest bruise on a left knuckle, a broken nail. She followed his glance; he was looking at the phone.

"No charge for local calls," she said. "But out-of-town ones, I have to charge for, of course. You'll want to call your wife, I'm sure." Her hands trembled as she said it; she squeezed them together in her lap.

"Just local calls." He stared into the drink as if he'd see something there, a vision. "My wife, yes. That's why I'm here."

And suddenly he was up, nervous, gripping his hands. "I flew, you see, from Chicago. That small plane into the Burlington airport! I'm full of Dramamine. I get airsick." He laughed, a self-deprecatory laugh. "I need a walk, really, around the place. To clear my head. You know."

"Those shoes," Fay murmured as he rose from the table. They were dress shoes, black and shiny-new; she imagined them wading through manure. And now the ground was slippery with wet leaves and a dusting of fresh snow. "They'll get ruined."

"Agh." He waved away her worry, then plunged outside.

FIVE

EMILY WILLMARTH was trying to be patient. She wasn't getting very far with Glenna Flint. Frustrated, she pricked her palm with the sharp point of her pencil. She was sitting in the shabby living room of the Flint farm, on a black horsehair sofa that looked as though it had been whipped too often. Across the room, Glenna was ensconced in an ancient overstuffed chair in purply red plush, her feet planted on a Turkish carpet worn from decades of shambling shoes.

But the old lady kept digressing. One minute, she'd talk about her mother: "Bit of a thing, four-foot-ten, but tough as the beef she cooked to death—ninety years old and out there chopping wood. That's how she died. Chopping wood. Keeled right over into the kindling. Is that a way to go or not?"

Emily wasn't sure, but she nodded politely and shifted position. The horse hair sofa was torturing the backs of her legs.

Then with no transition at all, Glenna was talking about her horse Jenny: "As pretty a mare as you ever saw, took me all over the county when I was a girl. Once, we rode right into church—you should've seen that old minister's face!" Next, she'd hop to the present, her nephew Homer's wife: "That biddy, trying to put me in a home. I wouldn't be alive five minutes there, I tell you, can't breathe in those places. Well, I kept Mother with me till the last. Never mind she thought I was Father, told me to 'shave that mustache, Henry, it don't become you.'" Glenna laughed hugely.

"I heard you married when you were working down in New York. He was a newspaper man?"

"Huh." Glenna snorted and crossed her legs. Her pants wriggled up her thighs when she moved. "He was no reporter—though he wanted to be. Kept writing up articles for the *New York Times* op-ed, but they never took a one. I used to wish I could get a piece in there just to show him. But I never got around to it, I guess. No, he didn't know what in hell was going on—at home or in the world.

He was just a proofreader, that's all. If you asked him, though, you'd've thought he'd just won the Pulitzer."

"Did he like it up here—when you brought him to Vermont?"

Glenna was quiet. Her mind seemed to make a trip back into time, and get stuck somewhere. She drew a hand through the thick nest of her hair. From the neck up, she looked dramatic, Emily thought, like an aging actress with a romantic past. "Well, he hated my horse, that's what—Jenny Two. 'Cause he couldn't ride her, that's why. Got on her once and Jenny threw him. Right into a heap of manure. Why, he went and dug her grave!" And when Emily gasped, Glenna said, "Oh yes, he did, oh yes. Dug it right beside the hired man's shack, facing the barn, right where I'd see it every day when I went to milk. We only kept two cows then—for Mother really—she still pretended to farm."

"But he didn't...kill her...Jenny Two?"

"Not exactly, no, no, he didn't kill her. I'd've killed him first." Glenna stopped, seemed confused by her words, her memory struggling out of a long-ago abyss. "He just wanted to upset me. He was good at that. Upsetting people."

She paused again, blew her long nose into an oversized handkerchief. "Did I tell you about my great-grandfather? This was his farm. An acre down by the creek—they called it 'Petticoat Strip,' you know that?"

Emily whipped over a page in her notebook to write down the story of old Matilda, who sued for breach of promise when Glenna's great-grandfather ditched her. But because of the lawsuit, he had to promise an acre of his land—the best acre.

"And then he got his revenge when he fertilized the hell out of a rocky strip and she fell for it," Glenna said. "Was she mad!" Glenna thought the tale hilarious; she laughed and laughed. Emily smiled, tried to take notes, until Glenna struggled up from the sofa and said, "Enough said, girl. Is there no privacy around here? Can a woman keep her life to herself?"

"I'm sorry, it was just..." Emily jumped up, hugged her notebook to her chest. "I mean, this is so we'll understand the past—that's what my teacher says. They're going to print it up in a booklet."

"Print it up!" screeched Glenna. "You let me see it, hear? Before you go printing it up. And I'll decide. Go see somebody else, you want a whole life printed up. Some of them love to prattle on about themselves."

"I am interviewing someone else," Emily said, tears springing to her eyes in spite of herself. She wanted to be out of the house now, away from this volatile woman. "Alwyn Bagshaw. He lives up the mountain in East Branbury."

"Bagshaw! I know where he lives. He has a brother, too." Glenna was suddenly quiet. Then in a minute, she said, "Anyway. I get them mixed up. Alwyn Bagshaw. He's a fool." Glenna stood up, leaned close to stare at the girl; her voice softened. She looked frightened, confused. "You stay away from him. Young girl like you. He's mean, hear? Your mother know you're going to see him?"

"She knows. She didn't say anything."

"You take her with you, then, when you go. Don't sit in there alone with him. Not with a Bagshaw."

"Why? What would he do? He's in his seventies now, my teacher says."

"Your teacher's a fool, too. Tell her I said that."

"Him."

"Whatever." And Glenna padded out of the room and upstairs on those long, thin bare feet, without looking back.

"Thank you," Emily hollered up. She took a deep breath to summon up courage. "Can I talk to you again? Maybe once more?"

But she got no reply. Discouraged, she sat down on a kitchen chair—no one was about except the cat, asleep on top of the refrigerator—and tried to make sense out of her notes. She had to get a good grade on this project. She'd had a slow start in history this term—all that worry about Wilder and the diamond nose stud. Well, she'd catch Glenna in a quiet mood sometime—after she saw Mr. Bagshaw. They were almost of an age, she guessed. Her mother had said Glenna must be around eighty years old, so she'd write that down. Funny: Sometimes the old lady seemed out of it, and other times right with it. But the way she dressed! Just didn't seem to care how she looked. Or couldn't see. Those tiny spectacles she peered out of. She was such an odd duck. For one thing, Emily wasn't used to hearing old ladies swear.

Well, of course she'd go alone to the Bagshaw place. She wasn't letting any cranky old lady intimidate her.

ALWYN BAGSHAW was spying through his binoculars. He'd got them for the grackles, so he'd know when the fall flock was on the wing. See, the critters dropped all over his barn and garden, polluting, gobbling up his stored cattle corn. And he needed the corn to sell to the farmers. Well, he'd give 'em their comeuppance, sure. But now the binoculars had another purpose. They could see into the main room of the house next door. The Healing House, they called it; they'd been over to "make his acquaintance" when they started up the place. Some fool woman, buttering him up so he'd keep quiet about their shenanigans. Isis, her name was—no Christian name at all, like she was some priestess—as if women could be priests. Alwyn had no use for the Pope; he'd been brought up in the white church in town—before his ma dropped dead one Sunday coming out of that church, and he'd never set foot in it again, not even to bury her. But by Christ, the Pope had the right idea about women. A priest—hah! And a midwife? Worse still. He'd seen a pamphlet she put out—it was in the local grocery. Witches they was, midwives. Ma'd said so. She took to the hospital to have him and his brother born; she didn't hold with midwives.

And now this healing place, all women—it was unnatural. First thing you knew, they'd be committing some mass suicide and he'd have to smell the bodies. He wasn't having none of that. The grackles—hundreds of 'em sweeping through his land, spring and fall, pecking at his crops—was enough. Why, he lived off that vegetable stand, and what he could sell to the local grocers!

So he was keeping an eye on next door.

Eight, ten of them now maybe, squatting on mats in the big room, heads down. Unnatural, he called it, and it was. No one saying a damn word, seemed like. Meditating on the devil most likely. No children there at least. First young'un in there, he'd be over in a shot, see firsthand what was going on. He knew the dangers, his only child gone west to join some guru, got hitched along with two hundred others. Mass orgy after, he supposed. He'd disowned that one. She wasn't getting none of his land.

Land. That's all that mattered now. What was left of what used to be a hundred acres of land—no more'n twenty acres now, less even. But his own, since the Battle of Hubbardton, yessir, when his great-great-great-granddaddy put in his claim. Indians camped here, yes they did. He'd found things. It was old, old land. And they wanted it, that sect. That's why that priest woman'd come over, asking questions about his land. Wanting more land, more victims to sacrifice.

Maybe a human sacrifice at that. He'd read of it. It happened. By Christ, it did, too!

He felt chilled all over to think on it; his chest ached, legs trembled. His legs, getting weak, his whole body sliding downhill. No more strength the way he used to when he was a young fellow and women running after and he had his Ford, rode all over town, and then the truck when he got the job as milk tester. He was young and randy then, sure, the women heating up to see him coming.

Those women getting up now, folding up the mats, walking single file out of the room. He lowered the binoculars. Christ, he was trembling all over. But it was his duty. His duty. His mother would've wanted it. To keep watch.

HARTLEY FLINT was moving into the trailer—she didn't care. That man was occupying her room, and she couldn't sleep one more night with Aunty's mumblings. Something screechy last night about a "booby"—what was a "booby" anyway? Hartley was so sleep-deprived today that she didn't even feel like walking. So she piled up the sweaters and jeans and books she'd brought from home and loaded them into the Colt. A pretty small pile, actually, but what did she need, really, except Tolkien and a change of underwear now and then? For good measure, she threw in a pail of soapy water, a broom, and a dustpan.

But when she was all ready to go, the Colt wouldn't start. It growled and grunted and squealed. It didn't like this Vermont weather—too cold. A freezing rain last night had killed even the stiff orange marigolds Fay had stuck into the ground in front of the farmhouse. Now they looked like a row of old people, sitting cock-eyed in their wheelchairs.

She pumped the pedal, yelled, "Shit, shit, shit!" and the Colt came to life with a roar and a jerk. It flew forward: past the outhouse, the empty henhouse, past the—hey! Something white and furry came dashing out. She braked. The car screamed, then skidded on an inch of black ice, spun about, and crashed, rear-end-to, into the side of the trailer. The ancient structure sagged like a popped balloon; she could hear the foundation crumble into the icy dirt. Aunty's cat slowed to a dignified walk and hopped up onto the farmhouse porch. She could swear it was grinning.

"Look what you made me do!" she yelled out the car window. But the cat just sat there, pulling burrs out of its tender paw.

She looked around to see if anyone had heard the crunch, but all was quiet. Aunty was inside being interviewed by the girl next door, so she wouldn't have heard. And Fay was in the barn, probably cursing the old cow. Only Gandalf came trotting out of the barn, excited to see her. "Good boy." She was safe for the moment anyway; she'd inspect the damage later. She hugged the dog, unpacked her stuff. No, she'd sweep first. She didn't want to sleep in mouse turd, did she?

"There's one, Gandalf. A mouse, see? In the grass over there. Go sic 'em. Good boy!"

And she smiled to hear the dog digging as she swung her broom.

She was mopping up the bedroom floor of the trailer—it sloped more than ever since the car had hit the side—when she heard a scream nearby in the barn. She arrived, to find a pail of milk knocked over and streaming along the sawdust-covered floor. Fay was doing some kind of dance, one foot in the air, and the other solidly on the floor—oh, and pinned down by the Holstein's left rear foot!

"Get off. Off you miserable beast!" Fay screamed, and the cow looked beseechingly at Hartley, like she'd forgotten how to move her legs. Hartley tugged on the foot while Dandelion bellowed and Fay hollered, her face a mask of pain. But the foot wouldn't move. Until Hartley pulled an apple out of her pocket and rolled it on the floor. Dandelion stared at it a minute, then lifted her hind leg and scooped up the fruit with her plump lips. She turned, chewing, the yellow juice oozing out of the corner of her mouth, to stare innocently at Fay.

"She didn't mean it," said Hartley, patting the cow's rump. "Your foot just got in her way, that's all."

"I'm sending her back." Fay sank down on the three-legged stool. "I don't care if I paid a six months' rent. Jesus, I can't feel my toes." She stuck up a limp foot at Hartley.

"I'll milk her, then," said Hartley. "I like the old thing. That farmer girl next door will teach me. The one you said helped you—that Emily."

"She's here now, interviewing Glenna." Fay was clinging to Hartley's shoulder, massaging the numb foot.

"I know. Poor kid. Aunty's so unpredictable. She'll be all sweetness and love and make up a dozen stories, or else slam the door on her—who knows?"

"Uh-oh, what did I tell you?" she went on, hearing the farmhouse door slam. "Aunty's thrown her out. Rescue mission number two coming up!" She whirled about. Or was it the trailer, fallen in on someone's head? She'd have to fess up about that.

"Don't leave me with this beast!" Fay cried. "She'll sit on *me* next."

Hartley just laughed.

EMILY WAS on her way home, the notebook under her arm, when she saw the greyhound at the side of the trailer, peering into what looked like a large hole. She was amazed at the size of the hole; one would think the trailer itself had dropped into a pit. Or was it an earthquake? The foundation appeared to have caved in. Vermont was on a fault, she'd heard. She wondered if the B and B woman knew about it, or that girl Hartley, whom she'd met briefly the night before when she came to set up a time for the interview.

Emily turned back to take a look. Actually, she was interested in the greyhound; she'd heard about its plight, how badly it had been treated—not unlike putting that old lady in a nursing home, she guessed. She remembered her grandmother before she died—her mother's mother, who had died of a brain tumor. She'd looked awful at the end, like a shrunken white mouse. A wave of sympathy swept over her for Glenna and the greyhound; they even looked alike, with those pointy noses, though Glenna was whiter and the greyhound grayer. Well, she was sorry already for thinking ill of Glenna. Poor thing.

Her mother, now she was still young enough to put things right.

Pull the family back together. But her mother did nothing, never even asked her father to come back. Just felt sorry for herself, that's all. One of these days, she and Emily would have a showdown.

The hound was practically in the hole now. Its gaunt rear end stuck up like the back of a bulldozer. It was good-natured, she'd heard, but she'd keep her distance anyway. The dog looked up when she approached, ears back, like it was afraid of *her;* then it crouched in the dirt, as though guilty of something.

"What have you got there, big boy? A nice juicy bone?" She risked a hand, but the dog retreated. She peered in the hole. For a moment, she thought she was seeing double. The bones were connected—and covered with dirt and shreds of discolored clothing. And something like a pointed rock stuck through a filthy shirt! She put a hand to her nose, though there was only the thick smell of earth. A gust of wind blew a pile of dead leaves in her face, and the bones seemed to move. She shivered.

And then she screamed.

GLENNA WAS TAKING a walk across the back pasture. Sun out bright after a night of freezing rain—everything shining: rocks, the rusty maples, the white birches, their leaves spinning like gold coins. The mountains, gleaming purple and black. God but she loved it here. She loved Vermont, and she loved her farm, shrunk though it was now. It was once five hundred acres, rich with merino sheep brought from Spain by Glenna's great-grandfather; he'd sold their fine oily wool as far off as Argentina and South Africa. Glenna still had a yellowy news clipping of her great-grandfather mourning the loss of Gold Nugget, his best ram, valued at $25,000. She'd like to have that kind of money now! But after World War I, her grandfather turned to dairy cows; when she was a child, a herd of Jerseys grazed in the meadow that still stretched to the foothills of the Green Mountains. Glenna's father had been no farmer, though. No businessman, either—he'd had a talent only for making the wrong investments.

Now there were a mere hundred acres, a single ragtag cow rented by that Fay creature, standing like a silhouette in the noon sun. Even her mother had kept a few cows after her father's runaway horse dragged him over the ledges that time and cracked open his head.... They'd laid him out on the horsehair sofa—her white dress got splashed with blood. But it was horses Glenn loved. And then her nephew Homer went and put down her beloved Jenny Two. And drove Glenna down to the city. She'd hardly wanted to live after that.

She had a stick, for the meadow was full of chuckholes. No one to keep it up the way her mother used to: out all day picking stone, mending fence, a tiny woman with muscles like small round rocks. Glenna had to admire her. Herself, Glenna used to ride through the meadow—bareback, too, no saddle for her! She was young and fit then, free as a wild finch; she and Jenny'd take any of those damn fences like a stallion. Should have been one—her parents disappointed she turned out a girl. Even so, they made a boy out of her. Kept her close to the farm: chores every day, turned away any boy came near, though not many did—that Flint nose! The tall, flat Flint body with its size-eleven feet. Till one day, when she was eighteen, the body blossomed. Boys came around then. She had to give two or three of them that big foot.

One of them had it in for her after that, kept hanging around, stuck on himself—stuck on something else he wanted from her—couldn't think now who, what it was. One day he—or someone else, some other man... Her mind blurred. Something that happened, that kept coming up, from somewhere in her past—trapped now in the bottom of the mind.

But no local boy was ever her match. No one was, not even the college boys—to them, she was just the "local girl." Though she did all right in college, hard as it was when she had to live at home. Won a writing prize once, swore she'd be a journalist—though nothing ever came of it. Other things took over her life. But those college boys! She didn't hold with their foolishness anyway. Fraternity boys, acting like children.

Till Mac MacInnis came along. She was working in that New York printers' union, riding the train to work—missing the farm. She called home every weekend, worried about Mother. Mac was plug-ugly—she was a Venus by contrast. He was a good two inches shorter than she, fringe of rusty hair arranged around a bald spot, those bad teeth. But for all that, he had something. He could talk—never mind it was mostly lies. It was a power struggle from the start. Who could outwit whom. He could talk a streak all right! He'd made Mother laugh now and then.

But he didn't like the farm. When Glenna told him she was moving back, fed up with cities, Mother needing help—Parkinson's bending her in half, the poor eyesight—he put his foot down. He wasn't going. "All right, then," she'd said, "don't. Stay here with your damn proofreading. Let 'em pay you ten cents an inch, exploit the hell out of you. I'm going home."

But two weeks later, there he was, unannounced. He'd been fired by the *Times*. She found him squatting in the farmhouse kitchen, his dainty small feet up on the table; he was guzzling her best scotch. Mother smiling at some joke he'd told. "Hi, there," he said, "got any vermouth? I'd really prefer a Manhattan."

And that's how she remembered him best. Feet up, guzzling booze. Her booze. Lost his job, so he lived off her. She made him sleep alone, of course—who'd want a liquory-breathed man to sleep with? She never cared for that part of marriage anyway. Way he did it, he just stuck it in, no sweet words, no preamble, just bullish. And thought he was some Don Juan. Oh, sure. A whole six or seven years it was till she got fed up. Even Mother agreed. He wouldn't throw a stick on the woodstove while she and Mother were out with the cows. And then one night they had it out. Hard to remember exactly—her mind did quirky things these days—but it was bad, she remembered that. It began with that open grave—the hole he said he'd dug for her horse; he wouldn't fill it in. She had to step around it to get to the barn. Then they'd had a cow down with mastitis; she was giving it penicillin. Another cow freshening at the same time, in trouble. Tried to call the vet—he'd have to drag the calf out with a chain. But the vet busy somewhere else, so she begged Mac to help; he came, but just leaned against the stanchion and watched. Complained about the smell, the manure on his New York shoes. She was furious. The cow died. The calf lived, but Mac just shrugged, said how homely it was.

"Better-looking than you," she'd said, and he'd laughed. "Or you," he said. "You look more like your mother every day."

It was too much for her. She went at him with a stick. Took him by surprise—she was bigger, stronger than he was—he keeled right over backward. The cow kicked up a pile of sawdust then and she

couldn't see. A minute later, Mac was up. He was going in the
house to pack; he was leaving, he yelled, then stomped off. She
went back to the cow. Someone standing in the barn door then.
Who was it? Someone she knew anyway, a man. She couldn't think;
this was where her mind blanked. Where the nightmares began.
Time passed; things happened. She just remembered riding off on
Jenny Two, and when she got back, Mac was gone. And then that
anonymous letter, someone who saw, saying she'd killed Mac.

But that hole. Who had filled it in? Herself? The letter said she
had. She couldn't remember. Couldn't bring herself to dig it up and
look. "Don't go digging up trouble," her mother had said. "Might
not be anything at all in there. Mac just filled it in 'fore he left. Go,
girl, make love to your horse."

Glenna missed Mac, though, after that. Funny, but she missed
the old bastard.

She'd reached the fence now; it divided her land from the Will-
marths'. The other side was cleared pasture, not overgrown like hers
with nettles, furze, goldenrod, black-eyed Susans. Smart, that Ruth
Willmarth: She worked hard. But that daughter of hers, asking personal questions, Glenna didn't like that. Meant well, she supposed.
Glenna recalled how she'd had school projects, had to do them or
flunk out. Well, she'd talk to the girl again sometime. Couldn't let
Alwyn Bagshaw have the upper hand, do all the talking. He'd better
not talk about her, better not! You couldn't trust a Bagshaw. Aw,
the girl would come back. Glenna would see what she'd written.
She liked that girl, to tell the truth. Seemed honest, practical—not
so flighty as her nephew Homer's girl, Hartley.

There was a lot of hollering back by the barn and trailer—Hartley
again, she supposed, running after that fool dog. They said Glenna
couldn't see for the cataracts, ought to have them removed: No way!
She saw enough. She supposed she'd have to go back and put a
stop to the noise. Though she needed a nap—she was getting old.
Didn't like to think how old. But they weren't putting her away like
they tried with that greyhound. No ma'am. She'd fight. She'd die
before she went to any Lands' End.

"CALL THE POLICE," Ruth shouted over the barn phone, and Emily
said, "I wanted to, but they wouldn't let me."

"Who wouldn't let you?"

"That woman Fay, for one. She said the publicity would scare away her new boarder. And Glenna, too. It has nothing to do with her, she says; she doesn't know how it got there. That girl, Hartley, dug the whole thing up—it was mostly covered with dirt when I saw it. But it's too big for her husband, Glenna says. 'It's not Mac,' she said. But she's scared stiff of any police. Says they'll come and put *her* away. Mom, everyone's in hysterics here. Please come. Now."

So Ruth left in the middle of cleaning stalls—droppings everywhere, Zelda's calf mewing, needing to be bottle-fed, with Jane Eyre out in the fields now—she might have to call the vet, God forbid. She ran back to the barn and phoned Colm Hanna, just in case. She might need his help to calm that mad crew.

Colm would meet her there, he said. She'd caught him in the process of laying out a corpse for his father. "Don't panic. Don't let them upset you. I know Glenna. She had a to-do with Dad once, over her mother's demise. Wouldn't let him cremate, but wouldn't bury her in one piece, either. 'What'll we do, keep her on ice till you make up your mind?' Dad said. Glenna didn't think that was funny."

Colm obviously did; he even got Ruth laughing over the phone. He was good for her, Colm was, lightened her up; she tended to be overly serious, her dour Scottish genes. Sometimes, though, Colm's joking around was too much. He didn't always know when to stop. She flung an arm into a plaid jacket and ran out again.

She found the situation even worse than Emily had said.

"It's not mine," Glenna was squealing, her hair a storm cloud around her face, "got nothing to do with me or Mother. Get that thing out of here!" Then Fay Hubbard shouting, "I can't have a skeleton lying around a respectable B and B! Bury it up in that field. Mr. Crowningshield'll be back any minute. He'll tell the chamber of commerce. Then what?"

"I'll get his room," Hartley said. "Mice, I don't mind. But I'm not sleeping with a dead man outside the door."

"Do we know it's a man?" said Ruth, trying to bring logic to the scene, placing a firm hand on Glenna's trembly shoulder.

"It's Mac. We know it's Mac, right, Aunty?" said Hartley, grin-

ning into her great-aunt's face. "Admit it, it's Mac. So he had a
heart attack and you buried him. Saved a lot of money, right, Aunty?
None of that funeral home stuff for you?"

"No, it's not right," yelled Glenna. "That's not Mac. It's too—
too—it doesn't even look like him, not one bit. He was smaller than
that. He had rusty-colored hair."

"The mice got it," said Hartley.

There were fringes of dirty ashy hair on the crest and sides of
the skull. The teeth looked equine; the bones were brownish and
spongy-looking; a thin vine had wound itself about the anklebone,
where the weathered boots had fallen loose. The fingernails were
long and thick and yellow—they gave Ruth the shivers. Yet the
bones appeared to be separate, disconnected. And something that
looked like a pointed rock—an arrowhead?—was stuck into the
sternum. Was it an Indian, as the girls were shouting? Was the
skeleton really that old? What was left of the clothing had been
nibbled at by something—though still recognizable as dungarees
and a plaid shirt—the standard uniform around town. It was no
Stone Age Indian. And a mildewed cap on the skull, like a plaid
Scots bonnet, half-chewed, or merely worn away. When Hartley
picked it up—ignoring Ruth's warning—Glenna screamed and said,
"Burn it!"

Still, one thing was obvious, as Colm Hanna pointed out when
he arrived, breathless, in baggy brown cords and a green tweed Irish
cap—one of a hundred hats he owned—and stopped to examine the
pile of bones: "It's missing a finger bone. The rest of the limbs are
accounted for." Ruth looked back at him, feeling her face get hot.

"A finger with a gold ring," Emily whispered, and Hartley made
a hissing sound; her face flushed bright pink with wind and intrigue,
and her chestnut hair danced in the wind: "What? What ring? What
ring, Emily? Whose ring? Whoa, tell me."

"That's what we have to find out, right, Mother?" said Emily,
ignoring the other girl, and Ruth nodded, while Colm wheeled about
and ran up to the house, shirttail climbing out of his pants and
flapping loose in the October breeze.

"What's he doing?" shouted Fay. "He's not calling the police!
He can't do that. I'm running a business here."

Aunty joined in the protest then, her hoarse voice riding low under the others. While in the barn Dandelion bellowed, and the greyhound lifted its nose and wailed.

"It's him," Hartley whispered to Ruth. "I know it is. It's him. It's old Mac. She did him in."

Fay clapped a hand on her shoulder. "Shut up, girl. You want our aunt to fry?"

"'Our' aunt?" said Hartley. "You're owning up now?" And then she said, "'Fry'? You mean—oh no, oh no. Aunty, no!" She lunged at Glenna, threw a possessive arm around her shoulders.

Glenna stood frozen in her niece's embrace. "It's not Mac—is it?" she whispered, and dropped her head onto her grand-niece's quivering shoulder.

SIX

RUTH WAS CARRYING WOOD down the basement steps when her load was suddenly lightened. She looked up, to see Kevin Crowningshield, the B and B guest from next door. She'd met him briefly the night before. "Oh, hello," she said. She was tired—she'd had an unscheduled barn inspection that morning from Agri-Mark. The fellow had a list of complaints, was "put-out" by Vic's chickens in the barn. "I'll see that they stay out," she'd said, knowing it was impossible, what with people and animals in and out all day.

"A woman shouldn't carry that load," Kevin Crowningshield said. The voice was quite thrilling actually, deep; the man could be a baritone soloist. "My—well, my wife used to say that," he apologized when she glanced up at him. "It crushes the organs or something."

Ruth had to smile. "I've been carrying wood for twenty years, and my organs are still intact—far as I know." Actually, she was two years overdue for a physical—Pap smear, mammogram, all that female business. She had no health insurance, for one thing: It was a rip-off, Pete always said, and she had to agree for once. Of course, health insurance probably came with his new sales job. But she and the children wouldn't benefit—only that would-be actress "friend," if he married her, as he evidently wanted to do. She swallowed, hard.

"So I see," said Kevin, with an admiring glance that should have annoyed her but somehow didn't. How long since a handsome man had looked at her in that way? There was Colm Hanna, yes—but who could call that pepper-haired, sunken-cheeked, bony Irishman handsome? Colm was, well, Colm. Comfortable. A savior, really, since Pete's defection. "Back off," she'd tell him on occasion, and he would. She was grateful for that.

Kevin had come over to talk—if she had a free minute, he said. He'd finish the stacking job with her to create that minute. There was something familiar about him. Had she seen him before? But, of course, he'd lived here once, he said, in town, years ago, worked for a company up in Argennes. She and Kevin had probably encountered one another in the post office or the local hardware store. She would have been in her twenties then, not looking at anyone but Pete. Oh but Pete was gorgeous then: tall and lanky, that dark brown hair curling all over his head....

Pete was growing bald now, the hair receding above his temples. She was glad, wasn't she?

Kevin had a dimple in his left cheek when he smiled. A self-deprecating smile, crooked—a relief really; she was suspicious of "perfect" men: They were usually stuck on themselves. Too many people in the Flint kitchen—that's why he'd come over, he explained: to use the phone. His eyebrow questioned, and of course she nodded. "All shouting at the top of their lungs over there," he said, smiling. "How could I make a phone call?"

They made short work of the wood stacking with his help, heaving the logs up in tiers in her dank basement. He didn't seem afraid to soil his clothes, though he wore a clean blue shirt, dark pressed pants, nice shoes. In short, he dressed "city." So why wasn't she suspicious of him? Was she sex-starved? Well, she'd better make it clear she wasn't.

"I just need someone, uh, rational to talk to," he said, the brief phone call over. He settled into a kitchen chair, hands cupping the apple cider she offered. He didn't drink coffee, he said—he had high blood pressure. Already she sensed his vulnerability.

"I'm not much on advice. But I'll listen. I mean, until the cows—you know. Tim, the hired man, he's had flu. I made him go home early. My daughter Emily's bogged down with homework—she claims. And my son, Vic—well, he's upstairs. Worn-out from building a pen for his chickens. So they'll stay out of the barn—Mother's orders. And then, he's worried about a hawk he found in the pasture. He calls the vet every day."

"A hawk?"

"Red-tailed hawk, yes. Poisoned—we don't know how. Pesticides, the vet seems to think. But not from here. Already we have another victim, a crow. Vic found it; we took it to the vet's. She's understandably upset about it."

Kevin nodded in sympathy. "I promise not to overstay."

At least, she thought, he was still staying next door. Hadn't been put off by that skeleton. He'd encountered it yesterday, just as the police came to remove it, to send it on to the forensics lab up in Burlington. Along with the separated hand, of course—though the bones in general looked pretty well deteriorated. But she'd kept the ring. What would the forensics people know about a ring? Of course, the police would want to know about the ring now. But that Indian arrowhead in the breastbone. Someone had jammed it in there. Was it Glenna?

Outside, it was raining, a cold October rain. At least it was melting the ice left over from an earlier freezing rain. She'd have to bring the cows in soon, for the night anyway. She hated doing that. So much extra work, feeding and hoeing out the manure.

But it was warm in the kitchen—she dropped another log into the woodstove; the cider she shared was comforting. She could spare another ten or fifteen minutes, couldn't she? His eyes begged. He was talking about his wife.

"And so she left with another woman, to join this group, this healing center or whatever it is. Just left me a note. 'You'll make out,' it said. Or something like that. I couldn't reread it; I tore it up in a fit of frenzy. I couldn't imagine her leaving like that. She'd always been so...easy to get along with, so loving. I was devastated. You know."

Ruth nodded. She knew. Though at least Pete had had the courage to confront her before he left. But then, he had three children. "Children?" she asked Kevin, but he shook his head.

"Angie couldn't have any. For one thing, she has this, um, bleeding defect—something genetic. Supposed to take a blood thinner. Her own mother died in childbirth—a second pregnancy—hemorrhaging. I didn't want Angie to get pregnant! So she wanted to adopt, but I—well, you hear things about that. You never really know where they come from. A neighbor was shot by an adopted child."

"It can work out. So many children, needing a home. I've thought of it myself."

"I guess. But. Well, she agreed with me later, didn't want to take the chance herself. She got quieter and quieter. Joined this religion."

"What is it exactly? This religion? I mean, is it a religion?"

He shook his head. "She'd never explain, though I asked her. Her stepmother runs a so-called healing center in California. I blame her for Angie's defection—Angie took a trip out there, came back...well, different. Angie calls it 'meditation.' Healing. Something about the hara, words I'd never heard. New Age stuff. The head woman here's a disciple of Angie's step-mother. So after that California trip, Angie took up this meditating, squatting on a mat on the floor. I couldn't watch. Say, could I have another cider? We still have"—he consulted his watch—"five minutes. Don't get up. I'll get it."

Vic came halfway down the back stairs, saw she had a guest, and halted on the bottom step, a scrawny boy in last year's tight jeans—she saw him through the stranger's eyes.

"My son," she said. "He's glad you're here. You've saved him from ten orders. Right, Vic?"

"That magazine come today?" he asked, retreating a step.

She knew what he meant, and she smiled. "Sorry, Vic. Maybe tomorrow. Astronomy," she told Kevin. "He saved his money for a telescope. He made a perfectly good one, but it wasn't strong enough, he said. He wants to see into the universe."

"Good for him," said Kevin, "I wish I could." He leaned his elbows on the table. "I worry about Angie. That's why I'm here, you know. I have to get her out. I don't know how. You seem a sensible woman, grounded, I thought you might—"

Now she was wary. What did he want of her? "Me? I mean, I can't just go and invade..."

"I meant, some thoughts on how I might...I heard about—your husband. I thought you'd understand what it is to be left, you know."

She flushed. She was glad of Vic, who was in the kitchen now, fumbling through a pile of letters, ads, flyers—junk mail! He gave the stranger a side scowl. "How's Zelda's calf doing?" the boy demanded, butting into the conversation. "It looked bad this morning when I left for school. It's not getting what it needs."

"I know. It has milk fever. Calcium deficiency," she explained to her son. "I gave it an intravenous shot this morning. You'll have to bottle-feed it yourself. It's your calf, if you want it. Obviously Zelda doesn't."

"You mean that? Jeezum." He started out the door in his shirtsleeves.

"Vic, come back. Put on a coat."

He backed up, reluctantly, grabbed a denim jacket, and hooked it onto one arm. "This is Mr. Crowningshield; he's staying at the Flint farm."

"Huh," said Vic, and flung out the door, letting it slam.

"Boys," she apologized, hands over her ears. "I'd better—I mean, he'll need help. And that calf isn't right. It's true—maybe it got dehydrated early on, with its mother leaving it."

"She died?"

"No, just refused to feed it. Defected, you might say."

"Ah." He understood what that meant.

She considered. "Maybe I shouldn't have called it Vic's, in case—"

"It dies," Kevin said, looking sympathetic. He has cow eyes, she thought, deep brown; she looked away quickly. "That's what worries me," he said, "about Angie. You know, she abandoned her pills, the blood thinners, after she came back from California. Didn't trust doctors anymore. Who's going to take care of her in that place? Healing House, they call it! I keep thinking of that cult—Heaven's Gate? They had a suicide pact. I don't trust this place, Ruth."

When he used her first name like that, there was a small explosion in her head. He stood up, followed her out onto the porch; his shoes made a crunching sound on the old boards where they'd tracked up leaves.

"Maybe you'd better go over there," she said. "Talk to the head woman. Make an appeal. Or, I don't know, just wait. Till your wife comes to her senses."

Wait, she thought, when Kevin had gone; she was running to the barn through a swirl of orangy-brown leaves. Was that why she couldn't agree to the divorce Pete wanted? She was waiting for him to come back?

HARTLEY COULDN'T stand it. Another reporter at the door, and Fay in town at the Food Co-op. Aunty had refused to talk to the others; of course, she wouldn't want to see this one, either, even though the woman was from the *New York Times*. Some Albany paper had gotten hold of the local *Independent* and blown up the skeleton find out of all proportion. Aunty was angry. Aunty was another Harriet Sedley, their cartoonist said, who took an ax and gave her parents forty whacks. Only this time, it was a pitchfork: "Glenna Flint, she popped her cork—and stuck her husband with a fork!"

Actually, Hartley had had a good laugh over that—until she realized the seriousness of it. But the *New York Times*—whoa. Her parents got the *Times*. And now they'd read about Aunty. "She's busy—she's taking a nap," she told the reporter. "She can't see you." But the woman said, "Oh, she knows I'm coming. I called," and she shoved right past with a wave of her hand, as if Hartley were a fly on her nose. Behind her, a man with a camera on his shoulder like a gigantic chip muscled his way in. He spun about, photographing the kitchen, taking a hundred shots a minute. "Hey! Who gave you permission?" Hartley cried. But the man went on shooting.

"What is it?" called Aunty from the living room, and before Hartley could answer, the woman announced, "Cheryl, from the *Times*," gave the photographer a nod, and the pair shouldered their way into the living room. Hartley waited for the uproar. Aunty would have them out of there in seconds.

Or would she? "Why, hello there," Aunty said with an ingratiating laugh. Apparently, she wanted to see them! Hartley hung in the doorway. Aunty would need someone to defend her. Never mind that the police had no proof, and Aunty kept changing her mind about whether it was Mac in that hole or someone else. Today, evidently, it was Mac.

"I did it," Aunty was telling the woman. "He was planning to kill my horse. Why, he'd dug a hole."

"It was self-defense?" the woman suggested, hoisting a thin black-stockinged leg over the opposite knee, a greedy little smile on her hot pink lips.

"No," said Aunty, "I just did it."

"It was self-defense," said Hartley, barging in. She couldn't stand it one minute longer. "You know that, Aunty. You told me yesterday. He was shoving you around."

"I said nothing of the kind," said Aunty sweetly. "Now who's being interviewed here?'' And the camera flashed, then flashed again—this time in Hartley's direction. The girl threw up her hands.

"Tell us about Mac. Your husband. What he was like? Why did you strike him—was it really an arrowhead?'' asked the woman. Hartley felt the vomit lump up in her throat. Whistling to Gandalf, she ran outside. She stuck a finger down her gullet but couldn't get anything up; instead, she swallowed hard, flopped down on the porch step, and sighed heavily. She couldn't believe how this skeleton had changed their lives—how Aunty had denied it was Mac at first, and now was making a turnabout, seeming almost proud she'd done it. Why, it was as good as a confession. When the Branbury police saw it, they'd lock her up. Unless Hartley's parents got here first. They'd throw Aunty right in the funny farm. They would! Either way, it spelled disaster.

Hartley dropped her chin in her hands. If she hadn't brought Aunty up here in the first place, there wouldn't be all this hoopla. Already, the police were gathering things, fingerprinting, taking tiny bits of earth and rock and analyzing the clothing, that Scottish cap. What if they found Aunty guilty? They'd lock her up for life.

But these reporters were exploiting her. They were killing her! Hartley ran back inside to tell them so, but they were already leaving. Aunty was posing for one last picture, her chin uplifted, a hand shoving back her heavy hair. She looked like an aged movie star. Hartley burst into frustrated tears.

"I can't believe you did that,'' she screeched when the crew had raced off in a red Fiat. "I can't believe you told them you did it. We don't even know it was Mac in that hole.''

"It was Mac,'' Aunty said, sitting down, slapping one trembly hand on the table. "There's no denying it. He had on that plaid bonnet. It was his clan's plaid; he sent all the way to Scotland for it. It looked ridiculous on him, but he wore it anyway.''

"Oh,'' said Hartley, sinking down beside Aunty. "But why do you have to tell everyone? Who would know that except you? That doesn't prove you killed him. Bad guys do things like that all the time. Planting stuff.''

"I know,'' said Aunty. "But...'' She put a hand to her quavery, wrinkly cheek. Her hair was especially wild today. It resembled a mass of racing clouds. The *Times* would love that, they'd call her a Vermont loony. They'd make up things. The media always made up things, her father said.

"Then tell me. Tell me just what happened. Blow by blow." The girl amended her words. "I mean, from the beginning."

"I can't," said Aunty. "There was too much going on."

"You don't know, then. You don't know!"

"I know. They told me. In a letter. They saw."

"Who's 'they'?"

"How would I know?" said Aunty, flinging up an arm, shoving away from the table. "How would I know?" She stomped upstairs, her slippered feet banging out a tattoo on the splintered steps.

"It's murder, Aunty. You don't realize it, but you're telling the whole world you killed somebody. They'll put you in prison. That's worse than Lands' End."

Aunty paused on the step, turned. The green eyes blinked behind the shiny spectacles. "Over my dead body they will." She climbed another step, then turned again, pointed a shaky finger at her grandniece.

"Mac was always wanting to get in the *Times*. He'd send them words, more words! But they just sent them back. Now I'm in the *Times*. My picture, too." She threw her head back and laughed. "Hear that, Mac?" she shouted. "You hear that?"

Then she sank down on the step and dropped her head into her pale veined hands.

ALWYN BAGSHAW'S PLACE was even more run-down than the hired man's trailer at the Flint farm. Emily wondered how many skeletons were buried in *his* place. It was an old yellow house with faded blue trim, a yellow veggie stand out by the road: FRESH CORN, TOMATOS, CUKKES, the sign read. The porch sagged; there were dead petunias in a hanging planter, an ancient cracked swing at the far end—sit on it and you'd fall through. A black Dodge pickup was parked askew in the driveway. Alwyn Bagshaw probably had twenty, thirty acres of land, but you could see that healing place to the south, its sign swinging in the wind. Later, she'd bring her new friend Hartley; they'd barge in together. She could use a little healing, to cure her of Wilder Unsworth and his diamond-nosed friend.

She knocked, but no one answered. It would be just like an old

hermit to forget she was coming—or ignore her arrival deliberately.
She knocked again and then turned the knob. The door swung open.
"Well, come on in," a voice croaked from somewhere at the rear
of the house. "I only lock at night. Don't just stand there." She
followed the sound. "Never locked then, neither, till them kookies
moved in next door. Though it don't keep out the— Well, git in
here, girl. Come on."

"Where are you?" she said. She felt like Alice with the Mad
Hatter. She was intruding; she wasn't wanted.

"In the kitchen, of course. I ain't got all day. Got an errand to
run."

He was seated in a black rocking chair, his bony body squeezed
between its spooled sides. His hands jerked in his lap as if he had
some disease of the nerves. She saw he had a pinkie finger missing
on his right hand; the middle finger of his left hand stuck up like a
pencil.

"Well, get to it. What'd'you want to know?" Without waiting
or inviting her to sit down—although she did anyway, in a straight-
backed chair with a cracked seat at the end of a white kitchen
table—he said, "I'll give you facts, that's all. I don't hold with that
psycho stuff. I was born December, nineteen-twenty in a snowstorm.
Father worked around different farms—left town after my brother
was born. Mother bought me and Denby up. Not sure Denby was
Pa's boy." He glanced sideways at Emily, smirked. She bent to her
note taking. Vic had left his tape recorder at school.

"Hardworking woman, Ma. Took in washing. Cleaned other people's dirt so's we could live. I made it up to her. Got a job selling
fertilizer. Later, I was a milk tester, drove round to the area farms.
Did my job. Fixed up this place good, sure—well, it's run-down
again. Live on Social Security now; government takes the rest away.
Denby died; it shook Ma up. He was the favorite. She couldn't
see through him. Well, I got married, but then she left. Ma didn't like
her nohow—Flora, that is. No loss. The girl I had with Flora run
off with some crazies. Ma and me made out fine, the both of us."

"No other children?" Emily asked, pencil in hand. He was talking so fast, she'd lost half of it.

"Don't interrupt," he said, "I gotta take corn to town."

"Sorry."

"But they was others. Other women. They"—he gave a cracked laugh, "took to me."

"Was Glenna Flint one of them? She said she knew you." She reddened. Why had she asked that?

He was furious now; he rose up out of his rocker like a genie out of a bottle. She shrank back in her chair. "Kee-rist. That bag of bones! Thought herself so damn clever 'cause she went to college—though they laughed at her, them college boys." He sneezed—or was it a laugh? "Took herself off to the city after that. Like she was some important lady!"

"Did you know her husband, Mac? They came back here to live."

He took a step toward her, and she cringed in her chair. His face was a volcano. He shook all over—chin, hands, knees under the patched overalls—then appeared to think it over, stepped back to his chair, groped for the sides, and lowered his trembly body into it.

"Seen him hangin' around when I went to test the milk. Flatlander, sure. She did him in, you know. Sure. Whole town knows that. Ask any old Vermonter. If you can find one in this town. A takeover by flatlanders, that's what. Nothin' the same no more. And he was one of 'em, Mac, whatever his real name was. A flatlander. And that's all I'm tellin' you. No more."

He appeared spent by his fury, his skin paled and blotched; the rocking chair went still, his hands, too, except for an occasional twitch in his lap. She started to talk about the skeleton, then stopped herself. He might not have read the local weekly.

But safe out on the porch, the road only fifty feet away, a house across the road, she couldn't resist. She wanted to shock him, the way he'd tried to shock her—she knew that by how he kept looking up into her face, the barest smile, the curse words.

"They found his skeleton," she yelled back to where he stood in the doorway. "Mac's. Glenna says it definitely was."

Bagshaw's face split open like waxed paper ripping apart. His laugh was weird to hear, like someone sick and gagging. Wanting to stop the laughing, wanting to shock him further, she hollered, "We found its finger on our land. It had a ring. A ring like..." She looked over at the healing place. The wooden sign was a bone crossed with an arrow, a moon. "Something like that sign next door, not exactly. Where do you think they got that?"

"Don't go there. Don't ask!" he shrieked, moving toward her now. "You want to get trapped? Took by the devil? That's what they want, young girl like you. My daughter, my own girl—"

She ran out into the road. A car was coming and she was relieved to see it. She stuck out a thumb (her mother would kill her if she found out), but it passed her by. She had to get to a telephone, ask someone to pick her up—she'd come by school bus. She started down the road; she could outrun that old guy all right.

She glanced back. He was standing on the porch. Porch and man appeared to be leaning in opposite directions, or was it her eyes? She might need glasses; she couldn't always see the blackboard. But she didn't want to give her mother any extra expense—her mother had a poor risk rating at the bank. "I don't believe in a devil," she shouted back. And she turned at the sign, ran up to the door of the Healing House, just to spite the old man. They were all women there, she'd heard. Who could hurt her? At least they'd have a telephone.

SEVEN

WILLARD BOOMER was at Fay's door. He'd read the papers, and he thought she might need cheering up. Then, afraid his visit might be misinterpreted, he said, "Want to check that sign, you see. Um, all that wind lately, thought it might—"

"But it's okay; it's fine," she said, stepping back to let him in. She was hooking a rug, a rooster, had just drawn the design on the burlap; the wool strips were in a bag at her feet. She was using an antique homespun instead of new wool; it gave a more primitive look to the rugs. He stood over her for a minute, admiring the design. He smelled of soap and fresh air.

"It's a rooster all right," he allowed, turning his cap in his hands. She saw the green bike, the empty cart behind, outside by the step. When he turned back, she put down the work, touched his sleeve. "Tea?" she said. "I have some nice wine." She really needed someone to talk to. She'd just had a call from her ex, who had accused her of taking the new sheets he'd bought for the double bed. "When have I been in Cabot," she'd yelled, "and why would I need sheets for a double bed?" But his voice just rolled over hers: "With you gone, I have to hire someone to collect the eggs." And he hung up.

"A small glass, yes, oh yes." Willard gave a little laugh, edged his way in, sideways, like a crab, and lowered his lanky body slowly into a chair.

"I, um, read about...what you found here," he said, and she understood why he'd come. "Said to myself, She'll be upset, seeing those bones. The new business and all."

"That's not the half of it," she said, clunking down bottles of red and pink on the kitchen table, two glasses. She pushed the bottles toward him. Finally, he pointed to the red. "Winter coming on. I drink red in winter."

"Good for you. So do I." She wanted to discover things in

common. She needed a friend. But the skeleton grinned between them, needed to be cleared away before the small talk.

"Colm Hanna—that friend of Ruth Willmarth's—"

"Mortician's son," Willard said, "I made his daddy's sign. Simple, you know, no frills. No frills in that business, right?"

"Shouldn't be. Though I read about the bronze sarcophagi they bury the rich in down in New York for eighty-five thousand dollars. Anyway, the police drove it up to Burlington. Some guy there who knows about skeletons. How to discover its age, other stuff, I don't know—like if it—he, she—got hit on the head or something, I guess. I mean, besides that arrowhead in the breastbone."

"Oh, oh. Good idea. Very good idea. That'll explain things." He peered sideways at her, sipped his wine, made a slight burping noise, then peered at her again. "I think he must have been, don't you? Hit on the head, I mean. Or somewhere. They said the arrowhead wasn't very big.... Odd, about that arrowhead."

"You knew him? I mean, if this *is* him. Glenna says it's not—Mac MacInnis, I mean."

"Well, once when I came out to touch up the sign—you know what weather does to a sign—there was, um, a small disagreement. He didn't want a sign—too, um, commercial, he said. Wanted to sell her horse, in fact. Yes, I remember something about a horse. The mother just sitting there, looking from one to the other, not interrupting."

"Whose side was the mother on?"

"Glenna's, I suppose, but then, the husband was kind of a tease. I'd see the mother smile at him, make Glenna madder still." He laughed. "I can see it now, Glenna's face red as a tomato, Mac threatening—" He stopped abruptly.

"He was threatening?" Fay poured another drink. A skeleton found on her premises. She had a right to question.

"Maybe...maybe I shouldn't use that word." His big pale face blossomed to pink. "Said he'd leave, go back to the city, that Glenna could have her effing—pardon my French—horse. If Glenna wanted him, she'd find him there. Some city bar he mentioned—I can't recall now. It wasn't pleasant, not pleasant at all. She was a nice lady, Glenna, always kind to me. My mother liked her." He threw down the second drink, his face a shiny beet, then waved his arms when she picked up the bottle. "No, no, I've work—home, you know."

"Where exactly is home?"

"Well, at the moment"—he laughed, hiccupped—"I've taken over Mother's garage—no electricity, of course. That's a drawback, but I make the signs by hand, you see; I don't need drills. Years ago they didn't—anyway, it saves paying a bill."

"I see what you mean." Fay knew what it was to live without electricity. The first ten years, she and Dan had had no electricity or plumbing in the house Dan bought up in Cabot. Jesus, she'd hooked her rugs by candlelight, took her exercise running out to the outhouse. Even after they got plumbing, he'd never put in a bathtub—unnecessary expense, he said. She took a hot bath every night now, wallowing in it for a half hour. Did her serious thinking in that old copper tub.

"Look," she said, "I've got it here—electricity. You need to drill holes or something, you just come over, okay? I mean it." And she did. He looked adorable, really, hanging over the table in his paint-stained shirt and baggy jeans, his vegetable face, with all that rumpled white hair like daisy petals.

Something banged outside and Hartley burst in, Gandalf behind her on a leash. The dog would run off, they'd discovered, given too much freedom—like it was on a high, not that she blamed it. Willard Boomer sprang up at the girl's entrance.

"Hey," Hartley said, "you two getting loaded?"

Willard's face was maroon now. "Oh, I, well, you see—"

Fay introduced them and Hartley grabbed his hand. "Enchantée. This doggy's hungry. Got any food in the house?" She lunged at the old fridge. Gandalf knocked Willard into the door as it loped behind. "Sorry," Willard said.

"Willard's a sign maker; he made our sign," Fay said. The bottles had been bought on Hartley's credit card. She felt a teeny bit guilty.

"I make them all over town," Willard explained; "there's not much competition. Someone will come along, though. Oh, you bet they will. I'm not as, well, fast as could be. I don't, um, have a car. On principle, you see. The pollution, you know. Why contribute?

And then my sister..." His voice choked up. Fay waited. "Your sister?" she said finally, wanting to know.

"Drunk driver," he said. "She never had a chance." And before Fay could commiserate, Willard said, "Well, have to be going, yes, I definitely do. I just stopped, um..."

"Say, you make a sign for that new Healing House?" Fay asked, following him out onto the porch. "Emily Willmarth told me about a ring. On the skeleton's finger. Said it had a design like the one on that sign at that Healing House. You make that one?"

"Oh, yes, yes, I did, oh my, yes. And then did it again, just this fall, when someone painted out the arrows. Imagine that! Came up at night and painted them out. But a ring on the skeleton's finger? Goodness." And he hopped on his green bike and pedaled off down the driveway, veering aside for a pair of town police who'd come to check the trailer. The area was cordoned off with tape, off-limits they'd said, so Hartley was sleeping on the living room couch for the time being, and Fay had to use a roundabout route to the barn. She watched now as he bumped off down the dirt road.

"Don't forget we've got electricity," she hollered after him, then ran back into the kitchen, where Gandalf was finishing off two cans of dog food in practically the same number of gulps.

"Don't worry," said Hartley, "Daddy's paying for it. For now anyway. Oh, Lordy, they'll be back home tomorrow. They'll find Aunty gone. Then what?"

THE FLOORS WERE so highly waxed that Emily had to tiptoe across them—in her socks, of course; a sign at the door warned REMOVE YOUR SHOES! It was the exclamation point that made her do it. She found the inmates—was that the right word?—all at tea in a scrubbed white kitchen. She had to blink; she held on to the door so she wouldn't slip on the shiny pale gray linoleum. Three women were preparing a meal: She saw carrots and rice and—yuck—tofu. A woman swiveled about in a wheelchair when she entered. She looked younger than Emily's mother, but her face was scarred. She frowned at Emily from where she sat, a yellow bowl balanced on her plump belly.

"The door was unlocked," Emily said, adding defensively, "I knocked, but no one answered."

"I told you to keep that door locked," a second woman told the first, "after—that last...incident." When Emily asked for the phone, the first woman said, "That will be thirty-five cents." It was the wheelchair woman; her body filled the chair to overflowing, but her legs hung thin and useless in black cotton socks and red Chinese slippers. Her arms, though, were strong and muscular, and with quick, deft motions, she sliced the tops off half a dozen carrots. Emily took a step back, remembering Alwyn Bagshaw's warning. But when she searched her pockets, she came up with only two pennies and a five-dollar bill; she held it out. "I'm sorry, but..."

The woman shrugged and whirled over to the sink. But a third woman jumped up, a thin woman with a drawn look, like someone had squeezed her features together—eyes, nose, mouth. Yet one could see she had been pretty; a wreath of curly brown hair crowned the chalky white face.

"I'll pay," she told the wheelchair woman, "when the bill comes. None of us have any cash here; we pool our money," she explained to Emily in a high, sweet voice. "You call your mother, child," and she sat down on a high stool. She looked like she might fall down if she didn't. The three faces, white as new milk, stared at Emily.

She dialed her number, but her mother was probably out in the fields, and she had to leave a message. Though she didn't like the idea of waiting here in this place with these silent women, all of them sitting around a table now, sipping what appeared to be green tea—not offering her any, either—like she'd accept if they did! It was as if each were in her own serene green sea world.

If it *was* tea they were drinking. She remembered Alwyn Bagshaw's warning.

"If you don't mind, I'll wait out on the porch for my mother," she said, but no one responded.

After she hung up, the women suddenly went, single file, after the wheelchair woman, into another room, ignoring her presence. A moment later, she heard gongs, and then a low, tuneless chanting, like women keening when they'd lost their loved ones—she'd heard people do that on TV. The smell of pine incense spilled into the kitchen. They are really quite rude, she thought, treating me as if I'm not here at all, and she decided it was her right to cut off a hunk of bread that was sitting on the spotless counter. She crammed it into her mouth; it was really quite delicious. The chanting went on and on, and she thought she'd look around a bit; after all, there was no telling when her mother would show up, and if she started to walk, she'd miss the green pickup altogether.

The adjacent room was filled with books, with titles like *Living with Abuse, Rites of Healing,* and *Meditation for Mental Health;* and there were candles—hundreds of them, though unlit, in various slumped shapes—all red or white candles, like it was Christmas already, when, in fact, it wasn't even Halloween. Back in the kitchen was a door that led to a well-stocked pantry and a huge freezer—one could lock up a dozen people in it, she thought. She'd heard on the news recently of that very act of horror somewhere in Los Angeles. A wave of chill air hit her, and she ran past and out another door, which led to the backyard. Emily was startled when a bent-over shape—probably a raccoon—darted into a clump of berry bushes. She squinted, but saw only the sway of twigs. She hated the way the world got dark so early these days. This very weekend, daylight savings time would end, and then it would be black by five in the afternoon. Black when she got out of the barn from chores. Even the cows disliked the dark: They'd start bellowing earlier and earlier, wanting to be milked, wanting to go back into the warm, lit barn.

On the back porch, she saw a large kettle of soup—it looked like seaweed actually, but she presumed it was soup. She straightened the cover, which something—that raccoon?—had knocked awry. But she couldn't bring herself to go back into that gloomy scrubbed house with those sad-faced women and their chanting. And so she ran around to the front and hunkered down by a maple tree until a car drove up. She was surprised to see that man, the one who was staying at the Flint farm, get out of a rented car and bound up the steps. He nodded at her politely—well, he'd only seen her once maybe, and then in the evening, so he wouldn't know her, and she wasn't about to reveal herself. Though if he came out soon, she might, and get a ride down the mountain to Branbury with him. He could let her out if she saw her mother coming.

Kevin Crowningshield knocked on the door. "Sorry, but no men allowed in here," a voice called through a crack in the door. "But my wife," he hollered back, sounding upset, and the voice said, the words evenly spaced, "She can't see you. We have a rule. And please, send no more packages." Then the door slammed shut.

"It was only chocolates," he shouted. "Angie loves chocolates. Hey, I'll get a lawyer. You can't keep me from my wife!"

He was back in minutes. He looked stunned, like an animal transfixed in a pool of headlights. Emily could see that he was almost crying, and she felt sorry for him, but she didn't dare ask for a ride then. She leaned, frozen, against the trunk of the leafless maple while he ran out to his car and sped off.

Moments later, a Toyota arrived, its right-front fender battered in, and her sister Sharon's face appeared in the open window: "Hurry up, get in. Mother sent me. I'm feeling like a sick elephant, and I still have to get supper. What're you doing here anyway? Why aren't you home doing chores?"

Her sister was in her last month of pregnancy and looking huge, haggard, and put-upon—her naturalist husband not due back from Alaska for two weeks. Her little boy, Robbie, was whimpering in the car seat. But it was so good to see someone normal, someone familiar, that Emily laughed out loud. "Thanks," she said, "thanks for coming, Shar. I love you, Shar," and Sharon said, "Oh, get the heck in the car, will ya, dumbbell? Just 'cause you've got all day to gallivant around..."

COLM HANNA found Ruth practically nose-to-nose with that old smoothy who boarded over at the Flint farm. Colm had come to give Ruth the forensics report; he'd wheeled it out of Chief Roy Fallon, who was still trying to get Colm onto the local force full-time. Colm's grandfather had been a hero in the department before he got killed up in Burlington while trying to stop a band of booze smugglers. But Colm was only available for short-term assignments—after all, he had the mortuary, he had real estate, and he had the part-time police work. He thought of a bumper sticker he'd seen—MOONLIGHT IN VERMONT—OR STARVE—and he smiled at the irony. He'd buy the bumper sticker for the Horizon.

"It was definitely foul play," Fallon had said, a can of Pepsi in hand, "in regard to, um, the skeleton—I mean, skull—you know, *bango!* Puncture in the breastbone from that, um, arrowhead, um—'' His big red face gleamed with intrigue, even though it had happened twenty-odd years before. '' She?'' Colm said, and Fallon smiled.

"Well, that's the rumor, you know—old lady Flint. Even she says so. And that skeleton—fifties at the time of death, the coroner says, like old Mac, you know. But if it's not Glenna Flint, well, the murderer may still be around. Twenny or so years can't stop the wheels of justice, you know.'' Fallon loved to watch crime films on TV; he imbibed the dialogue like the Pepsi he was addicted to. But he did his job, Colm had to hand him that.

Colm agreed, of course: They'd have to find the murderer—if he was still alive: the name of the victim, too, although the authorities were already calling it Mac MacInnis. "The whole town knew about Mac's disappearance," said Fallon, who had been on the force when the scandal blew. "Same time as the other, um, Bagshaw, drowned; we think maybe Mac did *that* one in—you know, jealousy rears its ugly—at least that was the, um, rumor.''

As for Glenna Flint, Fallon said, "She's handy with the shovel as well as the lip. But, as I say, we had no proof, no, um, body— just hearsay. But we got a body now, don't we?'' He giggled. "Well, bones anyway, um...'' He adjusted the beeper on his left shoulder, massaged under it. He was getting near retirement age; he had arthritis, he said, and to prove it, he'd heaved up out of his chair with a groan. And then Colm had headed for the Willmarth farm.

"What could I say?'' Colm told Ruth when she protested Glenna's involvement. "I know she's an old lady, but—''

"If it *is* Mac,'' Ruth said. "We don't know that, do we?'' Colm saw her smile at her "guest''—Kevin, his name was, an Irish name, but the guy looked more British to him: those close-set English eyes, something about the aristocratic set of the jaw. Colm couldn't see much good in the English; his grandfather had talked Irish history to him. "Proddy Orangecoats,'' his grandmother had called the men who controlled Northern Ireland; she was a fierce Republican. Crowningshield: The guy's name proved his suspect origins.

Colm tried to be civil to the man, to include him in the conversation, though it was none of Crowningshield's business, was it? The man was just a visitor here. "Staying long?'' he asked, noting with distaste the gleaming Florsheim shoes (Colm's sneakers were developing vents); and then he said to Ruth, "They're doing X rays, having the dental work looked at, a bite mold. Couple of teeth missing—from the impact of the blow maybe. We'll know if it's Mac—he had bad teeth, according to Glenna. If it's not—Glenna have any lovers she wanted to get rid of, you suppose?"

"That's not funny." Ruth shoved her chair back, then tucked in her shirt where it had worked up from her jeans.

Colm thought she looked sexy as hell: those freckles, the thick flyaway hair, that pink button-down shirt open at the neck, the full breasts. You could see the muscles moving in her lightly perspiring throat.

"I don't know," Crowningshield said, as though continuing a conversation he'd begun with Ruth before Colm arrived. He couldn't seem to get comfortable, kept shifting position. "I mean, it depends on my wife. They've got her a virtual prisoner in that place." He looked at Ruth for sympathy, and Colm was disturbed to hear her make a kind of clucking sound.

"Kevin's been to that healing place three times, and they won't let him in," Ruth told Colm, as if the fellow couldn't speak for himself. "It's a shame. It's not the wife herself—she may not even know. It's the woman who manages the place."

"And it's my wife's property, too," said Crowningshield.

That was a surprise. Colm took a quick breath. "How come some other woman can speak for her, then?"

"His wife started the group, got this woman to run it," Ruth explained. "She's a massage therapist and a midwife. Has this amazing upper body, according to Sharon's midwife, who knows her. She just assists other midwives now, though, since her accident—whatever that was."

Crowningshield looked skeptical; he reached for the doughnut Colm had his eye on. Colm was getting annoyed now. Ruth was so one-tracked that she didn't refill the plate, either. "Kevin thinks the woman's got the others hypnotized, brainwashed. Including his wife. And she's not well. Emily said they all looked...well, chalky, she said."

Crowningshield was hanging his head, a gloomy Eeyore. Like an animal waiting for a rival to leave so he could get to his feed. But

Colm wasn't leaving, no sir. He was sticking it out until the other guy left. He rocked back in his chair. Ruth always shook a finger at the kids for that. Would she scold him in front of Crowningshield? Probably not, too intimate a scene.

If it wasn't Mac in that grave, he thought (these non sequiturs in his head), then where *was* Mac? Maybe that was the next step. To find Mac. Before that crazy Glenna got herself in deep water. He'd heard about the *Times* reporter. The young Flint girl had called him—Ruth's line was busy, she'd said. But he wasn't about to tell Ruth in front of this guy.

"Want a trip to the city?" he asked Ruth.

"Burlington?" She glanced at him sideways, an amused smile on her face. Her skin was openly perspiring now. Why? Because of the woodstove? Or was it Crowningshield?...

"New York," he said. "The Big Apple. Our apples are small up here. Check in with the *New York Times*. Couple of dentists. In case they don't have any luck with the Vermont torturers." Fallon had authorized the trip.

"If we can take thirty cows with us," Ruth said, glancing at Crowningshield.

The intruder snorted. Thought the remark so cute, Colm figured. Now Ruth was bringing out more doughnuts. She was offering the plate to the rival.

Colm decided he wouldn't stay after all. Something about the atmosphere.

THEY WERE HERE, Hartley saw. The turquoise Blazer, with the New York license and the pink stripe along its side, her stepmother's precious stripe—she'd had it painted on specially. The girl's first impulse was to run, hide in the barn, hide Aunty. The article had come out in the morning *Times;* Fay had brought home a copy. Hopefully, her parents hadn't seen it yet. Aunty hadn't, either; she was out walking the fields, the way she did more and more often these days, and now Fay was drinking wine again with that guy who made signs. But Fay was her only hope.

"She's not here—Aunty's not here. *I'm* not here," she told Fay while Willard Boomer looked on, amused. "It's my stepmother," she pleaded. "With Dad. Steer them off!"

"But they'll worry." Fay stroked Gandalf and he slobbered her cheek with his long pink tongue. "I remember when my daughter, Patsy, disappeared one time. I was out of my mind. And all the time, she was with three girlfriends, camping out."

"Oh, yes," said Willard Boomer, who had no children of his own. "My mother worries. Even now. Oh, absolutely."

Hartley dashed upstairs with the *Times*, stashed it under a pillow. She heard them entering the kitchen, her stepmother's high-pitched voice: "A friend saw the Colt, heading north. Now it's outside, in the mud. She's here. Oh, yes, I thought so. Homer, Glenna's kidnapped the girl!"

Hartley grimaced. She had forgotten about the Colt, parked outside where the police had trampled the early snow into mud. She was caught. She sank down on the top step, trying to think it out, what she'd say, what excuse. She saw her stepmother's lower half, one shiny red shoe tapping. She always did that when she was angry, probably had been for the whole five-hour trip north. Fay was stuttering. "Who? What colt? No horses here, but we have a cow. This is a B and B you know, a farmhouse."

"My aunt's house," said Homer Flint. "I assume you're the one I rented it to." He stood there solidly, in brown gabardine pants with a wide brown leather belt, scuffed brown shoes with worn-looking salesman soles. He was looking apologetic.

Hartley drew a shuddering breath and scuffed slowly down the stairs. She loved her father dearly, though he made her angry the way he gave in to his wife. She couldn't rely on Fay. The woman would just make things worse.

"You were going to put her in a nursing home. She didn't want to go. She wanted to come home. She's happy here, Dad." Standing in the kitchen now, Hartley appealed to her father, stroked his sleeve. He was a pushover really, if she worked it right.

"We called the police," her stepmother said. "To find *you*. Can you imagine what you've put us through? And they told us about that—that thing you found. It was her husband—it was Mac. Homer knows. Oh Lord, oh God! We've been frantic, haven't we, Homer? Where is she? We've made arrangements."

Fay said, "I'm Fay Hubbard—your third or fourth cousin, and

this is Willard Boomer. He made the sign out there. It was very reasonable; he's the best sign maker around.''

"The only one," said Willard, looking modest. No one was looking at him, though, so he got up, stuck out his hand to Homer, who took it absently.

"You haven't finished your tea," said Fay. Hartley noticed the tea was a suspiciously reddish color. Fay picked up the cup and followed Willard out on the porch with it.

"Arrangements," Hartley repeated, the word sinking in.

"For Glenna, of course." Her stepmother started to sit down, but then, spotting a pat of butter on the chair, straightened up. She gave a little shriek when she saw the dog, and Hartley patted the frightened animal. Matilda Flint turned back to her stepdaughter. "How else is she going to get off? How's she going to explain—oh, Homer knows; he heard the fights. Glenna and Mac. He'd have to be a witness, wouldn't you, Homer? Oh Lord. We've called the state mental hospital—Rockbury. We'll take her up tomorrow. Of course they'll find her crazy. Crazy as a loon. Don't worry, we'll see that she gets her scotch. They'll make that concession, won't they?'' She drew a shuddering breath and sank down on the pat of butter.

"Dad?" Hartley took a step forward, held out her hands. But Homer let his fall to his sides.

"I don't know what else we can do, babe," he said. "It looks bad."

There was a shriek from Matilda Flint. She was holding a *New York Times* in one trembling hand. It had lain on the table the whole time, folded over to page sixteen, and Hartley hadn't seen it, hadn't known Fay bought two copies.

"She's already confessed. Confessed to everyone. Oh my God. To some reporter!" Matilda threw herself at her husband, and he patted her shoulder absently, then looked apologetically at Hartley. "We'll have to take her this minute. We have to get her out of here. Up to Rockbury. Glen-na, where are you?" she screeched. "Glen-naaaa?"

"Gandalf—he wants out," Hartley said, and banged out the door in her SAVE THE GREYHOUND T-shirt, the dog dashing on ahead. It was raining, a warmish drizzle, but she hardly felt it, she was running so fast. Out into the fields, to warn Aunty.

EIGHT

ANOTHER FLOCK of grackles—second this fall, swooping down out of the sky like a black cloud, crashing into Alwyn Bagshaw's garden, crushing his empty cornstalks, the last lettuce he'd covered up so careful with old sheets. Now they was sucking up his sunflower seeds, squeezing through the broken window of the barn, where he stored his winter squash.

Thieves, he thought. Black thieves! A miserable bird they was with those long wedge-shaped tails, the mean yellow eyes, the bronzy backs. A dirty bird, pushing the bluebirds out of their holes. The female the worst. He'd seen her one time, after she left her nest, circling over the East Branbury brook, squatting on the log, tail up, wings spread. All quivery, like a woman wanting sex.

"Git, git!" he cried, running in circles, flailing his arms. But still they came, a hundred, two hundred maybe, blacking out his land. Come to torture him, force him out of his home—like those females next door. They wanted his land, his house, they did. It was them brought the onslaught of grackles, he told himself. Brought the Willmarth woman—for here she was now, green pickup squealing to a stop next door—coming to see him? What had the girl told her? She better not come round no more. Got nothing to say to her. Damn the woman anyways, looking over the hedge at me, waving, smiling, like she's my good buddy. Looking at what I have in my wheelbarrow. Can she see what?

She'll tell, oh she will. Like Denby, a little tattletale when we was growing up. Always putting the blame on Alwyn, like the time Denby shot the frozen long johns down the road full of holes, then planted the .22 in my room. Ma locking me in the cellar a whole day and night without food.

He kicked the side of the wheelbarrow—it was in his way. Now he'd hurt his foot. He yelped with pain—and the pain spread to his chest.

"They's killing me," he cried aloud, "them busybodies!"

WHEN RUTH ENTERED the Healing House, past the sign with the
arrow aiming at the moon, she felt a cold draft on her neck. The
windows were wide open, though there'd been a heavy frost this
morning: You could see it outside on the grass, like a pale glaze on
a smooth pot. A pale glaze on a smooth pot, she repeated the words
to herself. There was a time back in college when she'd done pot-
tery, thought she'd like to have a kiln, make things with her hands.
Funny she should think of that now. But marriage used up the hands
in other ways: cooking, cleaning, milking cows. At least Tim was
back to work, doing the milking; he'd practically forced her to take
a morning off. And here she was, in spite of Kevin Crowningshield's advice not to come—he'd only needed her as a sounding
board, he'd said. "She'll see me—she's got to see me," he'd said
of his wife, the sweat springing out on his brow like drops of fine
rain.

The place was as spotless as Emily had said; you could eat off
the floor—if that's what you wanted to do. It looked as though
they'd even scrubbed the walls. There was an odor, though, about
the place, beyond the incense—as if there was sickness here, a
contagion, something they wanted to air out, exorcize. And no one
seemingly about, though she heard a high hum in another room:
like wind whistling, or a teapot coming to a boil. She followed the
sound, peered in. She stood in the doorway, shocked.

A woman was lying on her back, on a low massage table, eyes
tight shut—or was she dead? Her face was a mask under a tangle
of brown curls. A dozen other women sat cross-legged on straw
mats, their bodies wrapped in brown cotton robes. One of the watch-
ers was wheezing even while she chanted something unintelligible.
One woman at the side of the table—seemingly the leader—sat, tall
in a wheelchair, her eyes shut, head flung back; you could see the
purply veins taut in her neck. Her black hair was pulled tightly off
her forehead; her scarred skin was the yellowy white of curd; her
breasts bulged under the scarlet robe. There was a white drape over
the supine woman's body, except for one protruding foot that the
wheelchair woman was slowly, deeply, blindly—it seemed—massaging.

Was it a house for the sick? Kevin had every right to worry;
Ruth was glad she'd come. But she didn't dare interrupt. There was

some intensity, something deeply private, even solemn, about the ceremony; about the room itself, with its colorful Japanese lanterns, the soulful music, the incense. She decided to wait; she glanced through the brochures piled up in a rack on the kitchen wall. "Isis Blue Moon: R.N., M.Ed.: spiritual healings, holistic healings, soul therapy, psychotherapy. Chakra balancing, cranial-sacral work, chelation, foot reflexology, and therapeutic touch. Energy work."

Whoa! Where was the dictionary for a poor farmer who did her healing with hot mustard pads or the old Vermont cure, whiskey with lemon and honey? Her daughter Sharon laughed at her, of course. Sharon was a vegetarian; each day she swallowed ten different vitamins and minerals. She and her husband slept with the baby between them—Robbie hardly a baby now, but almost two years old. When had they had the privacy to make the new child? It could come any day now—along with a calf or two—and in her bed.

Calves and babies, babies and calves. Once she'd dreamed she was giving birth to a calf—and in the dream she became the calf, a bull calf. She woke, shrieking, could still see the ax, gleaming, above her head.

In the other room, the chanting had stopped. The group was circling the sick woman, touching her forehead, her cheek, her bare toes, which stuck out from under the drape. Suddenly, the woman opened her eyes and vomited a bloody froth. The onlookers gasped, one cried out, and another ran for a bucket. The leader, Isis, Ruth assumed, remained calm. She instructed two of the women to help the sick woman sit upright. They held a vial to the woman's nose. But the face turned paler still, greenish yellow in the slant of morning light from the south window.

"That woman needs a doctor," Ruth cried. "Call an ambulance!"

The sick woman opened her eyes then, pale blue eyes that seemed to swallow up the face. "No," she said in a high, firm voice. "I won't have a doctor."

"Of course you won't," said Isis in a flat midwestern accent. "Of course not, dear." Frowning at Ruth, she said, "Can't you see this is a sick woman? She wants a spiritual healer, not a doctor. Now please go."

"No doctor. Go. Please." The sick woman's eyes, intensely blue
now, pleaded with Ruth. Isis carefully wiped her forehead, while a
woman with a long black braid scrubbed the floor, on hands and
knees, with what smelled like ammonia. Ruth could see the spinal
vertebrae through the woman's thin robe.

As Ruth ran out, feeling light-headed, she heard the chanting start
up again, the sound mixed with a light rain; she smelled smoke in
the air. Raindrops spattered the swinging sign, making it seem as
though the arrows were moving, up into the sky, into whatever was
waiting there. Surely the woman would die! She only hoped it
wasn't Kevin's wife. He'd spoken of a clotting problem, his wife
on blood thinners—the medicine she'd left behind in Chicago. One
could hemorrhage, bleed to death, Kevin said, from a simple cut.

A thought entered her head as she climbed into the old green
pickup: If the woman died, if this *was* his wife, who would inherit
the house, the land? The woman in the red robe? Isis—who
wouldn't call a doctor?

Alarmed, she headed down the mountain toward Branbury. She
usually loved the drive; the road followed the curve of the river. At
each bend, rocky cliffs and waterfalls, bordered with scarlet swamp
maples—though they'd lost most of their color now. The tree limbs
looked black and sterile in the cold drizzle; the fallen leaves had
been raked into crumpled damp piles. There were no children playing in front of the houses. She should have phoned Colm at once,
from the country store—he might be on volunteer duty today with
Branbury Rescue. She would have, except for the sick woman herself, her own words. "No doctor.... Please." Didn't Ruth herself
get angry with doctors who interfered with living wills, with the
desires of sick patients? A woman had the last say over her body,
didn't she? Choice! For life—or death.

Still... Was it suicide this woman was committing? Or was it
something else? The word *homicide* came to mind. And Ruth felt
the rain enter her bones.

She kept on going, too fast, down the mountain, veering north at
the main road, toward home. She felt somehow bereft, half a person
away from the farm, as though the farm were an island, a self-
sufficient yet vulnerable island, at the mercy of the weather, the
market—forces beyond her control.

Well, Tim was in control today, although there was enough to do for ten people: hay to mound up into bales, mower in need of repair, tractor with a broken gear shaft. That was the frustration: She could envision where she could take the farm—the new genetics, new machinery, advances in nutrition. But there wasn't money for it, too little help from the state, and so it seemed she was moving backward into the future.

"Backward into the future," she said aloud, almost smiling at the oxymoron as she drove right past her own farm, as though the pickup, like a stubborn horse, refused to enter. Spacey Ruth. Well then, she'd go on to the Flint farm. It was probably an unconscious wish. She'd see Kevin. Something had to be done for that woman, something short of a doctor.... If, that is, the sick woman was his wife....

Or even if she wasn't!

"YOU KNEW HIM, Dad? Glenna's husband, Mac. You knew Glenna, too, you said?" Colm Hanna stood in the doorway of the embalming room, where his father was bent over a corpse, aspirating the body—an open-coffin procedure. He was inserting a trocar into the heart's right atrium. The body was that of an adolescent boy; he'd been in an auto accident, a drunken buddy driving, careening into the wrong lane, showing off. The girlfriend still in the hospital. "The driver was unhurt, of course," William Hanna said, sounding bitter. "They always seem to get off."

"But he'll have to live with the guilt," Colm said, thinking of the myriad horror scenes he'd witnessed as a volunteer with Branbury Rescue. He grimly watched the trocar plunge in and out of the body, like a knitting needle into wool—breaking up organs and intestines, vacuuming out the blood, replacing it with a preservative. When Colm went, he wanted his body *burned*.

His father said, "Guilt, huh. You bet he will."

Glenna, too, Colm thought, if she really was guilty, as people said. What mental hell, he wondered, had she gone through? Or had she simply blocked it out? He'd heard of people doing that: blocking out what happened to them—abuse; what they did to others—murder? That rumor about the hole Mac had dug for the horse. How true was it? Was it motive for killing the man?

"Painted tin," his father said, the aspiration complete. He removed a silver ring from the boy's finger, held it up to the window glass, squinting, the horn-rimmed glasses down on his nose, the skin white and puffy under his Irish eyes. In spite of the work he did, there was a humorous glint in his eyes. Like he'd rather be at the local pub with the boys than aspirating a cadaver. "Five-and-dime. The girlfriend gave it to him, I suppose."

"And he cherished it." Colm pictured the ring Ruth had given him in high school. It, too, was a five-and-dime ring. Impulsively, she'd stuck it on his finger one night, after they embraced. He didn't take a shower for days, afraid the gold would wash off. The thrill of it.

But here he was, in a room of death. "What was he like, Dad— Mac? Crotchety, like Glenna says? Mean-spirited? Sharp-tongued?" He didn't know why he had to know—except that Ruth was concerned. Glenna was a neighbor; Mac had been. Colm had never married himself, not after Ruth gave him the final no sophomore year in college; he could only know relationships secondhand. It made him feel inferior, as if he were anomalous, because he lived alone. Though he knew what they said: "When his dad goes, all that responsibility, then he'll marry." And maybe he would. When Pete left with that actress, he'd silently celebrated—a shot of his favorite Guckenheimer whiskey. Then kicked himself, knowing the hurt for Ruth. Christ but we're self-centered animals, he thought.

And now there was this Crowningshield fellow, insinuating himself into her life, slurping up her cider. Why, the guy had a wife! Though Ruth still had a husband—he had to remember that. The split wasn't official yet. He and Pete were on the same side for once: both hoping for a divorce.

"All that, I guess," his father was saying about Mac, motioning Colm to help lay out the body in the satin-lined coffin. "I only saw him once or twice. Your mother was alive then; we met them in the diner. Your mother just plunked herself down in their booth— she knew Glenna from some planning commission they were both on, liked the woman. But uninvited. Oh, she was always doing that, Roseanne—your mother. Impulsivelike. Not thinking of the reception we might get."

It was painful to look at the boy after they laid him there. Colm's

father had to be more inured to death than Colm was. The boy's
face was a rosy color from the pink embalming fluid; any minute,
it seemed, he'd get up and hit a home run.

"I guess! Walk in a restaurant, your mother'd know everybody's
business before we'd leave. Me, I'd cringe." William draped a
white sheet over the body. "He'll hold for now, poor kid, till the
makeup lady gets here. Get me a cup a coffee, huh? These kids,
they do me in."

"Decaf, Dad. You know what the doctor says. That high blood
pressure—I saw your chart. And that disk problem, in your back.
Doing anything about it?"

"Hell, they discounted that," his father said, and Colm laughed—
though the pun was probably unintentional.

"How many miles you walked this week?"

"Hundred times around the house. Inside. When I'm dead, then
I'll worry about it."

"Sure, Dad." Although not a churchgoer—he did catch the
"early show" now and then at St. Mary's—his father still believed
in an afterlife. The priests got to them early; hard to break old habits,
old beliefs. Colm would tell him it was this life that counted—the
only sure thing—but the words floated past his father's ear. Nice,
really. He wished he could believe, too.

In the kitchen, he put a spoonful of decaf in a flowered cup. It
was thin bone china, cracked on the handle, probably the last of a
set that had belonged to his grandmother. He stirred in a spoonful
of sugar, though his dad liked two. He put two in his own cup,
though—what the hell. He had thirty or more years yet to go. Knock
on wood.

"So, Dad, tell about that diner encounter. What did you talk
about?"

"Jeez, Colm, it was a quarter of a century ago. Well, I don't
know—his work mostly, I suppose. Mac was a talker. That New
York accent, you know, like a certain rep we got up here in Vermont—though damn, I voted for the guy. It was thick Brooklyn.
You'd think he wrote the whole *New York Times*. He had an opinion
about everything."

"He was a proofreader, Ruth says."

"Never know it from him. Wanted something more, awful bad,

I don't know what. Not a contented type, you know? One of those
questers? Hey, you really going down there, Colm? To that crazy
city? They tell me the taxi drivers don't speak English anymore.
You got to point out where you're going on a map. Look, kid, the
guy's nothin' but bones now. What's the use?"

"It might not be Mac, those bones. For one thing, the forensics
people thought the guy was a younger man than Mac. Well, anyway, I want to know Mac better. Anyone who'd marry Glenna,
move back to Vermont with her, he must have some kind of guts.
What do you suppose he saw in her?"

"The farm? Land? A listening ear? I don't know. Well, suit
yourself. Just stay out of the subways, okay? They got kooks just
waiting around to shove you down in the tracks."

"Dad, there are kooks everywhere. Up here, too." He finished
his coffee; he needed the caffeine. He'd take Amtrak, he guessed.
Didn't want to have to drive into the city. "You gonna wheel that
boy into the showroom?" His father frowned; he didn't always like
Colm's kidding around. Colm took the initiative anyway, pushed
the coffin in on its gurney. They'd bought the gurney a year ago,
along with a small elevator to get down to the cremation chamber,
a kind of dumbwaiter (an ironic name, he thought). No more lifting
for his father. It had cost a fortune, but Colm had helped out. His
father was growing frail—osteoporosis, it looked like, the way the
shoulders hunched forward, the back a humpy curve between.

William heaved himself up out of a chair with a grunt and followed Colm into the parlor.

"Family coming this afternoon for the wake. That's the hard part.
I need you here, son, not in any damn city. But if you gotta go,
don't stay long. They're talking about freezing rain again tomorrow.
You never know who'll crack up, way they speed around here. I
can't do it alone, Colm."

"I've told you that, Dad. You need to hire someone."

"Well, I'm telling you, Colm," William replied, a non sequitur.

There was no use pursuing that subject again. Anyway, his beeper
was sounding off. And he was on duty. Jeez. He hoped it wasn't
another crazy kid.

KEVIN CROWNINGSHIELD called Ruth at her barn. He said he'd been
seeing a lawyer, was sorry he'd missed her when she stopped by.

When she blurted out her story—what she'd seen at the Healing House—he panicked, said "Angie," told her to wait out front, that he was calling Branbury Rescue. He told her she had to come. Would it bring Colm Hanna? Ruth wondered.

She felt swept away; she was, literally. Yanked into Kevin's car after he whirled up to her barn. In seconds, it seemed, they were speeding up the mountain road. Kevin pulled over momentarily to let the ambulance scream past, then shoved his foot all the way down on the accelerator. He didn't speak; his mouth was an inverted U. *Desperate*—that was the word. Ruth felt a wave of nausea welling up in her throat. What kind of reception would an ambulance find? She kept hearing that woman's voice: "No doctors.... Please." Now Ruth was interfering, in the worst way.

Colm was already inside when they arrived. He glanced at her, then at Kevin. Why did she feel guilty for being here? A second medic, in overalls and boots, was jumping out the back of the ambulance: Tom LeDuc, a farmer. When did he have time for this? Ruth wanted to shrink into the woodwork, but Kevin motioned her onward; she was committed.

But it seemed the residents had been waiting for outside help; the house was in pandemonium, ten women talking, all at once: They weren't wearing robes now, just ordinary clothing: T-shirts, jeans, sneakers.

"She was only paring apples.... For lunch...to make us a strudel—she was always doing extra for people...."

"Why did she do that?... Mother told her not to...."

"Cut herself. Such a tiny cut and then..."

"Oh, look, is she dying? Please help!... It's Angie.... In there..."

It was a fight between Kevin and the medics to carry Angie out and into the ambulance. She was alive. Ruth saw the blue eyes open, unfocused, the vomit coming again and again, blood streaming from the finger cut. "Internal bleeding, as well," Colm said, though Ruth didn't know how he'd know. It seemed a sea of blood; even the walls had a bloody tint from the late sun, though it was still raining a little. Would there be a rainbow? Incongruous thought. Ruth could smell, taste the blood.

They wrestled Angie onto a stretcher, the medics elbowing Kevin away. He cried out her name, over and over: "Angie, Angie, it's me, Kevin—Angie..." Angie's lips appeared to struggle with words, but failed; her eyes closed, she gave herself to the medics. The last Ruth saw of her was a blur of white being shoved into the rear of the ambulance. Colm was all business; it was a side of him she'd never really seen. He leapt into the back, Kevin behind him, and the ambulance shrieked off and down the mountain road.

It seemed they would drown in the silence. Three of the women were weeping. Isis was slumped in her wheelchair; she kept running a hand through her uncombed hair. "I can't understand it," she moaned. "She's been taking the blood thinner. Oh, yes, I made her do it. I got the prescription myself. Why should that tiny cut—a mere slip of the paring knife..." She held her head in her hands like a fallen fruit; her belly ballooned. Around her, the women were starting to clean up, banging about with pails and scrub brushes, working frenetically, as if it would help them to comprehend all this. Isis's denim work shirt was stained with blood; she looked like a distraught housewife with a child who'd had a bad accident. "Take Marna to the hospital, would you?" she begged Ruth. "I have to know—about Angie. Her stepmother will want to..."

She was too exhausted to finish the sentence. One of the women—Marna, Ruth assumed—ran up, pushing her thin arms into a blue wool jacket. She followed Ruth out to Kevin's rented car. He'd left the keys in it; it was an automatic, easy to drive. Ruth felt small in this big car, not quite in control, like a child on a merry-go-round horse. But no parent to hold on to her, keep her from falling off.

She edged out into the road, glanced back through the rearview mirror. Alwyn Bagshaw was in his yard, watching, unabashed. If she didn't know better, she'd think he was waving. The acrid smell of smoke pushed through her passenger window. Bagshaw, burning his trash again, she supposed. It seemed the town just closed their eyes to his civil disobedience.

Ahead, as she rounded a curve—Marna silent and tense in the seat beside her—she glimpsed the rainbow, a double rainbow, slanting down into the rocky mountain brook, one color bleeding into the next: lilac, red, orange.... It was strangely beautiful.

Nature was full of ironies these days.

NINE

EMILY HAD an important message for her mother. And she wanted to deliver it alone. So she waited until Vic left the barn that evening with his two chickens. Personally, Emily despised chickens. They were such silly creatures, running around in circles on those wrinkly feet. She preferred ducks—ducks had personality. But her pet Quack had got run over by a tractor, and her mother had never allowed another. Ducks got in the way, her mother said, unreasonably. And it was her mother who had been driving the tractor that ran over Quack. Even now, the tears shoved into Emily's eyes. She remembered how Quack would waddle out to meet the school bus. Which was more than her mother ever did. Emily wasn't feeling at all good about her mother. Not today.

Here was Vic now, a chicken clutched, squawking, in either hand, a frown on his bony brow. "Why can't they stay in the barn?" he accused Emily, as though she'd made the rule.

"Because the inspector said no. They contaminate." Emily heard her voice grow weary; they'd had this conversation before.

"How, tell me how!" the boy argued, and without waiting for an answer, he launched into a diatribe about his poisoned hawk. "Mother won't take me there. I want to see it." He moved closer on his bowed legs and Emily backed off; she didn't want those chickens pecking at her new pink mohair sweater. She was going over to see Hartley Flint. The girl had some "mission" in mind; she needed Emily's "immediate" help—something to do with Glenna Flint, up in Rockbury, where Hartley's parents had stuck her, poor thing. *Ambushed* was the word Hartley'd used. Emily wanted to help out, she really did! She was quite fond of the stubborn old lady. And Glenna had known her dad; he'd fixed a fence at the Flint farm once, and Glenna was grateful.

"If it were Dad, he'd take you to that vet," she said softly. She had her own personal mission—it involved her parents. She might need Vic on her side.

But, as usual, Vic was no help. "He would not. You know he would not," he said. "He never took me anyplace except to the feed stores, where he had to go anyway. Then he called it *my* outing."

She gave up on Vic. "Put the dumb things in the chicken pen," she snapped, "right now." And she pushed past him into the barn.

"Dad called," she shouted at the shadowy blue-jeaned figure at the rear of the barn. "He's coming up Halloween weekend. He wants to see me and Vic. He wants to see *you,* Mother."

She moved deeper into the barn. The stench of manure and urine shocked her nose; the bellowing calves jarred her ears. What was she doing here anyway? Why did her mother have to keep running this farm? Her father had gotten away. The farm wasn't going anywhere, he'd told Emily once. It was like running and running in place and not moving beyond the next fence, he'd said. It was wasting his life. And who cared? People thought their food came from the Grand Union. They never thought of the farmer.

"Mother," she said to the shape bent over in the rear of the dimly lit barn, "are you listening? Can you hear me? I said, Dad is coming. He's coming soon. Can you answer me, Mother?"

But when she shuffled through the sawdust and the blown hay and the manure patties, which hadn't been swept up yet—it was Vic's job to sweep, and he was goofing off with his silly chickens— her mother still wouldn't answer. She was bent over Zelda's calf.

"I think it has mastitis," she said, as if Emily had never spoken at all; like the only thing her mother cared about in the whole wide world—more than her younger daughter, obviously—was that foolish calf of crazy Zelda's.

"Mother, we have to talk. Talk to me, Mother!" she said, and rubbed her face where the tears were drizzling down either side of her nose.

Her mother turned then and stood up. She looked at Emily as if she were seeing a stranger. And then, unaccountably, she lunged at the girl, threw her arms around her, squeezed.

But Emily couldn't hug back. She couldn't. Because of what her mother was saying.

"That woman is dead," her mother said. "The one at the Healing House. Angie. Colm called. She died an hour after they got her to the hospital. Then Kevin called. He says they murdered her. Did they, you think?''

Well, Emily couldn't answer that. She remembered those pasty-faced women; she couldn't pick out an individual face. She pulled away, looked down on her mother's brown head, threaded with gray, with hay wisps. Ruth had sunk back on her heels. Her mother didn't know that woman, either. What was all this sudden grief? Or was it that man, that Kevin? He'd been to the house three times already. Trying to pull her mother away from her father. Her father, who was coming this very month. Maybe to stay.

"I want you to see him, Mother. I want you to think of us. Vic and me and Sharon. I want my father back.''

She did, too! She didn't care what her mother wanted. She was beyond reason now. People worked things out. Wilder's mother had. Wilder's father had left just a year ago, after his older son got in all that drug-related trouble, and then he came back. And Wilder's mother let him. Because of Wilder and the youngest boy, Garth. She had a big heart. She understood.

But Emily's mother only said, "Angie was younger than me, too. She made the most unusual jewelry. Kevin showed me a piece. All that talent, wasted. Who says there's a caring God!''

On that note, Emily gave up. She left the barn, holding her breath, then gasped for air when she got outside. She ran, stumbling, through the south pasture toward the Flint farm to see about this "immediate" mission for Hartley. Her mother had let the cows out again after milking, and off in the twilit field she saw Zelda, grazing under a crescent moon, apart from the herd.

"That's Mother all right," she said aloud, and jammed her knuckles together in frustration.

IT WASN'T FREEZING RAIN that brought the next victim to the mortuary. William Hanna couldn't believe this one. And his son out of touch, and his own arthritis kicking in. Sciatic nerve bothering, too, the way the pain traveled from the hip down into his stiff toes. It was definitely getting time to retire. If only he had a son willing to take over the business. But it seemed there was nothing for it but to carry on.

This one was female: not young, but not old, either—mid-to late forties maybe. Cut her finger with a knife, paring an apple, and bled to death, the woman who called told him. Stoic-voiced, she said they'd broken a rule, sent the stricken woman off in an ambulance; the voice faltered as she spoke. What rule she'd broken was beyond William. If you need help, call the ambulance—that was his dictum. The Branbury Rescue number was taped to his phone. Though he knew it by heart, Colm being a volunteer himself. If he could get to the phone when he needed it, that is. The stubborn joints! Doctors didn't know from zilch. He'd go see a chiropractor.

Pale as ice, this body was, except for a slight skin rash. Early rigor mortis in the jaw and neck by the time he got her; that stiffness depressed him every time—it happened so fast. Like the soul couldn't wait to get rid of the body, to break loose. He wanted to open all the windows, restore the rose to her cheeks. And him in this business forty years now. He had to get out soon, had to...

What made it worse: husband charging in a couple of hours later, weeping, keening like a woman. William Hanna didn't hold with men crying; he didn't care what his son said; it wasn't for men to give in like that. Hell, his job was to cremate her, that's all, and the husband wanted it done at once, fast. Couldn't bear to look at her all rigid like that, he'd told William. Well, "fast" wasn't William's way of doing things these days. "You want to assist me?" he'd asked the husband—Crowningshield his name. "You know anything about this business?"

The guy got out of there "fast" then, wiping his eyes, didn't want any part of the nitty-gritty. Aw, they were all like that. Most of them wanting the faces dolled up, death disguised or denied altogether. As if anything could wipe it out.

Himself, basically, he'd gotten used to it, hadn't he? The old ones he put through the paces without a quiver. It was the young ones who got to him, ones who died before their time, like that boy yesterday, this one today. This one had been quite lovely: good bone structure, strong cheekbones. He peered closer at her neck and breast. Something about the tint of the skin, though, more than just the blue-gray of the average corpse. There was something greenish yellow showing up, a kind of jaundice. As if it had been more than hemorrhage—hemorrhage of the larynx and lungs, too, they said. Like something had helped her along. Doctor might not have noticed it right off—whatever it was. *If* it was. But he'd done enough corpses to know when something wasn't right. No, something wasn't right.

He would photograph, yes, but he'd better call the doc back in on this one. Maybe the police, but the doc could call that one. What was it about that Healing House? Didn't sound like it was all healing to him, fatal hemorrhages and all.

Drat that son of his! Off on a wild-goose chase in New York City, when the real need was here. Here, in Branbury, Vermont. With his own dad.

AUNTY TURNED her face away when Hartley came in the room. She looked like a bundle of old clothes, hunched over in the black leather chair. Her head was sunk into her chest; her feet splayed out on the floor. A second bundle of old clothes sat slumped beside her, asleep and snoring. A TV was blaring in one corner of the room, but no one was looking at it. Aunty never watched TV. It was phony, she said, all those advertisements. They just wanted your money, and she'd rather read a book, she said. Hartley went over to turn it off, and then, thinking better of it, turned it up even louder. So if Aunty made a fuss, an aide wouldn't hear.

She stood over her aunt, hands on her hips. "Now listen here, Aunty, I had nothing to do with this. It was my parents again, and you know it."

If Aunty knew it, she wasn't saying so. She just pursed her lips, beaklike, and stared into her lap.

"I'm here to get you out, Aunty," she whispered, not wanting to wake up the roommate. "Now listen to me. Emily's waiting outside to help. I had to sneak in past the guards. This place is like a prison. God, they've got bars on these windows, like you're some criminal! You don't want to stay here, do you?"

Aunty looked up then, the irises of her eyes like hard green apples. "Don't forget my red sweater," she said. "It's in there." She pointed to a white-painted bureau. A photograph in a thin leather frame sat on top: Hartley recognized the family at a Vermont Thanksgiving dinner: a younger Homer, a plumper Hartley, and Glenna toasting the photographer (it must have been Matilda) with her glass, looking about the same as she did today—that is, frazzled.

Glenna had cooked the turkey. It had been raw and pink inside, Hartley remembered, but they'd all nibbled at the outer pieces and pretended it was delicious. Later on, her stepmother had recooked it for three hours.

Hartley grabbed the red sweater and a couple changes of underwear and crammed them into a Grand Union bag. "Well, get up, then, Aunty." And then, louder, for the sake of the roommate, who was shifting in her chair, she said, "We're just going for a walk, right?"

Aunty started to protest, but then she caught her grand-niece's drift. "Sure, a walk," she said. And then, halfway to her feet, Glenna balked and sank down. "Where we going anyway? To the farm? They'll just put me in the car and bring me back here." She dropped her head in her hands, and Hartley wanted to pat it. But Hartley wasn't the touching type. None of them were, not even her father. They loved one another, she supposed, but at a distance. One day, she'd get therapy. But right now, she had to get Aunty out.

"I have a hiding place," she whispered, kneeling at Aunty's feet—you had to do that with Aunty sometimes. "It's neat. A little cabin in the woods. You'll like it, Aunty, you will. It's got a rocking chair and everything."

Glenna looked up, licked her dry lips, considered. "Has it got a bathroom?"

"Sure," Hartley lied. Actually, she hadn't thought about bathrooms. It was Emily who'd come up with the cabin idea. It was a place up in the Green National Forest, a cabin her father and another man had built for when they went hunting. But it wasn't hunting season yet. Not until mid-November, so Aunty would be safe. "You can have your scotch, too," she said. "And we'll cook tofu loaf for you, and cheeseburgers."

"Cheddar cheese," Aunty said. "That's the kind I like. I hate that processed stuff. It tastes like glue."

"Sure. Cabot cheddar. Sharp." Hartley mounded up Aunty's bed to make it look like she was sleeping there, stuck a white-haired wig she'd bought on the pillow. She smiled at her ingenuity.

"Get my black wool coat, too; it's in that closet. They took away my scarf. Thought I might hang myself. They treat me like some loony. I don't tell them a thing, mind you. They want to know who's president of the United States, I tell them it's Calvin Coolidge.''

"Right on, Aunty. Now, here's your coat. And put on this big old black scarf to cover your hair. So if they spot us, they won't think it's you.''

"Extra sharp is the way I like it,'' Aunty said as they stole out into the corridor. "A little excitement in your cheese.''

Somewhere at the far end, a woman screamed and footsteps ran toward her. "Hurry,'' said Hartley. "This way.''

"Bye-bye,'' said Aunty to the door of her ward, and let herself be hustled down a back stairwell.

FAY WAS painting over Glenna's room. Stark white, but she'd add a rose-colored quilt, rose-trimmed curtains. It was strange without Glenna around. First, the old lady had been an irritation, an embarrassment to the business, an interruption to her work. Now Fay rather missed her. And even the niece was gone half the time, visiting Glenna in the funny bin they'd taken her to. "She'll die in that place without me,'' the girl had shouted as she raced out that morning, leaving Fay, of course, to answer a call a minute from the stepmother. And Fay without a credit card with any financial backing. So Fay was on her own.

Well, at least the parents had gone, Homer apologizing, poor guy, saddled with that officious woman but too weak to assert himself. And he'd refused this month's rent: an apology for the presence of daughter and aunt. Wait till he gets the MasterCard bill, Fay thought; he'll be sorry. But Sweet Jesus, she was practically destitute; Dan had all the money up there, wasn't about to part with it. The woman always came off second-best in a divorce; Fay needed any handout she could get.

And worst of all, no word from Patsy. No answer on the phone. Patsy could be difficult at times, but Fay loved her. She wanted her child; she wanted her baby back. She wanted her grandson. Was she homesick? Paint dripped on the floorboards, and she stooped to wipe it up with her rag. She wasn't any better a painter than a milker. The stuff came off in a thick white glob, like spoiled milk.

Or was Patsy right? Was Fay to blame for her daughter's lonely childhood? She'd been busy, it was true: trying to put purpose into

her life, trying to make it as an actress in a small-town theater—
three plays a year, out nights. Though she'd given it all up for rug
hooking after she and Dan saw that counselor one time, tried to
stitch the marriage together. And failed at that, too. She'd told Willard Boomer about it.

"Never had one of my own," he'd apologized. "I mean"—he
laughed that sweet, ingratiating laugh of his—"never been married,
you know. But my dad, I never knew him. Locked himself in the
garage, turned on the gas—that's another reason I don't own a car.
He had lung cancer, you see—all those Camels. He couldn't stand
the treatment, the pain. Mother and I, though, we've managed."

"Of course," said Fay, and he patted her hand, as though he'd
help her manage, too.

There'd been no hugging yet. Willard was shy; it was obvious
he'd been with few women. Fay could wait. She wondered what
the mother was like. Mother and son, living under the same roof.
Had they become entwined, like that elm beyond the barn where
two trunks grew out of one? She imagined the mother a sweet lady,
though; Willard said she was shy, spent her days upended in her
garden.

Downstairs, a door slammed. Someone went to the refrigerator;
it opened and clicked shut. "Hello?" she called down, spreading
her hands, which now were pockmarked with paint.

"Kevin," he called back, already climbing the stairs: *click, clack,
click* in those polished shoes of his. He stood in the bedroom doorway, head tilted like a thoughtful Hamlet, his lips a bow that someone had just untied. "I've been to the undertaker's," he said, and
waited for her response.

What was Hamlet's reaction to the news of Ophelia's death?
Rather indifferent, she recalled—he was too preoccupied with other
matters, his father's ghost, the murder. Why, Shakespeare wrote
murder mysteries, he did! Old blood-and-guts man, he was.

"How awful for you," she said aloud. "We're all so sorry. Ruth,
next door—she phoned me. I suppose you'll be leaving soon, then?
Will you bury her back in, um—"

"Chicago," he said. "A suburb actually, Winnetka. I will, yes.
I had her cremated. She would have wanted that."

"You said she came from here, though. No relatives?"

"Relatives?" He drew a hand through a falling sheaf of hair, made himself comfortable in a chair. "No, no, not here anymore. She left Branbury when she was twenty-one. That's when we married. She'd just come back from Rochester, New York, actually—some school there to study jewelry making. I...well, I rescued her, you know."

"From jewelry making? But it sounds interesting. I hook rugs a little. Lately, with so much going on..." She picked up her brush and it dripped across the floor. "Jesus." She bent to dab it up. She wanted to weep. Oh, the mess! She wished he'd go away so she could concentrate on the work. It wasn't a time to receive male visitors.

"She wasn't always happy with it really." He gave a little laugh. "All those boring craft fairs, shut up in a tiny booth for hours and nobody buying. And the competition? It wasn't anything she'd make money at, she realized that. I could offer her a home where she wouldn't have to make money."

"How nice," Fay said, and he smiled, having missed her irony. "You'll be leaving...when?" She turned to look at him; she was worried now, her only boarder—and a handsome one at that. His eyes were red-rimmed, as if he'd been weeping. She liked a man who could weep. It would be hard to lose a spouse, if you really loved the person. But there hadn't been love on both sides, had there? The woman had chosen to leave him? Of course, he couldn't accept that. It was a blow to the ego. Her ex hadn't either, could never understand why she left him. Then he'd rushed her into a divorce so he could date again with impunity: "How can I bring a woman here when we're still married?" he'd complained. Now he had three women he ran around with. In one sense, she'd made him young again.

"Tomorrow," Kevin said. "That's what I came to tell you. But I'll be back. There's the matter of her land, you see. The place that so-called Healing House is on. It's mine now, that land, legally. I'll hire a lawyer. They'll have to leave."

"Oh," said Fay, and bent back to her painting. She wasn't going to get involved in this one.

Kevin finally left, his footsteps growing firmer, quicker as he moved on to his room. But other feet came clip-clopping up the stairs. She recognized them, ran to shut the door. But too late. Already he was inside, Gandalf, the victim, her partner. He'd been outside in the wire run Willard had fixed for him; apparently, someone had let him in. He smelled of fresh October air, a slight aura of skunk. He was thrilled to see her. He leapt up—and the paint can slid off the ladder. "Out, Gandalf, out!"

"It's me," Hartley hollered upstairs; "we're back. Just to get food, and Aunty wants her black shawl, a couple of books, her scotch. I've got Aunty."

"And I've got white boots and a white floor," Fay yelled back. "Call off that dog."

Then, catching her breath, she shouted, "What? But you can't. You can't just haul her out of that place without permission!"

"She's got *my* permission. That's enough," Aunty yelled up. Fay heard the pair laughing like conspirators, as if they were watching a film of the Marx Brothers. *A Night at the Opera,* she thought, surveying the mess. A skeleton, a dead woman, now a kidnapped one. Let the Marx Brothers match this one.

"Glenna," she said aloud. What were they going to do with her—escaped from the funny farm? Would Fay be an accessory to the crime?

"You can't do this, Glenna," she hollered down. But already the door was slamming. Fay went to a window, flung it open. "Come back! Where are you two going, anyway?"

They were getting into Hartley's Colt, along with that girl from next door, Emily Willmarth; Hartley shutting the door on the hem of Aunty's black wool coat, then opening it, stuffing the coat inside, laughing, closing the door again. "Hey, Fay. We're going into hiding. We're going to the Edge of the Wild."

"The edge of *what?*" yelled Fay.

"Read Tolkien," Hartley hollered back. "And Fay, if my stepmother calls, you haven't seen us."

Fay leaned on the windowsill and watched the dead leaves fly up from the rush of wheels. It was all the same, she thought, all the same. *Plus ça change, plus c'est la même chose.* She was left with the excuses, the white lies. She might as well be back in Cabot, lying to the zoning guys about why Dan had put up yet a third shack on the property without the proper sewage. "He's not planning to rent; no one will live in it,'' she'd say, her nose growing longer. Dan out-Thoreau'd Thoreau when it came to civil disobedience. He reveled in it.

Well, she had to admire him for that.

But who was left at the ranch to face the authorities?

TEN

THERE WERE HUNDREDS of dentists in New York City and at least six in the area around West Forty-first Street, where Mac had lived in his boardinghouse. It wasn't far from the offices of the *New York Times*. Colm had to walk up and down Forty-first in a cold drizzle for several grimy blocks before he found it. And it wasn't a boardinghouse anymore, but a pizza "palace." The owner recalled the previous owner relating its history: "But I don't know no Mac Maginney," he said, hurling a cheese pizza with mushrooms, peppers, and salami onto the grill. "You'll have to look someplace else. Now move over, you wanna get burnt?"

"Sorry," said all six dentists in the immediate area, and launched Colm into a wider circumference, where there were at least one hundred and fifteen dentists. With the twenty-fourth, he seemed to have scored. Mac was still a client, the secretary said, a busty woman with blue hair. The doctor had done a root canal only last year.

"Last year? You sure of that? We're talking about Robert MacInnis? A man of—well, he'd be in his late seventies now. At least." MacInnis was a common-enough name, it seemed. He'd already run into three Robert MacInnises—none the right age. Apparently, this was one more false lead.

"Oh, no, not this one. This MacInnis is a young man. Yeah, I remember, he's a writer. Detective novels, I think. Yeah, it's a series. Let's see, yeah, gave us a paperback—if it's still here in this pile of magazines. Hey, here it is. Mac MacInnis, the Mac O'Doughall detective series...

"Can you give me his phone number? It might be a relative."

"Oh, no, hon, I can't do that. We don't give out phone numbers. Privacy, you know. In this town? Well... But wait. You want his publisher? They'd know maybe. You could write to him there. It's right here in the front. St. something—must be a Catholic press. You can write to him there. Uh-huh."

Write to him, Colm thought. And wait a month or more for a reply. He took off his glasses, wiped them on his sleeve. There was still a spot of tomato from the pizza. The lenses came out doubly smeared, and he took that for an omen.

That night, he phoned Police Chief Fallon up in Branbury, Vermont. "Fax me a credibility note, will you, Roy? They think I'm a farmer down here." And they were probably right. He was paid peanuts for these jobs—was it worth it?

"Keep looking. The guy never went near a dentist up here," bawled Fallon, who always bellowed on the phone, as if he didn't trust the message getting across through the wires. "And guess what? That woman has disappeared from Rockbury, yup. Glenna. She's hiding out somewhere with that kid niece of hers. She's guilty as hell, that old broad. Why else would she run off like that?"

"Would you like to be shut up in Rockbury State Hospital, Roy?"

There was a silence. Something that sounded like a laugh—or sneeze. "Even so," said Fallon. Colm waited. "But just two days. You don't turn up something, you're on your own."

"Fair enough," said Colm, and giving the number for the cheap hotel he was staying at, he hung up.

RUTH SAT BY her son's bed: If he could only cry, it would help, but he wouldn't break down. "There'll be another," she said, knowing the words wouldn't help. He'd fallen in love with Zelda's calf—maybe because it was undersized. Like himself? The shortest boy in the sixth grade? He'd gone in to bottle-feed it that morning, the way he did every morning; found the calf dead, flies buzzing around its bony head. The other cows had turned away from it, like it was some trash, some excrement. Zelda was out in the pasture. "I hate her. I hate that cow!" he yelled.

Was this what happened when someone died? Like that unfortunate woman at the healing center, Kevin's wife. But a poor analogy, that. Kevin was beside himself. He'd come slumping into her kitchen, wanting her sympathy. Sympathy that had to be divided today. But there was something appealing about Kevin. Something almost tragic.

"I don't want another calf," Vic said. "I wanted that one. She had a star between her eyes, that white spot on her nose. When she sucked on the bottle, she'd look at me, like I was her—'' He stopped, not wanting to say it. An eleven-year-old boy couldn't be a mother.

"Fathers feed their children, too, Vic."

He was thoughtful. "Dad fed me?"

"Sure," she lied. Pete had been afraid of his children until they could walk. Then he'd take them out to the barn while he worked. He'd been a help that way. Until they'd begun to reason, though, the children were hers. But words weren't lies if they comforted. Vic lay there, staring at the window, a small vulnerable figure outgrowing his clothes, it seemed, even as she watched. It was a clear, cold night. A half-moon sent a shaft of light into the room, striping the pine floorboards.

"I forgot to tell you," she said, thinking of moons, pulling the quilt up around the boy's shoulders: "Your astronomy magazine came this afternoon. I intercepted the mailman."

He sat up. "You didn't tell me."

"It went clear out of my head with all—you know." They'd had to bury the calf, Tim and Joey straining into the frozen ground; Vic looking on soberly, his lips set in a straight line, his hands locked against his small hard belly.

"There was a telescope, a wide field one, advertised last time. It's bigger, better than the cheap one I got. It was only three hundred fifty, I got ninety dollars saved already. There might be a—a sale or something." He was coming back to life. She smiled.

She ran downstairs to get the magazine, then back up again. He reached for it as though it were a gift from heaven.

"I hear the phone. You better go answer it." He glanced up coyly. She knew what he wanted.

"All right. I'll give you fifteen minutes. Then lights-out. Promise?"

"Promise," he said, with a crooked little grin.

It was Colm calling, down in New York. Her heart raced a little as he spoke. He'd phoned his father; there was news she might want to hear. His voice was quivering with whatever he had to say. She'd felt his discomfort when Kevin was here; relished it maybe—

some perversity in her? But the news was a shock; she sat down to hear it out.

"That's right, they did an autopsy. Something funny—Dad suspected it when he saw the dead woman, the color of her skin. The coroner confirmed it."

"What then?" She was thinking of those women circling the body on the bed, not wanting her to come close. They'd been abusing her, had they?

"Poison. She was poisoned. Something that worked slowly. Jeez—think of it."

"My God," she said. Colm didn't mention Kevin's name after that, but she knew what he was thinking. Her cheeks were hot with it. Anger? At whom? Kevin's distraught face burned in her mind's eye. He loved his wife; she felt that in him—she couldn't be wrong. He wasn't a man who would poison his wife.

Colm went on about his search for Mac, the dentists he'd visited: "My own teeth were squealing," he said. "I wanted to crown every dentist who said 'No.'" He paused to let the pun sink in, but she wasn't in a mood for his levities. For one thing, she was thinking about those other women, at the Healing House. They'd all looked unhealthy, to tell the truth.

"My God," she said again when he'd hung up—out of quarters, he called from a pay phone—and gripped the sides of her chair till her knucklebones went white.

"IT'S COLD IN HERE," Glenna complained where she sat huddled in a split wicker rocker. She pulled her shawl close around her shoulders. The novel *Bleak House* slid off her lap and onto the plywood floor.

"Emily's bringing a heater. She'll be here any minute, Aunty. Have patience."

"You might have gotten it ready before you brought me here. Old people can't take the cold; their bodies freeze up."

"You know you don't like to be called 'old people,' Aunty. You said so last week."

"That was last week. This week, I've got old."

It was true; Hartley could see it. Her great-aunt seemed more frail, more brittle than ever, as if she'd break in two if you sneezed in her presence. For this, Hartley blamed her stepmother. If they'd waited to see who that skeleton really was before they rushed Aunty off to Rockbury, making Hartley go through all that trouble to get her out of there—sneaking her down the corridor, dragging her through the bushes to the car, with Aunty complaining the whole way—why, then...

"Look at this bruise," said Glenna, interrupting the girl's thoughts. "You did that."

"Be grateful, Aunty. I got you out of there."

"Got me where?"

Hartley looked around. It was true: The place was a shack. Ten by ten feet at the most, on the edge of the Green Mountain Forest— "Lonely Mountain," Hartley called it. A hacked-together log house, the wind knifing through the chinks. No rug, just a pair of cots, a couple of log chairs and a plank for a table, teetering on a pair of splintery sawhorses. But it was isolated, a sanctuary in that sense. It was Emily who'd suggested it. She said her father used it for hunting; he'd helped build it, in fact. Emily and her boyfriend would come up here and neck. Ex-boyfriend, Emily had insisted, something about a city girl with a diamond in her nose. Of course, in a month or so the hunters would be in here, deer season, but by then Hartley would have found a better place. Or by then—hopefully— Aunty would be cleared of suspicion and could go home. Even now, Emily had said, her mother's friend Colm Hanna was down in New York City, studying charts of old teeth.

Besides, Emily had remarked, this wasn't far from that healing place where the woman died. They'd have a look around. Hartley was interested in that. It was Bilbo into the dark woods. It was fantasy; it was future. Not the dead past that Emily was so wrapped up in with her local history—dullsville! Anyway, Emily said she'd borrow her brother's telescope. That at least was helpful. The thought of spying intrigued Hartley. She might join the CIA one day.

But what if Aunty was guilty? What if she really had murdered her husband and stuck him in that horse hole? A delicious irony, she thought. What guts.

"Aunty," she said, "come clean. What'd you hit him with?"

Her aunt didn't answer, just sat there like a bundled-up snowman, her lips stuck together like marshmallows. Her gold-rimmed glasses had gone crooked in the escape: The right glass angled up above the shaggy eyebrow like a question mark. The eyes were grassy slits in the plump pouches of skin. "I want my cat," she said, "I want Puffy."

"Fay's got him. You know we can't bring him up here. He'd make noise. Someone would come by, maybe steal him. He's better off at your place."

"I want to go back, then. To my place. You call this safe? I saw a catamount up here on the mountain once. I really did, when I was a girl. Came up with Father to cut a Christmas tree—not that he wanted one, but Mother did. She was the one kept the holidays; Father couldn't care less. He was a Flint. So we came. And surprised it. There in a tree. Snarling down at us."

"Aunty, they're afraid of people, those big cats—*if* they're still around. You probably saw a bobcat. I bet it ran."

"It did." Aunty giggled. "It was scared to death of us. That's when I went home and looked in a mirror. For the last time, too. I didn't like what I saw."

"Mac must've liked what he saw."

Aunty dropped her chin into her chest, considered. "It must've been my charming personality. He liked an independent woman. I didn't tell him what to do all the time like those other females."

"He wasn't a bad guy, then?"

Glenna licked a tongue around her chilled lips, and her hands flew up, like wild birds. "He was okay—sometimes."

"Then why did you kill him? Put him in that hole?" But her aunt just looked hard at her, then turned her head away.

Someone rapped twice on the door, and then twice again. "Don't answer it!" Glenna hissed, but Hartley laughed, opened the door, and drew Emily Willmarth inside.

"I brought the kerosene heater," Emily said, struggling in with a large cardboard box. "I remembered there was no electricity in here."

"Well, set it up, then," cried Glenna. "You want another corpse on your hands? I'm frozen."

"'Many are cold, but few are frozen,'" declared Hartley, quoting her father.

"Stop talking and start that damn thing."

"Yes, ma'am." Emily poured in the oil, fumbled with her mother's kitchen matches. Her hands were bluish from the cold. But it wouldn't light.

"Give it here." Leaning forward, Glenna grabbed the match and lit it, her hands sure on the wick. "I was brought up with kerosene. You kids are spoiled." A moment later, the heater was glowing, a slow warm-up in the chilly cabin.

But Hartley was more interested in a second object, wrapped up in a paper bag. It was the telescope. One could see deep into the woods through its scope. Beyond the window, she thought she saw something—a large animal, deer or catamount, staring in at them.

And squealed with delight. "Aunty, come look. Eyes!"

ROBERT B.—"Mac"—MacInnis turned out to be a nephew, son of Mac's half sister, Doris; he'd met Mac at a family reunion in Brooklyn. MacInnis had even modeled a character on old Mac. When Colm told him on the phone about the skeleton, he bellowed—a slight speech impediment, or was it too many martinis?—"Chrish, it's gotta be a quick death, then. I jush interviewed the old man lash week—he's not so good, but Chrish, wouldn't turn into bones this soon. Must be somebody elsh ya got up there in that hole."

Of course, the writer wanted to hear more about it. Gave him an idea for a plot, he said—he was having a dry spell. Colm promised to let him hear the outcome in return for old Mac's address. Why not? Young Mac was willing; he laughed again. That phone call had made his day. Colm could hear the pages of the address book rattle as young Mac shuffled through. Then he said triumphantly, "Got a penchil?"

Colm found Glenna's husband in an old journalists' home down in the Village. At least, he thought, Mac got his wish: He was among UN translators and Pulitzer Prize winners. They'd worked at the *Times,* the old *Herald Tribune,* the *Post.* If they didn't know Mac had been only a proofreader, he certainly wasn't going to tell. For one thing, they all looked like they'd fallen on hard times: split slippers and shabby trousers. The place was clean enough, although seedy, the furniture scratched and faded, a rug of uncertain hue on the floor, raggedy shades at the windows. The plump uniformed aide who scuttled about like a vacuum cleaner had suspicious yellow stains on her skirt.

Mac sat scrunched up in a black vinyl wing-back chair. It wasn't a case of what he'd seen in Glenna, Colm thought, but what had she seen in him? He had the look of someone who'd been old at birth. He couldn't be more than five-foot-six, even when he struggled up on his worn-down slippers—though age had probably shrunk his bones. "You from the *Times?*" he said hopefully.

"No, no. I said I knew *you* were. I'm from Vermont—Branbury, your old...I think you knew my father. William Hanna—the funeral home? Well, I'm here because of Glenna, your wife? She's back in Branbury, you know."

Mac sank down into his chair again. His prune face looked wary; his hands tightened into fists. "I didn't know as she'd left," he said.

Colm explained about Homer Flint and his wife. How they'd threatened to put Glenna in a home, and how Hartley had taken Glenna back to Branbury. How Glenna was in Rockbury now, the state hospital for the mentally ill. "Well, she's not there now," he amended. "She's gone already. We don't know where."

Mac chuckled. "Not surprised. You don't coop that one up. She was a free spirit all right. So what do you want me to do about it? She threw me out. Years ago."

"The reason I'm here, Mr. MacInnis, is to find out if you're still alive. And obviously..." When Mac snorted, Colm explained about the skeleton, the hole; he watched the man carefully for any reaction. And he got one, though he couldn't interpret it. Just a quick tongue darting, snakelike, up to the sharp nose. "You see, if it's not you in that hole, and we know you dug it—common knowledge, right?—then who is it?"

"Sure, I dug it," Mac said. "That goddamn horse of hers. Kicked me in the balls one time. It did! Threw me off when I tried to ride it. Sat on me. But hell, I dug that hole just to scare her. I wasn't gonna shoot the blame thing. She just liked to react. Shoulda been an actress, that one. Always putting on shows. Got me fired, barging into the office one day, wanting a raise for me. Sure, I wanted one; wasn't going to stick my neck out, though, get myself fired. But I was, anyway, wasn't I? Fired? It was Glenna's interfering. What could I do then but follow her up to that godforsaken clay pile she calls a farm.''

"You didn't get along?"

He shrugged. "You married?"

"No."

"Then you don't know. It ain't easy. She had a problem. She shoulda married that horse."

"That's why you left? It had nothing to do with a hole in the ground, somebody in it?"

"Look." The tongue darted in and out again. The body drew up to its full height, like a garden snake uncoiling, fixed Colm with a glassy eye. "We had fights, yeah, every day. There were problems. But if you think I stuck somebody in that hole over some fight with Glenna, think again." The eye squeezed shut; the hands had a life of their own in his lap. "Maybe you should ask Glenna who's in that hole," he said coyly.

"You don't read the *Times* anymore, Mr. MacInnis?"

"Not since they fired me. What then?"

"She's confessed to killing you. And the police believe her. It was rumored around town, you see, after you left, that she'd killed you. You," Colm said, pointing a finger. He was almost enjoying the confrontation. His grandfather used to love it, he'd said; it was like twisting off the stuck top of a bottle. The satisfaction of prying it open. And this old guy, he felt, was keeping something inside.

Now Mac was snickering. "That's funny, funny as hell. So I'm dead, am I? To those hidebound Vermonters?" He stuck a finger in his mouth, bit it, as if he'd prove he was still flesh.

"Not anymore. They'll want to see you. Somebody was buried in that hole, and they'll want to know who. You'll have to help them find out."

Now Mac was annoyed. "I left. I got out of there. What do I know about who's in that friggin' hole? I'm seventy-nine, you know that? I got pernicious anemia. I got osteoporosis. I got osteoarthritis. I can't leave."

"You haven't got Alzheimer's," Colm told him. "And you're going to have to go. It's here in a fax from the Branbury police. If I find you, alive, you'll have to report to the station for questioning."

"Kee-rist," squealed Mac MacInnis. "Just don't let it be Glenna.

I can't face Glenna. I had enough of her tongue all those years we were married. Not Glenna. Kee-rist!''

ALWYN BAGSHAW leaned into his rake, though the fire was still smoldering, giving out a stench that made him sick to his stomach. He sat back on a stump to ease his aching back—he wasn't the man he used to be. Used to be he could hold his brother, Denby, down for hours—Denby had been a pushover, sure. And lazy, couldn't keep a job. Denby'd been a juggler, juggled his ma till she give him what he wanted: pocket money, choice cut of meat, that stray mutt—when it was Alwyn that the bitch'd come to first, wandering in one day off the street: Lab mix, good legs, good for hunting. Got part of that piece of mountain land she owned, when she knew Alwyn wanted a hunter's shack—then Denby up and sells it to Willmarth. Only thing Denby'd ever hunted was women.

Denby took away the one woman Alwyn had wanted. She was a good-looking one, curly black hair, mountains of it; in bed, the hair floating around the pillow like thunderclouds. Thunder and lightning, that's what it was like to have her. And she'd give back. She was waiting for a divorce; then she'd marry Alwyn. His mother didn't care; Alwyn could marry the town pump—just so's the woman didn't live with her. But Annie wasn't a whore—at first, anyways; she was a decent woman, had a bad marriage, guy had cheated on her. Alwyn knew him; he was a no-good. Annie was a hairdresser, independent, planned to have her own place. Though Alwyn would stop that: Married woman belonged home.

Then Denby decided *he* wanted her. Whatever Denby wanted, he took. He was a looker, Denby: taller than Alwyn, same color hair, but he slicked his shiny with grease. Women loved that grease. Alwyn found it disgusting. One night, he come back from hunting. He'd bagged a buck, a six-pointer, planned to freeze the meat so he and Annie'd have a Thanksgiving feast. His ma didn't hold with holidays, but Annie did; she liked all that hoopla. Well, why not? He couldn't wait to surprise her, told Ma he'd cook the venison.

Wasn't out long; bagged the buck early, took it home, expecting only Ma. Only it wasn't Ma. Annie there, too—with Denby. On Alwyn's bed. His bed! Stark naked but for that cloud of hair. The pair wrapped up together like a Christmas package.

"You're early" was all Denby said. "Annie was bored."

Annie just laughed. Laughed and laughed there in his brother's arms.

But Denby tired *quick* of women he could have. Then Annie wanted Alwyn back, she said. Sure, she cried and cried and wrung her hands. She pulled her cloud of hair till some of it fell out. But Alwyn didn't want a used package. Twice used, come to think of it. After that, there was only Flora, from down the road. She was a warm body, that's all. A companion for Ma when Denby was gone. When the baby came, that's all she cared about, that baby, fussing around it all day; shut her legs to Alwyn. Then one day, she packed her bags and left, and that was all right, too. He was all Ma had then. Denby was gone; they said he drowned in the Otter. That was a time when Alwyn was content: He had his job, he had the occasional woman, and he had Ma to take care of his needs. He was content, even after Ma's heart gave out three years ago.

Till that group moved in next door and let loose the devil.

He jumped up off the stump and waved his arms. "Git! Git, you devil. Leave me be!"

The wind swirled the ashes; bits of grit flew up in the air, then slowly settled back on the ground, some in his hair. He shook his head, disgusted. Time to dig now, he thought; he took up his shovel. Then looked up, to see that Willmarth girl spying on him, through some kind of tube.

Angry, feeling invaded—when would they leave him alone?—he ran at the fence, shook his fist. "Git out of here. None of your business round here. Git out, I said!"

She ran then, back across *their* land; there were two of them he saw, two young girls. He pushed through a clump of dead peonies to have a better look. Now the other one was peering through the tube. He didn't like it. When they ran off, suddenlike, through the twilight, he heard them giggling. Stupid girls! Into everybody else's business. Like in Annie's hairdressing place, the gossip. He didn't hold with gossip. Alwyn was a private man. What he did was his own business. Till that bunch next door brought him bad luck. The flocks of grackles, the girl coming round to interview him, that skeleton over to Flint's—especially that.

They were walking now, slower, up the dirt road; up the shortcut

to the mountain. His mountain, for it was now—a patch of it anyway. With Ma gone, it was his, he reckoned. They was trespassing;
sure, it wasn't right. He heard them laughing up ahead, poking each
other, laughing and laughing. Like Annie that time in his brother's
bed. He'd let her go then, though he'd wanted to kill her. Strangle
her, sure, slow... But he'd let her go.

He'd regretted it since.

ELEVEN

RUTH TOOK Dr. Colwell with her. He was one of those old-fashioned, compassionate doctors: a tall, balding, big-boned man who still made the occasional house call. Though even he was skeptical. "The whole lot of them poisoned? Come on," he'd said.

But when they entered through an unlocked door in the rear—no one had answered their knocks out front—they found only one woman ill, in a bathroom, retching. She'd gotten into chocolate—the last in a box of chocolate-covered cherries that had come to Angie, a woman informed them. "Isis would be mad if she knew," she said.

Isis—the name related to corn. Ruth had a vision of a goddess with great curving cow horns. But when Isis wheeled in now, she looked more like a housefrau in her brown polyester slacks and short tan sweater, which only accentuated her belly. She swept Ruth back into the kitchen. It was spanking clean, just like the last time. A loaf of homemade bread sat on the counter and a pile of greens was soaking in a sieve. Isis supervised the cooking herself, she told Ruth as she spun about, opening and slamming all the drawers and closets she could reach with her robust arms, while in an adjoining room the doctor examined Ellen, a chubby, sweet-faced woman whom Ruth remembered from her last visit.

No, not a morsel of anything she hadn't sampled herself went down anyone's throat, Isis insisted—"Caffeine!" she said with a grimace, and pointed to the can of Cafix on the shelf, a coffee substitute made of figs and beet root. "That's what we drink here."

"And you can see *I'm* perfectly all right. It was the clotting problem that did in poor Angie; I worried about it when she came here. But I thought, with the blood thinner I insisted she take—well, it didn't work, did it? But it was her place; I couldn't send her away. And she needed the therapy."

"Oh?" said Ruth.

"Well, part of the therapy was my teaching her massage. Especially to do the back and leg work. You have to stand over the person for that. I can only do the head and neck now, you see, the energy work, the foot reflexology." When Ruth raised an eyebrow, she explained. "There are reflexes in the feet that relate to most parts of the body. Push in a certain way on a toe and it can help relieve a headache." As she spoke, she was twisting a plain gold ring on her thick finger.

"You're married."

"Was. I left him to come here. He was glad to see me go, frankly. He had a girlfriend, you see. After the accident—he didn't need... this." She nodded at her wheelchair. Then, as if to prove the degree of separation, she yanked off the ring, dropped it into a pocket. The corners of her dark eyes curved up into the fluid sweep of her shiny black hair.

"I do see." Ruth looked down at the ring on her own finger, a thin silver band with *RM* and *PVW* engraved on the inside. Why was she still wearing it? For the children, she supposed. For Emily, who'd been on a mission lately, it seemed, to reconnect her parents. Well, Pete's arrival was days away. Still, the ring was tight where her finger had thickened with hard work: a reminder of the decision she would have to make.

"We're all without husbands here, as you can see," Isis said, and veered over to a table to snatch up a teapot. "Chamomile. Want a cup? Good for stress."

Was it that obvious? Hearing a groan in the next room, Ruth shook her head. Was she superstitious, not wanting to drink from a cup in this house? "You know Angie's husband has been in town, wanting to see her. He was upset that she'd left. You wouldn't allow him in, and now..." She looked hard at the woman.

The black eyes took hers in calmly. "Angie didn't want to see him. It wasn't for me to let him in."

"You're sure of that? I mean, why? It wasn't you who persuaded her? I'm convinced he loved her. He was broken by her death."

Now the eyes looked away. "She had reasons, or she wouldn't have been here. I don't know what they were. All of them, anyway. It was her idea you know, this healing center for abused women."

"Abused?"

"Yes, of course! That's the raison d'être for this place. Angie wanted it that way. A sanctuary for abused women."

"But there were no...marks on the body, no evidence of abuse. Just the discoloration, the poison."

"Abuse isn't only physical."

"Of course not." Ruth thought of her sister-in-law, Bertha: "God's plan, God's idea," the crazed woman had said when Vic was kidnapped. All that anguish. The trauma for the boy. Ruth's hair already going gray.

But she couldn't imagine what the abuse was in this case. With Kevin Crowningshield, who seemed like compassion itself? He'd loved his wife—was that abuse? Perhaps there'd been some other problem with Angie. Some illusions, delusions, some pathological concerns.

"She seemed perfectly normal, Angie? I mean, nothing..."

"Mental? As normal as the rest of us, I guess." The woman gave a cynical smile. "What's 'normal,' anyway?"

Dr. Colwell came out into the kitchen. His face was grim. "I'm pretty sure, almost positive," he said, "that you're right, Ruth. Something has poisoned another woman here—maybe the lot of them. But the others won't let me near them." He shook his head as if to say, What can you do with a bunch of stubborn females?

He yanked open the refrigerator door. "Better not throw anything away. Milk, broccoli, this white stuff—" He made a comical face; obviously, he was a meat-and-potatoes man.

Isis looked weary, her shoulders collapsing under the thick neck. "The police called just before you came," she said. "They're sending someone from—what do you call it? Forensics. But we can't starve while they sort things out! We'll keep on eating, you know, though I admit we've had little appetite since Angie..."

"You bought the food in town?" Ruth asked.

"At the health-food store?" It was presumably an answer.

"I shop there myself, off and on," Ruth said. "And I'm perfectly healthy. My daughter Sharon won't go anywhere else."

"How do you account for poison, then?" said Isis, a trace of pink in her ivory cheeks.

"How indeed?" Doc Colwell said to Ruth when Isis spun about, at his request, to call an ambulance for the sick woman—they'd have to pump her stomach at the emergency room. Ellen was a frail woman, according to Isis, allergic to "everything": pollen, bees, strawberries, hay. "Chocolates," she added significantly. "I know. She sneaked them in. Caffeine."

"Keep her away from my farm, then," said Ruth. "Hay and caffeine. I live off both."

RUTH WAS RELIEVED to be home. She flung out her arms, breathed in the good farm smells; the round bales of hay stacked neatly in the fields fed the eye. She laughed even when she found things in a turmoil. Zelda had gone on a rampage, as if she knew her calf was dead, had torn through the fence that Tim and Joey had recently mended, raced into the pasture on the Flint farm. Fay Hubbard had found her in the barn, munching alfalfa with Dandelion.

"They're soul sisters," said Tim, emerging from the milk room, pulling on his salt-and-pepper beard. "I couldn't drag her out of there for ages. And you should see the mess she made of that fence! Joey and me had it fixed up good after she broke through to have her calf, didn't we, Joey?"

"Yup, we had it fixed up good," said Joey, who loved to repeat Tim's words.

"And now it looks like a herd of buffalo galloped through." Tim mopped his forehead; his face glistened with sweat. Though Tim had "found himself" in farm work, he'd admitted lately. He is lucky, she thought, wishing she knew who *she* was: mother, farmer, sometime wife—or now, it seemed, some kind of interfering neighbor? She'd found herself for the second time in that role, and felt...well, not exactly comfortable in it, yet stimulated by it: There was the satisfaction of digging out the truth—justice! For someone else anyway, if not herself.

"And this place needs serious work," Tim reminded her.

Of course it did, the house starved for paint, and the barn, too. They'd built it back up after last spring's electrical fire but then ran out of money before they could give it a second coat of barn red. What they had put on was already peeling. The two cement-block stave silos looked as if they'd been underwater and drudged up out of the sea. There was a blight on the baby balsam and Scotch pines Tim had planted as a way to diversify. The sheep on the pasture she rented to her friend Carol Unsworth had practically munched it bare, but she couldn't turn Carol out.

"Tim, you know as well as I that we can't afford it. Not yet. When the place falls down, then we'll jack it back up. Look, winter's coming," she conceded. "We'll have more time then for repairs."

Repairs to her life, too, she thought. Another letter from Pete in the mail today. Hints he'd start proceedings when he arrived in Branbury. "What are you waiting for?" he wrote. "You want to get on with your own life, don't you? Remarry? Have a little fun, a little sex? I want that for you, Ruth."

So solicitous, she thought. Worrying about her welfare, her sex life (he loved to address that in his letters; his own was "terrific," he constantly reminded her). Well, he could wait. He could just wait. She thrust out her lower lip.

Then she remembered Emily, watching her read the letter. "A letter from Dad?" she'd said with an insinuating little smile.

How much do we sacrifice for our children?

Tim was smiling at her, waving as he revved up the John Deere. "Better keep old Zelda in the barn till we get the fence fixed." Joey waved, too, important beside him in the bucket seat. *Feeling* important, she could tell. Nice. Nice for Joey. A person needed to feel important, to be needed. But she was, wasn't she—by her children?

She ran back to the barn to check on Zelda. A moment later, Kevin Crowningshield appeared; he'd been waiting for her in his car. He seated himself on an upside-down pail, the toes of his shiny shoes pointed up to avoid a pile of dung. "I need to talk, Ruth. I need your ear. I..." He didn't finish; apparently, he was too distraught. He buried his face in his hands.

She waited. Zelda was lunging in her stall, battering her head against the stanchion bar. "Serves you right," she said. "Oh, not you, Kevin," she added when he looked up. "I was talking to my cow. She's broken through the fence again."

He had seen her, he said listlessly. "In the Flint barn. She made a shambles of that, too."

She waited, leaned against a splintery beam; she felt Zelda's warm breath on her back, now and then a thump where the old girl was butting at her. Mad as she was at the cow, she felt a certain affinity—that lust for open spaces.

"The police have been back," he said, looking hard at her, spacing his words, halting between them as though searching for the right ones to explain his troubles. "Asking questions, going over and over the same ground. Not accusing exactly—they've no direct evidence. But it's clear what they think. They're at that healing center now. My God, all I did was send a box of chocolate-covered cherries—Angie's favorite. And they think I poisoned her? My own wife!"

She could hear his quick breathing. "I'm sorry...I'm sorry. I don't mean to break down. It's all this—everything." He waved his arms in a wide arc. "Everything that's been going on. Her not wanting to see me. Her pain, her death. When I've . . ."

He was out of words. He looked pathetic, without defenses. It was almost as if it was her problem, too: as if it was Pete who had died—and someone blaming her. She was suddenly outraged. Zelda gave a bellow and lunged at the bar, banging and banging her head as though in penance. "Sorry, old girl, sorry," Ruth said.

She took Kevin's arm. Led him, unprotesting, out of the barn, up to the house.

"All right," she said, settling down in a kitchen chair, "let's talk. Don't think I haven't worried—since we found out about the poison. But they're just grasping at straws—anything. Look, Kevin," she began, then got up to pour coffee. She couldn't sit still anymore, it seemed; the coffee might help to get his story out. "You've got to tell me everything. Angie was there at that place for a reason. Or what she thought was a good reason. Maybe I can help you. I mean, I'll try. If you're completely honest with me."

He looked affronted. His voice rose a decible. "What else can I be? Why else am I here?"

"Then tell me about Angie. You and Angie. Your life together."

He cupped the mug she offered in both his hands, rotated his neck inside the confining collar. He was wearing a blue-striped shirt with a stain on the sleeve. His eyes were a muddy brown; there was a grayish stubble on his chin, as though he hadn't given a thought to shaving, to appearance. His shoulders slumped, making him look wholly vulnerable. She had an impulse to put her hands on his shoulders, to steady him. But, hearing the grind of the John Deere returning to the barn, she held back.

"We got along, so that's what I don't understand about all this. She was such a giving woman. If I said, 'Let's go to a movie tonight,' she was ready, even if she was in the middle of a new design. That was the one thing she insisted on, in spite of my misgivings: her jewelry. And I let her do it. I did. I couldn't give up my room for it, my study, because that was my work. I'm an investor, you see, and I work mostly out of my house. I wanted to be near Angie, knowing her health problem. I didn't want her alone in the house. I...well, I have a lot of equipment: PC—I'm on-line; fax, files, endless files. You know. I was with a Chicago firm at one point, but I gave that up for Angie—I'd be away too often. I wanted us together."

"Where did she do her jewelry, her designs?"

"In the basement. I gave her the full run of it; I gave up my workshop, or most of it. She didn't mind I kept a few tools about. We shared some of them."

She waited while he thought what to say next; sat down across from him. Her brain was muddled today, with the Healing House crisis, problems with Zelda, and now this suspicion of murder. Poor Kevin! It was hard to concentrate fully, ask the right questions. She was more farmer than sleuth. Definitely.

When he didn't speak, she asked about the design on the Healing House sign, wondering if it had come from Angie. She didn't mention the ring on the skeleton's finger, a finger that forensics had found matched the "Flint Farm Skeleton," as the police called it. To Colm, it was simply "dem bones." Oh, that Colm.

Kevin looked blank. "I don't know about that. I don't recall a design like that. A bone crossed with an arrow? Definitely odd. But then, I didn't always look at her designs."

"She didn't show them to you?"

"Well, in the beginning perhaps. After a while, she discovered how obtuse I am." He gave a short laugh. "I mean, I'm not an artsy type, I'm afraid." He spooned a second helping of sugar into his coffee, sipped it. "She was so willing, so ready to drop everything for me. I like to go out for dinner, you know; it's one of my pleasures. The right place, the right meal. And she'd always come, though she was vegetarian. I used to kid her, call her 'the Tofu Kid.' She'd always find something to eat, though—an omelette, or pasta.''

"They don't serve tofu in the best restaurants.''

He smiled at the obvious. "Anyway. She'd come. She'd dress up. I felt...well, good. Sipping wine out of a thin-cut glass—I do appreciate that sort of thing. A beautiful, well-dressed woman at my side. Makes a man feel...well, you know.''

Ruth wasn't sure she did know. She imagined herself that woman. What would she wear? Boots and a jean skirt—her only dress-up clothes? Though Pete must have encountered the problem down in New York. Did that woman pick out his clothes? Pete was never a dresser. It wouldn't be easy for him down in that city, a seventh-generation Vermonter. There would be problems he wasn't letting on about.

"So you got along well. You saw no reason for her defection?'' She recalled something he'd said earlier. "A child—you said she wanted a child. And couldn't have one.''

"There was some blockage, although she tried. I tried to make her feel it was all right, though I worried—about hemorrhaging, you know—that bleeding defect. But then, frankly, I was so damn busy, what time did I have for a child? Though I knew it would have given her something to do, besides the jewelry. She tried an outside job once, you know, didn't even tell me. I wasn't too pleased, mind you. Her health! She got a position in a women's clothing store, thought she'd please me, I suppose—it was a quality store; she'd get a discount on things. But after a week of it, she got overtired. She agreed with me that she was better off at home.''

"You said she wanted to adopt.''

"Oh, yes, that was a temporary phase. I soon talked her out of it. She wasn't strong enough anyway, for a baby? Really! Lifting it in and out of places—I mean, they turn a house upside down, don't they? I had a maid for her; that was another thing. She didn't have to lift a finger in my house.''

"In *your* house.''

He nodded, didn't get the innuendo. Why had she said that? He was being honest. There was a fringe of sweat on his upper lip, a tic in his dimpled cheek. His throat looked wrinkled; the whites of his eyes were pinkish. This man was suspected of poisoning his wife?

"And then..."

"Then?"

"Then she began to...well, retreat. Into herself. Not that she was hard to please, no—I mean, she still went out with me the odd Saturday night, and we'd have a few friends in off and on—not too many. We didn't have time for a lot of socializing, you see. But she didn't talk much, sing around the house like she did when we were first married. I do miss that, the singing. She had a lovely voice. She sang for a time in a church choir, but then—that was too much for her, we felt; it was best to keep the singing in the house."

"But she stopped singing."

"Stopped. Yes. Stopped eating—practically. Got thinner and thinner. Almost anorexic. We didn't go out to eat much anymore. And then the stepmother—"

"She lives in California, right?"

"Yes, thank God. A real kook. I blame her for a lot of Angie's problems. I mean, Angie was lucky I got her away. Melanie, the stepmother, is into all that New Age stuff, you know, a kind of priestess or something. I only met her once or twice. She wasn't at our wedding; she was in Tibet. But she'd call up, you see. At least once a week. The father was dead—she'd killed off two husbands!" He smiled grimly, his dimples showing. "When she'd call, I'd have to say, 'Angie, I have to have the line free'—for my work, you know."

"And would Angie hang up then?"

"Oh, yes. Yes, she was always thoughtful that way. She thought her stepmother a little nuts, too."

"She said that?"

"Well, not in those words, but I know she thought it." He waved his hands, palms outward, as though to push away the stepmother.

"And then she got involved in this healing center."

"Well, it was her land, you see. Her dad came from here; he died of a heart attack—heart disease in the family, too, on his side anyway. Early on, that was—she was around twelve. He left the land to Angie—once she was eighteen, that is. The stepmother was in control till then."

"How much land? Like several acres?"

"Five plus, I think. It goes a ways back behind the house, abuts the property next door. Bagshaw, the man's name is." He made a face. "Unpleasant fellow."

"Yes. He's squeezed in there between the Healing House and the Wilcoxes on the other side, though his land goes back a long way. Always complaining about it; Colm has heard him."

"Colm? Oh, yes, the thin fellow who was here the other night. Father's a mortician."

"Yes. Colm's mainly in real estate. Does a little investigative work—his grandfather was on the force. He helps his dad out when he can."

But Kevin was back on an earlier thought, rubbing a red spot on his forehead. She saw the fatigue in the eyes, the sagging skin underneath. "Yes, yes, I remember now. He called up Angie once, wanting to buy a couple of acres. For privacy, he said, afraid of what Angie would do with it—develop it, he thought."

"I hadn't known that." Ruth sipped her coffee; it was cool, but she hardly cared. Alwyn Bagshaw hated—feared—that healing center; he'd made that clear all over town.

"You don't...think I did it?" Kevin said, lurching toward her, elbows on the table, his face anguished, looking old. "I loved that woman. I love her still. There'll never be anyone else. What it was like to come home to her! Even before she turned...odd. She was always there, waiting for me. My drink made up. I like a good Manhattan, you know, after a long workday. She knew just how I liked it. Until one day—"

"She wasn't there."

His words came out in a whisper. "She wasn't there. Just a note. She'd taken a flight out. To this healing place, on her land, some friend of the stepmother's running it—I'm not quite clear on that. They'd never let me in, you see."

"And you came here after her."

"Well, not right away. I gave her a few weeks. To get it out of her system. Whatever it was she was...well, unhappy about."

"She seemed unhappy then before she left?"

"I mean, she was...well, withdrawn. That's what I'm talking about. I didn't understand why! She wouldn't talk to me. And now. Now they won't let me leave town. They're keeping her body. Why? Why? They've done an autopsy; that was bad enough. That beautiful woman! Why can't I take her body home?"

"It takes time, I understand, autopsies. I mean, where there's poison involved. Homicide. Someone—something was responsible, Kevin."

His eyes pleaded; his hands were clasped as though in prayer. "Why would anyone want to kill my wife?" He laid his hands on the table, palms up. His chin was lifted as though he'd keep his eyes from brimming over. She felt sorry for him, a little overwhelmed from the long emotional interview, the day's hectic events. For all his possessiveness, she couldn't believe this man was a murderer. And yet—there were other things she had to sort out in her mind. She touched each of his open palms with a finger. But he didn't take advantage. He frowned down at his hands, surprised, as though he couldn't move them, as though they were a pair of soiled gloves lying on the table and he didn't know how they'd gotten that way.

TWELVE

WHEN COLM slowed down by the Flint farm, Mac wouldn't let him stop. "No way," he said. "I'm not setting a foot on that bloody place. No telling who might be there." He shrank down into the front seat of the blue Horizon, stuffed the remains of his cigarette into the ashtray. Colm had indulged him, bought the pack of Kents. "Glenna hates facial hair," he whispered to Colm. "I grew it once; she tried to shave it off, middle of the night. I caught her standing over my bed—a razor in her hand!"

"A razor?" Colm said thoughtfully.

"Sure." Mac's voice sounded eager. "If I hadn't waked up, no telling what she'd've done. Now, drive on, man, drive on. Anyplace but here. A motel maybe. I could use a night's sleep. How could I nap on that damn train?"

"But Glenna's not here. I told you that."

"Even so." The old man crouched, sullen, immobile in his seat, like a marionette, its strings unattached. Wrappers surrounded his feet; he and Colm had munched on pizza and fries after they got off the Amtrak at Whitehall, New York, just over the state line, where Colm had left the car.

"Even so," Mac said again.

Giving in, Colm drove on to Ruth Willmarth's. This time, he was the nervous one, didn't know what he'd find there. That Crowningshield fellow, buttering Ruth's ear? Pulling on her sympathies? He'd still be around of course. "It was poison," Roy Fallon had said on the phone last night. But he'd said they had no solid evidence against anyone.

Colm smiled. How he'd loved telling Fallon about Mac, that he was still alive, that it wasn't Mac whom Glenna had killed. And what motive had the woman for killing someone else—whoever that skeleton was? He could picture Fallon's face, the slow red creeping up the neck; the man had been so cocksure, so positive in his analysis.

There was no one in sight when he pulled up in front of the farmhouse. It was early for milking; Ruth would be in the fields, he supposed, though only Tim was visible in the distance, raking wood chips around the new young trees; Joey was cavorting about behind him, swinging a pail. Colm smiled when he saw some of the chips fly out. He moved on into the kitchen, motioning Mac to follow, though the old man lagged, then refused a hand to get up on the porch. It was early; Emily and Vic wouldn't be home from school for at least another hour. He and Mac would establish a beachhead, wait for Ruth. Talk. Bone up on the skeleton business (ha). He'd tried to get Mac talking on the Amtrak, but the man was closemouthed. Colm wanted to know more about Glenna; he suspected that she knew who was buried in that plot. He was immensely curious now, for some reason. For one thing, Glenna had known his mother. His mother had liked Glenna. And since the body wasn't Mac, then it might have been Mac who put it there. Another reason for leaving town?

And there was Ruth, of course. Glenna was Ruth's neighbor. In Vermont, neighbors helped out neighbors. Even when skeletons fell out of their closets, rose up out of their holes.

"You knew Ruth Willmarth?" he asked Mac when he got him settled in a chair. "No smoking in here," he ordered, and the old man shrugged, stuck the pack back in his pocket.

"To speak to, that's all. Good-looking broad. She'd just come on this place when I left. I knew the father best."

"Ruth's father?" No, he thought, Ruth's dad died when she was in high school, her mother not so long after—breast cancer. Ruth had wondered about the pesticides some of the area farms used. She'd taken her mother's death hard; her grades went down. Colm had cornered her in the corridor once, told her about his mother. That was after they'd stopped dating, when Pete horned in. Colm said that he'd be her brother if she couldn't return his love—what a nerd he was in those days! She was dating Pete full time then, of course. She accepted the "brother" thing. Had the relationship ever changed, in spite of a period of going out together in college? Could it now?

"Old Willmarth," Mac said. "His father alive, too, then, but bent over like a warped rake. Some spinal disease, I don't know. Crusty old bastard. Guess Pete was glad when the old man kicked the bucket.''

"Pete's gone now. Down in New York. Some woman grabbed him. Some would-be actress.''

"Hah.'' Mac sniggered. He thought it amusing.

"That surprise you?'' Colm wanted to hear more, wanted his own opinion corroborated. At least Kevin Crowningshield wasn't around. Until the thought struck him that they might be out together, Crowningshield and Ruth. He clenched his fists; a vein bulged up in his arm. Jeez.

But Mac only shrugged. "Seemed an okay fella when I knew him. But then I didn't really know him, did I? Bad enough living on the Flint farm, I wasn't about to hang around this one.''

Colm saw an opening. "Living on the farm wasn't all that bad, was it? What about Glenna—she liked it, didn't she? Other guys hanging about the place maybe? Anyone else could have been in that hole you dug? I mean, whoever dropped him in there?''

Mac shrank back into his chair, munched on a doughnut. His lips were furry white; he looked like an elf, peering out of his hole. A smile played on his lips. "You want me to solve this one for you, hey? Yeah, it was that guy who drove the milk tank, picked up the milk from the skinny Flint cows. He and Glenna were having this wild affair, see? Only he got seduced by somebody up the road and Glenna got mad and bopped him on the head and dropped him in that hole.'' He added, "After I left, that is. Look. There was no one, I said, no one in that hole when I left.''

"Okay. We drove all the way up here, you're going to play games?''

Mac was still smiling, if one could call a smirk a smile. He pulled at his whiskers. One could hardly call it a beard; Colm could almost count the white hairs. But it made the old man feel manly, he supposed, offbeat. He obviously liked being offbeat. Glenna, too. They seemed made for each other. And yet...

"If we can't find who put the man in that hole, you're the likely suspect, Mac. So anything you can tell us will help you.''

Mac ran a pale tongue around his sugary lips, considered. Colm waited.

"Well I'm gonna die anyway. I mean, what can they do to an

old guy like me?'' He sighed, held on the edge of the table as if it were his life. "Let's see. Needs a little digging, you know—memory's full of loose ends."

"Try."

"I need a smoke first, okay? Out on the porch?"

Colm relented. But just in case, he watched the man out the kitchen window. But Mac wasn't going anywhere. He sank down on the steps to smoke the cigarette. He'd inhale and then cough. They didn't allow it in the journalists' home. He was obviously out of practice. He stubbed it out before it was consumed, stomped back in.

"Glenna, well, she had friends, you know. Everybody knew the Flints, one of the old families. The grandfather was bounced outta the local church for swearing on Sunday—I mean right in church— loud! So they say—disagreed with the sermon." He chuckled. "Once that crazy Glenna rode right up the church aisle on her bloody mare, you know that? Before I came on the scene, that was, but they still talk about it around here. She was...well, a legend you might say. I suppose that's one reason I was, um, interested. Might make a story you know, personal-interest piece. I got one or two published in my day, before the *Times* dragged me into...you know."

"Uh-huh." Colm had discovered that an occasional noise, a grunt, an "uh-huh," helped an interviewee to go on. Real estate was full of trauma: divorce, death, abuse—all the reasons why people changed houses. Sometimes it wasn't divorce, just some guy looking for a private place to keep the lady friend. You asked questions—but you didn't move in too close.

"Did they like her?" Colm asked. "Or was she just an item of conversation? The eccentric neighbor?"

"Oh, they liked her all right. I mean, the men did. Glenna liked men. You bet. She was more comfortable with men than women. Women bored her, to tell the truth, most of them. I mean the la-di-da ones who mostly kept house and talked about their female problems. She had a couple women friends who'd gone out and done things; she'd give them the time of day."

"My mother knew her. Not well, but they were on a planning commission together, Dad says. They evidently saw eye-to-eye."

Colm pictured the scene: Glenna in her overalls and size-eleven boots, nose-to-nose with his ladylike mother in her crisp cotton housedress and tidy flat shoes. But his mother had her own mind. Glenna would have recognized that.

He went on with the questions, while Mac was in the mood. "What kind of, uh, relationship did Glenna have with these men? I mean, any particular man—before your time, of course. You were in your forties, you two, when you married?"

"I was forty; she was forty-one, I think—well, older'n me; she never let me forget that." He gave a brusque laugh, took a large bite out of a second doughnut. Colm hoped Ruth had no plans for those doughnuts.

"No relationships, then—that would worry you."

"Nah, she wasn't much for the pillow play, if you know what I mean." He winked at Colm. "With me, anyway. She didn't like 'em hanging around for too long. Although..." He paused.

"Although?"

"There were one or two hot on her. She was a woman, if you get my drift. She wasn't bad-looking in those days, no jewel, of course, but big boobs, you know, a farm woman's hips—"

"Farm women are larger-hipped than other women?"

Mac snorted. "Well, they get to look like their cows after a while, you know. Ever look at a cow from the rear? Those bony hips, wide apart? Those big tits hanging down?"

Colm guessed he had. Men's talk—he couldn't hide a smile. Ruth would frown, of course; Ruth would be furious. But Ruth wasn't here. Though any minute she could be, and the old man would button up.

"Who were they? These one or two men who were interested in Glenna?"

But Mac wasn't ready to say. "Listen, I could use a drink. She got any whiskey around here?"

"A beer in the refrigerator maybe. She's not a big drinker, Ruth." Though she did keep a little whiskey around, a quart of Guckenheimer, for him, he knew that. But wasn't about to give it up to Mac! He popped open a can of Otter Creek Ale. Ruth drank it now and then—to keep her spirits up, she said, when she was down. There were several cans, in fact, in the fridge, so he wasn't depriving her. He wiggled a can past the orange juice and soy milk. A dairy farmer drinking soy milk? Or maybe it was Sharon who'd left it there.

"It ain't Seagram's, but it'll have to do." Mac lifted it to his lips, guzzled it down. His Adam's apple moved up and down with each swallow; the scraggly whiskers were brownish with spill. Colm waited.

"They were mostly guys who came round to sell stuff, repair things—that sign maker, 'Don Quixote,' I called him, like Glenna was some Dulcinea. Ha! One of the vets, guy named—hell, I can't think of it now, but I think she was sweet on him. Leaning over him when he inspected the cows—they only had a couple when I came on the scene. Farm was going downhill fast. I'd hate to see it now. Cripes, that mother of hers! Four foot something and did the work of three men. But then she got some disease, I don't know. Stiff as a frozen sheet when Glenna had to take her to potty. But Glenna kept her home, I gotta hand her that."

"Try to remember that vet's name if you can. I can get a list from the animal hospital here. Joggle your memory."

Mac's eyes were on his beer, as if it held memories under the foam. "Then there was Bagshaw. Not the fertilizer Bagshaw. She hated that guy; he was a pincher. But that other one..." He shrank deeper into his chair, appeared to cruise his memory. His face twisted with the effort; he looked like he was on the rack. In the background Colm heard a car come up, Ruth's old Ford pickup; it was unmistakable, that grinding, grunting noise, squealing brakes. He worried about her driving the old clunker—it was twenty years old if it was a day. He'd looked at the mileage once, panicked.

Bad timing. "What other one? What other one, Mac?" Outside, the pickup door slammed, like pieces of rotting metal clanking together.

Mac heard, too. "That her? What's she gonna think, me drinking her beer? We shouldn't've come here. We should've gone right to that motel like I said. If you're gonna pay for it," he added softly.

"Me?" said Colm. "I don't think so."

"Well, take me to Flint's then. Glenna's not there anyway."

"That's what I kept telling you. Coming here was your idea."

"Shit," said Mac, and Ruth threw open the door. She stopped

on the threshold to stare at the old man slumped in her chair, devouring her doughnuts, swilling down her beer.

Colm stood up, smiled sheepishly. "I think you two have met. Ruth Willmarth, Mac MacInnis. Glenna's husband," he added, although it wasn't necessary. Ruth's face was dawning: rainy and cool.

EMILY WISHED she had her notebook. For once, the old lady seemed in a talkative mood; she was wearing the black scarf Hartley had brought her, and a black sweater decorated with Puffy's white fur. She'd answer anything you asked, though Emily wouldn't take too many chances. Not about the skeleton anyway. Glenna Flint would close up on that one.

"So tell about way back," she said, wriggling about on the plywood floor. It wasn't exactly comfortable, but if you got into one of the grooves, it wasn't too bad. "About how your ancestors got up here to Vermont. Where'd they come from?"

"Connecticut, someplace. That was old Homer Flint, your father's named after him. He buried three wives, Homer did." Glenna rocked back in the chair, stuck out her skinny legs, and Hartley rushed to put a straight chair under them. "That's better now. Just a sip of that scotch and my tongue'll be well oiled." She grinned.

"This is the last bottle, Aunty," Hartley warned. "I stole it from the kitchen. I can't go out and buy it, you know. I'm not eighteen. Though almost."

"And you're in college?" Emily said.

"I skipped a grade way back. I'm a freshman—the local college. I'm on parole." She winked at Emily.

"So what happened to the three wives?" Emily loved true stories. She was beginning to love history. "When was this exactly?" She didn't have her notebook; she'd have to take it into her head, try to remember it. Tonight, she'd write it down. She couldn't stay much longer, though, she had to get back home, her mother would worry. Her mother worried all the time now. There wasn't anything her mother wasn't worried about.

"Indians. Back in the 1600s. That's what happened. Well, one of 'em anyhow. Scalped. An arrow stuck in the stomach. Run right through to the back. And pregnant! Yep, she was. Eight months pregnant.''

"God," said Hartley, one hand on her belly. "But it wasn't the Indian's fault, right? They were being run off their land? But how could they do that to a pregnant woman?"

"They could, and they did," said Glenna, looking triumphant.

"An arrow. Through a half moon," Emily murmured, and thought of the ring on the skeleton's finger, the sign on the Healing House. Somehow everything seemed connected. The past repeating itself in the present. She sucked in her lower lip.

"What about the other two?" Hartley asked. "What happened to them?"

"Oh, they died," said Glenna with a dismissive wave of her hand. "Childbirth, I suppose, overwork. The men chasing around after the Indians while the women scrubbed and cooked."

"That much hasn't changed," said Hartley.

Emily imagined it: the wife, alone in a log hut, pregnant, like her sister Sharon, surveying the mountain of washing: husband's shirts and breeches—did they ever wash those? His "smalls," like they called underwear back then. And the mending heaped up in a corner, the dirt to be swept up off the sandy floor. The baby sunk low in the belly like a bunch of green apples. She'd walk outdoors, oh, just for a minute, needing sun and air. Out to the cornfield: her responsibility too, with her man away. And suddenly, there they were! Leaping out of the forest: three Indians, with hatchets in their hands, feathered arrows on their backs. She'd scream, race for the house, whirl about once to see if they were still there—and in her belly—ooh, oww!—an arrow. Blood spilling out of the moon...

"God," she said, dropping her head in her hands, her stomach gone queasy. "God, I can't even imagine it. That poor woman, that poor, poor woman."

"Rachel," said Glenna. "Rachel was her name. Rachel Flint. She was nineteen when she died." Glenna seemed pleased to be gaining control of her memory.

"God," said Emily again, "only two years older than me."

"Let's change the subject," said Hartley. "It's over now, all that old stuff. Wal-Mart's moving into Vermont, you know that? They got it through. Wal-Mart, the wave of the future, dah dah!'' She hoisted her diet Pepsi.

Hartley liked to shop: Emily was adding up the negatives of her new friend; shopping was a suburban trait. Emily, now she hated shopping of any kind, like her mother. Even the Grand Union was a chore. Wal-Mart! ''They don't want it up there in Saint Albans,'' Emily said. ''The people don't. And that brazen company, just shoving its way in. Mother's disgusted.''

''Well, isn't it about time we shoved our way out?'' said Glenna, banging down her empty glass. ''Scotch gone and it's billy cold in here. That heater doesn't work worth a damn. I'm going home, that's where I'm going.''

''Aunty, you can't. The boobies'll come and get you again.''

''What! What boobies?'' She paled. ''Don't say that!''

''You know—Dad and my stepmother.''

''Oh. Those. No, they won't. Last time they fooled me, said we were going out for lunch at some fancy restaurant. We'd have a drink, they said; we'd have a scotch. Oh, we went there all right. But then where'd we go? Headed for that death camp. No more. No ma'am. I'm not moving out of my house.''

''Then the state will make you, I promise. Aunty, let's think it through. Let's not rush it. There has to be a safe place.''

''That healing center?'' Emily suggested.

Hartley looked interested. She licked her tongue up around her lips, smoothed down her jeans where they'd wrinkled up around her chubby thighs.

''You said they were all sick down there,'' Glenna said, ''you said that, Emily Willmarth.''

''Not all, I don't think. That woman died of a hemorrhage or something. You know, that boarder's wife, the guy who stayed at Fay's B and B.''

''Oh, that one,'' said Glenna, with a twitch that crooked her glasses into a new angle. They made her look, Emily decided, like one of those *Star Trek* people Vic liked to watch—the ones with pointed ears and slanted eyes. Emily didn't care much for science fiction. She wasn't a Trekkie.

She thought of their excursion to the Healing House. ''What'd you see anyway?" she asked the girl. "You were going 'Mmmmm, ahhhh.'"

"A woman," said Hartley, "in the kitchen, taking stuff out of the refrigerator, putting other stuff back in. Then something funny—"

"What?"

"Mixing something in the first batch she took out. Then tasting it. Then sticking her finger in her throat and throwing up in the sink. Then sticking the bowl back in the fridge. It was weird. She was smiling the whole time. Suspicious, right?"

"She's probably just bulemic," said Emily. "I've a friend like that in school. She stuffs herself, then throws up. What I thought was really weird, though—"

"What?"

"That guy next door. What was he doing anyway, burning up all that stuff? Didn't look like leaves to me. Looked like...well, bones. Tiny bones."

"God," said Hartley. "Not another skeleton—I can't stand it!"

"Could've been," Emily said thoughtfully. "Well, look, I gotta go. Mom'll have a cow."

"She already has, hasn't she? Thirty of 'em?"

"Not funny. You sound like Colm Hanna."

"Who's he?"

"You know, Mom's friend. He came over to look at the skeleton. You saw him. He's a sort of detective-Realtor-undertaker. I can't quite figure what he mainly does. But he's nice. He's got a thing for Mom. But Mom's still married. Dad's coming back. He might want to stay. Colm Hanna's got to realize that. So does Mom."

"Does she? Anyway, some combination, all those jobs. Do they link up?"

"I guess so. Hey, I'm off."

"I'm coming with you," said Glenna, frowning, pushing up from her rocker. "We'll find a nice motel somewhere."

"No, Aunty. One more night here. I've brought extra blankets. Then we'll make a decision. I promise. How'll you get home, Emily?"

"I'll go back down to that store, call Wilder. He owes me one. He'll pick me up."

"If he's not home?"

"He'd better be."

Hartley laughed. "Wait. I'll walk you down to the store. Pick up some tempeh. You like tempeh, Aunty?"

"I don't eat tem-poo—whatever it is."

"Oh. Well, I'll find something. It's not that far. I'll be back in twenty minutes. Less. Don't you go anywhere now, Aunty. Promise?"

"No, I won't promise."

Hartley winked at Emily, then ran out the door. "She'll be back," Emily called to Glenna, then added, "Thank you," as though they'd just concluded a second interview. Outside, though, she was glad Hartley was with her. It was a cold black night, no wind, not a glimmer of a star. She shivered. "What is it about darkness," she thought aloud, "that changes your outlook on the world? Makes you feel unsafe?"

"Yeah," said Hartley, "Wilderland. I mean, sorry, I'm talking about Tolkien, not your old boyfriend. Anything can happen if you get off the path. They're all out there, the weirdos. Ooo-hh-h. And it's almost Halloween."

"Oh, help! Indians!" joked Emily, flinging up her arms, dancing into a clump of bushes. And she was yanked back to the path by her giggling friend.

GLENNA WAS IN AND OUT of time. Nodding off in the wicker rocker and then waking. What was wake and what was sleep? She didn't know. Age slowed time, changed it. Till it wasn't chronological anymore. It was increasingly a struggle to hold to the present. Mac...Mac was dead. Wasn't he? She'd killed him after...after something—a fight? Mac was jealous, so jealous. It was his worst fault—and over what? Nothing *she'd* done. She had no interest in that other one—which one? Forgot his name already. It was long ago now; she couldn't conjure up a face in her head, didn't want to....

She was a prudish woman when it came to talking about sex—she couldn't help it. That other business in the barn—she kept trying to piece it together, but her mind would stall. He'd come at her, some man...after she'd run at him, with what, the pitchfork? Teasing at first, then angry, shoving her down in the stall... What'd he want anyway? She was almost sixty then! After that—blank place in her head. What had happened? Only that anger, that sense of violation, something she'd blanked out. Then Mac suddenly there, she remembered now, grabbing the fellow. Grabbing her. Her! And that was when she killed him. Must've been the pitchfork again, or the shovel—an arrowhead, they said? Where'd she get an arrowhead? She'd ridden off on Jenny; that much was clear. When she came back, Mac was gone. The hole filled in.

But who—*who?* Her tiny mother, who had Parkinson's—the body falling down around the spirit? She had a spirit, her mother! More than Glenna. Glenna, she thought, seeing herself from a distance, was weak. Oh, she put up a good front. But now she was afraid. Afraid of change, afraid of old people's homes, afraid of death. Not death of the body, no, that's not what she was afraid of. Afraid of the dying spirit, yes, its slow paralysis.

For one thing, she'd never been able to bring herself to open up that hole, look in. Why? Because she'd been sure it was Mac. And someone else had been there. Someone had seen, had sent her a letter. "LOOK IN THE MIROR FOR MACS KILLER," it said in bold black misspelled capital letters (she never held with misspellings; she and Mac were alike that way—wanting it right!). She'd burned the note. But the letters stayed on in her head, bold and black, just behind the eyes.

She heard a sound outside, by the window. If she couldn't see so well as she used to, her hearing was still sharp. She shoved forward in the rocker, and, oh, felt her groin full and leaking. She hated the feeling, the old body, humiliating her. And no toilet in this damn cabin. She pushed herself free of the chair, listened again for the noise. But she heard only the wind, a hooting somewhere. She knew an owl when she heard it.

Outside, the quiet was almost audible. She held her breath, then let it out slowly. Squinted into the night. Agh, foolish. When was Glenna Flint ever afraid of the dark? Even so, she wouldn't go far. Just out beyond the cabin, a clump of brush there, thinly illuminated by the open door. She found a spot, pulled down her britches, squatted, felt the pee spill down her left leg—might as well have done it in her pants! Then what? A leaf? She hadn't thought to bring a

Kleenex, couldn't think ahead these days, just lived for the moment. Like some monk. Hah. She waddled over to a bush, holding up her pants in one hand, snatched off a bunch of leaves, hoped it wasn't poison ivy, wiped.

Thought she heard something. A giggle? Those girls, spying again! "Who's there!" she squealed. "Who's it? Come out and show yourself." She hurried to pull herself together, got her underpants hitched around wrong, hoisted up her trousers, fumbled with the zipper.

"It's me," the voice said. Whose voice? It wasn't one of the girls. Familiar? Could be. She squinted, could only make out a dark shape. "I saw you," the voice said, sounding angry.

She knew the voice now. It was the Booby. That's who it was! She grabbed at the underbrush, broke off a switch—flew at him with it, smacking him, the strength back in her hands now. Whacked him on the head, the chest, the legs. The stick caught his groin; he yelped, grabbed at it. She heard it gather air, speed, like a sound of rushing hooves, and then, like Jenny tripping that time, jumping the pasture fence, her head striking a post, she was down in the leaves.

THIRTEEN

HARTLEY FLINT'S STEPMOTHER was on the line about Glenna, and
Fay, squatting by the phone in jeans and a T-shirt stained with
freshly squirted milk, was, admittedly, lying through her teeth.
"She's with Hartley, Ms. Flint; we know that at least. Your daughter
will see that she's all right. Don't you worry now."

But it wasn't Glenna's physical well-being that was worrying
Matilda Flint the most; it was the fact that the old lady had escaped
from the state hospital. The notoriety, the embarrassment! "What
will we tell people?" she wailed. "And that girl, she should be in
school. We worked so hard to get her into that college. She was
underage; she didn't have the grades. Oh, she's bright—*too bright*—
but she never studied. Always reading, imagining things, into that
fantasy—that bobbit, or hobbit, or whatever they're called."

Through the dusky window, Fay saw Willard Boomer buzzing
along on his bicycle. The wheels wore a phosphorescent strip, and
a good thing, for it was dark out in spite of a three-quarter moon.
Minutes later, in the middle of Matilda Flint's harangue, he came
lumbering up the steps. "I have to go now," she told the woman.
"I've a guest driving up. But don't worry now, please; we're doing
everything—"

"You know where she is. You're holding back on us."

"I don't know," Fay said honestly. For once, she was glad she
didn't know the exact whereabouts of the pair. Fay was not a pre-
varicator by nature—she'd probably blurt out the truth if she knew
it. "But you'll be the first to know if I find out."

"It's my husband's only child," Matilda wailed, Glenna evidently forgotten; and Fay, remembering her own daughter, whose
whereabouts she knew but lately couldn't penetrate, said, "I know,
believe me. But everything will work out; I'll see to it."

And she hung up the phone, for Willard was already in the house,
his big perspiring face grinning to see her—her, Fay. She ran to get
him a cool drink. Gandalf, who liked Willard, and vice versa, leapt

up from his corner, stuck his narrow gray muzzle in the sign maker's face.

"Well, well, howth sweetie pie," Willard lisped, putting his own face to the dog's. And then he said, "Oh, oh" when the dog peed on the floor. Fay ran for the paper towels. "You do have a way with dogs," she said. "It misses Hartley, though. It whimpered all last night, then slept on her bed. The mattress lists now, north to south."

"Oh, but I saw the girl, up the road a bit, running. I thought she was just exercising. I was coming the opposite way or I'd've stopped, offered a ride on the handlebars—least I think it was her." He took the drink of iced tea and lemonade Fay offered him— "Kickapoo," she called it—smiled, looking grateful.

That's what Fay liked about Willard: He was grateful for things. She'd never known a grateful man before—unless it was for sex. Her ex-husband took things for granted: her, the meals, housework, even sex; her simply being there, until that day she wasn't. She wished she could have seen his face when he read the note. But, well, she hadn't hung around long enough, had she? Couldn't. Couldn't breathe, suddenly stifled, as if she had a bad case of asthma.

"It might have been Hartley. I rather think so, yes. Definitely, yes," he said as the door burst open and the girl hurtled in, hair and shirt flying, her face flushed and angry. "Where is she? Is Aunty here? She just left. She just took off on her own. I was only gone fifteen minutes—well, twenty maybe. I went to the store, to get her something to eat. The ungrateful old—"

She dashed upstairs, three steps at a time. Gandalf raced up after, his white feet a blur. "Aunty? I know you're there. How'd you get here anyway? Aunty? Answer me. Aun-tee!"

"She's not here," Fay hollered up. "Hartley, come back down. Where was Glenna anyway? When did you last see her? Your stepmother called; she's furious. You can't get away with this, Hartley. You can't postpone fate."

"No, no, you can't! You can try, but it comes running after you," Willard echoed. "Like that greyhound," he said as Hartley stomped back down again, the dog's angular head pushing her onward.

"Like Gandalf. Like fate," Willard repeated, "you think you've buried the past, and up it pops."

Fay was impressed with Willard's grasp of metaphor. Maybe he was right. The greyhound was fate. Her fate. She reached down to pat the animal and he gazed up at her with damp eyes. She'd tied an orange scarf around his neck. He was really quite handsome. The curve of belly, of tail, the way the rear legs angled back and then down into sturdy white paws—never mind the missing nails. She hugged him and he thumped against her.

"You don't understand," said Hartley, plumping her rear end on the kitchen table. Willard hastily removed his glass. "She's gone missing. Maybe she's walking back from the cabin."

"What cabin?" Fay asked.

Hartley gushed out the tale. "But we were only planning to hang out for a couple of days. Then, when things calmed down, I'd bring her back here."

"A couple of days? Your stepmother says she's notifying the police. They'll be out looking for Glenna. For you," she modified.

"Oh, yes, absolutely. For you, too, dear," said Willard.

"Gleeps," said Hartley. "I didn't think about police."

"You're learning," said Fay. "And I suggest you call your folks right this minute and tell them you're safe. But say that Glenna—"

"I never thought she'd walk out like that. She likes to be contrary, make threats. But it was dark. Pitch-black."

Now Fay was wholly alarmed. She ran for the phone. "Wait," Hartley cried, "call that other guy first—before the fuzz. You know, that Colm. He knows Aunty. If Aunty's on the road somewhere, she won't want the police coming after her. Aunty hates police."

But Colm wasn't at Hanna's Funeral Home. It was his father who answered. He only wanted to talk about Colm. "He's been on a wild-goose chase down in the city. Colm's not a city boy. He's no detective. Never mind his grandfather was a cop. He was crazy to go down there."

So Fay dialed Ruth. It was an old-fashioned phone; her fingers got stuck in the black holes of the dial. Finally, it rang.

"Colm's here," Ruth told Fay. "He's got Mac."

"What?" Fay envisioned the bones heaped up on Ruth's kitchen table.

"He's alive. He's here. It has to be somebody else, that skeleton."

Fay was quiet a moment, trying to absorb the news. "Mac's alive," she yelled to Hartley and Willard, and Hartley shrieked. "I was talking to Willard and Hartley," she told Ruth. She realized she was breathless. She couldn't seem to absorb any of it: Glenna gone missing, really missing, and now Mac, alive? Fay just wanted to be with Willard and Gandalf. She wanted to see her daughter and her grandson. She wanted peace in her life. She didn't need any of this bones business. Though she did want Glenna back. Yes, yes, she did, in spite of herself.

"Then Mac's got Aunty! What do you bet?" Fay heard the girl jump up, the chair crash back on the old floorboards, the dog give a short unaccustomed bark.

"What about Glenna?" Ruth shouted over the line. "You told me she got out of that home. I put Emily on the case—she's friendly with Hartley now. But Emily's been looking smug lately. She's up to something, I think."

"Glenna's gone missing, Ruth, really missing. Hartley had her, up in some cabin. Now Glenna's taken off, alone, in the dark. Tonight."

"The police?" Ruth was saying, raising her voice over Fay's.

"Hartley says no police. She says Glenna would have a heart attack if she saw a policeman."

"Well, they'll have to be called if she doesn't come home. Tell the girl to stay put," said Ruth, sounding resigned. "We're coming right over," and the line clicked off.

Peering through the kitchen window, Fay imagined Glenna, that crazy, passionate old woman, alive, out there in another black hole.... Alive?

"Oh Jesus," she said. "Sweet Jesus. Glenna." And Willard got up, put his hands on her trembly shoulders.

"Now now, now now," he said. "That man in the hole is gone; he can't hurt Glenna anymore. Glenna will be all right. You'll see. She'll walk through the door any minute." And he squeezed her aging clavicles.

GLENNA WAS dropping deeper and deeper into a black hole, her flesh melting, bones waxing; she was Mac, shrinking into a skeleton.

"Mac," she cried aloud, "I didn't mean it. I didn't want to, Mac!"

Someone was shushing her, warning her—something about a handkerchief, a gag—but her voice was weak, her muscles limp and aching, her head separated from her feet. She couldn't see. Where were her glasses?

Now she was nauseous, angry. It was Mac dug that hole, wanting to bury her horse, her Jenny Two. "You can't, can't—what right— you have?" she yelled, though it came out a long sibiliant hiss. She tried to lift her head, and the pressure came down again on her mouth. Her teeth squealed; her head was a screaming ache on her neck. She couldn't see. *She couldn't see!*

"Why you do it to me, why-yy..." The voice was almost weeping now.

She was too weak to make him understand: She was Glenna Flint, at the bottom of a hole. It was filling in on top of her; she was being buried, alive....

But he kept on whining. "Why? Why?" His voice getting angrier, heavier, as if his tongue were shovelling dirt on her, heaping it on—till it took—her—breath...

"IT WAS MY IDEA, Mom, the hunter's cabin," Emily confessed on the way to Fay's with her mother and Colm. "She couldn't stay in that awful place, that state hospital. She was a prisoner there."

"Where is she now then, Em? A prisoner somewhere else— where we can't even visit her? Feed her? What were you girls thinking of? Em, are you listening? It was irresponsible of you! And you've missed school again. Oh, yes, Emily, you can't fool me. Your bookbag is still in your room!"

Teenaged girls were so full of false ideals, so unrealistic, though as girls went, Emily was a practical one. It was this crazy city girl, Hartley, Ruth decided, who was leading her astray. But there wasn't time now for regrets. They had to find the old lady. They'd left Mac at the farm with Tim; all they needed now, Colm had said, was for *Mac* to disappear. If that happened, who would believe that he was still alive? "He needs to be watched," Colm argued when Ruth wanted to send an overworked Tim home. So she'd given in.

At Fay's, they found Fay and Hartley ready to leave for the

search; Willard, too, insisted on going along. "I've real good night vision," he said, "My mother calls me a tomcat." He laughed: "I didn't mean..."

"Never mind," said Fay. "Just let's get going."

They went first to the hunter's cabin, found it deserted as Hartley had said, though Glenna's black wool coat was still there, the black scarf. "Would she have gone outdoors without it?" Colm asked, and the others were quiet, realizing what that suggested. Beyond that, there were only the crusty remains of a cheese pizza, a carton of soda, a small case of clothing, the kerosene heater, Vic's telescope, Glenna's shawl, a Dickens novel, and a tattered copy of *The Hobbit*. Outside, as well, there was nothing unusual. Ruth supposed a forensics team would find evidence: hairs, threads, fingerprints inside or out, on the door perhaps—prints that weren't Glenna's or the two girls'.

"Don't touch or move anything," she ordered. "If it comes to police, they'll want things just as they were."

"No police, please, no police," Hartley murmured, but she was shushed by Emily. "Mother's right, for once," Emily said. "Do you want to find your aunt alive?"

Ruth smiled grimly at the "for once."

"There's no outhouse," Colm said. "It's possible she went in the bushes to, um, pee, and then—"

"A warg," said Hartley. "A catamount! Oh God..."

"Come on," said Fay. "There's been no catamounts in this state since 1860 something."

"No, no," said Willard, "I heard one, oh yes, a high-pitched cry, like a woman screaming. But it wouldn't come near Glenna. No, those big cats are shy. Yes..." His voice trailed off as though he was linking himself up with that cat. He curled his fists quietly into his chest.

"We all know Glenna," said Ruth. Someone has to be sensible, she thought. "Most likely, she set out down that path. You said, Hartley, she wouldn't promise to stay. Though we ought to see if there's any disturbance—like broken twigs, in case—I mean, it was dark out. She could have gotten disoriented, wandered off the path. Her poor vision."

She divided them into pairs: Fay with Willard, herself with Emily;

Colm with Hartley and the greyhound—the girl had insisted on bringing the dog. "The cat, you know. Aunty's got Puffy's scent on her black sweater," Hartley had explained and now dog and girl plunged into the woods. Colm touched Ruth's arm, gave it a squeeze. "Thanks a lot, Ruthie," he whispered sarcastically, and ran after the pair. Ruth didn't care what Colm thought. The girl needed guidance. Whose fault was it, anyway, that Glenna was missing?

Each pair took a different direction, flashing lights into brush, and cleared out muddy areas, where the old lady might have stumbled, her vision dimmed by cataracts. It was Willard who found the muddy spot in the snow where someone had recently peed. He said, "Oh, oh," but couldn't get any more words out. Fay said, "She peed here, or someone else did. Yanked these leaves off to dry herself." And Willard sneezed.

Ruth and Emily moved on down the path, Ruth trying to hold back her annoyance at Emily's complicity; after all, her daughter seemed genuinely upset about Glenna's disappearance. "She's a great old lady," Emily whispered. "I got a neat story for my project. She was really into telling stories about the old days. You, know, Mom, I kind of enjoy hearing about what life used to be like. I mean, even our own farm—it was in the family—how many generations?"

"Five, your father said. He knows the history; you should ask him. When he comes."

"Halloween," Emily whispered, glancing at her mother meaningfully. "But I asked him once. He didn't want to talk about it."

"That's because...well, he needed some excuse for leaving the place. Painful to think about leaving the farm, I suppose. Guilt? Maybe that's why he wants to sell. This could be the last generation. Sharon's not interested. Unless you or Vic—"

"Mom, you're evading the issue. You're always evading the issue. When Dad comes, I want you to be open. I want you to listen to his side. There're two sides to everything. Wilder says his mom—"

"Never mind that now. We have a missing woman. She may be in the bushes somewhere. Trying to call out."

"Evading again, Mom. Are we ever going to face this?"

"October thirty-first," Ruth said, feeling something sour in her stomach. "Then you'll have answers. But be open yourself, my dear girl. They may not be the answers *you* want."

They were at the road now. Ruth shone her flashlight to the west side of the path. She'd thought it a bare spot, but a closer inspection showed the brush was trampled down, as though something had been dragged there. She pulled at Emily's sleeve, and together they explored the terrain. The scrubs had been knocked down by an object the size of— She couldn't say the word. But Glenna's frail body rose up behind her eyes.

"Signal Colm," she said, and Emily gave the soft hoot they'd agreed upon. Moments later, Colm was there, breathing hard behind Ruth. She smelled the sweat on him. His glasses gleamed in the circle of her flashlight; she saw that he'd torn his shirtsleeve on something sharp. She touched it, and the blood came off on her fingers. He waved away her concern.

"It might have been somebody dragging a deer. We shouldn't jump to conclusions."

"Deer season doesn't start till Thanksgiving," Ruth reminded him. "Not that that deters some of the hunters around here."

"Right," said Colm, and they followed the path to its end in the dirt road, flashing their lights at the surrounding brush. But they saw no further disturbance beyond a scattering of leaves and twigs at the edge of the road itself. "Dragged into a car maybe?" Ruth whispered. "Someone pulled her into a car after she was hurt and had lain there in the bushes?"

"Oh God, a rapist," hissed Hartley, suddenly crashing in sight with Gandalf. The dog was panting, straining on its leash, but glad to see them. It leapt at Colm, and he stumbled against Ruth with a whispered oath. For a moment, there was that warm pressure of his body and she couldn't move.

"Sorry," he said, and of course he wasn't.

"But it could have been someone helpful, and right now she's at the hospital," said Emily, and Ruth was grateful for the girl's optimism, the break in the mood.

"Rape," Hartley said again, and Ruth turned on her. "No! Rape? Of an old woman?" But Hartley came from the suburbs; terrible things happened there: muggings, rapes, killings—age wasn't a deterrent. Though crime was creeping into Vermont, too. Ruth should know that, shouldn't she? What kind of world was her young grandson growing up in—and a new one coming along. Sometimes she hated the world, really hated it. Couldn't bear to read the newspapers. At this very moment even, Sharon could be in childbirth. What was Ruth Willmarth doing here, anyway? She was needed at home, home.

Fay and Willard appeared on the path, but had nothing to report. "Looks like we reached a dead end," said Fay, though her eyes shone; Ruth saw she was holding Willard's hand. "I tripped. A willow root in the path," she said, and dropped his hand. "My, yes, head over teakettle," Willard mumbled, then laughed softly, glancing at Fay.

"Not a dead end, don't say that," and, dropping her head in her hands, Hartley sobbed. Fay put her arms around the girl while Willard looked on, hands dropped at his sides like broken twigs, his big face woebegone.

"I've a hunch she's just fine," said Ruth, squeezing Hartley's arm. "We'll check the hospital. What do you think, Colm? Try out Emily's suggestion? And if not—"

"The police," said Colm, "we'll have to inform the police." And Hartley squealed.

"It'll be all right, all right," Fay soothed, and she wrapped the girl in her arms as if Hartley were her own child and had had a bad dream, that was all, but now was awake and everything was all right.

"She'll be all right," Ruth echoed, and felt it to be a lie.

IT WAS BAD ENOUGH to be baby-sat by that hired man and his half-brained Joey, who turned up *Wheel of Fortune* so loud, even the Willmarth boy upstairs screamed for quiet. But now, the hired man had gone and the older sister, what's-her-name, had taken over. Mac didn't like the principle of the thing. He should be baby-sitting *her* for pete's sake, she was young enough. And big as a house! What could he do if she went into labor? And her grilling him, like she was some kind of detective: "Why'd you leave Glenna? Why'd you come here in the first place if you didn't like it? Why didn't you write when everybody thought you were dead? Why, why,

why?" He wasn't about to give an answer. Time passed, that was why. Simple as that.

And that kid of hers, staggering around the living room, switching lights on and off, the black-and-white TV (black and white in this day and age?)—just when there was finally a decent show on, though it was a repeat, and Inspector Morse was about to make a breakthrough and nab the guy jumping off the church roof. Mac liked Morse, liked his cynicism; he was Mac's kind of guy: Don't trust anybody, give 'em all a sneer. Give 'em an opening? Hey, they'll do you in.

After what seemed an hour, she looked in on the kid. "Robbie? come out of there. Right this minute, I said." When the kid turned a deaf ear, she steamrolled in, scooped him up like a heap of laundry, and marched upstairs, her brown braids bobbing, her bare feet punishing the scuffed steps. Pretty agile, after all, for that fat belly.

He had a stabbing memory. Glenna'd thought she was pregnant once, and when she told him, he was floored. Christ, he was almost fifty, for crying out loud—what'd he want with a kid? "Take some castor oil or something," he'd said (words to that effect), and she'd got all in a rage and banged around the room, knocking things off the shelves. "You've got no romance in that skinny body, not a damned ounce," she'd shrieked, and then, to really get his goat: "What makes you think *you* could make a kid anyway?"

Well, he'd caught the drift of that; he was one mad guy. Picked her up and threw her down on that scratchy sofa and told her he had a kid, down in the city, grown up now—how'd she like that piece of news? And she just looked him back with those big green eyes and called him a liar, said he wasn't "man enough."

"Then who is?" he'd demanded. "Who else you been screwing around here? Answer me, who?" He was a jealous man, he had to admit it. But there really had been a woman once, before Glenna. She got pregnant but then aborted it. He didn't ask her to, either. He wasn't that kind; it was her decision. The question was: Was it really his or not? He'd seen how she acted with other men. He couldn't stand promiscuity—it was like a disease. His own mother'd had it, left his father, one fling after another. It grabbed him in the pit of the belly, festered like stomach flu. Himself, he never cheated on anyone. No! Well, he never saw that woman again, and glad of it. She went to work on another newspaper, women's news, that kind of trivia.

It turned out Glenna wasn't pregnant after all, just going through menopause, her periods screwed up. He was surprised she had any periods at all, ever—all that horseback riding. Still, you never knew; he found himself looking closely at the men who came to the farm. Never realized how many they were—remembering now that Hanna had asked the question: the grain salesman—forgot his name—guy who picked up the milk, plumbers, roofers, electricians, the sign maker, that milk tester. Hungry looking kind of guys, reminded him of that Shakespeare character—Mac liked Shakespeare—something about a "lean and hungry look"? Probably screwing every farm wife around, or trying to. Some gave in, he supposed. But Glenna?

She was crazy enough to do anything when she was in a mood. Just to get back at *him*. Look at the way she rode that effing horse. Christ, he hated that horse! Never mind he couldn't ride it himself. Jenny Two, she named it. Stubborn as Glenna. It was like masturbating, he told her once; she got her kicks, rubbing her cunt in the saddle. And then she socked him hard, in the gut. Knocked the wind right out of him—and him with weak lungs. He just laughed after he got back his breath. He'd dug a hole for that mare. He was going to do it in, too, he really was. Till one of them came—who? One of the Bag brothers? He never could tell one from the other, both with that spiky yellow-gray hair, though they weren't twins, Glenna said. She knew them apart. That said something, didn't it? Knew them well enough to tell them apart? "What's the difference, a mole on the butt?" he'd asked once, and instead of getting mad this time, she just laughed. You could never tell about Glenna. Maybe that's why he hung out with her in the first place. She was unpredictable. Fun, even.

Anyway, there was that knockdown fight, time he found Glenna on her back in the hay. What other conclusion could a man reach? And that asshole running off. But first—memory foggy now—he grabbed Glenna and struck her, and she got that shovel, or rake or whatever, and hit him with it. Then ran, damn her. Last thing he heard was the horse galloping off; knew she was on it. She didn't even stop to see if he was dead. Though she must've thought he was, according to that Hanna fellow, the guy who'd dragged him up here. He was as good as dead for a time, though, head like a bucketful of mud, he remembered that.

Then someone else was groaning, not just him. Like *Hamlet,* act 5, the whole stage full of groaners, dead men. He'd clobbered the guy before he went to Glenna, he remembered now. He'd killed that guy. He was still mixed up about the sequence. Anyway, he was fed up, it was the final straw, her rapping him like that. He left town. Just took what was his: the typewriter, tape recorder, his O'Brian sea novels—all fifteen of them. Rented a room in Montreal till it blew over. Month, two months later, no one coming after him, and he went home—his old rooming house in the city. No one ever called.

That skeleton, though—did he put the guy in there? The one he killed—whoever it was? In that horse hole? He must have, but he couldn't recall. Though Hanna said it was Glenna put him in it. He chuckled. Thought it was old Mac MacInnis in that hole, and she'd killed him. Wished he'd seen her face! Was she sorry? Or glad... Well, he guessed he wasn't always so great a husband. But what'd she expect, dragging him up here, out of the city? He was a city boy, born there, raised there, right in Brooklyn, where his dad ran a meat market. Nobody rode horses then in the city—except the Irish cops. Nobody kept cows. The only tits he knew were on the streetwalkers.

But here he was. What was going on anyway? What kind of mix-up here? When she sees him again though, she'll know it wasn't him in that hole. She'll know he just up and took off. She'll be in a fury. Christ! he doesn't want to see that. Doesn't want the police finding out about the one he killed, either.... Mac doesn't want to be here, that's all he knows.

He heard that young woman upstairs, singing off-key to her kid—squeaky voice, putting him to sleep. Heard the older boy, her brother, yelling at her to "shut up," he was "trying to do his homework." And that did it. Mac wasn't hanging around here another minute. He went to the phone, called a taxi; he'd meet it out by the road, he said. "Hurry up. I gotta make a plane in Burlington."

And swiping a tenner he saw lying beside the phone—he'd pay the woman back—he was no thief—he had, well, probably just the bus fare in his pocket, to Montreal maybe—Mac stumbled out.

FOURTEEN

SHARON WAS IN TEARS, but what could she have done? The toddler was crying; she had to pee; she was getting bigger and bigger—huge! "Mom, I think I'm having twins. I mean, they're in Jack's family, Mom. If I do, I'll shoot myself; we can't afford it."

Sharon had a way of turning a defense into an offense. Ruth gave up; impulsively, she hugged her: Sharon was bearing a second grandchild—new life. Ruth wanted to think about life, life... "Go to bed, darling, go to bed right here," she ordered her older daughter. Anyhow, Mac was gone, and Colm was mad—after he'd gone all the way to the city to get the man, and now the phone ringing and ringing. "Colm," she hollered downstairs, "pick up the damn phone." She wished she had one of those cellular ones she could carry around, but at what cost?

She glanced at her watch; it was already after ten. She had to be up by five, because she couldn't ask Tim to do the morning milking again. Another note from Tim on the breakfast table: "Zelda broke the west gate. Still mourning that calf she never fed? What is it about women?"

Humph. She'd ripped up the note. Women, indeed. They'd never really come to terms, men and women, would they? It seemed a grave difference, impassible. Try to break down the fence between the sexes and you landed on someone's ego.

"Jeez. Jeez," Colm was saying into the phone, "jeez, Roy. Well, hurry up forensics about that stuff in the cabin, will you? And find that old guy. No, I'm not making it up. He's alive; it's really Mac. He just took off on us while we were looking for Glenna. Yeah, I'm sorry, I know we didn't. It was just—"

Evidently the chief had hung up. Colm's face was a study in purple. "He's ticked off that we didn't let him know right off. About Glenna, I mean. He had to hear from Hartley's stepmother down in Poughkeepsie. And he thinks I'm kidding about Mac. Says it's Mac in that hole all right. Kept repeating what the forensics guys said.

Blow to the right temple, just what Glenna said she probably did. A puncture in the breastbone—that arrowhead. As for the teeth, Fallon said half of them were choppers—bad ones at that, not all his own teeth at all. Glenna verified that. And I wore out shoe leather looking for a damn dentist.''

"He might have identified the false ones." She tried to sound calm; she disliked controversy, arguments. With Pete, she was always the first to make up. Pete would blow, and then give her the silent treatment, face closed up like a coffin. When she couldn't stand it any longer, she went to him, apologized (For what? she sometimes wondered). He'd grab her and pull her upstairs. It seemed that sex was the only way to end an argument. Sometimes she enjoyed it, too, she had to admit. She still woke nights, missing it, wanting it....

But she and Colm weren't on that plane. They weren't on the point of ending a quarrel upstairs, though she knew he'd like to. She was the one holding off. Colm was sunk in a chair now, his chin in his hands. He was wearing that blue-striped shirt with the kelly green corduroys she disliked, that ridiculous Green Mountain Boy cap—he looked as though he was headed for a Saint Patrick's Day parade. His sneakers were blackish with dirt, and some of the dirt was on her floor, little triangular patches, from the rubber cleats. For some reason, she almost laughed.

He looked up, as though she had. "Both of them missing now. You think they had a rendezvous? Old lovers do sometimes. Rediscover each other?"

"Uh-huh. Not at the Flint farm, though—Fay would call." It was a silly thought, but she rather liked it. She liked the idea of people getting back together. Herself, though, with Pete—she didn't know. As long as she gave Pete no answer, there was no divorce.

"It's out of our hands, I'd say. At least we know Mac isn't far. He has no wheels," Colm said.

"Taxi?"

"Jeez. Yeah." He leapt up, fumbled through the phone book. His fingers were shaky on the dial. He told her she needed a Touch-Tone, and she thumbed her nose at him. He described Mac to Branbury Taxi. "Short, sort of a Grumpy the Dwarf look, if you know what I mean." He winked at Ruth. "Yep," he said when he hung up, "they took him into town. To the bus station. He'd catch that last bus to Burlington, maybe Montreal, depending on when—" He looked at his watch. "It's already ten-thirty. Jeez."

She wished he'd stopped saying "Jeez"; she hated the word. Now he was back on the phone, dialing the police chief. They'd have to stop the bus. "But suppose he got off somewhere in between?" He looked helplessly at Ruth.

"That would complicate things."

"Jeez."

When the phone rang again, they both lunged for it. Ruth got it first; it was her phone, after all. The call was for her anyway. It was from Marna, one of the women down at the Healing House. "It's Rena," Marna said, sounding like someone who'd just fallen into a pit. "We found her in the bathroom. I don't know what it is. She was slumped over on the floor. It was awful. I called the ambulance—though Isis wanted to wait. What else could I do? They're on their way. I remembered you came; I didn't know who else to talk to, I'm not from around here. I don't like what's been happening. We need help!"

Outside, a wind storm was blowing up; the phone crackled in Ruth's hand, and she dropped it. Colm picked it up, put an arm around her, led her to the living room couch.

"Let's neck," he said. "Till it all blows over." He put an arm around her waist and she let it stay. "Close your eyes and imagine Mac and Glenna, like this, on that horsehair sofa."

"Till he rubs her the wrong way and she slugs him. Like this." She shook a playful fist in Colm's face.

"Spoilsport," he said, and buried his face in her neck.

She relaxed—a moment's sheer pleasure. Until the phone rang again and Marna asked if Ruth could come. "Now?" the woman pleaded. "Could you possibly? Please? I don't know who else to ask!"

SOMEHOW the Healing House atmosphere was lighter with Isis gone—to the hospital to see about the two sick women. Anyway, Ruth thought, a visit would help to keep her mind off Glenna. Hours now and no trace of the old lady—but the police alerted and searching. What else could Ruth do? Except worry. She had a talent for that.

Three of the remaining women were playing cards in the scrubbed living room; two others were in the kitchen, whipping up a butter cake. "It's strictly illegal," one of them said, a woman in her twenties with long, straight black hair. "I have a sweet tooth, you see. She never allows it, even though my cholesterol's low, only one forty-two. I mean, it used to be high, high! I went on this oat-bran diet."

"Wherever did you find that mix, Grace?" a third woman asked, coming into the room. "I searched everywhere."

"The convenience store," Grace said, looking sly. "I sneaked out and bought it." She did a little jig in her bare feet. Ruth noticed the pink-painted toenails. Here was a hedonist, in the Healing House!

"With what? We don't keep money here," the third woman said, turning to Ruth. "We buy our food out of a common pool."

"It's not what you think, Jo," said Grace. "I didn't take it! I'd never touch the cache. I had some...well, hidden, I'd never turned in. I know it's illegal; Mother would have a fit—but I just felt I had to..."

Jo pretended a stern face when Grace looked anguished, then broke down and laughed, put an arm around her friend. "Don't worry, kid, I did the same. For a fag now and then. You can't break old habits. I had to hide money with Jake—he'd shake it out of me. Half-killed me once when he found I'd kept the sewing money. I still worry he'll find out where I am."

A fourth woman entered the kitchen, went over to Ruth, grabbed her hands, squeezed them; then she gave an embarrassed laugh. "You're here! I didn't know. I'm Marna. Remember me? I called." She wheeled about to address the cake makers. "I can't believe this. Rena's poisoned, Ellen barely recovered, Angie's...dead, and you're making a cake. Don't you see we're all in danger here? Someone's trying to kill us! One of the husbands maybe. Sneaking in and poisoning our food. Whose?" She glanced about wildly, her voice rising to a shriek. She clung to Ruth's hands.

Grace held up a dripping wooden spoon. "But Angie's was a preexisting condition. We knew she was fragile when she came here. Mother told us. And Rena—well, she always looked off balance, like she'd fall over her feet any minute. It's a symptom of brain damage, the boyfriend knocking her around."

The other cake maker agreed with Grace. "Rena was always the odd one. Didn't want to talk about her problems, even in talk session. Mother asked her once why she was here."

They keep using that word, Ruth thought. "*Mother?*" she said. "You mean Isis?"

"Oh, yes. We call her that. Her real name's Anna Smith, but she changed it legally to Isis Blue Moon. She looks motherly, don't you think? You hardly realize she's in a wheelchair. She's fierce about keeping up the massage therapy. We think of ourselves as a family here."

"Not always easy to think of Rena as family," said Jo. "Shrinking away from us all the time, not wanting to share what's inside, get it out. Mother's right. Why is she here, anyway? The rest of us share. That's part of our healing."

"Same as you and me, she's here," said a another woman, appearing in the kitchen doorway. She was dressed in a long green cotton skirt, bare toes sticking out from under; she had a pale pock-marked face, mousy brown hair parted in the middle. "I heard the story once, part of it anyway. First the stepfather—you know. Every night till the mother found out. Then the husband. He'd get drunk and hit her. When she cried, he'd hit harder. When she tried to leave, he'd throw himself at her feet, say he loved her—you know the bullshit. Then she was afraid to leave—keep quiet and you're safe, you know. They don't want to be found out, these bullies— they'll come back and kill you! My man, well, he never hit. He just wouldn't talk, that's all. Wouldn't have a telephone in the house, can you imagine? In this day and age? Said it was a nuisance, that the ringing made his blood pressure go up. He was a lawyer, said he had enough of the telephone daytimes. So I had to go out and use a pay phone to call a friend."

The others murmured in sympathy. Grace emptied her batter into a cake pan, shoved it into the oven. Ruth felt her own blood heat up. "He could have let her have it," Jo said, "could have turned off the ring when he came home."

The woman in the doorway shrugged. "Anyway, it got to her

eventually. I mean, in the house all day, no kids, the place still as a morgue. She'd pack to leave, and of course he'd threaten suicide. You know the kind.''

The others laughed. Ruth gathered that suicide was a common threat. "Most likely never carried out," she said.

"You got it," said Grace, clanging the oven door shut. "Homicide before suicide."

"So you think this sudden attack, whatever it is, was brought on by Rena's anguish, not letting it out? The husband brainwashed her too long—she couldn't speak out herself?"

Jo considered. "Or something more. Something from the outside. I mean, her husband sent a threatening letter. He hired a detective to find her." Marna shivered and peered earnestly at Ruth.

Everyone was quiet. Ruth could hear the vibrating hum of the refrigerator.

"Well, Angie was definitely poisoned," said Jo. "I mean, the police are questioning the husband, right? That guy who kept trying to get in here? Sent her that candy? I'm glad I didn't eat any of it. But they've got no proof, right?" She pointed a finger at Ruth.

"Of course they have no proof!" Ruth leapt to Kevin's defense. "He loved his wife, I'm sure of it. If you could hear him talk about her. Why, he's devastated. He's just gone in the hospital himself, did you know that? A breakdown of sorts. The police have driven him to it. He's not a well man to start with. And now..."

She looked up, to see the others smiling at her, ironic smiles. Pitying smiles. "Sure," said Jo. "They all love us. They really do. But only because they love themselves more."

The others agreed noisily. Grace banged a spoon on the edge of the sink. "Got to get this done before Mother comes back."

"But you don't think Kevin Crowningshield poisoned his wife?" Ruth said, backing off the love issue. She couldn't argue with six women who painted all men with the same batter.

"Well, he wouldn't have poisoned Ellen or Rena. Or the rest of us. I mean, we all had symptoms, but we got better with some stuff the doc recommended. I think it was something else we ate. And Angie's was—well, we've already discussed that."

"But we don't know," Marna concluded, "we just don't know.

I think someone's trying to do us in. Someone—among us even. Who can get at the food."

There was a hush while they looked down, almost to a woman. Not wanting to look at one another. Ruth felt chilled, the way she had when Pete left, not knowing exactly why, what she had done. Might have done, or left undone, around the farm. Wondering who might have spoken out against her, what child even. Or Tim, without meaning to, laughing with Pete at some inadequacy of Ruth's: leaving the barn door open, not completing an account, missing a meeting of Agri-Mark because she was chasing after a wayward animal. Not knowing. Not knowing—that was the worst.

They broke apart then. Grace gave up on a frosting—there wasn't any confectioner's sugar; said she wasn't hungry now. "Don't know why I started the darn cake anyway. Sugar makes me hyper." Jo went out to forage in the garden: "There're still some beet greens. We need vitamin C."

"There hasn't been anyone else here?" Ruth asked Marna as they walked out into the front hall. "Anyone suspicious? I mean, anyone at all you can think of?"

"Just the plumber, an electrician when we had a power outage. Seemed harmless enough, Vermonters—though looking at us like we're freaks, some weird cult, waiting to catch the next UFO. That old guy next door came over once. All upset about the sign out there. I'll bet he's the one defaced it that time. It was Angie's design. Have you seen her jewelry, by the way? She was planning to take it to the craft center when she...died."

Marna blinked, turned away quickly, and led Ruth to an adjoining room. There was a small table with gold rings and silver pendants. Ruth gasped. They were dazzling: full of loops and spirals and— *mystery* was the word Ruth would put to it.

"The designs look Celtic. My mother had a pin once, from the Hebrides, with intersecting circles like this one." She picked it up. It felt electric in her fingers. "I still have it, in a drawer. And Angie made up her own designs? Worked the metal and all that?"

"Oh, yes. Mother set up a corner of the basement for her. Then she'd try to give them away. To us. Said they were nothing, just designs that came out of her head, as if that didn't mean much." Marna fingered a silver ring lovingly. It had a pattern of exploding stars, a purple amethyst in the center. Amethyst was her birthstone, Marna said; Angie had wanted her to have it. She meant to speak to Isis about it.

"She didn't realize her own talent. Too bad." Another thought entered Ruth's mind, but she buried it before it worked its way into words.

"And here are Angie's designs, on paper. Mother had them framed. Here's the one for the sign. It was Mother's favorite; she had a funny fellow on a bicycle make it up for us."

"Willard Boomer."

"Willard Boomer?" Marna repeated the name, thought it humorous. "I remember he caught a fly in his hands while he was here in the kitchen, let it out the back door. A true Buddhist."

"But this logo. Your neighbor's interest in it. His family's been in town forever—the old mother almost reclusive before she died a couple of years ago, but decent people, for all that. I've never heard of any problems there." Though she recalled something about the younger brother drowning in the creek. But accidental, though townfolks joked it was the work of the old girlfriends, conspiring to do him in.

Now she'd lost the drift of her thought. "What I'm saying is, did he say why he was upset about that sign, that logo? Unless he was just using it to complain about the place as a whole. They say he complains publicly. He's not the only one, of course: Conservative Vermonters worry about places like this. They remember Island Pond, for one. Anytime a group of people stray from the norm— the nuclear family—there are suspicions. As though their own so-called family values don't hide a hundred sordid secrets!" Ruth thought again of her sister-in-law, Bertha, and shuddered.

"Hear, hear," cried Marna. And she added, "That's why Mother keeps a low profile, wants us to stick around, not go in town, you know. Partly for the healing, but also so we won't attract attention— or our men. She wants to make us forget we're outsiders. 'Cause that's what we are. What our husbands have made us. Outsiders."

Marna was quiet a minute; her head seemed to shrink into the collar of her print housedress. She seemed to forget Ruth was there. Ruth asked her how she'd interpret the logo.

"Oh. Well. Angie always said the meaning was in the eyes of

the beholder. So my personal interpretation, I guess, is that that arrow about to pierce the moon represents the abuse, the split in the family—what Mother is trying to heal. Mother wants it healed, but she doesn't want us to forget it. We carry those arrows inside us all the time—in our bones. It's hard to heal a heart with an arrow through it. It is!''

"I know," Ruth said. Then she thought of the skeleton that wasn't Mac, of the ring on its finger, bearing a similar design of moon and bone and arrow. Was it coincidence—or were the designs somehow linked?

And what was Alwyn Bagshaw's interest in that logo? Was there a reason he went after that sign? As she stepped outside, the lights next door blanked out, almost simultaneously. Well, too late for a visit now, and she had work piled up at the farm. There might be a call about Glenna. There would be; she was sure of that. Who would want to harm an old lady?

Tomorrow maybe, after milking and graining, if she could prevail once again on Tim, she'd pay a visit to Alwyn Bagshaw.

ALWYN BAGSHAW watched the house after the Willmarth woman's pickup squealed to a stop. But after awhile, he switched out the lights, sat down in the chair by the window. He kept that chair there now; he had watching to do. They never pulled their shades, those devil women, wanted him to see in, sure, get their kicks out of a man watching. Wanting more than a man—wanting his house, his land, what was left of it after Ma sold off that parcel. When Denby died, they got back the two acres up in the forest, but then Ma sold 'em back to the state. For what? For a year's rent, state fleecing its citizens like always, milking them. Ma'd had land in the swamp, too, but the state took that for sixty measly bucks. Though it wasn't worth anything, all muck and bugs. Been in the family two hundred years, though. Two hundred! The Bagshaws one of the first families up to Branbury, the ancestor a doctor. Doctor, sure! Indians shot him when he was building a cabin for the wife and child, shot him through the shoulder, front to back—on the spot where Alwyn sat now—and he set the shoulder himself. *Himself,* he thought. Alwyn admired that. That was self-sufficiency. Self-sufficiency was good;

his mother had taught him that. "Grow your own," she liked to say, "don't let them greengrocers fleece you. Live off your land."

Ma'd wanted Denby to be a doctor, like his ancestor, but Denby didn't have the hands for it, the head. All Denby wanted hands for was women. Alwyn, now he could of done it, sure, learned what it took. But there was no money for the learning. He finished high school, too, a sight more'n Denby ever did—Denby dropping out after ninth grade. Then went to work, Alwyn did. Next thing to being a medical man, testing milk. Seeing that milk had nothing contaminating, nothing to hurt the children. Alwyn liked children. Liked girl children, too. His cousin Oscar had one, cute little thing, used to set on his lap and he'd tell the story of his ancestor, about the arrow shot through, front to back, and setting it himself. She liked to hear it, too; she'd ask questions. "Did it get better, Cousin Alwyn? Did it heal?"

But they grew up, girl children. Changed. Turned into gossips, looking for men, sex. Ma no different, was she? Ma kept Denby in her bed long after Father took off, made Alwyn sleep alone. What'd they do in that bed? He shut his eyes, saw the hand stroking down the boy's belly, down to the sex there, fondling. Denby wriggling, liking it—that's how he'd got his sex drive, sure, that's how it'd started. Taught by Ma. Ma, who'd locked him in the cellar that time a whole day and night. Left him sobbing there, his blanket soaked on the old mattress. And Ma never came.

She was coming out of the place now, the Willmarth woman. He saw her, saw her hesitate on the walk, look over toward his place, take a step in his direction. He let the curtain drop, though she couldn't see him. It was dark inside, dark outside. She wouldn't come over in the dark, would she? No, she was turning back again, running to her car like something was running after: the Antichrist, chasing her into the green pickup; engine grinding, racing off down the road, down the mountain.

She'd come back. Sure, maybe tomorrow. When Alwyn wanted to be left alone. No one laughing at him, no one pushing him in the creek, no one saying, "Alwyn, wash your hands. Alwyn, go to the toilet—. Alwyn, go to the store, buy me some sleeping pills. I had another bad dream last night, Alwyn. I want it to stop; I get no rest."

He heard a squealing noise upstairs in Ma's room. For a moment, it sounded like Ma; he started up, hanging on to the dark wood banister. Ma would tell him what to do now. Ma had always helped him decide. She'd know what to do. Then he realized: It wasn't Ma. It was someone—something—else in that room? For a minute, he couldn't think what. But it wasn't Ma. Ma was dead. He had to decide on his own.

Then he couldn't think what he had to decide.

The tiger cat came thumping down the stairs then, mewling for food, and Alwyn guffawed. All that time, it had been the cat.

FIFTEEN

ROY FALLON HAD two messages for Colm when he called in that night from the mortuary phone. Forensics had found white hairs in the brush; they'd have to do a DNA analysis, match them up with Glenna's. They'd already sent a man over to the Flint farm. "Though that woman there, Fay, is nuts—a match for Glenna," Fallon allowed. "Wants to identify the hairs herself, not wait for the forensics report. I said, 'Lady, you must be a scientist.' She said, 'I know hair when I see it.' I mean..." Fallon's voice trailed off.

"Women," said Colm, and laughed. Fallon laughed, too. He had a chugging laugh: *chuk-chuk-chuk,* like a freight train. "So what's the second message? They check that bus?"

"Got the bus driver stopped in Burlington. Your Mac was on it all right, fit the description—if it was Mac." Fallon couldn't let go of his old assumptions.

"It is Mac," Colm said, excited. "You said 'was.' He got off, then?"

"In Burlington. Driver saw him walk off, um, brown scuffed suitcase. Doesn't know...um..."

"What direction? Jeez. It would have to be Burlington, Vermont's big city. Though better than Montreal. Look, I got a photo, too. Get the Burlington cops on the hunt."

"Get your ass down here, then."

"On its way," and Colm hung up. He took a deep breath, smelled the lemon polish the cleaning lady had lathered on the old mahogany woodwork, the claw-footed tables. At least it helped dispel some of the formaldehyde. The house was dark even in daytime. He thought longingly of Ruth's farmhouse, its wide pine boards, the white walls, the smell of apples and doughnuts. The smell of Ruth...

"You're not leaving me." It was a statement. His father had a "new one" coming in; they wanted "the works": open casket, old guy, complete with glasses on his nose—he'd been a librarian. "The back's bad today, worse'n yesterday. Rain coming, that's why. But I'll need help with the embalming.''

"Dad, you've got to get an assistant. You can't count on me so much; we've discussed all that." But his father didn't trust anyone new, didn't have the energy to teach a newcomer, wasn't comfortable with strangers. Colm had seen that a month ago when he'd hired someone on his own. The fellow had been through mortuary school, worked for his father two weeks; left when his father found the hundredth "fumble," as he called it.

"I'll be back, Dad, soon's I can. I'm just going up to Burlington to talk to the police. They'll do most of the running around. Call up your crony Ed Murphy; he can help lift at least. I have to go, Dad, or my efforts in the city are down the drain.''

"I told you so," his father said.

Colm ignored the comment. "We got a missing witness here, and Glenna Flint's life may depend on him."

"And where is *she?*" his father asked.

Colm sighed. "That's another chapter. Police are working on it." And he walked down the narrow front hall, one foot in front of the other; had to keep going, though his father sighed loudly behind, started coughing as Colm got to the door. Bad back, bad cough. It did worry Colm, to tell the truth.

"When're you gonna think about retiring?" He flung out the question as he heaved open the massive front door—and shut it mercifully behind. He knew the answer. His father would die with the embalming fluid on his hands.

Then who would embalm Dad? Not Colm! Jeez.

IT WAS GLENNA'S HAIR; Fay was positive of that. The officer didn't have the hair from the bushes in hand—but white? How many white hairs were crawling through the bushes up there on the mountain? They'd found a few gray hairs, too, but Glenna didn't have a gray hair left in her head. "That gray could belong to the guy who grabbed her," she yelled at the departing officer.

He didn't turn. He didn't need some nutty female telling him his business. In his handkerchief were the hairy scrapings from Glenna's pillow—along with cat hairs, no doubt. Glenna had a brush, but it had been left behind at Rockbury. And then, she hardly ever used it.

Hartley and Gandalf clomped into the living room and flopped down: Hartley on the sofa, the greyhound at her feet. Hissing softly, Glenna's cat, Puffy, leapt up on the curly-maple breakfront—you could see its claw marks. At least the dog stayed off the chairs—more or less. One pounce and the sofa would sag on the floor, as well. But the days were growing shorter, the air colder; November was just around the corner. Fay was in long pants. She had two pairs that she rotated: jeans and tan corduroys. Her daughter Patsy had undoubtedly appropriated what she'd left behind in Cabot: They wore the same size. When Patsy was a teenager, Fay would reach for a shirt or pants to wear for the day, only to discover them on their way to the local school.

"Aunty's dead," said Hartley, banging her head back against the horsehair. "I know it. Some guy's got her locked in his trunk, and with Aunty's lungs—all those Chesterfields she used to smoke, till I got them away from her! If we get that guy, I'm going to squeeze him dry, vein by vein."

She strangled the air with her stubby hands, kicked up her blue-jeaned legs. "And it's my fault. I did it. If I'd left her there in that Rockbury place... But I couldn't do that, could I, Fay? Leave her there with all those crazy people? Aunty's not crazy. She's just, just..." Hartley couldn't think of the right word. Her hands made frantic circles in the air.

"No, you couldn't," Fay agreed, patting her on the head. "It wasn't right. Aunty belongs here. In her own bed."

Hartley sat up. "Now you're criticizing me. You're saying I should've left her here after I got her out of that place. But then they'd've come and taken her back there. You know that, Fay."

"I know that." Fay picked up her hooking. She was hooking a cow design. Actually, it was Dandelion, looking ornery—that is, looking herself: head thrown back, tail up, eyes glinting cinnamon brown, with a touch of red in the centers. A pail knocked over in the right-hand corner, the milk a yellowy white that spilled out of the frame. It made Fay feel as if she had some control over the beast, hooking her into a rug like this.

"It's neat," Hartley said, "that woman leaning over to pick up the pail. I like her orangy hair."

"That's my daughter. She has light brown hair, actually, but she tints it orangy like that. She's a pretty girl." She corrected herself. "Woman. She's thirty-one."

"No kidding? You don't look that old."

"Yeah, yeah. She has a kid, too, a boy, ten years old. I told you that."

"Oh, well, my head's scattered these days. How come they don't come here to see you?"

"Another story." Fay tightened her lips. "I mean, she's busy, the kid, the PTA, that kind of thing."

"Then why don't you go there? I'll bet she'd like to see you. The kid would! So why don't you?"

Fay thought a minute. "Well, maybe I will. Maybe." She got up. She could almost hear new questions forming in Hartley's head. She didn't need those questions. She went into the kitchen, put away the supper dishes, clattering them noisily.

"If my mom was alive, I'd see her every day," Hartley said, coming into the kitchen. "I'd live with her, take care of her, wouldn't I, Gandalf?" She reached down to hug the greyhound. He nuzzled her hand, then rose and poked his long nose into Fay's behind. Wanting a handout, of course. And Fay gave it—$3.59 a can.

She poured herself a scotch. She hated the stuff, didn't know what Glenna saw in it, but she swallowed it down anyway. Afterward, it felt good in the belly. Spread to the kidneys. She had to pee, ran upstairs. She'd go to Cabot tomorrow—did she dare? After all, Patsy's house was only a hundred yards from Dan's. Yes. She would. Surprise Ethan, her grandson—just for an hour. He'd be glad to see her, wouldn't he? There was nothing more she could do for the old lady. Hartley would be here if they found Aunty. She sat on the cracked toilet and listened to the rain drizzle down through the pipes. By morning, it would turn to sleet, maybe, or snow; that was the forecast. And Glenna out there somewhere in it, was she? She could almost hear the old lady's voice calling through the pipes. Calling for help. "Help me, Fay, hel-l-pp..."

RUTH WAS READY to leave for East Branbury when for the umpteenth time Zelda broke through the same pasture fence. "Yep, she busted right through where me and Tim fixed it," Joey reported. "You better go git her. Me and Tim got other work to do."

Tim was right: She'd assigned the jobs. Cut the corn in the east pasture, for one. They were already late; it had snowed an inch last night, the temperature plunging down into the twenties. They might not save what they had. Jobs heaped up on jobs—she couldn't think straight. And on top of it all, Mac and Glenna both missing, and increased hysteria at the Healing House. How far did neighborliness stretch? She had her own life to think about, her family. Why was she running around to healing houses? What was Colm doing up in Burlington, chasing down an old man who didn't want to be here in Vermont anyway? She shooed Vic's chickens out of the barn— one of them, a large Rhode Island Red, flapped its reddish brown wings at her in protest, and she took the broom to him. Then, too lazy to walk, she drove the John Deere out into the north pasture. The day was brilliant with sun and snow and blue sky and red berries. She just wanted to sit down somewhere, drink it in.

But Zelda had broken through into land she rented out for sheep—to her city friend, Carol Unsworth. Carol had planted alfalfa, a patch of corn. Zelda would make short work of that. There was no time to enjoy nature.

Zelda swung her black head sideways at Ruth, as if to say, Ha. I got out, didn't I? You can't keep this old gal cooped up. A corn husk hung from her jaw; her mouth was moving sideways, her tail switching like a chorus girl onstage. "Chorus girl," Ruth murmured. Pete had taken Ruth to a nightclub once in Montreal, their yearly outing. "See?" he'd said. "That plump one on the far right. She's more desirable. Know why?" "Why?" she'd said, trying to please him, not really interested in why. Knowing why, actually. That plump flesh, for the grabbing. Pete had just laughed, poked her in the ribs, a good ole boy. She'd determined to stay in shape after that, not accumulate extra flesh. Well, the farm did that job for her, it wasn't hard. She ran her hands down the sides of her breasts, her hips. Soft, but hard flesh, both at once. She was still in the running.

Zelda had no spare flesh, either, her hips sticking up, all bone; you could count the ribs. She let Ruth pat her on the flank, then turned her head slightly, as if bowing. After the applause? Or was it a kind of "I told you so; you can't keep me in" look? The tough-lady stance. The free soul. "Zelda, you old reprobate."

Ruth lifted her chin, smelled the alfalfa Carol had planted, the purple aster. Overhead a small vee of Canada geese honked south, and she followed it with her eyes until it disappeared into a clump of low clouds. She laid her head against Zelda's bony skull. "I wish I could. I wish I could break through that fence," she whispered. And Zelda gave a long, soft bellow.

Tim was suddenly behind her. "You're spoilin' that cow rotten, madam. Anyway, thought you'd need help. Honest t'Jesus, I don't know what I can do to keep her in. Electrify a larger area, you think? The barbed wire don't stop her."

"No way," she said. She'd rather mend fence than have her children hurt. Besides, cows walked through electric, just as they did barbed wire. Now there was the grandson, running on his stubby little legs. "Just keep mending. She broke through a vulnerable spot, that's all."

"If there is one, she'll find it."

He walked her back with the cow. He was done with the last cut of corn. "What you think about growing hemp?" he asked.

"Hemp?" She'd read about it in the *Free Press*. There was a bill in the legislature. A way for farmers to diversify by growing industrial hemp. Use it for food, a kind of pepper, cloth, rope.

"Marijuana?" she said, winking at Tim. That, of course, was the concern. Marijuana was a by-product of hemp. Did she want marijuana on her property? Vic growing up, experimenting? As she had herself, back in college, before she'd dropped out to marry Pete? Well, once or twice, that was all, really.

"Hell, some kinds are low in THC," Tim said. "Marijuana's not a problem. It'd give you a cash crop here; I'd like to try it."

"We'll see," she said, knowing she was conservative, feeling she had to be. Funny, she used to be the liberal to Pete's conservative. The Democrat to his Republican. Not that she didn't consider herself liberal; it was just that she was responsible for the whole outfit now. She had to think things through, couldn't jump on every band-wagon. "I mean, we've got all these Christmas trees, haven't got a nickel out of them yet."

"They're only three feet high, for pete's sake." He laughed.

For Pete's sake, she thought. It was Pete's idea; he'd ordered ten thousand seedlings before he abandoned the farm for the city. Now he had no interest in them, just an "uh-huh" when she mentioned them on the phone.

Back in the pasture Zelda loped over to the other cows. At first, they ignored her; finally, reluctantly, it seemed, they assumed the old hierarchy, fell in behind her. Okay, girl, Ruth thought, you can leave your calf, leave your pasture. But if you want to be a matriarch, you'll have to stick around. One day, they'll butt you out altogether.

And what was it like, anyway, beyond that fence? Was it any better—or simply different? She felt a shiver of cold in her spine. Did she want to find out? She was safe—here on her island. God, what *did* she want, anyway?

She climbed off the John Deere; the engine sputtered and quit, and she heard the barn phone ringing. It could be anyone, anything. There were so many unanswered questions. She ran for it. It might be Colm, back from Burlington—he'd had no luck finding Mac, the last she'd heard from him. The police, with Glenna. Gasping for breath, she said, "Oh. Hi, Fay." The woman's voice was equally breathless; she'd been running after Dandelion. Wanted to tell Ruth about the hairs—Chief Fallon had called. "The DNA matched up with the hairs from Glenna's pillow. They were definitely Glenna's hairs on those bushes." But the iron gray hairs—they hadn't a clue.

"Tire marks in the road?" Ruth asked. "They haven't checked for those?"

"They're checking. I asked. But lots of people go by there, so it's hard, the chief said. But they've found some oil spill, too, near where someone might have picked her up. But..." Fay was quiet; her voice sounded tired.

"Get some rest, Fay. You've got Hartley and the dog. And that cow to hand-milk. That's enough work for anyone."

Fay sighed, then rebounded cheerfully. "Oh, and now I'm on my way to Cabot—to see the grandkid. I wanted to tell you that, too, just in case. I mean, Hartley's here alone. And Ruth—Kevin's back. He's checked out of the hospital; he's on Valium. Then he had to make a turnaround trip to Chicago. He's waiting now for the body. They've only just finally determined the poison—super something, they call it, um, superwarfarin—that's it. In humans, they say, it can lead to fatal hemorrhaging. I never heard of it, but what do I know?" Her voice lower now, she said, "Hey, here he is. He wants to talk to you. Sorry, I know you're busy, but..."

Ruth heard Hartley's high-pitched voice in the background, Fay's in response; then Kevin came on the line.

"Ruth? I'm back." His voice was intimate, breathy, as though he'd run back from the airport. "From Chicago." He gave a short laugh, as if he'd said something absurd.

She didn't know how to respond. "Oh, yes, and did everything, um, go well?"

"Relatively speaking. I mean"—he took a whistly breath—"arranging a memorial service is not my...well, you know."

"Yes. I'm sure."

"You sound out of breath."

"Well, I've been running after Zelda—the wayward cow? Not to mention Glenna."

"I heard. I'm sorry. I hope she's all right. She's a grand old girl. Eccentric but—"

"Interesting. Her own person. Something most of us never are."

He was quiet a minute. Then he said, "Yes, yes, you're right. I wondered about that while I was calling up people to speak at the service. But then, Angie didn't have many friends—close ones, I mean. Just an old college friend, wives of my friends, colleagues, you know. At least the college friend has agreed to say a few words at the service. The others didn't really know her, they said."

"Did you know her, Kevin?" She didn't know why she'd said that, but it was out. She gritted her teeth, waited.

There was a quick intake of breath. "Well, I'm her husband."

"I thought I knew my husband. And then he left. Like that." She snapped her fingers.

He thought it over, sighed. "When she left—I had no idea. No idea why. I guess I'm just finding out. I failed somewhere, Ruth. I'm realizing that now. Her stepmother called, you see. Talked about that Healing House. Why all those women were there. They were abused, or thought they were. Did you know that?"

"I think so, yes."

His voice rode over hers. "But why was Angie there? I mean, I gave her the silver spoon. My God, I did. She was my life; she was mine. How did things go so wrong?"

"Zelda broke through the fence again this morning," she told him. "She's one of those you can't keep in a stall. Some cows won't stand for it; you keep them in one place just so long and they...they break."

"What? The cow?" he said, taking her literally.

"Glenna, too. Someone's got her in a box. We've got to find out who. And where."

"I thought we could have lunch in town, that Inferno place. We could talk," he said, his voice pleading.

"Kevin, I'd love to but... I can't. There's something I have to do."

"It can't wait?" he pleaded. "The police, they want me back for more questions. Just the suspicion—that I might have hurt Angie, my wife. You don't know how awful..."

It would be awful. She sympathized. She understood. But she had to see Alwyn Bagshaw; the thought of the man nagged at her. There was something odd about his interest in that sign logo, when publicly, he talked down the Healing House. And she was sure he'd been watching her when she came and went—she'd caught a glimpse of him at his window. He'd been rude to Emily, too, Emily'd said so. On that score alone he needed to be talked to. She'd have to do it.

She could hear Kevin breathing. Waiting for her to speak. "I know, I know, Kevin, how awful it is for you. But you're innocent; they'll come to realize that. They'll find out who was involved, what happened. I'm sure they will." He was talking about lunch again. He needed to talk to her, now. "I'm sorry. But I have chores. And then I have to go to town. Rain check? Maybe tonight for a drink?"

Reluctantly, he agreed.

HE PLAYED in the basement as a child, Alwyn did; it was a large cellar, flooded every big rain. He'd built himself a little boat; he'd float around till his mother discovered the water and made him bail it out. The sump pump she finally put in didn't work now. But the cellar was dry these days, and there was that narrow room off it—

used once to hide a runaway slave in, when Branbury was on the Underground Railroad route. It was filled mostly with extra wood, stacked up in tiers. Alwyn was neat that way; he'd been neat as a child—not like Denby, who'd flung his clothes on the floor when he went to bed, left the wet towel after his shower for Alwyn to skid on while Ma scolded, loved his naughtiness.

He balled his fists, kicked a fallen log. It hit the pile and knocked off two more logs. That was what his life had been like, Denby hitting and hitting at him till the logs fell on top of Alwyn, crushed him. He'd dreamed back then of living alone, the only child, with Ma telling him what a fine drawing he'd brought home from school, Ma taping *his* pictures to the icebox instead of Denby's. "But whoever saw a green sun?" Ma would say of Alwyn's drawing. Alwyn overheard her on the phone once with a friend: "Takes after his father," she complained. "I don't know what I ever saw in Clifford Bagshaw. Good riddance to that man, I'd say."

"Good riddance," Alwyn said aloud. "Good riddance," he'd said when Annie left to live with Denby, till Denby got tired of her and came back home, and Annie wanted Alwyn back again. "Sure, if you want to live in the basement," he'd said. And by God, she would, too!

He'd leave some food, box of cereal—enough for a day, a pitcher of water. He'd show her what she'd done to him, cheating on him like that, killing his dream, unloving him—that's what she'd done, unloved him!

He lugged down a mattress from the spare room. The dust rushed up in his nostrils; he sneezed, banged it against the wall. There was a hole where the mice crawled in, but he didn't see any mice now. Though with winter, they'd be back. But not with a woman down there, not with Annie. He thumped the mattress down the cellar steps, threw an old quilt over it, sofa pillow where the cloth had split down the seam. It'll be a stopgap anyway, hold her for now, till I decide what to do with her more permanent, he told himself. "More permanent," he repeated aloud, sitting down on the mattress to think.

His back was killing him. His chest felt like it weighed two hundred pounds in and of itself. He rubbed it. But it went on aching. He got up finally, stumbled out. When he shut the door behind, you wouldn't know there was a room there.

SIXTEEN

Mac ROLLED HIMSELF up on the Church Street bench till his nose touched his toes, pulled the HOLY COW cap he'd bartered from a kid on the street down over his forehead, and lay there to plan a strategy. He still had a little money, but not much. Burlington was a bust; Montreal too cold, he figured. He had to get back to New York. He'd hitchhike south to Albany—had enough for a bus to the city. He still had his pension; he'd find a new place to stay. He never liked that old journalists' home anyway, bunch of stuck-up guys—"I did this; I did that." One of them from the *Times*, found out he was "just a proofreader." Spread the word; he was snubbed. He hated that. He could have been more; didn't have the education, that was all. Three brothers to educate, himself the youngest; he got the shaft. He was the only one still alive though—ha. Went to night school: He was smart, literate, got the job as proofreader, ready to rise in the ranks. But college guys coming on thick as spring leaves, pushing him back each time. It wasn't fair. Wasn't fair. That was part of Glenna's appeal: She went to college. The local college, yeah, but she went, got a job in the city—that printers' union. Glenna got away.

He'd been fond of the old girl; she'd help him move up, he'd thought, though he was in his forties by then. But it was too late. The college-bred journalists took over the paper. He was letting errors through, they said, readers complaining—when it was the fault of the typesetters, yeah, their fault, not his! So he followed Glenna north. For a time, it was okay; he was away from competition. It was killing his spirit, that competition. At first, he liked the mountains, liked the patchwork of fields, liked the quiet. He thought he might write again: articles, essays: He started a memoir—*Growing Up in Brooklyn*. Wrote maybe fifty pages on it. Till things started going wrong.

What went wrong? Hard to know exactly. Glenna's horse—he tried to ride it one day and it threw him. Maybe that was the beginning. Glenna's temper, his own short fuse, the old mother taking Glenna's side, seldom his. All those guys coming around—no privacy on a farm.

And then he killed one of them. Him, Mac MacInnis, who'd give up his seat on the subway for a woman, an old man, anyone on crutches, a cane.

How? Why? One thing leading to the next—no premeditation there.

But now they'd put him in jail; he'd spend his last days in a black hole. His heart drummed to think of it, his knees went buttery, and his bones sagged till he could hardly walk. But he had to—he had to walk away. Get out on Route 7, hook a ride—quick, before some damn cop saw him, that Hanna guy, sticking his nose where it shouldn't be. Hell, the guy had walked right past the bench, never saw him—Mac, in his new HOLY COW cap.

Hanna. Not too smart. The mouse catching the cat asleep. The cat waiting for the mouse to crawl out of the hole—only the mouse was already out, running for his life.

ALONG WITH the superwarfarin, a rodent poison, especially dangerous to a person already taking a blood thinner, the forensic pathologist had found evidence of tofu, cheese, rice, and greens in Angie's intestines. Colm recited this mixture to Ruth over the phone; she could hear the wince in his voice. Why was she so glad to hear from him? "At least the run to Burlington hasn't been a total loss," he said. "I even got to examine the skeleton; it's lying like a puzzle put together on the guy's gurney. He thinks the victim was already down—dead probably—when the killer got in the final thrust, that arrowhead. A crime of passion, you think?"

Ruth noticed he said "killer," and not "Glenna" or "Mac." Colm was at heart a sensitive man. Before she could speak, he said, "Jeez. It was like looking at myself twenty, thirty years from now."

"Colm, you're only forty-seven. Your father's still going strong at seventy something."

"Going," he said. "*Going* is the word. He has complaints. But if I stay another year in that business, I'll be a pile of bones—you can bet on it."

"Thought you wanted to be cremated."

"I was speaking metaphorically." Anyway, he went on, he hadn't found Mac, "the old buzzard. Disappeared. Cleanly. I met every bus. Hit the shelters. No sign of Mac." She laughed, and he went on. "Oh, we'll catch up with him sooner or later, I guess. But at this point, Fallon will just have to take my word for it. That there is a live Mac. That somebody put Mac's Scots bonnet on some other guy to make it look like Mac in that hole—nobody knows who yet. They haven't found any other dental records to match. Well, Glenna will have to identify Mac's picture from my photo.... Speaking of Glenna, is there anything..."

"Not a sign. The police are still searching. The townspeople have been wonderful. Scouts, Four-H, environmental groups—all looking. There've been twenty calls a day from people who've 'seen' her. One from Quebec, where she's been 'seen' running a brothel. Can you imagine that? *She'll* get a good laugh out of that if—when we find her."

"Brothel? She's a canny woman. She'd get her nickel's worth out of the pimps. Keep 'em under reins."

"Very funny. Anyway, I'm off to visit Alwyn Bagshaw in East Branbury."

"What do you want to see that old fart for? He'll just load your ear with complaints about the Healing House."

"That's exactly why I'm going. The Healing House. As if I have time! But—"

"That guy, Crowningshield. He's coming on to you."

"Quit that. It's just—oh, I'm not going into it again." She took a deep breath. She was mad now. At whom? Colm? Herself? Anyway. She explained about the arrow-moon logo, Alwyn Bagshaw's interest in it, how he'd tried to deface it. "They're pretty sure it was him. Remember that ring on the skeleton's finger? I wish I'd photographed it before I gave it to the police. I had to pull it off Emily's finger."

"You can go down to headquarters. It's part of their scanty evidence, along with the shreds of clothing, the Scots bonnet. Maybe the skeleton, whoever he was, stole it from Bagshaw."

"Which means Bagshaw is mixed up in this whole thing somehow. All these deaths are connected. You'd better get in and search his place. If he'll let you."

"Interesting thought. But how did the ring get to be that healing place's logo? Mere coincidence? Or is there a connection there? Look, Ruthie, want to wait till I get down there? I'll go to Bagshaw's with you. I don't want you seeing that old lecher alone. Letting him put the make on you."

"Uh-huh. If I can handle Zelda, he hasn't a chance. Anyway, I've got to get going. Tim has to leave at one, dentist appointment. Root canal or something. He's panicked about it."

Colm didn't want to talk about teeth. He'd had enough of dentists, he told her, in New York City. He wanted to know if she was free for dinner. "I mean, after milking. Let Emily and Vic do the barn cleanup for a change. You're too soft on those kids."

She ignored the innuendo. She couldn't, she told him. But she couldn't tell him it was because she'd finally promised Kevin Crowningshield she'd meet him at the Inferno for a drink. "I have other plans, Colm. I'm meeting a friend...."

There was a stiff "See you, then. Some other time." And he hung up.

She felt bad, she really did. But Colm wasn't being accused of poisoning his wife, hadn't lost a woman he loved. Or had he? He was such a romantic; told her she was the only woman he'd ever loved. Could she believe him? The Irish were known romantics, talked themselves into being in love forever, in love with an ideal. A paper doll. That's what the young Ruth was then: a paper doll. Hardly fleshed out—no idea who she was when she married Pete.

It seemed there was no such thing as a single "self." One kept changing identities. Why, she was an entirely different person now that Pete had left! She sat down, stuck her elbows on the table. She needed time out, now and then, to think.

Maybe she should give Pete that divorce. What was she waiting for, anyway? When he arrived—next weekend, was it?—she'd make her decision.

IT WAS a turnabout trip after all. Fay sat outside the house for an age before she got out of the car. It was a tiny one-bedroom house Dan had built on the property—to rent, of course, but after Patsy's divorce, at Fay's urging, he let her have it, for a small rent. Dan never gave anything away—unless it was an old toilet, a used carburetor. When she finally knocked and, getting no response, entered, Ethan said, "Hi, Gram," like she'd never been away. He was dressed in his red-and-white Little League uniform, ready for practice. He let her hug him, though she felt his impatience—he couldn't find his glove, he explained. And when she offered the present she'd brought, a set of Legos that built into a pirate ship—forty-nine dollars even at Service Merchandise—he just said, "Thank you," politely, dropped the box on a table, and then knocked off a porcelain vase searching for that glove.

"It didn't break," he said, as if Fay might scold him. "We practice every day after school. I just came home 'cause I forgot my glove. Mom," he hollered up the stairs, "where's my glove?"

"You left it on the kitchen table," his mother yelled down. "And hurry up if you want me to drive you. I'm meeting a friend at the caf."

Patsy's voice threw a fastball at Fay; she had to sit down. Ethan was already in the kitchen. "It's not on the table," he screeched.

"Well, look around. It might have got moved."

Patsy came running down the stairs, dressed to the nines: turquoise suit and hot-pink blouse. Her hair was still in that long orangy-blond braid—lighter than Fay remembered—but she looked more sophisticated somehow. "I thought I heard your voice," she told Fay, looking stern. "You should have told me you were coming." She gave her mother an obligatory hug. "I've got this man I'm meeting."

"A new man! No kidding? Tell me about him," Fay said, following her daughter into the kitchen. There was a time, when she was in high school, that Patsy had told her mother everything: the first kiss, the first fight, the first cigarette, which she nearly choked on. For a moment, the old excitement came back, the conspiracy, the thrill of mother-and-daughter talk.

But Patsy waved the question away. "Oh, he's just a guy. Out of a job at the moment, but looking, you know." She turned to Ethan, stuck her hands on her slim hips. "Up on the shelf. You have eyes in your head, dummy?"

"Oh. Yeah. But you said 'on the table,' so that's where I looked. Mom, I'm gonna be late."

"I'll take him," Fay said, wanting, needing to help, and Patsy said, "Would you? 'Cause I'm late, too, and Eddie doesn't like to wait. I'll pick you up at five-thirty," she told the boy. "Meet me by the bleachers. Bye," and she gave him a pat on the bottom, then whirled out the door. "Next time, call," she hollered back at Fay, "and we'll have a little lunch."

"Come see me," yelled Fay, but the door had already shut. Fay leaned for support against the refrigerator, heard it click on. She pulled her bones upright, hoisted her chin. "Chauffeur at your service," she told Ethan, but the boy was on the phone now. When he hung up, he said, "Bootsie Marino's mom will take me; he lives next door. You don't have to bother, Gram." He dashed out with his glove before she could give him a hug. He turned on the front step. "Thanks for the Legos. See ya," and he ran, leaping a shriveled shrub at the side of the driveway.

Fay sank into a black vinyl armchair, surveyed the dingy living room until it got too blurry to see. The whole house seemed smaller and seedier since she'd seen it last, all that vinyl furniture, the gaudy wallpapered walls. Oh, they didn't need her at all; they had their own lives. And all that time while she'd felt so guilty, daughter and grandson were playing ball and going to school and meeting a new man and...

"Jesus," she said aloud. "What a sap I am." She blotted her eyes with a fist, got up, straightened her skirt—she'd dressed up to come here, but for what? Of course she should have called ahead. Of course she should have known they'd be busy, have other plans. It's just that they seemed so self-sufficient! So contained, without her. Or was she misinterpreting? Had she called ahead, would the reception have been different? One never knew. Oh well. She'd try again.

She closed the door softly behind her and went out. Patsy's house had its own driveway, so she could avoid Dan—or could she? She heard voices over at the big house. Her old house. Even now she could smell the chickens, though the egg barn was at the bottom of the hill. Safely in the car, she peered over. Dan was standing in the driveway. With a woman. His arm around her, leading her up to the front door. He was definitely losing his hair; he was growing a potbelly. The woman was overweight. But they were laughing; they were having a good time. Fay sniffed back her remorse, her anger, her disappointment—whatever it was she was feeling. She rammed her foot down on the accelerator, lurched down the driveway and into the rutted dirt road that led to Route 2.

From Route 2, she entered the thruway, the thruway to Route 7. On an impulse, trying not to think, she swerved over to 22A at Argennes, singing loudly—"I'll Be Home for Christmas"—when it wasn't even Christmas; it was still October. "You can count on me..." So Patsy had a boyfriend now. *Lover* might be a better word, the way she was dressed. She was a grown woman of thirty-one; she could do what she liked. She didn't need any mother telling her what to do. "Please have snow or mistletoe..."

She slowed for a light in Argennes. Funny little town, called itself the "smallest city in the world." Mountains rising up lavender-blue all around, a stunning view in the late-afternoon sun. But the early settlers chose Branbury, with its waterfall in the town center, as their hub—Argennes was an outpost now. A derelict. Like that old guy in a feed cap stumbling along the sidewalk, thumb stuck out for a ride, the other hand munching on a candy bar. Looked like one of the homeless you read about. It seemed the light would never change. He lurched toward the car. He took her pitying glance for an affirmative, put his hand on the door handle.

"Okay, hop in," she said. "But I'm not going far."

He shrugged, got in beside her. He was a small man, monkeylike. Shaggy white hair and beard, needed a cut, a shave. Seemed harmless enough, civilized—a man down on his luck. He was thanking her. Usually, she didn't pick up men—not even women anymore; you never knew who'd pull a gun, a knife. But there was something needy about this poor fellow. A human being in distress. Actually, she could use the company right now. She really could.

"Okay," she said, remembering a line out of some play, "Where to, good sir?"

"As far as you're going, good madam," he said, turning gallant, doffing his cap, playing the game. She smiled. "As far as you're going. I'm a bit out of funds, you see."

And Fay said, "You can trust me, sir, to take you there."

RUTH PARKED by the Healing House; she didn't want to frighten Alwyn Bagshaw, have him drive off or wander out into the fields.

She'd go to the center first, then walk over to Bagshaw's. Knock on his back door maybe, take him by surprise.

On the way in, she stopped to examine the sign, was surprised to see that it was really quite different from the ring: The arrow tip was pointed up rather than down. And there was that half-moon. There were two tiny prongs, like the tines on a fork, at the end of the arrow. She didn't recall that on the ring. Of course, it might have been harder to put all that detail on a small ring. Or perhaps Willard Boomer had added the detail; he wasn't above doing that. He had embellished the Holstein on her sign, when all she'd wanted was the simplest WILLMARTH FARM: HOLSTEINS, with the outline of a cow's head. And then Willard had added something that looked like a smile on the cow's muzzle. Pete had laughed. "Good old Boomer," he said. "Leave it be."

The door opened while she was still examining the sign, and Isis called to her from the porch. She was wearing a sweatsuit; she'd been working out, she said. Her skin shone. It seemed any minute she'd rise up out of her wheelchair and run.

"Rena will be all right," she said, sounding expansive, pushing her hair back from her perspiring brow. "She'll live; they gave her the purge. I spent the night in the hospital—this wheelchair wasn't meant for sleeping." She leaned forward, smiling, put a hand on the small of her back.

Ruth was glad of the news; she inquired about the sign. She refrained from pointing, though—she thought she saw a window shade pop up next door.

"Well, it was Angie's stepmother, actually, who gave her the idea for the sign. It seems she knew old Mrs. Bagshaw, borrowed the idea from some hex sign she had. But Angie created her own version, of course. In an earlier design, she had arrow and bone inside a full moon, then thought it too much of a pregnant belly to suit her. She couldn't have children of her own, you know; it was a sensitive subject. So she made it a half-moon. The arrow, she said, meant healing, direction, creativity. It was important to her that it point upward. She sketched out the design and that sign maker with the green bicycle painted it."

Rolling back through the open door, she led Ruth inside. She wanted to talk about the Healing House, what would happen to it.

"The police have more or less shut us down, you know. We can't officially operate, that is, take in any new people—two of my women have already left!—till this poison question is resolved. How it got here, who was responsible. They've tested everything in the refrigerator. Tofu, soy milk, cottage cheese, bread. There was some talk about those chocolates—but not everyone ate them."

"Beet greens, lettuce?"

"Well, I don't know. The greens just came out of the garden, not the store. We ate all last summer out of that garden. How can you poison greens?"

"Can I take a look? In that garden?"

Isis waved her back behind the house. "Why not? It was Angie loved them, you know. It was practically all she ate. Fixed them with garlic butter and salt. Got some of the other women eating them, too."

"Rena?"

"Rena? Well, probably, I don't know. I don't recall. But don't go asking her yet. She's still weak, spent, since the hospital. She doesn't talk much anyway. To me, yes, but then I'm her confidante. She has no other relatives. She came here looking for sanctuary from her husband."

A gong sounded, and pine incense filled the air. Ruth heard Mozart on a tape in the meditation room. It was time for the healing session—Isis was going on with it in spite of police orders. She was swallowed up by six women, all chattering at once: "Mother" this, "Mother" that. Marna, who had called about her fears, tugged on Ruth's sleeve as she passed through the hall. "Mother says Rena's all right. But I'm still worried. I haven't felt well myself. We're so vulnerable here." She followed the others into the healing room, gazing back at Ruth as she entered, her violet eyes appealing.

A pile of beet greens caught Ruth's eye as she passed through the kitchen and she slipped a few into her handbag. It was silly— how could greens from an organic Vermont garden poison anyone? But something had; someone had slipped superwarfarin into the food, or drink—it seemed the most obvious way, an abuse of the old law of hospitality. But who? Surely not Kevin Crowningshield! He'd never been inside, he said. Was she that poor a judge of character? But then...she'd thought Pete stable, loyal, a man who would never leave her.... Okay. These things she had to find out. Had to! Some inner need, a way of giving back to her community maybe. It was so easy to live isolated on the farm; the farm work fulfilled her, recharged her. But she had to reach out. This was *her* religion.

She slipped out the back door, remembering why she was here: to see Alwyn Bagshaw, to take him unawares before he could leave—even now he'd be looking out his window. At her approach, he'd slip out another door. Vermonters were suspicious by nature, it seemed. They holed up in mountains, behind rocks, worried that someone would take away their space. She made a wide path to the west, behind a hedge, where Bagshaw couldn't see her from any of his lookout windows, moved cautiously back to where the hedge stopped, then ran the few spongy feet to the back garden. Had he seen her? She hoped not. There was a stand of sugar maples between them, a scattering of ocher leaves clinging to the limbs, but the branches were brownish black and thick. The fallen leaves crackled underfoot; ahead, the Green Mountain range loomed dark purple and brown in the cloudy light. Even so, she loved this time of year: It was sad and yet exciting, unpredictable. Anything could happen, for good or bad. Halloween came at the right season.

The garden had been planted in the spring; it looked tended, neatly put to bed for the fall. The old tomato plants had been pulled up, the earth patted down in their wake. Gardening would be part of the healing process for these women. She remembered how she'd worked her own kitchen garden after Pete left, hoed and raked furiously, planting peas, beans, radishes, corn. As if planting would make him come back, bring her spirit to life again! The next fall, though, he was still gone. And she'd pulled up the dead roots, the yellowed lettuce, raked it over, as though it had never been planted at all. As though Pete had never been. It was like a harvest of... bones.

"A harvest of bones," she whispered aloud, thinking of that dead garden, thinking of this autumn, too, and the yield from that horse hole next door. She felt suddenly chilled.

"Pull yourself together, Ruth," she said fiercely, and straightened her shoulders.

The greens, she saw, hadn't come from this garden; there was no evidence of beets, of okra, parsnips, any late root vegetables that would yield greens. Where then? She moved farther back—was this still Angie's land? She turned toward Bagshaw's property, though there were no posts to note where one property ended and another began. Then behind a clump of bittersweet, where the yellow-and-orange berries still clung to the dry stems, she found a second garden. If you could call it a garden. This one had been largely untended, but there were beet greens—someone had planted them. The ground was higher here, surrounded by a scraggle of bushes; the frost hadn't penetrated as deeply. And there was evidence of digging. More digging, oddly enough, than pulling up greens would warrant. That is, you simply pulled and the greens flew up. She was rewarded with a handful, a small beetroot on each end. Yet the earth was uneven, not flat the way you'd rake a garden before planting, but, rather, in the form of erratic hillocks, as though if she dug, she'd find more than just beetroots.

She should have brought a spade with her; she hadn't thought ahead, hadn't meant even to come back here. She'd intended merely to encounter Bagshaw. It was seeing those greens on the kitchen table that gave her the thought.

She snatched up a stick and dug a little with it: It yielded a black feather, iridescent in the cloudy sun. She stuck it in her shoulder bag, along with the handful of greens. She'd have a dirty bag now; at least her checkbook had a hard cover—but her hairbrush? Oh well, she'd wash it at home. She scratched deeper, and found, oddly, a pair of bird claws, brownish purple and wrinkled. What on earth, she wondered, would a dead bird be doing buried here? And how could its feet become separated from the body? She shrugged. Some animal, she supposed, a cat maybe, dissecting the bird, burying it. Did cats bury their prey? The inedible parts? Above, in a birch tree, a starling scolded her, gazing intently with a sharp yellow eye. A moment later, it flew off and the male, a handsome fellow, iridescent bronze and purple in a sudden shaft of sun, came to a perch on the branch and remained there, as if guarding till she returned. A perfect mating, she thought. Was this what Colm'd had in mind, wanting to accompany her here? She suddenly wished he had come.

Well, he hadn't, and here she was. She moved on to the Bagshaw place—that is, she assumed she was now on Bagshaw property. It seemed so sneaky to come this way, but she'd explain she'd gone to the garden, give some excuse, approach his side door. "I was next door," she'd explain. "I went to the garden; they told me about those beet greens, invited me to pick for myself. And then I came over to your back door, that's how come...."

She imagined his sour expression, his suspicion. And she almost laughed aloud. She thought of her father-in-law, who'd run the farm single-handed before Pete, and then drafted a reluctant son into the business. But when Pete wanted to try new ideas, new methods, his father balked, stood his ancient ground, suspicious of tractors, balers, milking machines. "It won't work. You'll see. I say no." That was Pete's father all right.

She knocked on the back door. And waited. When there was no answer—surely she'd seen his truck out front—she peered through a window, then moved around the house to the front door. Knocked. Again no answer, and now she was worried: He might have fallen, been hurt in some way. After all, he was an old man; anything could have happened. She tried the knob. It was unlocked. She twisted it.

Suddenly, he was there, a .22 in his quivering hands. "Outta my house," he said, but she stood her ground. He wheezed, and the rifle went off. A bullet zinged past her ear and through the top glass of the door. The glass splintered into her hair. She jumped back. The man was crazy; he'd lived too long alone. And to think Emily had been here.

"Hey," she yelled, "I only wanted to ask you a question—about that sign, that logo. It's interesting, and I just wanted to know the story behind it. I heard the design came originally from your family. I'm not trying to—"

A second bullet thudded into the floor at her feet.

"All right, all right, you've made your point," she said, her nerves shattering like the glass, and she spun out the door; she raced, crazy-legged, across the lawn to her car. Already the women were dashing out on the porch, panicked; they'd heard the shots. Marna was screaming at her. She heard someone say "Police"; they would phone the station. She ran back to the Healing House, tried to calm them. "It was just that old man; he's lived too long alone. He saw me coming the back way. I was prying. I can understand. Of course he wouldn't shoot me; he only meant to scare... Now calm down, Marna, calm down. I'll explain to the police. They've seen this kind of thing before.''

But Marna had flung herself into a sofa, was sobbing. Another woman dropped down beside her, cradled her in her arms. ''It's all right, Marn, we'll get to the bottom of this....''

But it wasn't, was it? Angie had been poisoned, maybe Rena. Glenna was still missing. And there was an unknown skeleton in the hole in Glenna's backyard. It wasn't all right at all.

BACK HOME, Ruth skipped her errands; she'd send Emily to the food co-op. She switched off the engine, ran straight for the barn. She just wanted to be with the cows, wanted to do the evening milking. ''Go home,'' Tim said. ''I've got it under control.'' But he didn't understand. She needed the work; she wanted to smell the cows, breathe them in, clean the manure off the floor, fork the hay into the troughs. She knelt down by Jane Eyre's calf. It burrowed into her, mooing softly. She put her arms around it, smelled it; its body was warm and full of throbbing blood. ''I love you, baby, I love you,'' she told it, and it stood absolutely still then in her arms. If it were a cat, it might purr. Purring, mooing—that was giving back, returning love. That's what she needed. Love. Work.

She sat there until a shadow fell over her outstretched feet. It was Tim. When had his beard gotten so gray?

''Well, make up your mind, lady, you gonna milk or not? 'Cause if you are, I got other things I can do. I'm still hurting from that root canal. This farm...''

She stood up, gazed out the barn window. ''I know. This farm. But we'll make it work. We will, Tim. We will.''

''Sure, we will,'' he said, his whiskery face softening. ''So go do the milking, will ya? The fences are holding—so far. Good luck!'' And he shook his head as she smiled. ''Women,'' he said, for the hundredth time. ''No man's never gonna understand 'em.''

This time, she laughed out loud. She didn't understand herself—so how could any man?

WHEN FAY ASKED the hitchhiker to tell about himself—she loved to hear other people's stories—she could feel him shrink back into his spine. "It's okay," she said, "you don't have to tell. We don't have to talk. It's just that—well, I've been to visit my daughter and grandson, you see. I left them, you know, and I felt bad about it. I mean, I left my husband, and that meant leaving them, too. Though she's not young, Patsy. I'd never have left her as a child, you know. I wouldn't—couldn't!—have. Though there were times I was tempted. Because of Dan, I mean."

"Dan's your husband?" She felt him coming back out of his shell, interested in what she had to say. What she felt compelled to say, like some ancient mariner, back from the murky deeps.

"Uh-huh. He's a good guy, really—everyone says so. It just didn't work out, that's all. I felt kind of, you know, squeezed in that relationship."

"Yeah," the old man said in his funny gruff voice. "I know that feeling. Had it myself. I suppose there was—pardon me—somebody else? Another woman? For—what's his name?"

"Dan? Now, oh yes. But not then. I mean, he adored women, and they adored him. Especially the elderly ones. He was always on call for coffee, bridge—I don't play bridge—he'd fix their furnaces."

"Their plumbing?"

She caught the joke, laughed. "Really, not that I know of, but he liked to be away, you see, out of the house—anyplace but in it, with me—even though he had all those chickens. We had an egg farm."

"Farm? Any horses?" the man said.

"No horses. But how'd you like to live with a thousand chickens? Roosters crowing every dawn, so you can never sleep in late when you want to. Dan loves those chickens, those hens, those roosters."

"No horses, though."

"No. You had horses?"

"The wife did. A horse. God, she loved that horse."

"More than you, you mean," Fay said, thinking of Dan's chickens, how he'd crow over them, their colors, their shapes, the size of their eggs.

He thought a minute. "More than me, yeah. Always pampering it, talking to it, riding off on it. Wanting me to ride. Calling me a sissy 'cause I didn't.'' He banged a fist on his knee. "Fuck," he said softly.

"You didn't talk to her about it? Make her understand the horse was coming between you?"

He chuckled. "Oh, I did. I...I, um, dug a hole, you see."

She braked quickly for a dog running across the road. The car swerved. "Sorry," she said, suddenly nervous. "You dug a hole for the horse. You meant to...bury it there?"

"I did," he said, pleased with himself.

"But one horse," she said, thinking of the thousand chickens back in Cabot. "Surely you weren't jealous of one horse?"

Now he was angry. She felt him rise up out of his backbone. "One horse. She slept with the damn thing. Oh yes, two or three times I woke up, and she wasn't in bed. She was in the barn, lying in a pile of hay—next to that goddamn horse." He stole a look at Fay. "Made me wonder what she did with it. You know about shepherds and their sheep, do you?"

Fay would have laughed if she hadn't been so nervous. She thought she knew who this man was. They were driving into Shoreham now. Soon the turn would come up for Branbury, where she'd planned to let him out. So he could hitchhike over to the thruway. Albany, he'd said. He had money enough for a bus to the city.

"And that wasn't all she slept with," he cried. "I could have swallowed that horse thing, I could have. But not those others!"

"Oh?"

"So I up and left."

"You left her? Your wife? Without saying anything?"

"I meant to. I think. But...things happened. I never got around to it. I just left. I didn't come back till—"

Fay felt the tiny hairs quiver on the back of her neck. It had to be old Mac, Glenna's husband, who they'd thought was in that hole, but who'd been found down in New York, brought back, and then disappeared. Someone must have done in the bones that were in that hole, and put Mac's hat on him. Her hands quivered on the wheel. She didn't want to alarm him. But she had to get him back to the farm. Or to Ruth's.

No, either way he'd be suspicious; he'd get out, run off. There had to be another way.

There was a small convenience store outside of Shoreham. There was a phone, a bathroom. She remembered her Philadelphia lover, his weak kidneys. She'd make a phone call.

"You mind if we stop?" she said, trying to steady her voice. "I'm dying for a soda. I've had this thirst since I left Cabot. They've got a bathroom, too."

"No soda," he said. "But you can buy me a Hershey bar. With almonds. I don't like the plain chocolate. Reminds me of Ex-Lax. My mother made me eat that crap."

"I don't blame you," she said, squealing to a stop in front of the store. She dropped the keys in her pocket, just in case. "Give me a few minutes. Sure you don't want to come in?"

He was slumped down in his seat. He looked exhausted; his eyes were filming over. "Take your time," he murmured.

And she did. She had to. No one answered at Ruth's or Colm's, so she left messages. It could be fifteen, twenty minutes before Hartley and Willard Boomer got here. Lucky Willard had dropped by the farm. But already Mac was snoring, little gusts of noisy breaths coming out of his mouth, like steam.

SEVENTEEN

ALWYN POURED a trickle of fenthion in the cocoa he was making. Oh no, wouldn't hurt a human, not a bit, said so, he recalled, on the label. Just keep her quiet down there when the police come. He was expecting them, sure. That Willmarth woman, she'd go straight home and call, yes, she would. He chuckled to think of the scare he'd given her. Wouldn't've hurt her, no, just a little scare so she'd learn to mind her own business. He added a spot of milk, stirred in the fenthion. Or was it that? He remembered now he'd used up the fenthion. When the second flock come along, he bought the other stuff—fellow he knew sold it. Put it in the same box, had he? But it was all the same. For rodents, birds, sure. He didn't want to kill her now, did he? Just wanted to make her realize. She couldn't laugh at him. She couldn't push him in the creek like that. Lock *him* in the cellar with no food!

Was it Glenna or Annie down there? He couldn't think. Comes down to the same in the end, sure, he thought. Women. They's all alike.

He descended the broken stone steps into the basement, opened the door to the underground room. She was lying there, quiet, Ma's pill still working, that white hair (for a panicky moment, he thought it *was* Ma) sprawled across the torn sofa pillow he'd gotten her when she complained.

"Here, uh, Annie, nice hot cup of cocoa here."

She grunted. "Wha?"

He yanked her up to a sitting position. "Cocoa," he said. "Now drink it. You won't get nothing else till suppertime. You'll have a long wait."

She didn't respond, just glared at him, like a hurt wild bird, reached out as if to strike him. He didn't need that. So he set it down on the floor beside her.

He heard a knocking upstairs. They were here. But he was ready, sure. His rifle loaded. He was angry now. He scrambled up the cellar steps, then locked the door leading down there. Had he bolted the secret door? He couldn't think. They were banging at the front door—hollering, top of their lungs. Two, three of 'em, he counted, peering out the corner of the shade. Sneaky sons a bitches. Wanting his space.

Alwyn sat. Sat in his mother's rocking chair; he'd pulled it out of the kitchen into the parlor. He sat and rocked, the old .22 across his knees, cocked. Let 'em come in and get him.

More bangs on the door, the old wood cracking. "Bagshaw? We know you're in there. Bagshaw! Open up now. We got a couple questions to ask."

He clasped his fingers around the metal gun. Middle finger on the left hand wouldn't hold; it stuck up—arthritis. But hell, he had four more on that hand. He was right-handed anyway; his ma'd made him be. Used to eat with the left, write with it, till she'd made him switch. The devil was left-handed, she said.

"Bagshaw! Open up or we're coming in."

Let 'em come. He'd show 'em a welcome all right. He picked up the gun, aimed at the front door. But it was quiet out there now. Had they moved? Gone around back? He rocked the chair back into a corner, where he could see the windows. If they'd passed by, they were crouching. Wouldn't see nothing in that cellar window, no. All dead weeds climbing up, and no window in that slave room.

Why, they had no right, no right to break into a man's home! What'd he done anyway, except kill a few worthless birds? Something else, too.... He pushed it out of his mind. His brother, Denby, now, he was the one they should've been after.

Denby only a half brother anyhow, sure. He knew. Ma couldn't hide it—never mind they both had yellow hair. That man, hanging around while Alwyn was growing up. Ma getting pregnant with Denby, the fellow taking off. He wouldn'ta done that, not with Annie. Not if she'd stuck with him. But she hadn't. Now she was paying. Christ, the door breaking, the pine splintering; he rose up out of his chair, the gun clumsy in his stiff fingers. He straightened it, aimed. They halted. He felt the power back inside; he moved ahead, the gun steady in his hands. "Git out," he said. "Git the hell outta my house. Git, I said!" He had the bead on them, two husky fellows, show-off badges on their shirts.

"Now Alwyn, we only want to ask some questions, that's all. Put down that rifle, Alwyn. You know you don't want to assault an officer, Alwyn—you know what that means."

The fellow took a step forward and that was it. Alwyn fired at his feet. "Next time," he shouted, "it's the belly. Outta my house." He was shaking now; he could feel it, like a fit coming on. The gun vibrating in his hands—and then it wasn't there at all; it was lifting out of his fingers, seemed to be levitating. Like it was the devil stealing it away—and when he turned, there he was. Big devil in a blue shirt, with a shiny badge. Taking away his gun, snapping handcuffs on his hands—couldn't get the cuffs over the stuck-up finger, bent it down. He screamed with the pain.

"Sorry," the devil said, "better see a doctor for that," and pushed him out of the house, out on the porch, down the steps, across the frozen lawn, into the backseat of a police car.

He thought he could hear Annie laughing as they drove off. Laughing and cackling like the devil was inside her. He'd warned them. "In the cellar," he'd said, "an Antichrist in the cellar."

One of the men had grimaced, but he'd gone down there anyway. And seconds later, he'd come up, holding out empty palms. "The Antichrist!" Alwyn had shouted again, but no one had listened. The devil had him, cock and balls, was bearing him off.

DOWN IN THE CELLAR, Glenna was riding her mare. Out of the damp barn, into the open pasture, across the narrow footbridge that spanned the creek behind her farm, into the fields beyond. She liked to ride in the open, in the wind, and Jenny did, too. They were a pair, sun in their faces, grass and clover in the nose. It was fall, Glenna's favorite season. Life smelled sweeter then: as if, with winter coming, it was a last hurrah for the senses. On they rode. The field stretched ahead; it had no boundaries, no fences. The grass unrolled like a green carpet under their pounding feet. She was free; she owed no one: not Mother, not Mac, not those others who were always pestering, wanting this, that from her: land, milk, honey, flesh. She was free!

Till she fell. It was sudden, the way a log dropped into your path, or a root reached up to grab you, unexpected, or a shot knocked you off your feet, catapulted you into a trap. *Bellowing, like the bull*

*her father had once when it met an electric fence, he dropped down
on her—the Booby. She saw him clearly now; it was like bolts of
lightning—breaching her everywhere: in the groin, thighs, breasts:
She screamed, and he slapped a hand over her mouth: His sex
inside her—the thing that had lain coiled like a snake in the bottom
of her mind all these years. The thing she had to get out, out into
the clean air....* For there was no grass now, only cold cement, the
place dank and reeking of mold, rot, dead mice, her nose in something wet—had she soiled herself? No—smelled like chocolate. She
remembered now: He'd brought it; she'd tried to drink it. She loved
chocolate, and now she'd spilled it. No—not all—half an inch
maybe in the bottom. She was in a cellar, trapped by a Bagshaw.
Trapped, like some skunk or fox.

Upstairs: voices, a shot! Someone coming to release her—footsteps nearby. She tried to scream, but only a hiss came out. "Here,"
she mouthed, "down here. Here. Here-re..."

And then the footsteps retreating, everything still. Somewhere
outside a car speeding off, a cat mewling.

She crawled toward the door. It was shut—had he locked it?
She'd get out somehow. He wouldn't keep her here, no.

And she stopped, almost there, but exhausted, sprawled on her
belly, on the hard floor.

In a far corner, a startled mouse dashed back into its hole. And
finally all was quiet.

EUSTACIA WAS starting to freshen for the first time, and Ruth was
at her side. Tim argued that the healthy cow would drop the calf
unassisted—hadn't Zelda done it? If there was any problem, though,
he'd be on call.

"Come on, you think I'm a Park Avenue lady? I can't take it?
I've had three of my own. How many've you birthed?"

"You got me there. It's just I know you got other stuff on your
mind. But you know where you can find me."

"Alibi?"

The Alibi was the local bar, and Tim was fond of it. Though
who was she to keep him from his small pleasures? He gave her a
hard week's work. He threw up his arms in surrender and strode

out, Joey trotting on his heels. "You call now, you want help," said Joey, echoing his mentor.

She turned over a pail and sat down to wait. Some births were quick, but some took hours. Ruth didn't hold with Pete's method, tying a rope around a calf's feet and hauling it out. It was like using forceps on a baby: hurry the birth, maybe damage the child. So she'd wait.

It was true, she had her mind on more than a new calf being born. Mac was back, although Colm would deal with that. Glenna was still missing. The police were investigating the back garden where the bird entrails were buried. They were checking the tires of Bagshaw's pickup against the prints on the mountain road; they'd searched his house after they took him, were interrogating Bagshaw himself. Of course he'd say he knew nothing, and maybe he didn't. He was a little crazy, but he'd never done anything criminal, as far as she knew. But human beings were unpredictable, even within families—she'd learned that, all right, in the past two years. She'd go back there when she had time, see for herself. At least check on that cat.

Eustacia was lying down now, breathing hard in her contractions, the amniotic sac bulging out from the birth canal. Ruth hoped it would break soon, hoped the birth would be normal, feetfirst. She didn't want to have to call Dr. Greiner. She had a pile of unopened bills on her kitchen desk.

Hearing footsteps coming through the barn door, she yelled, "Tim, please, I'm fine, I told you. Go do your thing."

"Can I?" It was Colm's voice, making out to be sexy; she didn't know whether to laugh or growl. Then suddenly, she laughed. Oh, but she was too prissy, getting worse with Pete's absence. She had to change her ways.

"You may not want to watch this," she warned as he stalked in. He was dressed in white cotton pants and a pale blue shirt, a blue feed cap. "What is this—Midsummer's Eve?"

"Only clean ones I own," he said. "I need a woman."

Another remark to ignore. The Irish in Colm, she supposed—generations of patriarchy. Eustacia was bellowing softly now with the quickening contractions, the calf's feet—for it was coming feet-first, thank heavens—emerging and then contracting, the birth fluids leaking out into the hay. "Draw up a pail if you're planning to stay," she told Colm, and then had to laugh when Eustacia suddenly urinated—she had to jump back herself.

"Jeez," said Colm, then added, "Why I'm here—if I can distract you a minute—Mac's at Fay's—safe." She nodded, she knew. "Oh, and the tire prints match. I just called headquarters. But Bagshaw insists he only gave Glenna a lift. He was driving by, he said, and she was coming down the path from the woods, waving her arms. Said he let her out at the convenience store in East Branbury, because he had to get home; he didn't know she'd disappeared from Rockbury. Didn't know she was there in the first place, he said. And then, according to Fallon, he went into a bunch of gibberish. Something about some woman named Annie. In and out of reality—poor old guy. Anyway, Fallon has sent a man to interview the clerk at the convenience store."

"Do you believe him—Bagshaw?" She wasn't sure that she did. After all, the man had taken a shot at her. There'd been something else going on in his head; she'd have to sit down and think about it.

"Well, I'm inclined to, I guess. But you can't rule him out. He did bury those birds—or at least the feet and beaks. I went with Fallon to have a look. We don't know whose property that garden's on—it's right between the two places. Of course Bagshaw says it's his land. We'll need a deed. But your friend Kevin Crowningshield holds the key to that. He says he owns the land the Healing House is on."

"He inherited it. Is that supposed to be suspicious?" She glanced at him, sitting there, leaning back against the stanchion, looking smug. Already, the metal pail was tipping back. She hoped he'd go plop in the dung; it'd serve him right. "And I know he didn't poison his wife. Alwyn Bagshaw did, I'll bet—those birds. How did he kill them anyway?"

"We don't know they were poisoned. He could have shot them."

"All those shots? The neighbors would've been up in arms." She got up, hands on her hips. "And Colm, Emily saw the birds in his wheelbarrow. Through Vic's telescope. She told me last night. She didn't realize at the time what they were, but now it adds up. She's ready to testify."

Eustacia was bellowing, Ruth had to shout to make Colm hear. It wasn't the time for polite conversation—if that's what they were having. It was time to break the amniotic sac. If he couldn't take it, he'd have to leave. "Watch out," she warned Colm, who jumped up at the spurting liquid; and then, "Okay, girl," she told Eustacia, "let's get going."

But the calf was in no hurry, and Ruth sat back down again to wait.

"He lived here a couple of years, in Branbury, right?" Colm asked, sitting back on his pail.

"Who?"

"Your friend. Crowningshield."

"Colm, he's not 'my friend.' I don't like the inference. He's simply a man who's lost a wife he loved. He needed someone to talk to. So I gave him an ear."

"That's all you gave him."

"Back off, Colm! What assumptions are you making here?"

But he was getting serious now; she knew the look—the black brows beetling. "He lived here in town for a time, right?"

"Before he married, that's all. He worked for Killian's Precision up in Argennes; that's how he met Angie. I mean, when they met. She lived here."

"Next to Bagshaw's?"

"No, I don't think so. Not then. She lived in town somewhere. Why do you want to know this?"

He leaned farther back on the metal pail; any minute, it would tip—irreversibly. She couldn't wait. "I'm just curious, that's all. Killian Precision, huh? They made airplane parts. For the air force."

"So?" She patted Eustacia's rump. The contractions were slowing. "This will be awhile longer."

Colm got up, wiped hay off his rear end, and the pail clanged down on the floor. He put out a tentative hand to pat Eustacia's sweaty flank. "Good luck, old girl," he said.

"That was sweet, Colm. She's eyeballing you, see?"

"Or maybe she wants to butt me. You think?"

"If she doesn't, I might." She grabbed his arm when he almost walked into a pile of dung.

"Jeez," he said. "This is a dangerous place. I hope you've got lots of health insurance."

She laughed. "Health insurance? For farmers, barns and cows come first. Forget the health insurance."

"Kill-i-an Pre-ci-sion," he said again, making six syllables out of it.

This time she let him walk, *plop*, into the manure.

She gave him one more volley before he moved out of hearing. "Colm, Pete's coming. Halloween, nice timing? Maybe he can tell you more about Killian Precision. He had a cousin worked there."

He didn't even turn around this time, but she was sure she saw his shoulders slump. She was sorry then. Suddenly, she wanted to run and hug him, but now he was out of sight.

COLM WALKED along the road, over to the Flint farm. He needed the walk; he was getting flabby: He slapped his belly and it wiggled. From now on...well, after today, anyway, he'd start watching his calories. His father did most of the cooking in their household—red meat and baked potatoes, night after night. Maybe a spoonful of peas—never a salad. The Irish diet. Ruth was trying to get him off red meat, of course—beef, anyway. *She* wouldn't even down a beef bouilon cube. Said she might be eating one of her own bull calves. Though she paid her hired man, in part, with a side of beef.

He'd put off seeing Mac since Fay called with the news of his return. He smiled. She'd put one over on the old man. Said he had a scowl a mile wide on his face when Hartley arrived with Boomer, though Fay suspected Mac was almost—almost—relieved to be found. The old man wasn't going anywhere now; Colm was pretty sure of that. Fay and Hartley were keeping a close eye on him. Mac seemed subdued, according to Fay. After all, he was anemic, and frail-looking—all skin and bones. And maybe, just maybe, he was worried about Glenna.

Jeez. Who should he meet coming out of the Flint house but Kevin Crowningshield, as dapper as ever. A smile on his face—"pumpkin grin," Colm called it. Thrusting out his hand to shake Colm's, as if they were bosom buddies. Reluctantly, he took it.

"The police called. Just now. It was Bagshaw all the time. Bagshaw used a poison called superwarfarin to kill those birds. They found it on the feet—that's how they absorb it from the feeding perch—through the feet. He'd admitted it, too, used some kind of perch he bought through a catalog—Killabird or something. It's illegal in this state." He withdrew his hand, grimaced. "But it doesn't bring Angie back."

"Killabird uses fenthion—that won't harm humans," Colm informed Crowningshield. "But superwarfarin will—especially if the victim is on blood thinners. He evidently used it when the fenthion ran out. That's why it took so long to recognize the poison in her system." He heard his voice expressionless. Crowningshield hadn't hurt his wife, so why was he so down on this guy?

The man's voice got throaty; his breath sounded raggedy. "She could have been saved. I blame them all. I blame those women at that Healing House for not letting me see her. I blame Bagshaw, blame the police for dragging their feet, blame the doctors...." His fists were clenched so hard, the bone shone through the knuckles.

Colm cleared his throat. It was unfair of him to judge the man this way, he supposed. Crowningshield was obviously in pain. He just didn't like him, that's all. With some men, you had bad vibes. Ruth, of course, would say he was jealous. Maybe he was.

"It was my land, too," Crowningshield went on, blowing his nose, lifting his chin, his shiny black shoes planted on the porch floor. "I showed them the deed; I got it from the lawyer."

"Already?" said Colm.

"Well...well, I have to settle things. While I'm here. I mean, I have to get back to Chicago. My work. I've been away from it too long. The work will help."

Colm nodded, went on into the house. He heard Crowningshield's rented car start up, and then turn off—engine trouble? He was sorry for the man, and yet angry. The guy would be contacting a Realtor next, he bet, but Colm was pretty sure he wouldn't be the one called. Selling the Healing House land out from under the women. Making a bundle, no doubt. With Bagshaw in trouble, maybe Crowningshield could buy up the land next door, as well. Develop it.

Jeez, but Colm hated real estate. Why was he in it—except to walk the land, escape the mortuary? Of course, it was nice to see a young couple's faces when they signed for their first home, though he winced at the mortgage they took on their backs. Like carrying a hump around with you for thirty years. Maybe he should go back into teaching. He'd tried for a time, but the kids ran all over him. He was a patsy for any excuse: "The computer ate my paper...." Yeah, right! He'd take a test, he decided. See what career he was really suited for. In his late forties? Still living with his dad? Jeez.

He found Mac slumped over the kitchen table, stirring a cup of hot cocoa, a soggy marshmallow in the middle. There were a couple of half-smoked cigarettes in an ashtray. The old man squinted up at Colm with a sly smile.

Colm decided not to scold. Anyway, he still had Crowningshield on his mind. "Ever seen that guy before? The one who just walked out the door? Ever see him back when you lived here?" He looked out the window. The man had the hood up, was peering in at the engine.

Mac shrugged. "Looks slightly familiar. Might have seen him around town sometime. Not around here, though."

"Killian Precision ring a bell? Got any more of those marshmallows?" Then he put a hand on his belly. He didn't need them. He slid into a chair across from Mac.

Mac thought a while, slurped his cocoa. "Couple guys I knew worked there, one of the Bagshaws, I think." And when Colm looked interested, Mac added, "I said, I think. *Think.* I don't *know.* Now let's get back to me. You got me; I give up. I can't run anymore. You wanna tell the police I killed that guy in the hole? I'm yours. I need a long nap."

"I don't *want* to tell them anything, Mac. I just want them to know you're alive. So Glenna won't be a suspect."

"If she's not a suspect, then I am. Ever think of that, buddy? I ran off—somebody put that guy in the hole. They'll point the finger at me, right?"

"If you didn't do it, you don't have to worry."

"Oh, I have to worry all right," said Mac, brooding into his cocoa. His whiskers dipped into the cup and came up brown.

"One of the Bagshaws worked at Killian Precision. Do you recall when?"

"Hell, I don't know. Time passes. It blurs. You can find out if you go there."

"It's no longer in operation."

"So? There are ways. I don't have to tell you; you're a—"

"Pseudodetective," Colm interrupted. That was his career now. Pseudodetective. Jeez.

Mac laughed, a wheezing sound that spit out cocoa onto the vinyl tablecloth.

Fay would be glad when Mac left, he bet. She wouldn't get any rent out of *him*. He heard her upstairs, running a vacuum.

Mac was looking serious again. "I saw him in Alibi—that's where I saw him. Younger version, of course."

"Who?"

"That guy who just left, Crown something. You asked me, right? He got in a fight, yeah, fisticuffs. Bartender had to heave the two of 'em outta there. It was a good one." He smiled at some image he was projecting on the white wall.

"Two? Who was the other? What was the fight about?"

"How the hell do I know?"

"Who was the other? I asked."

"Oh. Well, I think—one of the Bagshaws, the womanizer, that one. Maybe that's what the fight was over, a woman. Most likely."

"That's all you know? You don't remember when, or what they said to each other?"

Mac sighed, swallowed his marshmallow. Colm watched it lump its way down through his throat. Then he said, "It was just before I left. Month or so maybe, I don't know. Couple of weeks. Then that guy, that Bagshaw—he came here to the farm."

"Go on."

Mac stood up suddenly, spilling the cocoa. "Nothing, just nothing. Had business here, that's all, I guess. He sold fertilizer or something. That's all I know. I'm sick of answering questions. If we're going downtown, let's go. Get it over with. Show 'em I'm me, Mac MacInnis. Do I have to take out my teeth? Prove to 'em Glenna didn't kill me?"

"Hopefully, it will help Glenna."

"Yeah, hopefully," Mac said, his face a mask, and snatching a dark red cardigan sweater from the back of the chair, sighing loudly, he plodded to the door. "Let's get it over with, okay?" He pulled out a cigarette. "I need a nap."

CHIEF FALLON sat back in his swivel chair, unfolded a banana. Bananas contained fiber, iron, he told Colm; his chiropractor advised him to eat them. For one thing, he had a bad back: "Last week, I put something, um, out. The wife finds me flat on the floor—I can't move. I have to crawl to the, um—"

Colm repeated his request to see Alwyn Bagshaw, and finally Fallon sent him over to the jail, where they were holding the man. "Sure, ask away. And good luck. We can't get anything out of the son of a gun. He just raves on about some Antichrist. We got him a lawyer, but now the guy's telling him to plead not guilty. When we've got him against the wall. He's guilty as hell of offing those birds. That's crime enough around here. Wait till the Audubon Society gets hold of that one. Poisoning birds."

"What about those women? Angie Crowningshield? Two others with traces of it in their systems? Lucky for them we found out when we did."

"You got a point there," Fallon said. "You got a point." And as Colm left the office, he yelled, "That Flint woman, he swears he left her at the convenience store. The clerk says he never saw her. I got a man interviewing the neighbors. Okay, see if you think Bagshaw's telling the truth. He's senile, a little nuts. Raves on about some Annie, says she ruined him. There was an Annie, someone he went with back when. One of our detectives checked on it. She lives in California now. Alive and well, right? Hasn't seen old Bagshaw for twenny years. The old man lives in the past. So go, um, ask... At least your man MacInnis has his act together. If it really *is* old Mac." He grinned. "I've got him on hold here until..."

Colm shut the door on the rest of the sentence. He was concerned about Mac, and Glenna, too, yes, but obsessed—he had to admit it—with Kevin Crowningshield. With unanswered questions, like Denby Bagshaw's relationship with Crowningshield. Why would Crowningshield want to stay at the Flint place, a marginal farm? He had money, so why not stay at the inn? Was there some reason behind that? Nothing obvious—yet. Colm just wanted to know some things, that's all.

Though Fallon was right. Bagshaw just rambled on, raving about the Healing House. "It ain't right; it ain't normal," he whined at Colm. "Them women, prancing about half-naked. I don't hold with that. Where's the men? You tell me where's the men? Woman needs a man to keep her down. Like Annie... But I fooled her. I fooled Annie.''

"I want to know about your brother," Colm interrupted. He started up the small recorder in his pocket. Hoped the battery worked. Colm wasn't very good with machines. Of course, it wasn't an official interview. "Denby. He worked at Killian Precision?"

Alwyn slitted his eyes. "Why you want to know that for?"

"He drowned," Colm said. "Back in '75, it was in the *Independent*. I looked up an old copy. Wasn't that a bit odd? I mean, just the year before, he dove off the rock at the quarry and landed on some woman, half-drowned *her*. That was in the papers, too. Would he dive off if he couldn't swim?"

Alwyn considered, ran a hand through his white hairs. Colm noticed that his left middle finger stuck up, like he was always giving someone the finger. In a way, it was true. "Yep, yep, he could swim all right. But his truck couldn't. He drowned in his truck. Body floated off into the lake. Try dredging up that big lake?"

"You know Glenna Flint's husband, Mac?"

"Maybe I do." Alwyn slumped back on the bench. "Well, he's dead. Buried in that hole. Sure. Look, I'm tired. I got problems. Police took me outta my home. They can't do that. A man's got a right to his privacy. Get me outta here!" He stretched out a hand. The backs looked clawed, like bird feet.

"You didn't think of those women's rights, did you? When you burned those birds? Buried what was left in that garden?"

"It was my property. I got a deed, too. It's in my closet. If they let me out, I'll show 'em. They got no right coming on my property."

"It was *half* your property; we have a deed from next door." Colm was guessing. He needed time to go check on Crowningshield's deed. He'd go after this interview. "Some of the bird remains were on the, um, Crowningshield property." It was a nice lead-in. "Ever seen him before? Kevin Crowningshield? He was the dead woman's husband. He owns the property now. So he says." Colm held a photo under Bagshaw's nose. Fay had taken it, smart lady.

"No."

"Denby knew him, though. They both worked at Killian Precision. In the same year. Then Denby was fired. Why was that?"

Alwyn burst out laughing. It sounded like a rooster crowing. "He got that woman knocked up, that's why. She worked there. She come round to the house once. Looking for him, wanting him to marry her, that's what Denby said." He exploded with laughter. "Denby, he wasn't the marrying kind. He just took what he needed. Didn't need no wedding ring. Took 'em and then throwed 'em off." He looked angry now, jumped up and grabbed Colm's shoulders. "You son of a bitch, you bastard, you took my Annie. You ruined her. You got ever'thing you ever wanted. You just took it, you—"

Colm grabbed Alwyn's shirt. It was worn from washing, and a button shot off. Something gold shone through. It was a ring, on a thin chain. He pulled it out. A ring with a bone crossed with an arrow. "Where'd you get this?" he yelled.

But Alwyn was hollering now about the devil, spitting as he harangued; he shoved Colm's hand back. Colm gave up the questioning. He'd heard what he wanted anyway. He'd seen what he wanted. He knew now whose skeleton was in that hole. What he didn't know was who had buried it there.

But they'd want proof. More dental work, more X rays. Jeez. More dentists. Let Fallon handle it this time, some other full-time cop.

Now Colm was the one bedeviled. He blew on his glasses to clean them—where Alwyn had spit—but he only smudged them more. He called the guard to release him, walked out with skewed vision.

EUSTACIA HAD a bull calf. In the end, it shot out, like a rush of toothpaste you'd almost given up trying to squeeze. Eustacia rolled the calf over, licking it. She'd be one of the good mothers. But a bull calf would have to be sold, fattened up and eaten, unless it was used for stud—and how many bulls did the cow population need? Now if this happened to humans... Interesting concept, but rather dull, Ruth thought, considering Colm. A dull world without Colm. Without Kevin? But Kevin was leaving, just for an overnight; he'd left a message on her answering machine, apologizing about being unable to keep their date for a drink. He'd been cleaning up loose ends, seeing a Realtor about the Healing House land. He was short of cash, he'd said, and he needed to sell the land. Well, it was his business. Though Colm would make something big out of it. It had been kind of nice, actually, having two men around.

"Come on, Ruth," she said aloud. Kevin had loved his wife. He wasn't interested in Ruth. Was he? He was a handsome man, though. Strong square chin, those penetrating eyes—a warm chocolate color. They kept changing somehow, brown to black.

She needed a little healing herself after the ordeal with Eustacia. She'd go see Isis, see how the rest of the women were faring, now that they'd got the poison greens out of their systems, the rest of the "garden" pulled up, taped off by the police. She'd see what herbs she should be taking. Sharon had told her how important folic acid was. "You should take it, Mother, along with vitamin C. For an older woman..." She was, yes. Menopause just around the corner. Then what?

So. She'd look at that ill-fated garden again, determine, if she could, whose property it was on. That wouldn't violate the police ordinance, would it? Look in on Bagshaw's cat. The cat wasn't to blame for his shenanigans. She hoped it wasn't locked up inside— it probably didn't have a litter box.

At the Healing House, Isis said that Ruth needed a massage. She told Ruth that she could see the tension in Ruth's neck, in the tight way she held her shoulders. She offered to do the massage for free, assuring Ruth that she could do it from a wheelchair: "Nothing is impossible!" she said. Her arms were steely; she was working out with weights. Even before her accident, she had sat on a chair-on-wheels for the head and neck work. Ruth had been a help to her, she said. And she told Ruth that she, Isis, had been a suspect— questioned "to the point of exhaustion" by the police.

Ruth said, "I'm sorry, but you know the police had to question everyone involved. "And I *will* get a massage," she promised. "As soon as I have a minute for myself." When would that be? she wondered.

"That's the problem here, for all these women," Isis said, nodding her dark head vigorously. "They've never taken time for themselves. It's all gone into children, husbands, jobs, lovers—and how do they get repaid?"

Rena, standing in the doorway in a long rayon print skirt, her hair lank about her shoulders, burst into tears. Isis wheeled over to her, put an arm around the young woman's waist. "It's all right, dear. It's okay to be yourself," she soothed. And Rena, just back from the hospital, smiled through her tears. "I keep getting reminded, that's all, when you mention—you know."

"I'm trying to make her face what's happened," Isis confided to Ruth out on the porch. "With her stepfather, as well as the husband. Make her talk it out, break the silence, you know. That's when the healing begins."

Ruth could smell the piney incense even out on the porch; it was in Isis's hair. She supposed it relaxed the patient during a massage. Did they make an incense that smelled of hay? "You should try it, the massage," Isis repeated as Ruth descended the steps, and Ruth said, "Maybe I will. I'll call you."

"Do you think he'll sell it? This house, this property?" Isis called after her. Her face was suddenly a downhill slope. "Is there a will? I mean, Angie wanted this place to continue; she might have seen to that."

A will, Ruth thought. Kevin had said nothing about a will. After all, Angie'd been in her forties; she'd have thought there were years still to think about a will. Though she'd had that blood problem. She might have made a will. Might have stipulated that the place be kept as a healing center. Might even have left it to Isis. Who knew? After all, she'd left her husband. Ruth made a mental note to speak to Kevin.

The Bagshaw house looked dark—not just because of the peeling paint but also because of the windows, their heavy green shades. She imagined Alwyn and his old mother down through the years, huddled inside, peering out the raggedy corners at the world. She didn't have a warrant, or whatever it was you needed. She just wanted to see for herself—what? Well, the cat, of course, but something else, too. Something dark that had been hiding in the back of her mind since the discovery that the tire prints matched up: Bagshaw's, and the prints on the mountain road. They had Bagshaw; the police had already searched the house. Something more extensive was in the works. They clung to the idea that Glenna was out there—somewhere. Fallon doubted they'd find her alive; he'd made that clear.

It was odd that the store clerk where Alwyn had reportedly dropped Glenna off hadn't seen her. Surely she would go in for some reason—chewing gum for relaxation, a chocolate bar for energy. Glenna loved chocolate. Ruth had made her a chocolate cake once, for her birthday. Glenna would be exhausted after all her comings and goings. Oh, those adolescent girls! They felt themselves invincible, thought others should be, too. A woman of eighty—or thereabouts.

Something rubbed against her right leg, and she jumped, then smiled. It was the cat, a mangy-looking beast, but alive, purring: a spindly-tailed tiger. Wanting food. She ran back to her car, brought out the bag of Meow Mix she'd brought for it. But she had forgotten to bring a dish. She rummaged around on the front porch, then the back porch, but found only old newspapers, rusted chairs, a watering can minus its nozzle. The cat was crying for food now, and she dumped a little on the ground; the animal attacked it voraciously. She'd leave the rest with Isis, let one of the women next door come over to feed it as long as Alwyn was in custody. How long would that be? His was a serious offense: not first-degree murder, maybe not even second-degree. But they might call it manslaughter.

And what about the birds? Vic's hawk? That crow? How many other birds might have died in the chain of poison?

She walked around to the back, where the metal cellar doors jutted up out of the ground; she yanked on them. They gave a little, then banged back down again—rusted out. They hadn't been opened in years, most likely. She tried them again; this time, they came up a foot before they clanged back. She thought she heard something down there, a cry, a whistle. But she realized it must have been birds overhead in the tamarack tree. Chickadees—sweet-faced little fellows they were, with those soft-looking brownish feathers and the coy black cap. She yanked again, but no luck.

She walked back to the Healing House with the bag of dried cat food, knocked on the back door. Marna opened the door warily, a kitchen knife in her hand. She put it down when she saw Ruth. "I'm sorry, but I'm paranoid," she said. But she was pleased to hear about the cat. "Oh, I love cats. I've been trying to convince

Isis. But one of the women here is allergic to animal fur. I'll go over right now and make friends. Would you come with me?"

She sounded apologetic, but Ruth smiled. Anyway, it might be that with two of them tugging on the cellar doors...

She had to wait while Marna hugged the cat. "I adore tiger cats. I had one at home I fed. Used to let it in the house when my husband wasn't home. But he was fatter than this one. This little guy needs food. He needs love. Kitty kitty kitty? What's his name?"

"I'm sure he'll answer to any name you want to give him—just as long you have food." Ruth went back over to yank on the doors. They almost gave.

"You want to open that?" asked Marna, her eyes huge and filled with the sun that was already dropping behind the mountain peaks. "Isn't that...trespassing?"

Ruth explained about Glenna. "Oh, she's probably not here at all; the police have looked, after all. It's just that...well, Alwyn Bagshaw had evidently picked her up that time—I mean, he admitted that, said he left her at the store—and then she disappeared again. She didn't go home; that's where we'd expect her to be. So..."

Marna crouched down on her heels beside Ruth; together, they pulled, heaved, giggled, pulled again—and the doors swung open, throwing them off their feet. Marna thought she'd let Ruth enter alone. "Though call if you really need me," she said, and Ruth nodded. The basement was musty, dark, and dank; something skittered across her path as she reached the bottom step. She saw stacks of old wood and logs for the woodstove, a rusted bedspring, piles of rags, an ancient mower, but no Glenna.

The window was broken; shards of glass lay on the floor below. She hadn't noticed from the outside—all those thick vines growing everywhere. There's nothing unusual about a broken window, she told herself. She was about to leave, when she noticed a part of the wall slightly askew. Only it wasn't a wall at all, she discovered when she drew closer, but a gray door, made to look as though it were part of the cement wall. It was slightly ajar. She pushed through and, to her surprise, discovered a small room, filled with wood piled up in tiers, and in the far corner, something that looked like a mattress, with clothing heaped on it. She went closer, her heart drumming; and knelt down.

But it was just that, a heap of old clothing, a cup of spilled cocoa, a stained black sweater—a woman's sweater. She was outraged to see it.... But no Glenna.

She went back to the broken window. A rusted hammer lay on the floor below. The window was hardly big enough for someone larger than a child to get through.

"But Glenna did it—she must have; she's wiry," Ruth said aloud, and Marna called down, "What? Did what?"

"Got out! Maybe after they came for Alwyn," Ruth shouted, a little dizzy now with this revelation. "Only Glenna didn't know that."

"But you said the police searched the house."

"That was right after they took Alwyn. If that door was shut, they wouldn't have noticed there was another room."

"Where is she, then?" Marna shouted. "Why didn't she come to us, next door?"

And that, Ruth couldn't answer.

EIGHTEEN

THE POLICE CHIEF was getting his kicks—you bet your britches he was, the way he kept grinning, asking damn fool questions, repeating them even after Mac had replied. Who'd he think Mac was, some ignorant clod? When Mac was a journalist, he had at least three articles published, one in the *New York Times* itself—well, so it *was* a letter to the editor. But they printed it. The fifties it was, that Communist uproar, that McCarthy. Mac hated that SOB. Couple of his buddies in theater, indicted, summoned to Washington, made fools of. And all because they were artists. Like Mac. Could have been anyway—he just didn't get his share of old lady luck.

"And you admit you were quarreling, you and Glenna," the chief said. "The day you, um, disappeared."

"I just told you. Yeah, yeah, yeah. We were quarreling."

The chief folded his hands patiently, as if praying. "And what was this quarrel about?"

"Oh, come on, it was twenty years ago. Maybe more—I don't know. Ancient history."

"Was the quarrel over another man?"

"I just told you that I—yeah, well, I guess, come to think of it, it was. One of the Bagshaws, I think, fertilizer salesman—or was. The milk tester. Testing more than milk. I don't know which—They looked alike. Both with that spiky yellow-gray hair."

"That would be Alwyn; he was a milk tester. Denby sold fertilizer—for a time at least. At that time, anyway."

"I thought he worked for that place up in Argennes—made parts for war planes."

"Oh, he did, yes indeed, he did, but he was fired. Um, over a woman, I'm told."

Mac smiled. "That's what the fight was about, then."

"Fight? Another one?"

"In the Alibi. I told that guy about it, the one who got me up here. Hanna."

"Colm Hanna."

"Okay. I don't remember names anymore. They escape. You know how it is."

The chief rocked back in his chair; Mac heard the tape recorder whirring. He hated being recorded. Not when he couldn't play it back, change it if he didn't like what he'd said. That's what he liked about writing things down. You could make changes. Revise.

"So Alwyn Bagshaw was, um, making out with your wife?"

"He was, yeah." Mac remembered things clearly now. Some things stayed in your head, the big events. They'd argued and Glenna came at him with a shovel—or was it a pitchfork?—and he left. Got madder, though, sitting in the house, went back out. He'd walked in the barn—and she wasn't alone. She was on her back in the hay, yelling—well, she always yelled when they made love; Glenna was a yeller. Bagshaw on top of her, pants down to his knees, the cows bellowing like they were getting it, too. That was the clear part, the visual, brilliant in his mind, like a film running backward, then forward again. After that, things got shadowy. Mac grabbing Bagshaw by the churning legs, Bagshaw furious, Glenna lying there. Mac smaller than the other, but with the upper hand. Grabbed a shovel, hit him on the head, again and again, till he was quiet.

"It was self-defense," he told Fallon. "He would have killed me. Then Glenna—"

Fallon leaned forward, his upper teeth swallowing his lower lip, although he was still smiling. But he was excited; Mac sensed it. "Then Glenna," he urged.

"Glenna was hitting me. I called her a whore, a bitch. She didn't like that; she was mad—I'd interrupted her lovemaking. Bagshaw, that ugly idiot! What'd she see in a moron like that?" He smeared his palm across his forehead, and it came off wet; he could smell his own sweat.

"And Bagshaw—Alwyn, you think, was lying on the barn floor. To all, um, appearances...dead."

"Bleeding, yeah."

"Did Glenna go to him? Try to help? Call an ambulance?"

"She was fighting me, I told you. She had that shovel, or pitchfork. She chased me out of the barn. I ran. I kept running. I left most of my stuff behind—just grabbed my typewriter. The old lady was there in the kitchen—Glenna's mother. I remember her coming at me with a steaming kettle, had to push her off. I had a taxi waiting. Man, I left.''

"Knowing you'd killed Alwyn Bagshaw.''

"Thinking that, yeah. But he would have killed me.''

"Undoubtedly,'' said Fallon. "Interview ended,'' he said, sounding oh so important, Mac thought. Then the chief motioned to his officer to switch off the recorder. "You can go now, Mr., uh, MacInnis. If what you told us is true, um...''

"That I killed Alwyn Bagshaw?''

"That you didn't kill him, yes. You see''—Fallon cleared his throat importantly— "Alwyn Bagshaw is alive and in prison!'' He looked into Mac's face to see the effect of his words. Mac looked away. "For destroying birds with illegal poison, with contributing to the demise of a, um, neighbor woman. Of course...''

Mac waited. He was confused now; his memory was leaping about: from Glenna to Bagshaw, from Vermont to New York City, then to the retired journalists' home Hanna had routed him out of. He'd never complain about the food again if he could just go back there—get out of this confounded cow country. He'd been a fool, taking a ride from that woman—May or Fay, or whatever her name was.

"Of course,'' the chief continued, with the air of one about to play a trump card, "it might not have been Alwyn you struck. It might have been his brother, Denby. In which case, any way you look at it, it was, um, mur-der.''

Mac slumped in his chair, ran his fingers through his sparse hair. He wanted to go home. Home to New York City. Home even to those sons of bitches in the journalists' home. His eyes overflowed. He hated that, hated it. A man slobbering. He rubbed his cheeks with a sweaty hand, blew his nose into a blue Kleenex Fallon handed him.

"In which case, um, you'd better stick around,'' Fallon finished. And with his left hand, he picked up the phone that had been urgently ringing.

"Fallon,'' he said in his gruffest voice, then sighed when he heard who it was.

"Ms. Willmarth," he said, tilting his head to one side like he'd fall asleep any minute in his chair, "and what is it now, ma'am?"

"I DON'T KNOW how long she's been gone," Ruth told Chief Fallon. "But it's only been a matter of hours since you picked up Alwyn Bagshaw. And my guess is she only recently left. If you had only—" She stopped midsentence; there was no use provoking the man. What was done couldn't be undone. Where had she read that?

"Mmm," said Fallon.

"Please! get the Scouts, get out the Four-H, the firemen, the schoolchildren. Start the search in East Branbury. And check that cocoa—there might have been a sedative in it. Glenna could have fallen asleep somewhere, after she left—who knows? She's probably disoriented, at any rate. She could freeze to death. Roy, they're calling for a frost tonight."

"Is that so," said Fallon.

"You'll do it, then!" she shouted.

"I'm head of police, aren't I?" was Fallon's noncommittal response, and finally she hung up the barn phone, breathing hard. What more could she do? She had to have faith in the police. She had to get to the cows. They didn't care about a missing woman. Self-absorbed creatures! Suddenly, she was angry, angry at Bagshaw for lying about Glenna, angry at Fallon for his laid-back stance. Angry at the cows for just being cows. Angry at the world for being what it was: imperfect. Imperfect! When she needed a world in order, a world to hurl her own imperfections against, a world that would show her how to mend her ways, her life.

But the world wasn't perfect. And all her machinations, all her efforts to improve it were small and foolish. She might as well go grain the cows.

She suddenly felt trapped in this barn with its ribbed tin ceiling, the strung power lines, the windows dirty and hung with cobwebs, the central aisle a pool of dung and urine-soaked sawdust. The cows consumed the grain, poking out their tongues to clean up the last bit, then slop up the liquid from their water cups. That done, she went back to the barn phone to return a call from Colm; he'd left an "urgent" message on her kitchen machine. She apologized for not getting right back; the cows had urgent needs, too, she told him.

She told about Glenna, and he said he already knew. Fallon was giving one of his men hell for not finding that second cellar room.

"Look, Ruthie, she's a tough old bird; she'll survive—if she has to this point. Alwyn Bagshaw's in jail. I doubt he really meant to hurt her in the first place. He was just...well, confused. Not that that exonerates him! It was a devilish thing to do. But Glenna'll be all right. Probably walk into the Flint farm any minute. Or someone will recognize her, take her there."

"We hope," said Ruth, who couldn't always share Colm's optimism.

But Colm had something else on his mind. It was a rather delicate matter.

"Say it, friend. I have to get back to work. I want to see how the new bull calf is doing. We need the money for him, and he's kind of poorly."

"Just an hour, that's all. I need a woman. I mean, it's better if a woman does this. She'd be more open with you."

"Okay. You've buttered me up. Now what is it?"

He explained about the woman from Killian Precision, the one Denby Bagshaw got pregnant. He needed Ruth to talk to her, woman-to-woman, find out what really happened.

"Not that again. Not Killian Precision. Can't you let sleeping dogs lie? What has this to do with Denby's murder?" She had been thrilled, actually, when Colm told her that the rings matched: Alwyn's and the one on the skeleton's finger; that the police were doing a DNA analysis now—they had discovered a lock of Denby's hair his mother had kept in a small frame on a living room shelf. Amazing, she thought—DNA from a lock of baby hair! But what all this had to do with Kevin Crowningshield, she didn't know. Or want to know. The man had gone through enough.

Colm was playing possum, of course. She imagined him at his Realtor's desk, leaning back in his chair, glasses down on his slightly hooked nose, grinning. She could hear the grin in his voice. He was so transparent. (Oh, she was bitter tonight.) "Probably nothing at all, Ruthie. But you have to look at everything. You know, there might be a link. This woman could have been pissed off enough to stick a pitchfork—uh, arrowhead into the guy. Could have seen his truck, whirled in, killed him—and run."

"Then how did his truck get in the creek? If she was a pregnant woman, she wouldn't have that kind of strength."

"Who knows? She might give us a clue. Get Mac off the hook. They're holding Mac, Ruth. I've grown fond of the old bastard— that's why I'm doing this. You want Mac in for life? What's left of it?"

She rubbed her neck—something landing on her—a cluster fly. She knew that he knew that she'd do it. He was a devious one, Colm Hanna. "So what's this woman's name? Where does she live?" She pulled a pencil out of her jeans pocket to write it down. She couldn't remember anything these days without writing it down. She was definitely entering menopause. Memory loss was one of the symptoms.

Two hours later, maybe three, after giving Vic his good-night hug, after helping Emily with her history project, after a long conversation with Sharon, whose husband, Jack, had postponed his homecoming from Alaska one more week—some research he absolutely couldn't put off, the phone rang again. This time, it was Fay. She'd just heard about Glenna's second disappearance. "I mean, it *seems* a second one, Ruth—Jesus, I'd almost given up. So Hartley and Willard and I are joining the search. I just thought I'd tell you, in case you hear anything. Hartley has a cell phone; she bought it today with her credit card. You can call us, wherever we are—isn't that incredible?" She gave Ruth a number, hung up.

Ruth slumped down beside the new bull calf. Next week, a truck was coming for it; it would be turned into someone's dinner. It looked so vulnerable, its huge brown eyes gazing up at her. Those spindly calf legs.

But tonight she'd give it a little food, a little affection. At least it didn't know what was coming—the difference between beast and human. Though there were ways to live each day; Isis had told her that; and Sharon, too, who'd discovered some Zen center up in Shelburne.

One hour could equal one year, according to Sharon. Everything was relative.

"Poor baby," she said, stroking the bull calf. "Poor baby."

NINETEEN

RUTH GOT all the way over to the woman's house the next morning—Emma Stackpole was her name—and realized she had on her smelly boots. She worked so much in manure, she hardly smelled it anymore, but other people would. Especially the woman who lived in this pristine white house with the cute sign: STACKPOLE'S, HOME OF EMMA, WILLIAM, RACHEL, PAUL, HEATHER, WANDA, SUE. FOUNDED A.D. 1978. Which one of these, she wondered, was Denby's?

She was greeted at the door by a small dark-skinned girl, who announced that she was Wanda. Her mother was out back in the garden. Would the lady she said—staring at Ruth's boots—please sit down? She indicated a small side room with a sofa done in sturdy brown corduroy and several black vinyl chairs with end tables piled high with women's and kids' magazines. It looked more like a dentist's waiting room than a living room.

Ruth picked up a copy of *Good Housekeeping*—it was a year old—then set it back down again when two more children, older than the first, peered in. One was obviously of African descent, a rich dark brown skin; the other looked Chinese. "Hi," she said, and they disappeared. A moment later, a plump woman of fifty or so entered, a basket of ripe red tomatoes in her arms. Ruth was surprised. Her own garden had long since frozen, except for the brussels sprouts she hadn't had time to harvest. She wondered what would happen if she left them till spring. "You haven't had a frost here?" she asked.

"Oh yes," Emma said, squatting on a stool, arranging the tomatoes at her plump feet—for plump was the word to describe her: cheeks, face, body, knees. Pink and plump and pretty, Ruth thought—full of dimples, even in the knees. "But I hang the vines upside down in the greenhouse. The tomatoes keep coming. Here. Take three or four; I've plenty. Wanda, get a bag for the lady."

"A greenhouse. I've always wanted one. Probably never will."
Ruth felt an affinity with this plump tomato woman.

"Why not? I bought mine prefab. They're easy to assemble."

"If you have a handy husband."

"If you have an older son with handy know-how."

"The oldest is?" asked Ruth, making an opening, then explained
why she was there.

"Oh," said Emma, shifting back into the chair above the stool.
"I thought you were here for the cancer drive. That's what Heather
said when she took the message. I'm supposed to help. They were
sending someone around this morning to show me how and what."

"Sorry. But this is important. It has to do with a man we've just
discovered in a hole. I mean, he's been long dead. I understand you
knew him when you worked at Killian Precision. We're trying to
find his murderer. Any help you can give..."

Emma cried out, and three children came running to surround
her.

"Not you—no one's accusing you," Ruth cried over the hubbub,
fearing she'd blown this mission already. One of the children stood
guard at Emma's side, the Chinese one; the others stared at her
accusingly.

"Someone has already confessed to it. But we think someone
else did it—we don't know who; we're just looking for a motive.
We thought you could help us, tell us what you know about Denby
Bagshaw."

Emma calmed down, her plump cheeks finally going still. In her
upset, she'd squeezed a tomato; it oozed out onto her flowered
apron. She hugged the Asian girl fiercely to her breast. "These are
all mine," she said. "Adopted, or foster children. I have six now,
though the oldest is away at the university."

"The oldest—He isn't yours? We heard, you see, that you were
pregnant by someone, that he refused any responsibility..."

Now the blood was up in Emma's cheeks. Wanda brought in the
bag for Ruth's tomatoes, then climbed into her mother's lap, and
Emma buried her chin in the girl's frizzy black braids.

"You could help us so much, Ms. Stackpole," said Ruth. "I
promise anything you say will *not* go beyond our ears."

"Oh, people knew," the woman burst out; then, aware of the

children, she shooed them out of the room. "That's what was so hard. And I thought we'd marry—that's what he said. That's what he said before we—when we..."

"When you . . ."

"But then he wanted me to get"—she whispered the word—"an abortion. I'm Catholic, Mrs.—"

"Willmarth, Ruth Willmarth. Please call me Ruth."

"Mrs. Willmarth. Aborting a child, I felt I couldn't do that. When I found I was pregnant, I was so glad. I mean, we'd planned to marry, I thought—he said so. But when he said he wanted—you know—he'd pay he said, he had the money—I said no money in the whole wide world can make up for a lost child. I wanted that child. I was already thirty, Mrs.—"

"Willmarth."

"Mrs. Willmarth. I'd turned down two other men. Two! Because of Kevin..."

"Because of—" Ruth felt her heart flip into her boots. Kevin, the woman had said. Kevin? "You mean Denby," Ruth said. Of course she did; the woman was just confused, "Denby Bagshaw."

"Oh, no, not *him*. He came around—oh, yes, he did—but I kept him off all right. Oh, you thought... No, I'd never have let Denby Bagshaw touch me. Why, he was after every woman in the place; he was just a janitor. He drank! I don't know what else. All the secretaries, every lunch hour they'd talk about ways to keep him off. He actually got a receptionist pregnant. Oh no. No. It was Kevin I wanted. Kevin Crowningshield. I loved him, Mrs. Willmarth. He was the first man I really, truly loved, you see. You never forget that; you never lose touch with that first love. I still have those letters, even the cruel ones."

Ruth felt the tomatoes she held ooze into her lap. She couldn't seem to unclench her fists, let the tomatoes go. Her fingers were stiff, like pencils. Kevin Crowningshield. Was Colm right, then, in his suspicions? She felt a little dizzy, her breathing raggedy.

But what would Kevin Crowningshield have to do with a long-ago murder? What did he have to do with Denby? Denby was a janitor at Killian, Kevin a researcher, or fund-raiser, or something more white-collar. What would they have had in common to talk about?

She took a deep-down breath, and then another. Why was this turn of events affecting her like this? She had to keep calm!

"You had the child, then?" She waited for an answer. Wanda came back in the room and she let the girl put Ruth's bruised tomatoes into the bag, then sent the child off again. "Go see if the kitty wants food, sweetheart."

"I had the abortion. In the fourth month. It was dangerous, but I had my job to think about now, my reputation—though everyone at work knew. He'd left town; he got engaged to another woman, but he kept sending money. He'd support me if I wanted it, he said. But why would I want Kevin's child without Kevin? I was angry then, you see. Furious! And so guilty. I stopped going to church. I couldn't face the priest." She twisted her hands in her lap; her joints looked broken. "It was legal then," she reminded Ruth, as if Ruth were the law. "Abortion had been legal for a few years. After that—"

"You married?"

"Yes. But he died; he was an older man. He knew about the—you know—he understood. He was a good man. We started adopting. But then nine years ago, he died. I still have the children. Six of them. Starting with Billy, in college now. I mean, the youngest three are foster children. They won't let me adopt now, at my age...without a man." A pair of laughing children raced through the room and she looked after them, her palms upturned in her lap, as though she'd lost something but didn't know exactly what it was.

"That's all I can tell you," she went on. "I don't know much about Denby Bagshaw. He came around, that's all, before I was married. Asking questions about Kevin. He said he saw me and Kevin together. I didn't believe him. I let on it was someone out of town." She stared at her empty lap.

"Thank you," Ruth said. "Thank you so much, Emma. You have a beautiful family here. You've been lucky in many ways, haven't you?"

"Oh yes," Emma said, jumping up, a tomato rolling out of her apron and onto the floor. "I've been lucky. My husband was a good man. I have good children—most of the time." And she smiled as Wanda came in, holding a kitten by its stomach. "Not that way,

Wanda; you'll hurt its little tummy. Hold it under the feet, the whole body. We have to be careful of babies."

For some reason, Ruth wanted to weep. There was that disappointment, the feeling of being betrayed somehow. Stop it, she told herself. She was just tired; she was getting her period. Five bills this morning in the mail: from the vet, Agri-Mark dues, the repair shop for the John Deere. Her life was slipping away, her farm! She wanted to sit on her own threadbare sofa and have a good cry. She thanked Emma again and ran to her pickup with the bag of tomatoes.

When she got home, the bag was leaking; it had fallen off the seat, and she'd dropped her pocketbook on top of it. What she had was tomato juice. She wiped it off her skirt, changed back into her jeans, then dialed Colm's number. But he wasn't there, so she left him a message; she listened, in turn, to a message from Fay on the answering machine—no sign yet of Glenna, but they were still searching. And a message from Pete, who'd be up in a couple of days he'd said (a reminder she didn't need: They had some "down-to-earth talking to do," he said). Then she mopped the kitchen floor—it was filthy; she'd neglected it too long. She got down on hands and knees to scrub the corners and crevices.

Then she ran out to the barn, her anger vented.

COLM FOUND RUTH squatting beside the new bull calf, her hair matted with hay. The other calves, along with Deborah, who had diarrhea, mooed in sympathy from their stalls. "You think you have problems," he said, "think of that bull calf. About to be sold as chopped liver."

"I'd keep him," she said, blowing her nose, "but they grow so fast. I can't keep a bull on this farm." Though she might have to, she realized—the artificial insemination was getting too costly. But her homegrown bull wouldn't produce the good legs, the straight flanks, the volume of milk she needed. "It's a catch-twenty-two situation," she said aloud.

"What is? Let's take a walk," he said. "Let's talk about Kevin and Denby and Mac and Glenna. Let's sort things out. Let's have a think-out. I mean, I have work to do, too, Ruthie. I have to show land, houses—even if nobody buys."

"A walk—or a think?"

"Both."

She started to follow him out—she could use a break. The bull calf bellowed in protest, and she turned back to pat him. "How can I sell this little guy?"

"Exactly my feeling, Mama," Colm said, and made a bellowing sound that was echoed by the other cows. "See? They agree with me."

"Right. You going to walk in those shoes?"

He looked down at his shiny brown Rockports, then laughed and went to his car to change into boots. She was way ahead of him by then, her heavy brown hair a tangle of wind, her denim jacket billowing out behind, revealing the back of her pink work shirt. "Hey, wait up—jeez," Colm said. "We can't talk with you running a marathon."

She looked back, smiled. She is lovely, he thought. The freckles shone on her nose. He wanted to be Gregory Peck—what was that forties film? Running into her arms. Holding her close.

But already she'd turned, hands in her pockets, as if she knew his thoughts. He could only pick his way along the uneven ground beside her. The meadow was rich with decaying leaves, waves of purple aster. Overhead another vee of geese honked south—he'd seen them every day almost. Each time, they gave him a thrill; he could almost hear the whir of the beating wings. All the honking, he'd heard, was to keep the leader going, the guy with the toughest job. How he did it, Colm didn't know; he had a terrible sense of direction himself.

"Tell me about the interview," he said. "Everything. What you thought of Emma. Was she telling the truth? Was it really Crowningshield who knocked her up?"

She told him. "I knew you'd love it. That it was Kevin." She walked on faster.

He ran to catch up. Already he was tired; he was out of shape, and his lungs felt as if they were bursting. "But if it was Kevin," he said, pacifying her, "what would that have to do with Denby's death?"

"Exactly. I've been telling you. Kevin's not a killer. He got her pregnant, okay; she was obviously a consenting partner. Though I agree: It wasn't fair if he said he'd marry her—if she's telling the truth here. But I figure he met Angie, fell in love—really in love. The old triangle. Emma loved him, but he loved Angie, didn't want to hurt Emma, but—"

"So he let her have an abortion. Pay for the abortion—no guilt, right?"

"I didn't say that. You make it sound so...so black and white. Anyway, she only had the abortion after he left with Angie. Before that, she wanted the baby. She's happy now—she made a good marriage, has all those children."

He gave up on that score. He couldn't move her: She wouldn't want to lose faith in Kevin. In a way, he'd be sorry if it was Kevin. Maybe he should cool it. She'd lost faith in Pete; that was enough for one woman.

But he had to get Mac off the hook. *If* Mac hadn't done it. "Do you think Emma was really telling the truth? Could she prove in court that Kevin was the man? Could it have been Denby after all? I mean, that's the rumor that got around."

"Oh, Denby probably started that. He loved being the Lothario. I always heard that." She stooped to pick a stem of Queen Anne's lace, still alive at the end of October. It was a warm day—you'd think time had ticked backward.

He suddenly realized what she was saying. "Meaning he'd have known she was pregnant."

"Well, it got to be obvious, right? They both worked there at Killian? Anyhow, to answer your other concern: Emma kept his letters—Kevin's. I didn't ask to see them. But she has them, she told me."

"Suppose Denby got hold of them."

"How?"

"I don't know—blackmailers have ways." He didn't know why he'd said that. He was searching for a motive, that's all.

"Whoa, man." She turned to face him, shook the lacy flower head at him. "How do we know Denby was a blackmailer? Aren't we making grand assumptions here?"

"Maybe." A vision of Kevin and Denby arguing at the Alibi bar flashed into his mind. "Maybe not. But I'd sure like to see those letters. You might have—"

"Who do you think I am!" she cried. "Some kind of snoop? Reading other people's intimate correspondence?"

"If it helps find a killer—"

He could see she didn't want to deal with that. She lunged ahead, long-legged, through the tall grasses, through an unlocked gate, into the north pasture, where the herd was grazing. He followed, got caught in the wire; it snagged his best blue corduroys. One by one, the cows turned to face him; he could swear they were laughing.

The only one who wasn't laughing was Ruth. He'd struck a vulnerable chord. He'd as good as called Kevin Crowningshield a suspect in Denby's killing. Though he had no proof. He'd have to see Emma Stackpole himself, her letters. For now, he had only hunches. But he had to make Ruth understand.

"Ruth," he cried, wrenching at the wires, "help me!"

But she was hugging a cow. *A cow.* "Zelda, honey," she said, "he's caught. Should we help him or not?"

But the cow only swung her skinny white tail, then turned and trotted away, the other beasts following. Leaving him stuck in the fence.

KEVIN WAS BACK. He was coming over. Ruth had called him. Somehow she'd felt she had to. To tell him about Emma. Didn't he have a right to know? Even as she heard his footsteps on the porch, she felt guilty, wanted to say, No, it's nothing, nothing important at all.

But here he was. "Ruth?" He seemed eager to see her. There was an urgency about him, a nervousness. Though she understood, didn't she? He'd lost his wife, *his wife*...

"I'm glad," she told him again as he sat on the edge of a chair in the shabby living room (it looked especially shabby with elegant Kevin in it: the old slumpy sofa, the humpbacked chairs, the moth-eaten carpet), "glad you're absolved. That they found the source of the poison. Can you imagine that man Alwyn Bagshaw being so careless? So irresponsible?"

He nodded, but his face was a rock. "It was my wife he murdered. I hope they give him the book. Until they brought Mac MacInnis back, I was sure—and the police were, too, I understand— Alwyn had killed his brother, too."

"You must have met Denby, Kevin? He worked at Killian Precision, too, at one time. I think it was Alwyn told me."

She thought she saw his face turn pink, but it might be the sun, slanting in through the window and reflecting off the glassed-in bookcase. "Denby? Well, yes, yes, he was a janitor, I believe. Not a very prepossessing fellow. Quite the womanizer."

"Yes." There was a silence. Her skin was flushed because of the delicacy of the subject. She couldn't bring herself to speak of Emma. Not yet. But she needed to hear the truth from Kevin, his side of the story, how he felt.

Instead, she offered him a beer, a glass of Otter Creek Ale. "They make it right here in Branbury. Try it?"

He nodded. He could use a drink. He'd been to see his lawyer; they were trying to settle Angie's estate. Too much happening at once, he said; his mind was in chaos. Her stepmother was flying to Chicago next week for the memorial service, and he dreaded seeing the woman. He was flying out again tomorrow, and so he was glad she'd called him today. The ale loosened his tongue, his feelings. "It's hard being here, where Angie and I met. You can't know what she was like. So different from city girls, so refreshing—unsophisticated. She had dark brown hair, like yours—reddish highlights; she was lovely." He looked at Ruth. She felt a spasm in her cheek, covered it with a hand. "She was brought up on a farm. Like you, Ruth."

"Actually, I wasn't." She had to establish a difference. "My parents lived in town; Dad was an accountant, Mother a housewife, like most women in those days. I moved here when I married Pete. Grew to like it—I surprised myself."

"Pete doesn't know how lucky he was," he murmured, looking hard at her. "Ruth, I...I want to keep in touch."

She blushed under his gaze, had to turn the tables, talk about him—that was her purpose in bringing him here. She thought of Isis. She'd promised herself to speak to Kevin about the Healing House. It would put off the subject of Emma Stackpole for a bit. "That Healing House, Kevin. People get the wrong idea—anything offbeat, you know, people are suspicious. I'm sure Isis would make a good renter, pay what you ask. If you'd let her stay on."

"Ruth, times are hard; my investments haven't been working out the way they should. I've made arrangements with a Realtor."

"Colm Hanna?"

He gave a half laugh. "Coldwell Banker—they're the biggest outfit around. They hustle. They already have someone interested." He turned the glass in his hands, appeared to be polishing it. "Besides, you may not understand, but—look, Ruth, Angie died there. They could have called a doctor sooner; they never let me in so I could—Ruth, she might have lived if they'd let me see her. I'll never"—his lips tightened—"never forgive them for that."

She nodded. Although Angie herself had ostracized him. But this wasn't the time to bring that up again. The silence was almost palpable. In a minute, she'd scream.

"Did Angie make a will?" She had to break the silence. "Anything that would keep you from selling?"

"Is that why you called me? What you wanted to talk to me about?" His flat voice shattered her nerves.

"No, no, I just happened to think of it now."

"Oh, there was no will," he assured her. "She was only in her forties." He sounded condescending. But Ruth was in deep now. It was time for the real subject: Emma.

"When you worked at Killian," she said slowly, "you knew a young woman named Emma Stackpole?" She glanced at him, saw his hands tighten on the glass. "I happened to meet her—asking about Denby Bagshaw, you see. I mean, we'd just discovered it was Denby in that hole...."

"Go on," he said. "You happened to meet her. Or you went deliberately to meet her?" His words dropped like crushed stones. But she had to get it out now.

"Yes. I went deliberately to meet her. To talk about Denby. The word was that Denby had gotten a young woman pregnant—and we thought it might have been Emma. He bragged about it around town. It was shortly before he died."

"And what did she say—when you asked her? She's married now, I believe," he said, as though he'd postpone the answer to the first question.

"Her husband died several years ago. She takes in foster children."

"She's content, then; she likes children."

She looked carefully at him. His face was expressionless, but he was watching her intently. "It was you who got her pregnant, Kevin. You offered to pay for an abortion."

His face suddenly leapt to life. He buried it in his hands. "I tried. It was for her sake. I—I couldn't marry her, Ruth. I'd met Angie, you see. After that, there was no one else. It would have been heartless to marry her, loving someone else."

Ruth sank back in her wing-back chair. It had a bad leg because Vic had jumped on it once; it rocked a little with her weight. She felt seasick, but relieved at the same time. "Of course, Kevin, I realize that. You'd met Angie, fallen in love, that was why—I told Colm."

His face hardened again. "What does *he* have to do with it?"

"He's helping Chief Fallon, you see—a kind of moonlighting job? He and I are trying to find Denby's murderer. Because of Glenna, you see. She was our neighbor! Is," she amended. Though another day had passed since the "second" disappearance, as Fay called it. Fay had called again, saying there was no visible sign of Glenna Flint.

"Ruth," he said, leaning forward, reaching out to her as if she were a little girl needing a hand to cross the street, "Mac MacInnis has confessed. Did you know that? Oh, yes. It wasn't Glenna at all. It was Mac. He admitted it. What more do you want? He killed him out of jealousy, or some craziness. I'll admit I was surprised. I would have put money on Alwyn. But, well, you have your murderer. What are you dragging up this other stuff for? Making Emma suffer by talking about it again? Making me..."

"I'm sorry," she said, putting a hand on his. "I just had to know, that's all. I just wanted to hear from you. It was Colm who dug up the Emma business. He had to, I mean," she said, defending her friend, "in case it wasn't Mac. We're still not sure, you know; we've no definitive proof."

"You thought Emma might have done it, that Denby got her pregnant and she was getting her revenge—or her father, someone who acted for her—that it?"

"Maybe."

It was easier to let it lie like that. Easier than telling the whole truth. That Colm had it in for Kevin, wanted to implicate him. She was angry now, at Colm.

"If you knew how it was—I couldn't tell Angie about Emma—it made the guilt worse, keeping it in. Did Emma tell you I sent money? Every Christmas? Pretending to be an uncle so her husband wouldn't know? I did, Ruth, I did. If she'd had the child, if she'd insisted—well, I'd have paid for that, too."

"Of course," she said. She was glad when the telephone rang; when Vic called to her from upstairs, needing help with his math; when Sharon came home, big as the side of a barn, looking exhausted, dragging Ruth's grandchild behind her.

"Nana," little Robbie said, and Ruth scooped him up in her arms, hugged him to her. "Ice cream?" he said hopefully, and, ignoring Sharon's frown, Ruth said, "Yes, sweetheart, right in the freezer. Nana will get it."

"One spoonful, then," Sharon said, frowning. "And make it vanilla. I don't want him up half the night with a chocolate buzz."

"You know," Kevin whispered, following Ruth into the kitchen, "there was some question as to whether it really was my baby—she went out with some other guy just before she met me. Once even, I heard, with Denby. That's how the rumors started. I'm the one who took responsibility."

Ruth stared at him, couldn't think of anything to say. Something unripe in her throat.

After Kevin left, after she dished out homemade vanilla ice cream for her grandson—two spoonfuls, since Sharon was out of the room—she called Colm. But Colm was out, his father said. "Gone to see some woman. I'll have him call you back. Um, here it is: Stackpole, Emma Stackpole. I suppose she wants to sell her house. They call all hours of the day and night. If Colm would take over here for me..."

"Don't they die all hours of the night?" she asked, irritation building up inside at Colm's errand.

There was a faint laugh. "Oh, yes, absolutely. But they usually hold off bringing them here till morning. They're not going anywhere, anyway, are they?"

"I suppose not," she said, thinking of Glenna—wherever she

might be. In some ditch, on the side of a mountain, in somebody's barn, asleep, or worse...

When she put down the phone, it rang at once. But it wasn't Colm; it was Emily. "Mom, I'm at a football game—at the high school. They're undefeated, you know." Ruth didn't know—she couldn't keep up with things. "Great," she said.

"With Hartley, Mom. Hartley was on the search, I mean, but when her parents arrived, she had to take time out—they keep bugging her, you know."

"Well, all right, Em. But come home right after, will you? I'll need you tomorrow."

"Tomorrow? Tomorrow, I promised to go on the search with Hartley. I mean, it's more important than school, Mom! But Mom, Wilder's here. And guess what? Without Joanie Hayden. And he wants to sit with us. But I won't be too eager."

"I wouldn't be. After all, he left you for that diamond-in-her-nose." Ruth had to give her daughter *some* motherly advice. Was it enough?

But Emily had advice for her mother, too. "When Dad comes, you will be nice to him, Mom? You will...consider what he has to say? I mean, I'll listen to Wilder anyhow; I'll consider.... Mom? Answer me, Mom."

"Of course I will," said Ruth, feeling a headache coming on. "I'll consider. I've been considering—more than you realize."

"Thanks, Mom. Thanks. I gotta go now. Here's Wilder."

"Hi, Ms. Willmarth. How are you?" Wilder's voice cracked through the wires. "Hi," Ruth said, and then there was a peal of laughter, and Emily yelled, "Remember what I said, Mother," and hung up.

Ruth sat still for a few minutes afterward, couldn't seem to move her feet.

"Nana's cry-ing," little Robbie told his mother, who was coming out of the bathroom, and Sharon ran to Ruth, knelt down to put her arms around her. Ruth felt her daughter's hair warm and soft like spilled milk on her knees. "Was that Dad? Let him have it, Mother. What are you waiting for? He's not coming back. To stay, I mean. He's not. You have to face reality."

Ruth nodded. She couldn't speak, couldn't tell Sharon it wasn't Pete at all, but Emily. That somehow that made it even worse.

"Mother, I need help," Sharon cried, struggling to get up off her knees. "This baby's gravity is down. Help, Mom!"

Smiling through her tears, Ruth pulled on Sharon's arms. Together they got mother-cum-child up out of the chair. "Whew," said Sharon. "Any day now, this kid'll be knocking on the door. Jack better get his ass back here. What do you suppose it is—girl, boy, or calf?"

"QUICK," SAID HARTLEY, "there they are. Run, Emily!" She yanked on Gandalf's leash. Then she cried, "Whoa, baby, whoa. Not quite *so*-o fast."

"You can't avoid your parents forever." It was Emily, shouting, dropping behind. They were in East Branbury. Most of the searchers had given up on the area—for one thing, it was raining, a kind of sleet. Hartley's hair and shoes were soaked. But if she'd been drugged, Hartley figured, Glenna wouldn't have staggered very far from Bagshaw's.

"Besides," the girl confided to Emily, who had finally caught up, "I have an appointment at eleven-thirty for a head and neck massage. Some energy work, too. I made it days ago. In that Healing House. I can slip in—it'll only take an hour."

"You're kidding," said Emily. "A massage? Energy work? What do you need that for?"

"It helps you think," said Hartley. "It relaxes you so the brain cells can operate. So you can face the world. Face your parents, you know."

"I know," said Emily, "oh, I know."

"I know you know," said Hartley. "Your dad coming up, right?"

"Right. I'm a wreck thinking about it. My mother can be so, so stubborn sometimes. Not always thinking of *us*, you know."

"I know. Well, maybe she can work you in. Isis, I mean. After she's through with me. I mean, I'll lend you the money."

"Well...maybe." Emily leaned against a stump to catch her breath. They were on a dirt road behind the Healing House. "Can you slow that dog down a bit? I'm beat. I had to do chores before I came here. I'm so wet, it doesn't matter anymore."

They were on somebody's farmland, Hartley saw. She didn't know whose. The place looked run-down, "marginal as heck," she said aloud; it had a FOR SALE sign stuck sideways in the ground in front of a clump of frostbitten bushes. A mangy dog barked at them but wagged its tail when it saw Gandalf, and then ran off at a clumsy gait. Gandalf strained at his leash; he was a wet gray ghost. A single white silo leaned toward them ominously, as if it would strike if they came any closer. A gray barn badly in need of paint squatted beside it. Its cupola told of better days, before the pigeons took over. The birds squabbled and flapped over the girls' heads. Hartley peeked inside a dirty window and a workhorse swung its gangly neck in her direction. She had just turned away when a young boy burst out of the barn.

"Nobody here—they moved," he said. "I'm jest feedin' this old mare. She's mine now, but Mom say she got to stay here till somebody buys the place. And don't seem like nobody's gonna." He glared suspiciously at the two girls.

"You haven't seen a white-haired woman, have you?" Hartley asked. "She's disappeared, and we're part of a search party." But the boy just shook his head. "Seen nobody," he said. "Nobody wants out in this weather," and he trotted off down the road.

The house was unpainted, its windows boarded up; the porch had three slats missing right in front of the door. "Gandalf—come back!" Hartley whistled and clapped her hands. But the dog had pulled its leash out of her hands; he leapt across the hole in the boards, hurled himself against the door. It banged open from the impact.

"It's still somebody's property—in residence or not," said Emily.

"Aunty might be in there!" cried Hartley. "Are you with me or not?"

"I'm with you. But I'm thirsty. And I'd like to rest a minute."

"Come on, then. They'll have a kitchen faucet, anyway."

Gandalf was already in, racing around a small square room decorated mainly with dust and cobwebs. The walls were a bright pink, as if someone had tried to beautify the place. "Someone's been here," Emily said. "Look. Footprints on the floor. Big ones. I mean, there were men in here. Couldn't be Glenna."

"Glenna wears size eleven."

"No kidding?"

"She does. But she wasn't wearing boots when she left the hunting cabin. These are boot prints. Glenna was wearing sneakers. Purple-and-white Adidas. My stepmother bought them for her."

"Your stepmother isn't all bad, then? I mean, she worries about Glenna? About you?" She turned to face Hartley.

Hartley considered. "Well, she can be all right. Sometimes. She just doesn't understand me. You know?"

"I know."

"I bet they were here then, the searchers. Those are their tracks. And obviously—"

"They didn't find anything."

Hartley leaned against the wall, groaned. But Gandalf seemed excited. He stumbled up a set of rickety stairs, and the girls followed. There were two bedrooms, both empty, except for a faded lounge chair that the mice had taken over, and an ancient Victorian wardrobe. The single bathroom was clean enough, but empty of water. Though there was a yellowy puddle of what looked like urine in the bottom of the empty toilet.

"Some guy, probably, from the searching party. Could've gone outside. Disgusting," Hartley said.

"Basement?" said Emily, and they ran back down again. Gandalf knocked into Hartley and sent the girl sprawling. "Cut that out, beast," she yelled, while Emily giggled.

But there was no sign of life in the dugout basement—human life, anyway. Only a pair of mice skittering past a dead possum, its long pink nose flattened against the hard cement.

"No Glenna here," Emily said, and Hartley dropped down on the broken step.

"There's the barn. The silo?"

"But that boy didn't see her. Anyhow, why would she be in there when there's a whole house?" Emily argued. "I mean, why would she stay in a place like this? Why wouldn't she just go home? Old Bagshaw's in jail."

"Well, she doesn't know that. She obviously escaped, thinking he was still in the house."

"After all that shooting when they came to get him?"

"She was probably drugged then. There was poison in that cocoa, you know—that super something. The police found it. And God, Emily, you know yourself she was panicked she'd get put back in that mental place—that Rockbury."

Emily held up her hands in surrender. "Okay."

"But Gandalf," Hartley mused. "He was so superexcited."

"Mice. Aren't those greyhounds trained to catch rodents?"

"I guess." Hartley looked at her watch. "Hey, it's eleven already. The Healing House is only half a mile from here. I don't want to miss that massage. We'll come back here after, okay? Look in that silo? What do you say?"

"I say, good idea. My throat's a desert. At least they've got water there."

"It might be poisoned."

"Don't say that! I want to live to see my dad." Emily put a hand to her mouth and pretended to gag.

"Rest in peace." Hartley folded her hands, bowed her head. "Back on that leash, Gandalf, baby. We're heading for the goblins of the Misty Mountains!"

"Misty is right," said Emily, throwing up her jacket hood against the sleeting rain. "I wish I was back home in the warm cow barn."

"No, you don't."

"Yeah, you're right. I guess I don't."

JIMMY'S JUNKS the sign read. It was a graveyard for old cars, Colm saw, situated on a slope that led down to the New Haven River. He wondered how many ancient parts floated away each spring after the rains. Fords, Dodges, Corvettes—there was no class division here: All were welcome. You just had to be a derelict. The paths of glory lead but to the junkyard, he misquoted from some long-ago poem. Rust in peace.

And here was old Jimmy himself, sauntering out to greet him, waving a stick that served as cane, eyeing the '87 Horizon where it sagged in the driveway, its door dented in where Colm had skidded into a beech tree one icy day last winter. But Colm had another mission today. It was Jimmy's place that Denby's truck had gone to when they hauled it up out of Otter Creek back in '75. At least he assumed so: Jimmy's was the only junkyard in town at that time. Today, there were half a dozen crowding the landscape.

He was correct on that point, Jimmy acknowledged, grinning out of a gold-glinty mouth, thumbs stuck into a pair of red plaid suspenders. "Sure, they brought it here. But I ain't got it now." He guffawed. "I mean, that were over twenny years ago, man; I'd just got in the junk business. I knew Denby Bagshaw, never liked the fellow anyways. He almost done in my own sister, you bet he did. I'd of killed him for that, he'd knocked her up. Well, they never found Denby's body—just the wallet, washed up on shore. Never really looked, you ask me. Who in hell cared?"

Of course, the truck had long ago been broken down for parts: "It wan't worth fixing, all that time in the water," Jimmy allowed. "You want, I can tell you who bought parts. Got it all down in the book—well, in my head anyways. Don't pay to keep it all in the books, you know." He winked, and Colm knew what he meant. He paid his own snowplow man in cash. Some things never got reported.

Colm thanked him, but he couldn't see the point of chasing down every carburetor or clutch. He didn't know why he'd come really, just an impulse. Jimmy hadn't been at the Flint farm at all, it turned out; it was his son who'd hauled up the truck. "Howie," he hollered down the hill, where a middle-aged man was hunkering over a rusted Plymouth, "C'mon up here. Fellow wants to know about the Bagshaw truck. You know—back when? Howie, he got a better memory'n me," he explained to Colm.

But Howie, a replica of his dad but some twenty years younger, in a misshapen tweed hat, was no more help than his father. Sure, he'd hauled it up—"a back buster," he remembered. "Nuthin' in it," he said when Colm questioned him. "Well, not much—coupla old tools. I recall a wrench, jack, you know, all that kinda stuff. We sold 'em, right, Dad? Police said we could have 'em, right?"

"We wasn't doin' nothin' wrong," Jimmy said loudly, sticking a bit of chewing tobacco under his tongue. "Nothin' worth nothin', you can bet. Denby didn't have no money—though it were a new truck. That struck me as odd, a brand-new truck. Least was afore he run it in the creek. 'Now where'n hell,' I says to Howie, 'Denby Bagshaw got the money for a brand-new truck?'''

Colm was running late; he had land to show a customer. He thanked the pair, admired Howie's hat—looked like real Irish tweed. Howie doffed it, then remembered something. "Sure, it came outta that truck, but it weren't Bagshaw's. I woulda give it to Alwyn, it had been. Got some other name in it. Someone I never heard of. Figure Denby stole it." He held it out, looking put-out, as if he'd been accused himself of stealing the hat.

Colm looked in the band, yellow from years of sweat. The letters were faint, in gray thread, but still legible. It was a single name. *Crowningshield.*

He promised to return it. Afterward, that is, after the hearing, after the trial, he thought, his imagination leaping ahead of him as he ran to the Horizon.

"You could use a new door there," Jimmy called out after him, but Colm was already headed for the police station.

TWENTY

EMILY WAS WAITING with Gandalf on the covered front porch of the Healing House. She'd had her fill of water, but the smell of incense inside was too much for her; she preferred the aroma of hay and wildflowers. Hartley was getting her massage; she'd made an appointment for Emily, too, for the following week—Emily wasn't too sure about that, though. Alwyn Bagshaw was in the county lockup, so he couldn't poison anyone else now. She wondered if she really should include his story in her history project. And then she decided, Why not? No one else in the class would have such a dramatic story to tell. Murder? Well, the next thing to it, anyway. Secretly, she thought *he* might have killed his brother, Denby. She liked that grumpy old Mac; she didn't want *him* convicted.

Gandalf seemed uneasy; he jumped at the slightest sound. He whimpered now when a car pulled up in front. A man got out, followed by a woman wearing a red plaid suit. The man, she saw, was Kevin Crowningshield. He recognized her; she gave him a stiff nod in return. She'd seen him with her mother, and she didn't like that. She was hoping her father would stay when he came back; she wanted them all together, wanted her family back. Most of her friends had fathers! Though Wilder's father was never home. She smiled, thinking of Wilder at the football game. He'd asked her to a movie that weekend, and she'd put him off. So he'd broken up with Diamond Nose? She wasn't going to be that easy to get.

"Hello there," Kevin Crowningshield said, smiling, like he was already intimate with her, with her mother. He was dressed to the nines: regimental necktie, dark blue suit with wide lapels, and those shiny black shoes. He looked like an undertaker. That hair, slicked back—looked darker than usual. But you could pack a pair of shoes in the bags under his eyes, swing on the lines in his face. She said, "Hi," and, reluctantly, followed him and the woman back inside. She was worried about Hartley, for one thing. The girl was lying on her stomach, naked, except for her hipster underpants, on the low massage table. Isis was seated at her side, passing her hands over the girl's back—energy work, Emily guessed. It was as though the woman's shoulders and arms had grown an extra foot. All that smelly incense, and soft music on the tape recorder—Emily wouldn't want that.

She didn't know who the woman with Kevin was. Lawyer? Realtor? Trying to force the women out, close up the place? She'd heard her mother talking to Colm Hanna. The place might not be Emily's cup of tea, but she liked Isis, and she liked some of the women here. Mostly, she didn't like people who tried to interfere with other people's lives. One of her ancestors had fought in the Battle of Bennington, when Vermont called itself a Republic. And Emily was a Vermonter.

She felt a sudden wave of sympathy for old Bagshaw. And now he was in prison. Everybody trying to control him. Of course, he'd grabbed Glenna, but he was confused. Maybe he had a brain tumor. All that pressure. She'd heard of things like that. She'd make a case for him in her essay.

Isis had a sheet now over Hartley; she was working on one foot that stuck out of the sheet. Emily could hear Hartley humming to the music. Isis was poking and rubbing and stroking; Emily could see the muscles bulge in her arms. "You know how to relax," Isis told Hartley, "that's good. That helps me. Helps you to get the most out of a massage."

"Ma'am," said the plaid-suited woman, poking a snub nose in the doorway. "We called. There was no answer. So we just came. I'm Mr. Crowningshield's attorney, Karen Close. We have a writ to serve on you. We're giving you ten days to close up here. Mr. Crowningshield has a party interested in buying. They'll want to move in."

Isis went on rubbing and stroking; Hartley went on humming. "I think she's busy," Emily told the intruders, and Mr. Crowningshield gave her a superior smile. "I think we'll let *her* answer," he said.

"I'll be with you when I'm done," Isis shouted. "I've a client here."

Kevin laughed. "That child?"

Hartley sat up, clutching the sheet to her breast. "I'm not a child,

Mr. Crowningshield. I'm eighteen—almost. I'm a paying customer.''

"Of course," said Kevin. "We'll wait, then." He nodded at the attorney. *So-o* condescending, Emily thought.

He and the woman brushed past Emily, like she wasn't even there. Planted themselves down on a bench, spoke in hushed, urgent tones. Emily went into the kitchen, where two giant piles of greens sat in sieves, one of the women washing them. A tiger cat squatted on top of the refrigerator, washing its face—she'd seen it at Bagshaw's. "Oh, are those—I mean, you're not supposed to eat those, are you?"

"Oh, no," the woman said, indicating the left-hand pile, "these are fresh, bought at the local co-op."

"Could I have a few on a plate?" Emily had an idea. Just a joke, of course.

"Well, take these, dear. Not those," she said, pointing to the larger pile. "Those are from the poisoned garden, you know, where he buried the bird remains. We're digging them all up so no one else—human or animal—will eat them."

"Like my brother's hawk," Emily said, and explained about the poisoned birds. She dished up a few of the co-op greens, then went out and offered the plate to Kevin Crowningshield and the lawyer. Kevin was concentrating on something the lawyer was saying; he took a small piece, put it in his mouth. The woman, who had followed Emily into the hall to see what she was up to, glanced up at him, then shrieked, "Don't eat that. It could be poisoned!"

He blanched, while Emily giggled and ran back in the kitchen. A second later, Crowningshield stormed in, dumped the plate in the sink. "Oh, those were from the co-op," the woman said above Kevin's noise. "You're not poisoned, mister."

"It was just a joke," said Emily.

But he didn't think so. "You goddamn women," he hollered, his face churning like a washing machine. "Killing my wife, keeping her locked up here, brainwashing her..." He was out of control now, his words incoherent.

He was suddenly caught. Isis was behind him, in her wheelchair, her strong blue-knuckled hands on his elbows. She made him face her. "I have a copy of a will here," she said, "sent by Angie's

stepmother. You and your lawyer friend might be interested in reading it.'' She thrust it at the lawyer, who was standing, hands on her
plaid hips, in the kitchen doorway. ''Angie owned this place. At
her death, it reverted to the stepmother in California. Angie wanted
it kept as a healing center. To help other abused women, the way
we helped her.''

And when Crowningshield interrupted, Isis said, ''You might
want to read her diary, too. It would break your heart—if you still
have one.'' She rammed the man toward a chair with her wheelchair, tossed a small blue notebook at him. Emily was almost sorry
for him. He was holding the notebook close to his crumpled face,
trying to read it, his eyes blinking a hundred times a minute. It
made her ankles wobble. She'd seen Wilder crying once, when his
brother was involved in an assault on an old farmer. She'd felt so
badly for Wilder then, she'd let him cry it out in her arms. She'd
wanted to smash in his brother's head for doing that.

But there was no time for feeling sorry, because there was a
sudden commotion outside, a car door slamming, a pair of police-
men running up to the door. Hartley came out, pulling down her
Ben & Jerry's T-shirt. ''What's going on here?'' she said, her green
eyes shining.

''Wait and see,'' said Emily, and flattened herself against the
wall. Her heart was jumping, her palms sweating. Something important was happening here and she was in the middle of it. The
lawyer was standing between Crowningshield and a policeman,
shouting, gesticulating; another policeman pulled her away, grabbed
the man's arms, and snapped on a pair of handcuffs. It was like on
Murder, She Wrote. Emily watched the reruns—only this was for
real. She was breathless with it all.

''You can't do this. You can't arrest this man,'' the lawyer was
screaming. ''What has my client done?'' The policeman mumbled
something about ''new evidence,'' said she could come along to
headquarters if she wanted, that Mr. Crowningshield would probably need her. And before Emily could catch her breath or blow her
runny nose, they were gone, careening up the rainy street, the lawyer's red car racing after.

''Boy, will Fay be pissed,'' said Hartley, grasping Emily's arm for balance while she leaned down to tie her purple sneaker laces. "She's lost her only boarder."

KEVIN HAD SAID he wanted Ruth to hear before anyone else did. He'd had the lawyer call her, rout her out of the barn. So here Ruth was at police headquarters, though she felt uncomfortable, out of place, disoriented even. But she'd be there, for Kevin, who had broken down after the repeated questions, confessed to Denby's killing—or "half a killing," as he put it, saying Denby was already "half-gone" when he got there.

"But alive," Colm prompted, "in need of a doctor." Though Ruth wanted it to be a matter of self-defense, didn't she? She wanted Kevin to be absolved, to leave Branbury with impunity, go back to Chicago in peace, to bury his wife.

But she didn't really know what to think; she felt swept away into a limbo, bereft of judgment. She looked at Colm, but his eyes were fixed on Kevin. Colm had gone and ferreted out that letter from Emma, the letter that helped to prove Kevin was being black-mailed; established motive. She had to admit that Colm had been right to pursue the man—if right was always right and not some-times wrong.

"Alive," Kevin admitted, with a piteous glance at Ruth. "He was just coming to. He recognized me. I guess I wanted that. I wanted him to know I knew he was the one blackmailing me—he'd followed me and Emma once when we... Well, I wanted him to see me before I—before I struck him. I was half-crazy. I'd been looking for him anyway. When I saw his truck parked at the Flint farm—a brand-new truck he'd bought with my money—I knew it was the time to finish what we'd started at the Alibi. Get him off my back; I wasn't going to hand over any more money. I wasn't making so much then, and I wanted to get married. But then..." His eyes sought Ruth's, but she found herself looking away.

They all waited. Chief Fallon sat in his chair, tapping his fingers on the interview table. Colm was looking at his folded hands. Ruth sank down in a chair, her legs giving way. Kevin was gazing at her still with those sad brown eyes.

"Then I saw him—that fellow, Glenna Flint's husband. He was coming out of the barn, running. I pulled over into the grass. A minute later, I saw Glenna riding off on her mare. MacInnis didn't even go in the house; he just left in a taxi—must have called it earlier, I think the only car—a pickup—was Glenna's. But Denby's truck was still in the drive. So I got out."

He pulled out a large linen handkerchief, blew his nose, stuffed it back into his pocket. He was dressed for something other than this sort of confrontation, Ruth saw, right down to the regimental tie, the blue suit, those shoes—unfit for the Vermont climate. She saw how scuffed and stained Colm's loafers were, as if he'd been exploring some client's septic system, or wandering around a junk-yard....

"I surmised what had happened," Kevin went on. "A blow on the head. Mac had done it, I thought. Or maybe even Glenna—you know what a womanizer Denby Bagshaw was. And both of them taking off, leaving Bagshaw for dead. Only he wasn't dead; he was coming to, as I said. Groaning, you know. He looked so...ugly lying there, crumpled against the side of the barn. So...subhuman. That's the way he struck me. Subhuman. Even half-dead, he threatened to tell Angie about me and Emma. If she'd known about Emma, you see, she'd never have . . ."

He looked searchingly at Ruth; he was motionless, on the point of collapse, like an unwound doll. Ruth heard the creak of Roy Fallon's chair, the rumble of the tape recorder. She hardly breathed where she sat, motionless herself, at the other end of the table—trying to sort out her feelings, her sympathies. But her hands lay numb in her lap.

They waited. And waited. Finally, Colm spoke. Colm was anxious. Ruth could see that. He kept stealing little glances at her, his nails digging into the palms of his hands. He wanted the final confession out of the man. "Then what? Get it all out, man. Then what? Tell us and they'll go easier on you."

She hated him at that moment, hated Colm! Everything was so black and white for him. Couldn't he see how ugly Denby Bagshaw was? A womanizer, maybe a rapist. A blackmailer. Shoving his brutish way into someone's personal life. If it had been her he'd been blackmailing, would she have been angry enough to kill?

"Angie," Kevin said. "It wasn't just me—it would have devastated Angie."

Angie. Angel in the house. Why did that phrase suddenly come to her out of her school days? Ms. Manning, her feminist English teacher, junior year, that was it. It was what a Victorian called his woman. There she was, off balance, on a shiny marble pedestal. Angel in the house. Was this what Angie had wanted? What Ruth would want? She shuddered; she chewed the inside of her lip. She couldn't look at Colm, or Kevin.

"So I picked up the shovel; it was there on the ground. He tried to grab it; he was up on his knees. But too weak, he fell back down. I...I hit him. I couldn't have him telling Angie—that's what he was threatening, even as he lay there. I knew he'd never be satisfied. I'd already given him six thousand dollars, and I didn't have any more to give. Not to him..."

Chief Fallon said, "So? You dropped him in the hole? Convenient for you, that MacInnis had dug it already." He was looking at his watch. His cheeks were working in and out. He wanted this confession over with. It had all happened almost a quarter of a century ago; he had current affairs to deal with.

"I...I saw the hole. I'd heard about it—rumors—but I'd never seen it. But I didn't put him in it. In case he wasn't really...you know, dead. I mean, I just hit him, that's all. Out of anger. Frustration. But I wanted that truck out of there—the truck he'd bought with my money. I didn't want him to have that new truck, dead or alive."

Kevin looked self-righteous, as though he'd been accused of burying a live man. But he killed him, Ruth told herself; he killed Denby—a defenseless man, at least at that point. Mac was gone, Glenna off on her ride—it had to have been Kevin who gave the final blow. Her head felt the impact of that shovel.

"And you took his truck—must've had the keys in it? Or you took them out of his pocket?" It was Colm pressing now. Kevin's face was mottled; his hands were jerking in his lap. Ruth was torn between pity and her vision of a murder.... But Mac had hit him, too; if it had been only Kevin, that final blow might not have been fatal. Did they realize that?

Kevin only nodded. He drove the truck over to the river behind the farm, he said, his voice splintering. Drove it in, jumped out— the water turbulent, at least ten feet deep, he'd heard, at that place.

There'd been a lot of rain that October. Enough to destroy that truck. "I had to do it. I had to do that!" he cried.

They'd found the wallet floating in the water, Roy Fallon confirmed. It was assumed that Denby was drunk, drowned—a swift current would take a body out, eventually, into Lake Champlain. The truck was hauled off to Jimmy's junkyard—a canoeist had complained to authorities of not being able to row around it. The Flint mother and daughter had claimed no knowledge of it. Inside the truck was Kevin Crowningshield's hat, appropriated by Jimmy's nineteen-year-old son, who'd helped haul it out.

Fallon patted Colm's shoulder. "Good man," he said, and Colm glanced wistfully at Ruth.

"You came back afterward, got in your car, I assume, and, uh, left the, uh . . ." Fallon asked, and Kevin nodded. "No one saw you? No one else was on the premises?"

"Not that I saw. Unless—Mrs. Flint, Glenna's mother. But she was blind, I understood." Kevin's face was like a shattered plate; when he dropped it into his hands, Ruth could see the bald spot on the top of his head where the hair he brushed over it had gone askew.

"Then who put Denby in that, um, hole?" Fallon asked. "I don't think he crawled in all by himself."

And no one could answer.

Ruth was the first to leave the police station. She'd imagined before she came that she might go over and touch Kevin on the shoulder, show her support. The man was desperate; he'd been afraid of losing a woman he'd loved but had never really known, never really understood. It was the angel in the house he worshiped—not Angie, the woman.

And there was that other woman. Emma Stackpole's heart-shaped face moved toward her on the street, on the body of a younger woman. Kevin had given Emma money for an abortion. He hadn't given *himself.*

When Colm loped after her, called her name, she kept going. Down Seminary Street to her pickup, back to the farm. It was snowing, fat, thick flakes cooling her hot face, blanching her shoulders. She thought of her cows, out shivering in the pasture—the calves in their outdoor pen. The truck was coming for the bull calf Tuesday. She'd give it a last meal (she'd have to tell Vic). This afternoon, she'd do the milking. She wanted to; she needed that good, clean work. For no reason at all, she thought now of Zelda, wondered if she'd broken through the fence again. Crazy, recalcitrant cow.

"I MIGHT or I might not have that massage," Emily told Hartley. "For one thing, I don't have a credit card like you. I don't even have a decent allowance."

"I'll treat you," said Hartley. "It'll be a birthday gift."

"My birthday's not till June."

"An early one."

"We'll see." The girls were walking up the driveway of the deserted farm. Hartley doubted they'd find Aunty in the old barn, but she wanted to see the horse, and take a look in the silo, just in case. A quick look, that is, before the thing fell down with them in it. "Got that apple?" she asked Emily.

"In my pocket." They'd begged it from Marna at the Healing House. "Quit it, Gandalf," she said when the dog stuck its long nose into the folds of her coat. "It's not for you. You don't like apples anyway."

As if in protest, the dog sniffed at the air and, yanking his leash out of Hartley's mittened hand, ran ahead to the barn.

"Let him go," said Emily. "Probably a rat in there."

"It might crumble on top of him. Gandalf, come back here." Hartley grabbed the leash at the barn door. Gandalf threw his weight against it and the barn door caved in. They walked over it, like a castle drawbridge broken down before the enemy. It was a thrilling moment for Hartley. "Ho!" she cried, "Halt there."

But there was no answer, just the old mare, in her stall, chewing noisily on a hunk of dried grass.

"Gandalf, heel," said Hartley. But the worn leash snapped in her hand and Gandalf was away again, rummaging in a pile of hay. Bits of moldy straw flew up into the girls' noses, and Emily gave a whopping sneeze. Gandalf was crouched now in the hay, wagging his tail, whining. He was nosing something—a body, Hartley realized, in ripped slacks and burlap, grimy with dirt. "Aunty," she

TWENTY-ONE

WHO WAS THIS they were dragging in to meet her? Glenna squinted through her weak eyes. She was lying with her pink-slippered feet up on the horsehair sofa. They'd tried to make her go to the hospital, but she'd held firm. "No hospital," she'd told that interfering nephew's wife, "no damn doctor. Or I'll take off again."

Glenna had had two whole days away with Jenny. Or was it three? She'd lost track of time. Or regained it—the ride had been exhilarating. She and Jenny had galloped everywhere, all over the county, forging their own trails. And no one to stop them. Till the relatives. Oh, they'd brought her back, yes, but she wasn't the old Glenna. Oh no. She was in command of her own life now. No one was going to make her do things. Things they'd once forced her to do. Like that Booby, that Bagshaw, barging into the barn when she was with Jenny.... It was all out in the open now, exorcized. He'd raped her body but never her spirit. Never! She was free of him. She was her own woman; she didn't care how old. She might live to be one hundred. She might—just to spite them all. She clasped her hands together, bared her chipped teeth at the dark-haired man.

"This is Mac, Glenna," the man said, "I'm Colm. Colm Hanna. We met. The day we found that skeleton?"

"That was Mac," Glenna said. "I killed him. He came after me. He found me with that Booby."

"I don't think you killed him, Glenna. This is Mac, you see, and he's very much alive."

But Glenna knew better. She lifted her chin, straightened her glasses; it didn't seem to help her vision. Squinted. No. This scrawny bent-over creature with the straggly white beard was not Mac. Oh no. Mac had hair the color of a maple in November. Mac was a talker; Mac wouldn't just stand there. She'd killed Mac. *Suddenly, the Booby rose up, pants down around his knees, as if he were a marionette, jerked up by its strings, and she heard a howl, Mac's voice: She sat up to see the Booby—dragged out of the stall by his yellow hair; a string of oaths, bashings against the old boards, a high-pitched squeal, Mac's bawl on top of it all. He was shaking her then, her. She was hay in his hands, small hands, a small man, but she'd never known his strength till now, the depth of his anger. Shook the words right out of her; she couldn't explain. He wouldn't listen. The fury was in her then; when he let go, she grabbed a shovel. Swung, connected; Mac lay on the ground, bleeding. She ran back in the barn, untied Jenny, led her out without looking at the other, the one Mac struck. She rode and rode in the clean wind.... And when she came back, spent, Mac was gone, the hole filled in. Someone running, or riding, down the road—she couldn't see for the growing dusk. One of the ones who came around—to plumb, to fertilize, to buy syrup? "Good riddance," her mother said. "Nobody in that hole. Mac's gone, that's all. Good riddance."*

"Good riddance," she said aloud, then sank back down on the horsehair sofa. It was her grandmother's; she'd always meant to replace the scratchy fabric but had never gotten around to it. She wasn't one to worry about the inside of a house. It was the outside that counted: the silo, falling down now—they'd have to mend it; the barn, the fences, the tractor, the hay wagon. Not the cows, though. Horses were her love.

"Hello, Glenna," the whiskery creature said, and her hands fluttered up, out of control. Uh-oh. Something familiar here now: the voice, the smell of nicotine, the way he cleared his throat, coughed. He shouldn't smoke those things. They'd kill him; she'd told him so. At least *she'd* kicked the habit.

"Think you could kill me with that little shovel, Glenna? Knocked the wind out of me, okay, but kill me? Not a chance. I took off, was all. Hit that other guy, that Bagshaw. But I was entitled, right? A busted head for a tit?"

"It wasn't the way you thought," she said. "It was nothing *I* wanted."

The man who said he was Mac sat down beside her on the sofa. "You think I haven't thought about this for years, do you? Think I haven't gone over it in my head every goddamn night? I killed a man over a woman? Maybe over a mistake?"

"You were always so damn jealous. You had no good reason. I never once touched another man."

"I almost killed him for nothing, then. That what you're saying?"

"Not what I'm saying. I'm nothing?" She banged her fist on her knee, and winced with the pain. She had a bruise there. She had bruises everywhere. It was that man, that Bagshaw.... "He's alive," she yelled. "Look what he did to me. Kidnapped me. Locked me in his house. Shoved pills down my throat. Stuck me in that stinking cellar. I ruined my knee going down there, hit my head. I cut myself getting out. I could've bled to death."

"That was Alwyn Bagshaw, the older one; the other one's dead, the one who hurt you," the man called Mac said, pushing his whiskery head in her face. She smelled onions. Mac always ate onion sandwiches for lunch; the place reeked with them, and her eyes wept.

She reached out a hand, touched his arm. It jerked a little under her touch. "It is really you, Mac?"

Mac sighed. "I'm afraid so. 'Fraid so," he repeated, and laughed out loud. "You're something else, you know, Glenna?"

He always did have a laugh like a donkey, Glenna thought, and laughed herself. It was crazy. Life was crazy. But she was glad to be alive.

Both of us, she thought, back from the dead. And laughed again.

IT WAS the Willmarth woman got him released—on bail, they'd told him, though Alwyn suspected a rat: why'd she do that? Something about a cat, she'd said. Letting him go so he could feed a cat? Don't run off, they said; he'd go up before some judge. But, hell, where'd he run to if he could? Sure, he was home now. He wasn't going nowhere. No. They wanted to find him, they'd find him. He wasn't going to that Rockbury they talked about! Not to that place, full of loonies. He'd be dead first.

The cat looked fed enough, yelling sure, always did, even on a full belly. He poured the dry food into the dish; the cat rubbed against his leg. Like a woman it was; he didn't know why he kept it. Separate, ornery. No use for you when it didn't need food, a dry place to sleep. Annie, he thought—where was she? He was confused. How long he'd been away, anyhow? He recalled something about the cellar....

He was relieved. Nobody down there but mice. His imagination, carrying him off sometimes. Annie long gone—he'd watched her go. California it was. No woman in that cellar.

There was nothing much in the old Kelvinator. That Hanna fellow just dropped him off here, left him; they took his truck. He'd have to walk to the store to get food, a good mile. In a hurry, that's why, that Hanna, his beeper going. Somebody'd run a car up a pole somewhere; he had to go, he said. He'd be back, sure, he said, the Willmarth woman making up a supper. But go ahead and starve meantime.

He looked out the window at his corn. Couple of stalks still there, overripe, sticking out of the snow. Tomatoes, in their tires. Most likely froze while he was stuck in that jail. It was Halloween, Hanna said. He'd keep the lights out, didn't want kids hanging around, wanting candy. Bellies full of sweets. Alwyn's ma didn't hold with that, never let him go out Halloween. Though he'd wanted to. Once or twice.

Kids here already. And not even dark out—they ought be in school. Banging on his window. Faces staring in at him: ghosts, witches, devils. "Devils," he shouted, and banged back. The window shattered under his fists. The blood, spurting from his arm. "Devils!" He ran out the back door.

"Trick or treat," they mewled.

"I ain't got any. Now git, git, I said. Git, you devils!"

And they got, sure; he had 'em on the run. For there was more than one—they were everywhere, in the house, in the bed, the trees, bushes, one more of 'em rising up now out of his burning bush. He threw a rock at it; it turned and leered at him. He yanked at his hex ring, the clasp broke and it came off in his hand. Still the devil laughed and, furious, he hurled it after the fiend, chain and all.

Then stood there, panting, breath gone, ring gone—hex sign hardly working anyways since he cut off Denby's finger that time. Sure, he'd found Denby's body in that horse hole old Mac dug. Somebody killed him, hauled him over to that hole—who? Glenna or Mac, he'd suspected. He'd figured what dirty business Denby had in mind up there at the Flint farm. Alwyn found that Scotch hat on the ground, stuck it on Denby's head. Denby admired that hat; now he'd wear it all right.

But the hex ring. Tried to get the ring off, he did; he didn't want it buried with his brother. Let Denby go to the devil! But it wouldn't come, got stuck above the knuckle. So he pulled a jackknife out of his pocket—arrowhead he'd dug up, kept for good luck, came out with the knife. He sawed off the finger. Then, remembering things— bad things—his blood up, he raised his hand and jammed the arrowhead into his dead brother's chest. Clear as day he could see it now.

But then the old lady'd come out of the house—blind or not, she'd smell him, know it was him. Think he'd killed Denby— though he'd just come to test the milk. And suddenly sick to his stomach, blood on his hands, he'd dropped the finger in the stream, ring and all.

The old lady turned back then, into the house, and on impulse Alwyn filled in the hole. Seemed suddenly he should do something for a blood brother—though he was glad, glad, wasn't he, to see the last of Denby? But blood was blood. So he covered him up. For Ma. Ma would've wanted it. Then he drove off. He wasn't telling the police—they'd think he might of done it. Wasn't him drove Denby's truck in the creek, no. That's why he wrote that letter to Glenna Flint—though he never really saw her do it, just figured.

"Hey, kidnapper, hey, poisoner—got any poison candy, hey?" Still here, those devils. He scrabbled in the dirt for the ring. But one of the tormentors found it first, held it up; it gleamed gold in his fingers. "Finders keepers," the fiend yelled, and, shrieking, danced away.

"Gimme it. It's my ring. Stop, stop!" He stumbled after them, but already they'd reached the road. Enraged, beside himself, he chased them, screaming. Till the pain swallowed him up, his chest on fire, breath gone, and he fell, facedown, in a muddy rut.

TODAY WAS HALLOWEEN, and Fay wanted everyone there; she didn't want kids coming to surprise her alone, deface her new front door. She'd put on a full-length glass door from Grossman's going-out-of-business sale. Glenna objected, of course; she'd almost walked right into it, thinking it was open to the air. "I could've killed myself," she complained. "You've got a whole outdoors there, so why bring it into the house?"

"But think of winter, Aunty," said Hartley. "Think of how nice it will be to see the snow falling past that door and you're inside all cozy and warm in the house."

"You can't ride a horse in the snow," said Aunty. "Well, not anymore. It's deeper than it used to be."

"Hell," said Mac, who sat crunching a hot dog between his yellowy teeth, "the Northeast hasn't got half the winters it used to. I remember some years the snow up to the eaves—you couldn't ride at all that winter, Glenna. Who you kidding? Only peace I had was when you couldn't ride. You had time to make supper now and then."

"It's snowing out now," said Fay. "Well, a little anyway." She pointed to a few plump flakes drifting past the glass door. "Stick around and you can see who's right, you or Glenna," she told Mac, and Willard Boomer smiled, sitting at the kitchen table, sipping mulled cider.

But Mac was up; he was heaving his battered old Depression-era suitcase by the front door. He clomped back into the living room to wait for his taxi; he was heading back to New York City, to the old journalists' home. Fay had lost another boarder. First Kevin Crowningshield—on bail in Chicago to bury his wife; now Mac.

At least Aunty was staying on. Fay had promised Hartley's parents that she'd take care of her. They'd pay her, of course, but she'd even do it without pay. "To the death," Fay told Willard, who looked a bit panicked. Willard was spending the evening, having brought a bagful of lollipops for the trick-or-treaters—he loved Halloween. "I've got my mother and you've got Glenna," he whispered in Fay's right ear. "Should we move them in together—work something out with us?"

Fay didn't know. Too many things happening at once. She needed time, to clear her head. Ever since they'd found that skeleton in the horse hole, things had been happening so fast, she was running behind, like in one of those frustration dreams. Well, tomorrow she'd see Ruth, get all the details. It seemed two men—maybe three—had had a part in Denby Bagshaw's death: first, Mac, hitting him with that shovel; then Kevin, finishing the job—something about being blackmailed. Personally, she was sorry about Kevin. She'd rather liked him; he was good-looking, the right age. But it seemed they all had something wrong with them. If they hadn't spent their whole lives hatching eggs and ignoring women, or unscrewing their artificial limbs at night, why then it turned out they'd killed somebody—though this was an affair of passion; she knew that much from Ruth. Shouldn't passion count for something?

But Kevin Crowningshield never put Denby in that hole, he'd said. So how could they *prove* Denby was dead after Kevin hit him? She asked the question aloud, and got an unexpected answer.

"Oh he was dead all right," Willard said, reaching for a hunk of Fay's pumpkin bread. "Mmm," he murmured.

"What? How do you know? Were you there?" She gave him a skeptical smile.

"Why yes," he said. "I came to repair the sign, you see. All that rain, you could hardly read the lettering. They still had syrup to sell back then; the old mother put it up."

"And you saw Denby Bagshaw's body and you knew he was dead?" Fay was slightly incredulous.

"Without a doubt. I felt for a pulse, you see, and there wasn't one. I know how to do it. When my uncle passed on..."

"Uh-huh. Then what did you do?"

"Well, I saw the old lady coming out of the house. She was practically blind. Oh dear, I thought, she might stumble over the body—the shock of it for a lady! So I dragged it over to that hole—to get it out of the way, you see; it wasn't far. Besides, I saw it was Denby Bagshaw. Something bad must have happened, I thought, for someone to strike him like that. And I knew he'd have deserved it. Oh, indeed he would have. You see, it was Denby Bagshaw driving that truck that killed my sister! So I dropped him in. I'd have filled it in, too, but there wasn't time. The old lady saw me—my shadow anyhow. I waved at her. I told her I'd come to fix the sign, and she said, 'Well, get to it, then'—she wasn't one for long conversations. So I fixed the sign. And I left. I passed Glenna riding back down the road. I waved, as I recall."

"She waved back?"

He hesitated, swallowed the pumpkin bread. "Well, I really couldn't say. It was getting dark, you know, hard to see."

"But this is incredible. Simply incredible," Fay said. Jesus, she thought, there had to be four guys involved here! "So who filled in that hole?"

Willard spread his hands; he didn't know.

"And you never reported it. To the police."

Willard gazed up at her, his eyes innocent as a blue sky. "I didn't want to upset the teakettle," he whispered, glancing into the next room, where Glenna lay. "Break up a family. In case *she'd* done it."

"Oh, Willard," said Fay. "You sentimental, eccentric old fool."

Willard put his hand on her knee, and she let it stay. Her mind was racing ahead, though: If she had to put up bail—well, what better use for the Philadelphia widower's fur coat?

"Hey, Mac, your taxi's here." Hartley and Gandalf burst through the door; Gandalf, bright with snow, skidded on clicking nails to his empty dish. "Sure you want to go, Mac?" Hartley shouted at the living room. "I mean, we'd love to have you stay. Right, Fay?"

"Sure," said Fay, "we'll build an addition. Get out your credit card, kid." Personally, though, she'd be relieved when the girl left to go back to school. Though Hartley was talking of transferring to the local college, right here in Branbury. Jesus.

Well, all right, the girl could help walk the dog. It was killing Fay, running that greyhound up and down the road. Keeping him out of other people's corn. And now he had some stomach bug, a sensitive tummy after the bad stuff he'd eaten in his racing days. Though when Hartley suggested she might take Gandalf back to Poughkeepsie, something in Fay balked. She remembered the license plate on that New Hampshire car that had brought him here. *Live Free or Die.* For some reason, it had printed itself on her mind. Gandalf belonged here now. The way Glenna did. They were two victims, set free. No, she probably wouldn't marry Willard, even if he asked her. At least, not for the moment.

When Mac got in the taxi, she waved good-bye at the window, then turned, to see Glenna at the glass door, watching. She wondered what the old lady was thinking.

But Glenna just stood there, squinting out as the taxi zigzagged its way down the drive, a hand under her chin, as if she'd keep it propped up, come what may. And then she wheeled about on her fuzzy pink slippers and said sweetly, "Time for a little scotch?"

IT WAS SNOWING LIGHTLY when Ruth returned from the hospital where Colm and his ambulance crew had taken Alwyn. Marna, from the Healing House, had found him, though even then it was too late: a case of massive heart failure. Alwyn was dead on arrival— a kind of poetic justice? She'd suspected that Alwyn had something to do with Denby's death. Was he the one who had jammed the arrowhead into Denby's chest? The police had found a cache of Indian relics in his cellar. And was it Alwyn who'd filled in the hole? Well, they'd never really know now.

There were two cars in her driveway; she recognized Isis's white van, wondered what the woman was doing here, how they'd gotten the wheelchair in the house. Then she spotted another familiar car: Sharon's '84 Honda. But Sharon was supposed to be in Burlington today, at a home-schooling conference. Ruth's grandson wasn't two yet, but Sharon wanted to be ready. Vic greeted his mother at the door.

"It's Sharon—she's having the baby," he said, sounding mildly interested, as though it were one more cow having one more calf. "And the midwife is out delivering another one. So Sharon called that wheelchair person. She's been here a couple hours, I guess. Tim and Joey got her upstairs. Jeezum. It was like moving a tank."

"But it isn't due for another week," Ruth protested. "Jack isn't back from Alaska yet. He'll have to be called!"

"She did. Sharon called him. She was mad. She said it was his fault he'd miss the birth."

"Well, it is. He waited too long." And she started upstairs.

"Mom. Wait. The vet called. And she's coming over. With the hawk. We're going to let her loose."

"Now?" Ruth paused in midstep. What else could happen today? And wasn't it Halloween? Lord, who was going to hand out candy when the hordes came?

"I'll wait for her on the porch, Mom. Please?"

"Of course. Of course you don't want to be here." Ruth flew down the steps again, hugged the boy. What was a birth compared to a freed hawk? The trauma of letting it go. She thought of the bull calf again (dung and death...). "All right, darling. You wait out there. I'll put out a flag—have we got one? Well, a white tablecloth anyway, when the baby's born. So you can come back in. Get ready for Halloween."

Upstairs, there was a long moan, like a train rumbling through a tunnel. Ruth's heart leapt into her feet; she took the scuffed steps three at a time. Was the room ready? She'd meant to move out, sterilize, change the sheets. Where had she been? What had she been doing?

But already the room had metamorphosed. Candles burning in a window, the floor spotless, Ruth smelled Murphy's oil soap— Sharon's work. And there in the double bed she had once shared with Pete was Sharon, propped up on three pillows, naked from the waist down, legs wide apart—but at rest, the contractions slowing for the moment.

"They're coming every two minutes now," Sharon said, looking knowledgeable, looking beautiful with her honey-colored hair spread out on the pillow. Isis, at her side, pinch-hitting until the regular midwife got there, said, "She's doing fine. She's fully dilated now. Your girl is strong. The baby's hammering at the gates. It will go well, I promise."

But Ruth knew that. She and Pete had produced strong, independent women. She didn't regret marrying Pete, did she? Even though he'd left. But that was another part of her life now. She and the children were on their own. Pete was like a piece of the puzzle that had broken off. She had to let it lie. When Pete came tonight, she'd tell him so.

She knelt down to hug her daughter. Sharon was twenty-seven— was it possible? It had happened so fast, her chunky little curly-haired girl grown into a woman, a mother. And for the second time. But Sharon was grabbing her tightly now, impossibly so, holding on for dear life, grimacing, groaning.

"That's a good one, a good one. You're getting ready to push," Isis was shouting, and Ruth felt the pain gather in her own body, felt herself heaving, splitting. But bearing no fruit.

Suddenly, there was a new commotion, a door slamming downstairs, the head midwife sailing in, arms filled with emergency equipment, oxygen tent—in case—and Ruth didn't know what all. The noise picked up in the room, with both midwives urging, "Push, push now," and Sharon shouting, "Stop ordering me around! I need another pillow. I want soy milk. Someone get me a glass." Sharon was boss now; she was in charge of the birthing. They'd have to obey.

"I'll get it," Ruth said, and dashed downstairs. What else was she good for but to run errands?

The kitchen door slammed and Emily entered like a fresh wind. "Mom, it's Dad. He's here, at the inn. I went to ask for his room number. And the man said, 'They. *They* are in room sixteen. He brought that woman with him, Mom. How could he do that?" She burst into tears, and Ruth put a hand on her shoulder. "It's all right, I understand. Your father has to have a life, too." And something caught in her throat.

Upstairs, there was a shout, and Emily said, "What's going on here?" and when Ruth explained, Emily cried, "Oh my God! Can I go up?"

"Here. Take up this glass. She may throw you out. But if she does, try to understand. This is *her* show."

She followed Emily up. At the door of the bedroom, Emily paused, put her arms around her mother. The soy milk dribbled on Ruth's shirt, but it was all right. "Mom, I love you," Emily whispered, and Ruth burrowed her face into the girl's neck.

THE VETERINARIAN thought Vic would prefer to let the hawk go here, near the pasture where he'd been found. "This was her territory," she said, smiling at the boy, and Vic nodded.

"I found her in the east pasture," he said, "over by the fence." He pointed. "You know, flying around her mate. Though I guess they must've come from the mountain—where they got that poison."

"They have a wide range of flight," the woman said. "You want to hold her? I brought an extra pair of mitts."

She helped attach the jess straps so Vic could carry the bird out to the pasture. He saw she was wearing sturdy boots; she strode right along beside him, while the hawk rode silent but straining on his mitt, like it knew something was about to happen. If only he could tame it... But the eyes were wild and unblinking, and Vic knew it had only one thought: to fly free.

It was a beautiful afternoon for a flight—a light fluffy snow dusting the wild aster and the scarlet sumac. The trees that bordered the pasture were that golden brown color they got in November. The black-and-white Holsteins looked on as Vic and the hawk approached. Zelda was out in front as usual, the others grouped behind her, as if they were painted onto a canvas.

The vet unfastened the jesses from Vic's mitt, and for a moment the hawk didn't move at all, and Vic felt she'd stay, she'd stay with him! But the woman nodded, looking resolute, and Vic glanced once more into those fierce hawk eyes, and he knew what he had to do. He threw her up in the air and she let out a shrill scream and spread her reddish wings out full—like a huge unfurled fan—and soared upward. She was magnificent! Then she circled back, screeching—looking for her mate? Vic held his breath to see, thinking once more that the hawk might stay.

But she flew upward again, and Vic's heart beat like a hundred hawk wings as he watched her soar westward toward Bread Loaf Mountain, her tail feathers gleaming red in the late sun that was pushing through the snow clouds.

AFTERWARD, Vic ran to the barn to see the calves. He just wanted to see them, that was all. There were only three still in the indoor pen: two heifers and the bull calf. The bull calf was lying by itself in the corner; he whistled and it raised its head.

"Don't get to know it too well, Vic," a voice boomed behind him. Hands pressed on his shoulders and he squinted up, to see Tim looking down at him, his cowboy hat riding on the back of his head. "Just don't, now, I said," and the hands gripped harder, then released, and Tim moved on out into the milk room.

Vic stood there, feeling numb. He looked at the bull calf. There was a circle of white around the wide nostrils—it looked like a little kid that had dipped its head into a bowl of cream. Strands of hay hung from its moving jaw; it was lying in straw and dung. Vic was about to go when suddenly the calf stumbled to its feet and its eyes gazed into his own.

Vic couldn't seem to move his feet.

"Vic? Where'n heck are you, Vic?" a voice called from the barn door. It was his friend Gerry Dufours; he was picking Vic up to go trick-or-treating.

It doesn't know, Vic thought, looking into the soft liquidy eyes; it doesn't know.

But Gerry called his name again, and Vic got up, and without looking back, he moved toward the sound of the voice.

"Wait here," he told Gerry, and ran up to the house. Wondering why a white tablecloth was hanging out the bedroom window. And then he heard a baby crying upstairs. It was a soft *la-la* sound; above it, the chatter of women. So it was here. Okay. But how was he going to get his costume? He had to pass that room. "Mom," he shouted. But his mother held up a hand for quiet. She was in the kitchen, talking on the phone to his father.

"A girl, Pete," she was saying, "six pounds, five ounces. She's a week early, you know. Yes, yes, Sharon's fine. She'll want you to come over, see your new granddaughter. She's a honey. Red hair, yes, that's right. Well, my grandmother had red hair, Pete; that's where it comes from. But Pete, give her a few hours to rest first, okay? Come around eight? And alone, Pete. Leave *her* at the Inn."

Vic tiptoed past to his room; he grabbed his mask and red feathers and his candy bag. When he got downstairs again after a slight delay—Emily dragged him in to see Sharon and the baby, though it didn't look like much of anything—a baby calf looked a lot more robust—his mother was still on the phone. This time, it was Colm Hanna. She was telling him about some "decision" she'd made; he could hear Colm say "Hooray!" on the other end.

"I'll call you later, Colm, when Pete comes over. You can pick me up. So he can have time with the children alone. He'll be bringing papers for me to sign, you know. But those can wait."

She'd spotted Vic now, was grabbing his sleeve. "Your dad's coming over at eight—he'll want to see you."

"But it's Halloween," he said. "They're having a party at school after trick-or-treating. I can't miss the party. He'll be around tomorrow, won't he?"

"Sure," she said, sounding more agreeable than he could remember her lately. "I'll tell him. They'll have to stay one more day—that woman is with him, you know. But come straight home after the party, hear?''

She was still talking to Colm Hanna as he left, sounding flirty almost; it sounded dumb. But women were women. And here was Gerry, hurrying him up, and Garth Unsworth with his brother, Wilder, who was looking for Emily. Vic pointed upstairs. ''Good luck,'' he told Wilder. ''You got competition.''

''What's it supposed to be, Vic, that outfit? An Indian? The devil?'' Gerry said, standing at the foot of the porch in a sheet with holes for the eyes.

Vic didn't bother to answer. ''Let's get going,'' he told his friend, feeling excited now, although he didn't know why. ''We'll start with Larocque's, next door. He's always got red licorice. Then we'll go to Flint's.''

He raced on ahead, leaping, shouting ''Yee hoo'' into the air as he went. Like a bird. Like a red-tailed hawk.